A NOTE TO THE READER FROM W.E.B. GRIFFIN

Dear Reader,

With two long-running series, BROTHERHOOD OF WAR and THE CORPS, I have tried to accurately portray the inner workings of the military community. With BADGE OF HONOR, I created an all-new series based on one of my favorite subjects, the fascinating and complex world of law enforcement. Books One and Two were originally published under the pseudonym John Kevin Dugan, to avoid any conflict with my military novels.

However, the police force and the military share a number of unique traits: astonishing courage, loyalty, and camaraderie that unite its men and women like no other profession in the world. For this reason my publishers and I have now decided to release the BADGE OF HONOR novels under the W.E.B. Griffin name.

I hope that the readers of BROTHERHOOD OF WAR and THE CORPS will share my interest in the police community—from the cop on the street, to the detectives, to the chief of police. And I hope these books capture the spirit, the pressures, and the controversies that face these brave men and women every day of their lives.

Sincerely,

W.E.B. Griffin

Turn the p̶[...]
W.E.B. Griffin's bestselling series . . .

BROTHERHOOD OF WAR

"Griffin is a storyteller in the grand tradition, probably the best man around for describing the military community. *Brotherhood of War* . . . is an American epic!"
—bestselling author Tom Clancy

"Extremely well-done . . . First-rate!"
—*Washington Post*

"Absorbing . . . fascinating descriptions of weapons, tactics, Army life and battle."
—*New York Times*

"A major work . . . magnificent . . . powerful . . . If books about warriors and the women who love them were given medals for authenticity, insight and honesty, *Brotherhood of War* would be covered with them."
–William Bradford Huie, author of *The Klansman* and *The Execution of Private Slovik*

"A crackling good story. It gets into the hearts and minds of those who by choice or circumstance are called upon to fight our nation's wars."
—William R. Corson, Lt. Col (Ret.) U.S.M.C., author of *The Betrayal* and *The Armies of Ignorance*

"Griffin has captured the rhythms of army life and speech, its rewards and deprivations . . . Absorbing!"
—*Publishers Weekly*

THE VICTIM

THIRD IN THE BADGE OF HONOR SERIES

W.E.B. GRIFFIN

JOVE BOOKS, NEW YORK

For Sergeant Zebulon V. Casey
Internal Affairs Division
Police Department, Retired, the City of Philadelphia.
He knows why.

BADGE OF HONOR: THE VICTIM

A Jove Book / published by arrangement with
the author

PRINTING HISTORY
Jove edition / February 1991

ISBN: 0-515-10397-7

Jove Books are published by The Berkley Publishing Group,
200 Madison Avenue, New York, New York 10016.
The name ''JOVE'' and the ''J'' logo
are trademarks belonging to Jove Publications, Inc.

PRINTED IN THE UNITED STATES OF AMERICA

10 9 8 7 6 5

ONE

On the train from New York to Philadelphia, Charles read *Time* and Victor read *The Post*. Charles was thirty-three but could have passed for twenty-five. Victor was thirty-five, but his male pattern baldness made him look older. They were both dressed neatly in business suits, with white button-down shirts and rep-striped neckties. Both carried attaché cases. When the steward came around the first time, when they came out of the tunnel into the New Jersey wetlands, Charles ordered a 7-Up but the steward said all they had was Sprite, and Charles smiled and said that would be fine. Victor ordered coffee, black, and when the steward delivered the Sprite and the coffee, he handed him a five-dollar bill and told him to keep the change. Just outside of Trenton, they had another Sprite and another cup of black coffee, and again Charles gave the steward a five-dollar bill and told him to keep the change.

Both Charles and Victor felt a little sorry for someone who had to try to raise a family or whatever on what they paid a steward.

When the conductor announced, "North Philadelphia, North Philadelphia next," Charles opened his attaché case and put *Time* inside and then stood up. He took his Burberry trench coat from the rack and put it on. Then he handed Victor his topcoat and helped him into it. Finally he took their luggage, substantially identical soft carry-on clothing bags from the rack, and laid it across the back of the seat in front of them, which was not occupied.

Then the both of them sat down again as the train moved through Northeast Philadelphia and then slowed as it approached the North Philadelphia station.

Victor looked at his watch, a gold Patek Philipe with a lizard band.

"Three-oh-five," he said. "Right on time."

"I heard that Amtrak finally got their act together," Charles replied.

When the train stopped, Charles and Victor walked to the rear of the car, smiled at the steward, and got off. They walked down a filthy staircase to ground level, and then through an even filthier tunnel and came out in a parking lot just off North Broad Street.

"There it is," Victor said, nodding toward a year-old, 1972 Pontiac sedan. When he had called from New York City, he had been told what kind of car would be waiting for them, and where it would be parked, and where they could find the keys: on top of the left rear tire.

As they walked to the car both Victor and Charles took pigskin gloves from their pockets and put them on. There was no one else in the parking lot, which was nice. Victor squatted and found the keys where he had been told they would be, and unlocked the driver's door. He reached inside and opened the driver's-side rear door and laid his carry-on bag on the seat and closed the door. Then he got behind the wheel, closed the driver's door, and reached over and unlocked the door for Charles.

Charles handed the top of his carry-on bag to Victor, who put it on his lap, and then Charles got in, slid under the lower portion of his carry-on bag, and closed his door. Charles and Victor looked around the parking lot. There was no one in sight.

Charles felt under the seat and grunted. Carefully, so that

no one could see what he was doing, he took what he had found under the seat, a shotgun, and laid it on top of the carry-on bag.

He saw that it was a Remington Model 1100 semiautomatic 12-gauge with a ventilated rib. It looked practically new.

Charles pulled the action lever back, checked carefully to make sure it was unloaded, and then let the action slam forward again.

He then felt beneath the seat again and this time came up with a small plastic bag. It held five Winchester Upland shotgun shells.

"Seven and a halfs," he said, annoyance and perhaps contempt in his voice.

"Maybe he couldn't find anything else," Victor said, "or maybe he thinks that a shotgun shell is a shotgun shell."

"More likely he wants to make sure I get close," Charles said. "He doesn't want anything to go wrong with this. I had a phone call just before I left for the airport."

"Saying what?"

"He wanted to be sure I understood that he didn't want anything to go wrong with this. That's why he called me himself."

"What did this guy do, anyway?"

"You heard what I heard. He went in business for himself," Charles said. "Bringing stuff up from Florida and selling it to the niggers."

"You don't believe that, do you?"

"I believe that he probably got involved with the niggers, but I don't think that's the reason we're doing a job on him."

"Then what?"

"I don't want to know."

"What do you think?"

"If Savarese was a younger man, I'd say maybe he caught this guy hiding the salami in the wrong place. It's something personal like that, anyhow. If he had just caught him doing something, business, he shouldn't have been doing, he probably would have taken care of him himself."

"Maybe this guy is related to him or something," Victor said, "and he doesn't want it to get out that he had a job done on him."

"I don't want to know. He told me he went into business

for himself with the niggers, that's what I believe. I wouldn't want Savarese to think I didn't believe him, or that I got nosy and started asking questions.''

He loaded the shotgun. When it had taken three of the shotshells, it would take no more.

"Damn," Charles said. He worked the action three times, to eject the shells, and then unscrewed the magazine cap and pulled the fore end off. He took a quarter and carefully pried the magazine spring retainer loose. He then raised the butt of the shotgun and shook the weapon until a plastic rod slipped out. This was the magazine plug required by federal law to be installed in shotguns used for hunting wild fowl; it restricted the magazine capacity to three rounds.

Charles then reassembled the shotgun and loaded it again. This time it took all five shells, four in the magazine and one in the chamber. He checked to make sure the safety was on, unzipped his carry-on bag, slid the shotgun inside, closed the zipper, and then put the carry-on bag in the backseat on top of Victor's.

"Okay?" Victor asked.

"Go find a McDonald's," Charles said. "They generally have pay phones outside."

"You want to get a hamburger or something too?"

"If you want," Charles said without much enthusiasm.

Victor drove out of the parking lot, paid the attendant, who looked like he was on something, and drove to North Broad Street, where he turned right.

"You know where you're going?" Charles asked.

"I've been here before," Victor said.

Eight or ten blocks up North Broad Street, Victor found a McDonald's. He carefully locked the car—it looked like a rough neighborhood—and they went in. Charles dropped the plastic bag the shotshells had come in, and the magazine plug, into the garbage container by the door.

"Now that you said it, I'm hungry," Charles said to Victor, and he took off his pigskin gloves. "Get me a Big Mac and a small fries and a 7-Up. If they don't have 7-Up, get me Sprite or whatever. I'll make the call."

He was not on the phone long. He went to Victor and stood beside him and waited, and when their order was served, he carried it to a table while Victor paid for it.

"2184 Delaware Avenue," he said when Victor came to the table. "He's there now. He'll probably be there until half past five. You know where that is?"

"Down by the river. Are we going to do it there?"

"Anywhere we like, except there," Charles said. "The guy on the phone said, 'Not here or near here.' "

"Who was the guy on the phone?"

"It was whoever answered the number Savarese gave me to call. I didn't ask him who he was. He said hello, and I said I was looking for Mr. Smith, and he said Mr. Smith was at 2184 Delaware and would be until probably half past five, and I asked him if he thought I could do my business with him there, and he said, 'Not here or near here,' and I said, 'Thank you' and hung up."

"If it wasn't Savarese, then somebody else knows about this."

"That's not so surprising, if you think about it. He also said, 'Leave the shotgun.' "

"What did he think we were going to do, take it with us?"

"I think he wants to do something with it," Charles said.

"Like what?"

"I don't know," Charles said, then smiled and asked, "Shoot rabbits, maybe?"

"Shit!"

"How are we fixed for time?"

"Take us maybe ten minutes to get there, fifteen tops," Victor said.

"Then we don't have to hurry," Charles said. He looked down at the tray. "I forgot to get napkins."

"Get a handful," Victor said as Charles stood up. "These Big Macs are sloppy."

Officer Joe Magnella, who was twenty-four-years-old, five feet nine and one half inches tall, dark-haired, and weighed 156 pounds, opened the bathroom door, checked to make sure that neither his mother nor his sister was upstairs, and then ran naked down the upstairs corridor to the back bedroom he shared with his brother, Anthony, who was twenty-one.

He had just showered and shaved and an hour before had come out of Vinny's Barbershop, two blocks away at the corner of Bancroft and Warden Streets in South Philadelphia, freshly shorn and reeking of cologne.

The room he had shared with Anthony all of his life was small and dark and crowded. When they had been little kids, their father had bought them bunk beds, and when Joe was twelve or fourteen, he had insisted that the beds be separated and both placed on the floor, because bunk beds were for little kids. They had stayed that way until Joe came home from the Army, when he had restacked them. There was just not enough space in the room to have them side by side on the floor and for a desk too.

The desk was important to Joe. He had bought it ten months before, when he was still in the Police Academy. It was a real desk, not new, but a real office desk, purchased from a used furniture dealer on lower Market Street.

His mother told him he was foolish, that he really didn't need a desk now, that could wait until he and Anne-Marie were married and had set up housekeeping, and even then he wouldn't need one that big or—for that matter—that ugly.

"I already bought and paid for it, Mama, and they won't take it back," he told her.

There was no sense arguing with her. Neither, he decided, was there any point in trying to explain to her why he needed a desk, and a desk just like the one he had bought, a real desk with large, lockable drawers.

He needed a place to study, for one thing, and he didn't intend to do that, as he had all the way through high school, sitting at the dining-room table after supper and sharing it with Anthony from the time Anthony was in the fourth grade at St. Dominic's School.

The Police Academy wasn't school, like South Philly High had been, where it didn't really matter how well you did; the worst thing they could do to you was flunk you and, if it was a required course, make you take it again. The Police Academy was for real. If you flunked, they'd throw you out. He didn't think there was much chance he would flunk out, but what he was after was getting good grades, maybe even being valedictorian. That would go on his record, be considered when he was up for a promotion.

Joe had not been valedictorian of his class at the Police Academy; an enormous Polack who didn't look as if he had the brains to comb his own hair had been. But Joe had ranked fourth (of eighty-four) and he was sure that had been entered on his record.

And he was sure that he had ranked as high as he had because he had studied, and he was sure that he had studied because he had a real desk in his room. If he had tried to study on the dining-room table, it wouldn't have worked. Not only would he have had to share with Anthony, but Catherine and his mother and father would have had the TV on loud in the living room.

And when the guys came around after supper, his old gang, and wanted to go for a beer or a ride, it would have been hard to tell them no. With him studying at the desk upstairs, when the guys came, his mother had told them, "Sorry, Joseph is studying upstairs, and he told me he doesn't want anybody bothering him."

The Army had opened Joe Magnella's eyes to a lot of things, once he'd gotten over the shock of finding himself at Fort Polk, Louisiana. And then 'Nam, once he'd gotten over the shock of being in that godforsaken place, had opened his eyes even more.

He had come to understand that there were two kinds of soldiers. There was the kind that spent all their time bitching and, when they were told to do something, did just enough to keep the corporals and the sergeants off their backs. All they were interested in doing was getting through the day so they could hoist as much beer as they could get their hands on. Or screw some Vietnamese whore. Or smoke grass. Or worse.

The other kind was the kind that Joe Magnella had become. A lot of his good behavior was because of Anne-Marie. They were going to get married as soon as he came home from the Army. She was working at Wanamaker's, in the credit department, and putting money aside every week so they could get some nice furniture. It didn't seem right, at Fort Polk, for him to throw money away at the beer joints when Anne-Marie was saving hers.

So while he didn't take the temperance pledge or anything like that, he didn't do much drinking. There was no temptation to get in trouble with women at Polk, because there just weren't any around. And when he got to 'Nam and they showed him the movies of the venereal diseases you could catch over there, some of them they didn't have a cure for, he believed them and kept his pecker in his pocket for the whole damned time.

How the hell could he go home and marry Anne-Marie, who he knew was a decent girl and was saving herself for marriage, if he caught some kind of incurable VD from a Vietnamese whore?

The first thing he knew, he was a corporal, and then a sergeant, and a lot of the guys who'd gone into the boonies high on grass or coke or something had gone home in body bags.

Joe had liked the Army, at least after he'd gotten to be a sergeant, and had considered staying in. But Anne-Marie said she didn't want to spend their married life moving from one military base to another, so he got out, even though the Army offered him a promotion and a guaranteed thirty-month tour as an instructor at the Infantry School at Fort Benning if he reenlisted.

A week after he got home, he went to the City Administration Building across from City Hall and applied for the cops, and was immediately accepted. He and Anne-Marie decided it would be better to wait to get married until after he graduated from the Police Academy, and then they decided to wait and see if he really liked being a cop, and because her mother said she would really feel better about it if Anne-Marie waited until she was twenty-one.

He really liked being a cop, and Anne-Marie was going to turn twenty-one in two months, and the date was set, and they were already in premarital counseling with Father Frank Pattermo at St. Thomas Aquinas, and in two months and two weeks he could move himself and his desk out of the room and let Anthony finally have it all to himself.

Joe had laid his underwear and uniform out on the lower bunk—Anthony's—before going to take a shower and shave. He pulled on a pair of Jockey shorts and a new T-shirt, and then pinned his badge through the reinforced holes on a short-sleeved uniform shirt, and then put that, his uniform trousers, and a pair of black wool socks on.

He took one of his three pairs of uniform shoes from under the bed and put them on. He had learned about feet and shoes, too, in the Army, that it was better for your feet and your shoes if you always wore wool socks—they soaked up the sweat; nylon socks didn't do that—and never wore the same pair of shoes more than one day at a time, which gave them a chance to dry out.

Some of the cops were now wearing sort of plastic shoes, some new miracle that always looked spit-shined, but Joe had decided they weren't for him. They *were* plastic, which meant that they would make your feet sweaty, wool socks or not. And it wasn't all that much trouble keeping his regular, leather, uniform oxfords shined. If you started out with a good shine on new shoes and broke them in right, it wasn't hard to keep them looking good.

He strapped on his leather equipment belt, which had suspended from it his handcuff case; two pouches, each with six extra rounds for his revolver; the holder for his nightstick; and his holster. His nightstick was on his desk, and he picked that up and put it in the holder and then unlocked the right top drawer of the desk and took out his revolver.

He pushed on the thumb latch and swung the cylinder out of the frame and carefully loaded six 168-grain lead round-nose .38 Special cartridges into it, pushed the cylinder back into the frame, and put the revolver in the holster.

He didn't think much of his revolver. It was a Smith & Wesson Military and Police model with fixed sights and a four-inch barrel, the standard weapon issued to every uniformed officer in the Police Department.

It had been around forever. There were a lot better pistols available, revolvers with adjustable sights, revolvers with more powerful cartridges, like the .357 Magnum. If Joe had his choice, he would have carried a Colt .45 automatic, like he'd carried in the Army in 'Nam after he'd made sergeant. If you shot somebody with a .45, they stayed shot, and from what he'd heard about the .38 Special, that wasn't true.

He'd heard that people had kept coming at cops after they'd been shot two and even three times with a .38 Special. But department regulations said that cops would carry only the weapon they were issued, and that was the Smith & Wesson Military and Police .38 Special, period. No exceptions, and you could get fired if they caught you with anything else.

It probably didn't matter. The firearms instructor at the

Police Academy had told them that ninety percent or better of all cops went through their entire careers without once having drawn their pistols and shot at somebody.

Finally Joe Magnella put on his uniform cap and then examined himself in the mirror mounted on the inside of the closet door. Satisfied with what he found, he closed the door and left the bedroom and went downstairs.

"You sure you don't want something to eat before you go to work?" his mother asked, coming out of the kitchen.

"Not hungry, Mama, thank you," Joe said. "And don't wait up. I'll be late."

"You really shouldn't keep Anne-Marie out until all hours. She has to get up early and go to work. And it doesn't look good."

"Mama, I told you, what she does is take a nap when she gets off work. Before I go there. And who cares what it looks like. We're not doing anything wrong. And we're *engaged*, for God's sake."

"It doesn't look right for a young girl to be out all hours, especially during the week."

"I'll see you, Mama," Joe said, and walked out the front door.

His car was parked at the curb, right in front of the house. He had been lucky when he came home last night. Sometimes there was just no place to park on the whole block.

Joe drove a 1973 Ford Mustang, dark green, with only a six-cylinder engine but with air-conditioning and an automatic transmission. He owed thirty-two (of thirty-six) payments of $128.85 to the Philadelphia Savings Fund Society.

The Mustang was one of the few things in life he really wanted to have, and Anne-Marie had understood when they looked at it in the showroom and said, go ahead, make the down payment, it'll be nice to have on the honeymoon, and if you buy a new car and take care of it, it'll be cheaper in the long run than buying a used car and having to pay to have it fixed all the time.

There was bird crap on the hood, on the passenger side, and on the trunk, and he took his handkerchief out and spit on it and wiped the bird crap off. Somebody had told him there was acid in bird crap that ate the paint if you didn't get it off right away.

He opened the hood and checked the oil and the water, and then got in and started it up and drove off, carefully, to avoid scraping the Mustang's bumper against that of the Chevy parked in front of him.

He turned right at the corner and then, when he reached South Broad Street, left, and headed for Center City. He came to City Hall, which sits in the center of the intersection of Broad and Market Streets; drove around it; and headed up North Broad Street. There was no better route from his house to the 23rd District Station, which is at 17th and Montgomery Streets.

He found a place to park the Mustang, locked it carefully, and walked a block and a half to the station house and went inside. He was early, but that was on purpose. It was better to be early and have to wait a little for roll call than to take a chance and come in late. He was trying to earn a reputation for reliability.

At five minutes to four he went into the roll-call room and waited for the sergeant to call the eighteen cops on the squad to order and take the roll.

Nothing special happened at roll call. The sergeant who conducted the inspection found nothing wrong with Joe's appearance, neither the cleanliness of his uniform and pistol, nor with the length of his hair. Joe privately thought that some of the cops on the squad were a disgrace to the uniform. Some of them were fat, their uniforms ragged. Some of the cops in the squad had been there for ten years, longer, and wanted nothing more from the Department than to put in their time and retire.

Joe wanted to be something more than a simple police officer. He wasn't sure how far he could go, but there was little doubt in his mind that he could, in time, make at least sergeant and possibly even lieutenant or captain. He was prepared to work for it.

There was nothing special when the sergeant read the announcements. Two cops, both retired, had died, and the sergeant read off where they would be buried from, and when. There had been reported incidents of vandalism on both the Temple University and Girard College campuses, both of which were in the 23rd District. There were reports of cars being stripped on the east side of North Broad Street.

The Special Operations Division was still taking applications from qualified officers for transfers to it. Joe would have liked to have applied, but he didn't have the year's time on the job that was required. He wasn't sure what he would do, presuming they were still looking for volunteers once he had a year on the job.

On one hand, Special Operations, which had been formed only a month before, was an elite unit (not as elite as Highway Patrol, which was *the* elite unit in the Department, but still a *special* unit, and you couldn't even apply for Highway until you had three years on the job), and serving in an elite unit seemed to Joe to be the route to getting promotions. On the other hand, from what he'd heard, Special Operations was pretty damned choosy about who it took; he knew of three cops, two on his squad, who had applied and been turned down.

It would seem to follow then, since Special Operations was so choosy, that it would be full of better-than-average cops. He would be competing against them, rather than against the guys in the 23rd, at least half of whom didn't seem to give a damn if they ever got promoted and seemed perfectly willing to spend their lives riding around the 23rd in an RPC (radio patrol car).

When roll call was over, Joe went out in the parking lot and got in his RPC. It was a battered, two-year-old 1971 Ford. But that, having an RPC, made him think again that it might be smart to stay in the 23rd for a while rather than applying for Special Operations when he had a year on the job.

He had been on the job six months. He was, by a long-established traditional definition, a rookie. Rookies traditionally pull at least a year, sometimes two, working a radio patrol wagon.

RPWs, which are manned by two police officers, serve as a combination ambulance and prisoner transporter. In Philadelphia the police respond to any call for assistance. In other large cities the police pass on requests to assist injured people, or man-lying-on-street calls to some sort of medical service organization, either a hospital ambulance service or an emergency service operated by the Fire Department or some other municipal agency. In Philadelphia, when people are in trouble they call the cops, and if the dispatcher understands that the trouble is a kid with a broken leg or that Grandma fell down the stairs, rather than a crime in progress, he sends a radio patrol wagon.

In addition to the service RPWs provide to the community—and it is a service so expected by Philadelphians that no politician would ever suggest ending it—"wagon duty" serves the police in conditioning new officers to the realities of the job. When a cop in a car arrests somebody, he most often calls for a wagon to haul the doer to the district station. This frees him to resume his patrol and gives the rookies in the wagon a chance to see who was arrested, why, and how.

Joe Magnella had worked an RPW only three months before the sergeant took him off and put him in a car by himself. That was sort of special treatment, and Joe was pretty sure he knew what caused it: It was because he had come home from 'Nam a sergeant with the Combat Infantry Badge.

Captain Steven Haggerman, the 23rd District Commanding Officer, had been a platoon sergeant with the 45th Infantry Division in Korea. Lieutenant George Haskins, the senior of the three lieutenants assigned to the 23rd District, had served in 'Nam as a parachutist and lieutenant with the 187th Regimental Combat Team. Two of the 23rd's sergeants had seen service, either in 'Nam or Korea. An infantry sergeant with the CIB is not regarded as an ordinary rookie by fellow officers who have seen combat.

It was nothing official. It was just the way it was. Army service, particularly in the infantry, was something like on-the-job training for the cops. So when one of the guys on the squad had put his retirement papers in after twenty years and they needed somebody to put in his RPC, the supervisors had talked it over and decided the best guy for the job, the one it seemed to make more sense to move out of wagon duty, was Magnella; he was new on the job but had been an infantry sergeant in Vietnam.

So in that sense, Officer Joe Magnella reasoned as he started up the RPC and drove out of the parking lot, he had already been promoted. He had been on the job only six months, and they had already put him in an RPC by himself, instead of making him work a wagon for a year, eighteen months, two years.

He turned right on Montgomery Avenue, waited for the light on North Broad Street, then crossed it and drove East to 10th Street, where he turned right and began his patrol.

TWO

When Anthony J. DeZego, a strikingly handsome man of thirty years and who was tall, well built, well dressed, and had a full set of bright white teeth, came out of the warehouse building at 2184 Delaware Avenue just after half past five, Victor and Charles were waiting for him, parked one hundred yards down the street.

DeZego, who was jacketless and tieless, opened the rear door of a light brown 1973 Cadillac Sedan de Ville and took from a hanger a tweed sport coat and shrugged into it. Then, when he got behind the wheel, he retrieved a necktie from where he had left it hanging from the gearshift lever and slipped it around his neck. He slid into the passenger seat, pulled down the mirror on the sun visor, and knotted the tie. Then he slid back behind the wheel, started the engine, and drove off.

Victor put the Pontiac in gear and followed him. "What you said before," Victor said, "I think you were right."

"What did I say before?"

"About him probably fucking somebody he shouldn't

have," Victor said. "Those really good-looking guys are always getting in trouble doing that."

"Not all of us," Charles said.

Victor laughed.

Two minutes later he said, "Oh, shit, he's going right downtown."

"Is that a problem?"

"The traffic is a bitch," Victor said.

"Don't lose him."

"If I do, then what? We know where he lives?"

"We do. But I don't want to do it there unless we have to."

Victor did not lose Anthony J. DeZego in traffic. He was a good wheelman. Charles knew of none better, which was one of the reasons he had brought Victor in on this. They had worked together before, too, and Charles had learned that Victor didn't get excited when that was a bad thing to do.

Thirty minutes after they had picked up DeZego—the traffic was that bad—Victor pulled the Cadillac in before the entrance to the Warwick Hotel on South 16th Street in downtown Philadelphia, got out of the car, handed the doorman a bill, and then went into a cocktail lounge at the north end of the hotel.

"A real big shot," Victor said. "Too big to park his car himself."

"I'd like to know where it gets parked," Charles said. "That might be useful."

"I'll see what I can see," Victor said.

"You'll drive around the block, right?"

"Right."

Charles got out of the Pontiac and walked past the door to the cocktail lounge. He saw DeZego slip into a chair by a table right by the entrance, shake hands with three men already sitting there, and jokingly kiss the hand of a long-haired blonde who wasn't wearing a bra.

I hope she was worth it, pal, Charles thought.

The Cadillac de Ville was still in front of the hotel entrance when Charles got there, engine running. But he hadn't walked much farther when, casually glancing over his shoulder, he saw it move away from the curb and then make the first left. A heavily jowled man in a bellboy's uniform was at the wheel.

Charles crossed the street, now walking quickly, to see if he could—if not catch up with it—at least get some idea where it had gone.

Heavy traffic on narrow streets helped him. He actually got ahead of the car and had to stand on a corner, glancing at his watch, until it passed him again. Two short blocks farther down, he saw it turn into a parking garage.

He waited nearby until, a couple of minutes later, the jowly bellboy came out and waddled back toward the hotel. Charles followed him on the other side of the street and, when the bellboy came close to the hotel, timed his pace, crossing the street so that he would be outside the cocktail lounge. He saw the bellboy hand DeZego the keys to the Cadillac, then saw DeZego drop them in the pocket of his jacket.

He walked back to the parking garage and stood near the corner, examining the building carefully. Somewhat surprised, he saw that the pedestrian entrance to the building was via a one-way gate, like those in the subways in New York, a system of rotating gates, ceiling-high that turned only one way, letting people in but not out.

He thought that over, wondering how the system worked, how a pedestrian—or somebody who had just parked his car—got out of the building. Then he saw how it worked. There was a pedestrian exit way down beside the attendant's booth. You had to walk past the attendant to get out. The system, he decided, was designed to reduce theft, at least theft by people who looked like thieves.

He walked to the garage and passed through the one-way gate. Inside was a door. He pushed it open and found two more doors. One had ONE painted on it in huge letters, and the other read, STAIRS. He went through the ONE door and found himself on the ground floor of the garage. The door closed automatically behind him, and there was no way to open it.

DeZego's Cadillac was not on the ground floor. He went up the vehicular ramp to the second floor. DeZego's car wasn't there, either, but he saw that one could enter through the door to the stairwell. He walked up the stairs to the third floor. Same thing. No brown Cadillac but he could get back on the stairs. He found the Caddy on the fourth floor. Then he went back into the stairwell and up another flight of stairs. It turned out to be the last; the top floor was open.

He walked to the edge and looked down, then went into the stairwell again and walked all the way back to the ground floor. The attendant looked up but didn't seem particularly interested in him.

I don't look as if I've just ripped off a stereo, Charles thought.

He walked back to South 16th Street and stood on the corner catty-corner to wait for Victor to come around the block again.

Then he saw the cops. Two of them in an unmarked car parked across the street from the hotel, watching the door to the cocktail lounge.

Were they watching Brother DeZego? Or somebody with him? Or somebody entirely different?

Victor showed up, and when Charles raised his hand and smiled, Victor stopped the Pontiac long enough for Charles to get in.

"The Caddy's in a parking garage," Charles said.

"Penn Services—I saw it," Victor said.

"There," Charles said.

"I also saw two cops," Victor said. "Plainclothes. Detectives. Whatever."

"If they were in plainclothes, how could you tell they were cops?"

"Shit!" Victor chuckled.

"I saw them," Charles said.

"And?"

"And nothing. For all we know, they're the Vice Squad. Or looking for pickpockets. Take a drive for five minutes and then drop me at the garage. Then drive around again and again, until you can find a place to park on the street outside the parking garage. You can pick me up when I'm finished."

"How long is this going to take?"

"However long it takes Lover Boy to leave that bar," Charles said, and then, "How would I get from the garage exit to the airport?"

"I'm driving," Victor said.

"I'm toying with the idea of driving myself in Lover Boy's

car,'' Charles said. "I think I would attract less attention from the attendant if I drove out, instead of carrying the bag.''

"Then leave the bag," Victor said.

"I've already walked out of there once," Charles said. "He might remember, especially if I was carrying a bag the second time. I'm not sure what I'll do. Whatever seems best.''

"And if you do decide to drive, what do you want me to do?''

"First, you tell me which way I turn to get to the airport,'' Charles said.

"Left, then the next left, then the next right. That'll put you on South Broad Street. You just stay on it. There'll be signs.''

"If you see me drive out, follow me. As soon as you can, without attracting attention, get in front of me and I'll follow you.''

"Okay," Victor said.

Victor then doubled back, driving slowly through the heavy traffic until he was close to the Penn Services parking garage. Then he pulled to the curb and Charles got out. He opened the rear door, took out his carry-on bag, held it over his shoulder, and crossed the street to the pedestrian entrance to the garage, where he went through the one-way gate.

There is a basic flaw in my brilliant planning, he thought as he walked up the stairs to the fourth floor. *Lover Boy may send Jowls the Bellboy to fetch his Caddy.*

When he reached the fourth floor, he saw that there were windows from which he more than likely could look down at the street and see who was coming for the car.

If Jowls comes for it, I'll just have to walk down the stairs and get to the hotel before Jowls does, or at least before Lover Boy leaves the bar to get into the car, and follow him wherever he goes next. If the attendant remembers me, so what? Nothing will have happened here, anyway.

Charles took his handkerchief out and wiped the concrete windowsill clean, so that he wouldn't soil his Burberry, and then settled down to wait.

Four young men, one much younger than the other three, each with a revolver concealed somewhere under their neat business suits, stood around a filing cabinet in the outer office of the Police Commissioner of the City of Philadelphia, drinking coffee from plastic cups and trying to stay out of the way.

Two of them were sergeants, one was a detective, and one—the young one—was an officer, the lowest rank in the police hierarchy.

Both sergeants and the detective were, despite their relative youth, veteran police officers. One of the sergeants had taken and passed the examination for promotion to lieutenant; the detective had taken and passed the examination for sergeant; and both were waiting for their promotions to take effect. The other sergeant had two months before being promoted from detective. The young man had not been on the job long enough even to be eligible to take the examination for promotion to either corporal or detective, which were comparable ranks, and the first step up from the bottom.

They all had comparable jobs, however. They all worked, as a sort of a police equivalent to a military aide-de-camp, for very senior police supervisors. Their bosses had all been summoned to a meeting with the Commissioner and the Deputy Commissioner of Operations, and for the past hour had been sitting around the long, wooden table in the Commissioner's conference room.

Tom Lenihan, the sergeant who was waiting for his promotion to lieutenant to become effective, was carried on the books as "driver" to Chief Inspector Dennis V. Coughlin, generally acknowledged to be the most influential of the fourteen Chief Inspectors in the Department, and reliably rumored as about to become a Deputy Commissioner.

Sergeant Stanley M. Lipshultz, who had gone to night school at Temple, had passed the bar exam a week before his promotion to sergeant. He was "driver" to Chief Inspector Robert Fisher, who headed the Special Investigations Division of the Police Department.

Detective Harry McElroy, soon to be a sergeant, was carried on the books as "driver" to Chief Inspector Matt Lowenstein, who was in charge of all the detectives in the Philadelphia Police Department.

Officer Matthew W. Payne, a tall, muscular young man who looked, dressed, and spoke very much like the University of Pennsylvania fraternity man he had been six months before, was carried on the manning charts as Special Assistant to Staff Inspector Peter Wohl, who was Commanding Officer of the newly formed Special Operations Division.

It was highly unusual for a rookie to be assigned anywhere but a district, most often as one of the two officers assigned to a radio patrol wagon, much less to work directly, and in civilian clothes, for a senior supervisor. There were several reasons for Officer Matthew Payne's out-of-the-ordinary assignment as Special Assistant to Staff Inspector Wohl, but primary among them was that Mayor Jerry Carlucci had so identified his role in the Department to the press.

What Mayor Jerry Carlucci had to say about what went on within the Police Department had about as much effect as if Moses had carried it down from a mountaintop chiseled on stone tablets.

The mayor had spent most of his life as a cop, rising from police officer to police commissioner before running for mayor. He held the not unreasonable views that one, he knew as much about what was good for, or bad for, the Police Department as anybody in it; and two, he was the mayor and as such was charged with the efficient administration of all functions of the city government. It wasn't, as he had told just about all the senior police supervisors at one time or another, that he "was some goddamned politician butting in on something he didn't know anything about."

Officer Payne had been assigned, right out of the Police Academy, to Special Operations before his status as Special Assistant had been made official by Mayor Carlucci, and it could be reasonably argued that that assignment had been blatant nepotism.

The assignment had been arranged by Chief Inspector Coughlin, and there had been a lot of talk about that in the upper echelons of the Department. Officer Payne had grown up calling Chief Inspector Coughlin Uncle Denny, although they were not related by blood or marriage.

Chief Inspector Coughlin had gone through the Police Academy with a young Korean War veteran named John Xavier Moffitt. They had become best friends. As a young sergeant, while answering a silent burglar alarm at a West Philadelphia service station, John X. Moffitt had been shot to death.

Two months later his widow had been delivered of a son. A year after that she had remarried, and her husband had adopted Sergeant Moffitt's son as his own. Denny Coughlin, who had never married, had kept in touch with his best friend's widow and her son over the years, serving as sort of a bridge between the boy and his natural father's family.

The bridge had crossed a stormy chasm. Johnny Moffitt's mother, Gertrude Moffitt, whose late husband had been a retired police captain, was known as Mother Moffitt. She was a devout Irish Catholic and had never forgiven Patricia Sullivan Moffitt, Johnny's widow, for what she considered a sinful betrayal of her heritage. Not only had she married out of the church, to an Episcopalian, a wealthy, socially prominent attorney, but she had abandoned the Holy Mother Church herself and acquiesced to the rearing of her son as a Protestant, and even his education at Philadelphia's Episcopal Academy.

When Mother Moffitt had lost her second son, Captain Richard C. "Dutch" Moffitt, commanding officer of the Highway Patrol, to a stickup vermin's bullet six months before, she had pointedly excluded Patricia Sullivan Moffitt Payne's name from the family list for seating in St. Dominic's Church for Dutch's funeral mass.

The day after Captain Dutch Moffitt had been laid to rest, Matthew W. Payne went to the City Administration Building and joined the Police Department.

Chief Inspector Dennis V. Coughlin had been nearly as unhappy about this as had been Brewster Cortland Payne II, Matt's adoptive father. It was clear to both of them why he had done so. Part of it was because of what had happened to his Uncle Dutch, and part of it was because, weeks before he was to enter the Marine Corps as a second lieutenant, they had found something wrong with his eyes disqualifying him for Marine service.

The Marines, in other words, had told him that they had found him wanting as a man. He could prove to himself, and the world, that he was indeed a man by becoming a cop, in the footsteps of his father and uncle.

It was not, in Denny Coughlin's eyes, a very good reason to become a cop. But he and Brewster C. Payne, during a long lunch at the Union League, had decided between them that there was nothing they could, or perhaps even should, do about it. Matt was a bright lad who would soon come to his senses and realize (possibly very soon, when he was still going through the Academy) that he wasn't cut out for a career as a policeman. With his brains and education, he should follow in Brewster C. Payne's footsteps and become a lawyer.

But Matt Payne had not dropped out of the Police Academy, and as graduation grew near, Dennis V. Coughlin thought long and hard about what to do about him. He had never forgotten the night it had been his duty to tell Patricia Sullivan Moffitt that her husband had been shot to death. Now he had no intention of having to tell Patricia Sullivan Moffitt Payne that something had happened on the job to her son.

Shortly before Matt was to graduate from the Police Academy, at the mayor's ''suggestion'' (which had, of course, the effect of a papal bull), the Police Department organized a new unit, Special Operations. Its purpose was to experiment with new concepts of law enforcement, essentially the flooding of high-crime areas with well-trained policemen equipped with the very latest equipment and technology and tied in with a special arrangement with the district attorney to push the arrested quickly through the criminal-justice system.

Mayor Carlucci, a power in politics far beyond the city limits, had arranged for generous federal grants to pay for most of it.

The mayor had also ''suggested'' the appointment of Staff Inspector Peter Wohl as commanding officer of Special Operations. Peter Wohl was the youngest of the thirty-odd staff inspectors in the Department. Staff inspectors, who rank immediately above captains and immediately below full inspectors, were generally regarded as super detectives. They handled the more difficult investigations, especially those of political corruption, but they rarely, if ever, were given the responsibility of command.

There was muttering about special treatment and nepotism vis-à-vis Wohl's appointment too. A division the size of the new Special Operations Division, which was to take over Highway Patrol, too, should have had at least an inspector, and probably a chief inspector, as its commander. Wohl, although universally regarded as a good and unusually bright cop, was in his thirties and only a staff inspector. People remembered that when Mayor Carlucci was working his way up through the ranks, his rabbi had been August Wohl, Peter Wohl's father, now a retired chief inspector.

It was also said that Wohl's appointment had more to do with his relationship with Arthur J. Nelson than with anything else. Nelson, who owned the Philadelphia *Ledger* and WGHA-TV, had put all the power of his newspaper and television station against Jerry Carlucci during his campaign for the mayoralty. And it was known that Nelson loathed and detested Wohl, blaming him for making it public knowledge that his son, who had been murdered, was both homosexual and had shared his luxury apartment with a black lover. Right after that had come out, Nelson had had to put his wife in a private psychiatric hospital in Connecticut, and Peter Wohl had made an enemy for life.

Those who knew Jerry Carlucci at all knew that he believed "the enemies of my enemies are my friends."

Denny Coughlin was one of Peter Wohl's admirers. He believed that the real reason Wohl had been given Special Operations was because Jerry Carlucci thought he was the best man for the job, period. He was careful without being timid; innovative without going overboard; and, like Coughlin himself, an absolute straight arrow.

And Denny Coughlin had decided that the safest place to hide young Matt Payne—until he realized that he really shouldn't be a cop—was under Peter Wohl's wing. Wohl didn't think Payne was cut out to be a cop, either. He went to work for Wohl, as sort of a clerk, with additional duties as a gofer. It would be, Denny Coughlin believed, only a matter of time until Matt came to his senses and turned in his resignation.

And then Payne got the Northwest Philadelphia serial rapist. While he was delivering a package of papers to Wohl's apartment in Chestnut Hill late at night, he had spotted, by blind luck, the van everybody was looking for. The driver had tried to run him down. Payne had drawn his pistol and fired at the van, putting a bullet through the brain of the driver. Inside the van was a naked woman, right on the edge of becoming the scumbag's next mutilated victim.

The first car (of twenty) to answer the radio call—"Assist officer, police by phone. Report of shots fired and a hospital case"—was M-Mary One, the mayoral limousine, a black

Cadillac. Jerry Carlucci had been headed to his Chestnut Hill home from a Sons of Italy banquet in South Philly and was five blocks away when the call came over the police radio.

By the time the first reporter—Michael J. "Mickey" O'Hara of the Philadelphia *Bulletin*, generally regarded as a friend of the Police Department—arrived at the crime scene, Mayor Carlucci was prepared for him. In the next edition of the *Bulletin* there was a four-column front-page picture of the mayor, his arm around Officer Matt Payne and his suit jacket open just wide enough to remind the voters that even though he was now the mayor, His Honor still rushed to the scene of crimes carrying a snub-nosed revolver on his belt.

In the story that went with the photograph, Officer Payne was described by the mayor as both the Special Assistant to the commanding officer of Special Operations and "the type of well-educated, courageous, highly motivated young police officer Commissioner Czernich is assigning to Special Operations."

Matt Payne, who was perfectly aware that his role in the shooting was far less heroic than painted in the newspapers, had been prepared to be held in at least mild scorn, and possibly even contempt by his new peers, the small corps of "drivers." He had known even before he joined the Department that the "drivers," people like Sergeant Tom Lenihan, who was Denny Coughlin's driver, had been chosen for that duty because they were seen as unusually bright young officers who had proven their ability on the streets and were destined for high ranks.

Working for senior supervisors, drivers were exposed to the responsibilities of senior officers, the responsibilities they, themselves, would assume later in their careers. They had *earned* their jobs, Matt reasoned, where he had been *given* his, and there was bound to be justifiable resentment toward him on their part.

That hadn't happened. He was accepted by them. He thought the most logical explanation of this was that Tom Lenihan had put in a good word for him. Tom obviously thought that Denny Coughlin could walk on water if he wanted to, and could do no wrong, even if that meant special treatment for his old buddy's rookie son.

But that wasn't really the case. Part of it was that it was

difficult to dislike Matt Payne. He was a pleasant young man whose respect for the others was clear without being obsequious. But the real reason, which Payne didn't even suspect, was they were actually a little in awe of him. He had found himself in a life-threatening situation—the Northwest Philly serial rapist would have liked nothing better than to run over him with his van—and had handled it perfectly, by blowing the scumbag's brains out.

Only Sergeant Lenihan and Detective McElroy had ever drawn their Service revolvers against a criminal, and even then they had been surrounded by other cops.

The kid had faced a murderous scumbag one-on-one and put the son of a bitch down. He had paid his dues, like the two kids from Narcotics, now also assigned to Special Operations, Charley McFadden and Jesus Martinez, both of whom had gone looking on their own time for the scumbag who'd shot Captain Dutch Moffitt. They had found him, and McFadden had chased him one-on-one down the subway tracks until the scumbag had fried himself on the third rail.

No matter how long they'd been on the job, it wasn't fair to call kids like that rookies; doing what they had done had earned them the right to be called, and considered, cops.

The door to the commissioner's conference room opened, and Chief Inspector Matt Lowenstein—a short, barrel-chested, bald-headed man in the act of lighting a fresh, six-inch-long nearly black cigar—came out. He did not look pleased with the world. He located Detective McElroy in the group of drivers, gestured impatiently for him to come along, and marched out of the outer office without speaking.

"Why do I suspect that Chief Lowenstein lost a battle in there?" Sergeant Tom Lenihan said very softly.

Sergeant Lipshultz chuckled and Officer Payne smiled as Chief Inspectors Dennis V. Coughlin and Robert Fisher and Staff Inspector Wohl came into the outer office.

Coughlin was a large man, immaculately shaved, ruddy-faced, and who took pride in being well dressed. He was wearing a superbly tailored glen-plaid suit. Fisher, a trim and wiry man with a full head of pure white hair, was wearing one of his blue suits. He also had brown suits. He had three or four of each color, essentially identical. No one could ever remember having seen him, for example, in a sport coat or in a checked, plaid, or striped suit.

Matt had heard from both Coughlin and Wohl that Chief Fisher believed that entirely too many police officers were wearing civilian clothing when, in the public interest, they should be in uniform.

Coughlin walked over to the drivers and shook hands with Sergeant Lipshultz.

"How are you, Stanley?" he asked. "You know where I can find a good, cheap lawyer?"

"At your service, Chief," Lipshultz said, smiling.

"Matthew," Coughlin said to Matt Payne.

"Chief," Matt replied.

"Let's go, Tom," Coughlin said to Lenihan. "Chief Lowenstein had a really foul one smoldering in there. I need some clean air."

"We could smell it out here, Chief," Lenihan said, and went out the door to the corridor.

Chief Inspector Fisher nodded at Matt Payne, offered his hand to Coughlin and Wohl, and then walked out of the room. Sergeant Lipshultz hurried after him.

"Say good-bye to the nice people, Matthew," Inspector Wohl said dryly, "and drive me away from here. It's been a *long* afternoon."

"Good-bye, nice people," Matt said obediently to the others, the commissioner's secretary, his driver, and the other administrative staff.

Some chuckled. The commissioner's driver said, "Take it easy, kid."

The commissioner's secretary, an attractive, busty woman in her forties, said, "Come back anytime, Matthew. You're an improvement over most of the people we get in here."

Officer Matt Payne followed Staff Inspector Wohl out of the office and down the corridor toward the elevators.

There was no one else in the elevator. Wohl leaned against the wall and exhaled audibly.

"Christ, that was rough in there," he said.

"What was it all about?"

"Not here," Wohl said.

He pushed himself erect as the door slid open, and walked

across the lobby to the rear entrance of the building, stopping just outside to turn and ask, "Where are we?"

Payne pointed. There were four new Ford four-door sedans, one of them two-tone blue, parked together toward the rear of the lot. When they arrived at the roundhouse, Payne had dropped Wohl off at the door and then searched for a place to park.

There were five spaces near the roundhouse reserved for division chiefs and chief inspectors, and one of them was empty, but Matt had learned that the sign didn't mean what it said. What it *really* meant was that the spaces were reserved for chief inspectors who were also division chiefs, and that other chief inspectors could use the spaces if they happened to find one empty. It did not mean that Staff Inspector Wohl, although he was a division chief, had the right to park there.

None of this was written down, of course. But everyone understood the protocol, and Matt had learned that the senior supervisors in the Department were jealous of the prerogatives of their rank. He had parked the unmarked two-tone Ford farther back in the lot, beside the unmarked cars of other senior supervisors who, like Wohl, were not senior enough to be able to use one of the parking spaces closest to the building.

Unmarked new cars were a prerogative of rank too. Senior supervisors, Matt had learned—chief inspectors and inspectors and some staff inspectors—drove spanking new automobiles, turning them over ("When the ashtrays got full," Wohl had said) to captains, who then turned their slightly used cars over to the lieutenants, who turned their cars over to detectives.

When Special Operations had been formed and had needed a lot of cars from the police garage right away, the system had been interrupted, and some full inspectors and captains hadn't gotten new cars when they thought they were entitled to get them, and they had made their indignation known.

When they got to the two-tone Ford and Matt started to get behind the wheel, Wohl said, "I think I'm going to go home. Where's your car?"

"Bustleton and Bowler," Matt said. "I can catch a ride out there."

Special Operations had set up its headquarters in the Highway Patrol headquarters at Bustleton and Bowler Streets in Northeast Philadelphia.

"No, I have to stop by the office, anyway. I just didn't know if you had to go out there or not," Wohl said, and got in the passenger seat.

Matt drove to North Broad Street and headed north. They had traveled a dozen blocks in silence when Wohl broke the news. "There are allegations that—I don't have to tell you that you don't talk about this, do I?"

"No, sir."

"There are allegations that certain Narcotics officers have had a little more temptation than they can handle put under their noses and are feeding information to the mob," Wohl said.

"Jesus!"

"Several arrests and confiscations that should have gone smoothly didn't happen," Wohl went on. "Chief Lowenstein told Commissioner Czernich what he thought was happening. Maybe a little prematurely, because he didn't want Czernich to hear it anywhere else. Czernich, either on his own or possibly because he told the mayor and the mayor made the decision, took the investigation away from Chief Lowenstein."

"Who did he give it to?"

"Three guesses," Wohl said dryly.

"Is that why Chief Lowenstein was so sore?"

"Sure. If I were in his shoes, I'd be sore too. It's just about the same thing as telling him he can't be trusted."

"But why to us? Why not Internal Affairs?"

"Why not Organized Crime? Why not put a couple of the staff inspectors on it? Because, I suspect, the mayor is playing detective again. It sounds like him: 'I can have transferred to us anybody I want from Internal Affairs, Narcotics, Vice, or Organized Crime'—theoretically routine transfers. But what they're really for, of course, is to catch the dirty cops— presuming there *are* dirty cops—in Narcotics."

Wohl then fell silent, obviously lost in thought. Matt knew enough about his boss not to bother him. If Wohl wanted him to know something, he would tell him.

Several minutes later Wohl said, "There's something else." Matt glanced at him and waited for him to go on.

"On Monday morning Special Operations is getting another bright, young, college-educated rookie, by the name of Foster H. Lewis, Jr. You know him?"

Matt thought, then shook his head and said, "Uh-uh, I don't think so."

"His assignment," Wohl said dryly, "is in keeping with the commissioner's policy, which of course has the mayor's enthusiastic support, of staffing Special Operations with bright, young, well-educated officers such as yourself, Officer Payne. Officer Lewis has a bachelor of science degree from Temple. Until very recently he was enrolled at the Temple Medical School."

"The medical school?" Matt asked, surprised.

"It was his father's dream that young Foster become a healer of men," Wohl went on. "Unfortunately young Foster was placed on academic probation last quarter, whereupon he decided that rather than heal men, he would prefer to protect society from malefactors; to march, so to speak, in his father's footsteps. His father just made lieutenant. Lieutenant Foster H. Lewis, Sr. Know him?"

"I don't think so."

"Good cop," Wohl said. "He has something less than a warm, outgoing personality, but he's a good cop. He is about as thrilled that his son has become a policeman as yours is."

Matt chuckled. "Why are we getting him?"

"Because Commissioner Czernich said so," Wohl said. "I told you that. If I were a suspicious man, which, of course, for someone with a warm, outgoing, not to forget trusting, personality like mine is unthinkable, I might suspect that it has something to do with the mayor."

"Doesn't everything?" Matt chuckled again.

"In this case a suspicious man might draw an inference from the fact that Officer Lewis's assignment to Special Operations was announced by the mayor in a speech he gave last night at the Second Abyssinian Baptist Church."

"This is a colored guy?"

"The preferred word, Officer Payne, is black."

"Sorry," Matt said. "What are you going to do with him?"

"I don't know. I was just thinking that there is a silver lining in every black cloud. I'm going to give myself the benefit of the doubt there; no pun was intended, and no racial slur should be inferred. What I was thinking is that young Lewis, unlike the last bright, college-educated rookie I was blessed with, at least knows his way around the Department. He's been working his way through school as a police radio operator. Mike Sabara has been talking about having a special radio net for Highway Patrol and Special Operations. Maybe something to do with that.''

When they pulled into the parking lot at Bustleton and Bowler, Matt saw that Captain Mike Sabara's car was in the space reserved for it. Wohl saw it at the same moment. Sabara was Wohl's deputy.

''Captain Sabara's still here. Good. I need to talk to him. You can take off, Matt. I'll see you in the morning.''

''Yes, sir,'' Matt said.

He did not volunteer to hang around. He had learned that if Wohl had a need for him, he would have told him to wait. And he had learned that if he was being sent home, thirty minutes early, it was because Wohl didn't want him around. Wohl had decided that whatever he had to say to Captain Sabara was none of Officer Payne's business.

THREE

Matt Payne walked a block and a half to the Sunoco gas station at which he paid to park his car. Wohl had warned him not to leave it in the street if he couldn't find a spot for it in the police parking lot; playful neighborhood youths loved to draw curving lines on automobile fenders and doors with keys and other sharp objects, taking special pains with nice cars they suspected belonged to policemen.

"Getting a cop's nice car is worth two gold stars to take home to Mommy," Wohl had told him.

Matt got in his car, checked to see that he had enough gas for the night's activities, and then started home, which meant back downtown.

He drove a 1974 silver Porsche 911 Carerra with less than five thousand miles on the odometer. It had been his graduation present, sort of. He had graduated cum laude from the University of Pennsylvania and had expected a car to replace the well-worn Volkswagen bug he had driven since he'd gotten his driver's license at sixteen. But he had not expected a Porsche.

"This is your reward," his father had told him, "for making it to voting age and through college without having required my professional services to get you out of jail, or making me a grandfather before my time."

The Porsche he was driving now was not the one that had surprised him on graduation morning, although it was virtually identical to it.

That car, with 2,107 miles on the speedometer, had suffered a collision, and Matt had come out of that a devout believer that an uninsured-motorist clause was a splendid thing to have in your insurance policy, providing of course that you had access to the services, pro bono familias, of a good lawyer to make the insurance company live up to its implied assurances.

The first car had been struck on the right rear end by a 1970 Ford van. The driver did so intentionally, hoping to squash Matthew Payne between the two and thus permitting himself to carry on with his intentions to carry a Mrs. Naomi Schneider, who was at the time trussed up naked in the back of the van under a tarpaulin, off to a cabin in Bucks County for rape and dismemberment.

He failed to squash Officer Payne, who had jumped out of the way and, a moment later, shot him to death with his off-duty revolver.

The deceased, Matt learned shortly after the Porsche dealer had given him a first rough but chilling estimate of repair costs, had no insurance that a diligent search of Department of Motor Vehicle records in Harrisburg could find.

He next learned the opinion of legal counsel to the Philadelphia Police Department vis-à-vis the outrage perpetrated against his vehicle: Inasmuch as Officer Payne was not on duty at the time of the incident, the Police Department had no responsibility to make good any alleged damages to his personal automobile.

Next came a letter on the crisp, engraved stationery of the First Continental Assurance Company of Hartford, Connecticut. It informed the insured that since he had said nothing whatever on his application for insurance that he was either a police officer or that he intended to use his car in carrying out his police duties; and inasmuch as it had come to their attention that he was actually domiciled in Philadelphia,

Pennsylvania, rather than as his application stated, in Wallingford, Pennsylvania; and inasmuch as they would have declined to insure him if any one of the aforementioned facts had come to their attention; they clearly had no obligation in the case at hand.

Furthermore, the letter was to serve as notice that inasmuch as the coverage had been issued based on his misrepresentation of the facts, it was canceled herewith, and a refund of premium would be issued in due course.

He tried to handle the problem himself. He was, after all, no longer a little boy who had to run to Daddy with every little problem but a grown man, a university graduate, and a police officer.

His next learning experience was how insurance companies regarded their potential liability in insuring unmarried males under the age of twenty-five who drove automobiles with 140-mile-per-hour speedometers that were fancied by car thieves and whose previous insurance had been canceled. Five insurance agents as much as laughed at him, and the sixth thought he might be able to get Matt coverage whose premium would have left Matt not quite one hundred dollars a month from his pay to eat, drink, and be merry. At that point he went see Daddy.

The next Monday morning, a letter on crisp, engraved stationery, the letterhead of Mawson, Payne, Stockton, McAdoo & Lester, Philadelphia Savings Fund Society Building, Philadelphia, went out to the general counsel of the First Continental Assurance Company of Hartford, Connecticut. It was signed by J. Dunlop Mawson, senior partner, and began, "My Dear Charley," which was a rather unusual lack of formality for anyone connected with Mawson, Payne, Stockton, McAdoo & Lester.

But Colonel Mawson had quickly come to the point. Mawson, Payne, Stockton, McAdoo & Lester was representing Matthew W. Payne, he said, and it was their intention to sue First Continental Assurance Company for breach of contract, praying the court to award $9,505.07 in real damages and $2 million in punitive damages.

Six days later, possibly because the general counsel of First Continental recalled that when they had been socked with a $3.5 million judgment against the Kiley Elevator Company after a hotel guest had been trapped for eight hours in an elevator, thereby suffering great mental pain and anguish, the plaintiff had been represented by Colonel J. Dunlop Mawson of Mawson, Payne, Stockton, McAdoo & Lester, Matt had both a check for $9,505.07 and a letter stating that First Continental Assurance Company deeply regretted the misunderstanding and that they hoped to keep the favor of his business for many years.

A week later, after the Porsche mechanic told him that after a smash like that, getting the rear quarter panel and knocking the engine off its mounts, cars were never quite right, Matt took delivery of a new one, and the old one was sent off to be dismantled for parts.

It was generally believed by Matt's fellow officers that with a car like that he got laid a lot, so how could he miss?

But this was not the case. When he thought about that, and sometimes he thought a lot about it, he realized that he had spent a lot more time making the beast with two backs when he was still at U of P than he had lately.

He had once thought that if the activity had been charted, the delightful physical-encounters chart would show a gradual increase during his freshman and sophomore years, rising from practically zero to a satisfactory level halfway through his sophomore year. Then the chart would show a plateau lasting through his junior year, then a gradual decline in his senior year. Since his graduation and coming on the job, the chart would show a steep decline, right back to near zero, with one little aberration.

He had encountered a lady at the FOP Bar, off North Broad Street, a divorcee of thirty-five or so who found young policemen fascinating. He did not like to dwell on the aberration on the declining curve.

There were reasons for the decline, of course. In school there seemed to be a pairing off, some of which had resulted in engagements and even marriage. He had never met anyone he wanted to pair with. But there had been a gradual depletion of the pool of availables.

And once he'd graduated and shortly afterward come on the job, he had fallen out of touch with the girls he knew at school and at home.

Tonight, he hoped, the situation might be different. He had

met a new girl. He almost had blown that but hadn't. He had heard that God takes care of fools and drunks, and he thought he qualified on both counts.

Her name was Amanda Chase Spencer. She had graduated that year from Bennington. Her family lived in Scarsdale and they had a winter place in Palm Beach. So far he liked Amanda very much, which was rather unusual, for it had been his experience, three times that he could immediately call to mind, that strikingly beautiful blond young women of considerable wealth, impeccable social standing, and, in particular those who went to Bennington, were usually a flaming pain in the ass.

Matt had met Amanda only four days before, at the beginning of what they were now calling "the wedding week." He had not at first been pleased with the prospect. When informed by the bridegroom-to-be that it had been arranged that he serve as escort to Miss Spencer throughout the week, his response had been immediate and succinct: "Fuck you, Chad, no goddamn way!"

Chad was Chadwick T. Nesbitt IV (University of Pennsylvania '73) of Bala-Cynwyd and Camp Lejeune, North Carolina, where he was a second lieutenant, United States Marine Corps Reserve. Matt Payne and Chad Nesbitt had been best friends since they had met, at age seven, at Episcopal Academy. No one was surprised when Chad announced that Matt would be his best man when he married Miss Daphne Elizabeth Browne (Bennington '73) of Merion and Palm Beach.

"I told you," Mr. Payne had firmly told Lieutenant Nesbitt, "the bachelor party and the wedding, and that's it."

"She's Daffy's maid of honor," Chad protested.

"I don't give a damn if she's queen of the nymphomaniacs, no, goddammit, no."

"You don't like girls anymore?"

"Not when more than two or three of them are gathered together for something like this. And I've got a job, you know."

"Tell me about it, Kojak," Chad Nesbitt had replied.

"Chad, I really don't have the time," Matt Payne said. "Even if I wanted to."

"I'm beginning to think you're serious about this, buddy."

"You're goddamn right I'm serious."

"Okay, okay. Tell you what. Show up for the rehearsal and I'll work something out."

"All I have to do is show up sober in a monkey suit and hand you the ring. I don't have to rehearse that."

"It's tails, asshole, you understand that? *Not* a dinner jacket."

"I will dazzle one and all with my sartorial elegance," Payne said.

"If you don't show up for the rehearsal, Daffy's mother will have hysterics."

That was, Matt Payne realized, less a figure of speech than a statement of fact. Mrs. Soames T. Browne was prone to emotional outbursts. Matt still had a clear memory of her shrieking "You dirty little boy" at him the day she discovered him playing doctor with Daphne at age five. And he knew that nothing that had happened since had really changed her opinion of his character. He knew, too, that she had tried to have Chad pick someone else to serve as his best man.

"Okay," Matt Payne had said, giving in. "The rehearsal, the bachelor dinner, and the wedding. But that's it. Deal?"

"Deal," Lieutenant Nesbitt had said, shaking his hand and smiling, then adding, "You rotten son of a bitch."

Matt Payne had been waiting inside the vestibule of St. Mark's Protestant Episcopal Church on Locust Street, between Rittenhouse Square and South Broad Street in central Philadelphia, when the rehearsal party arrived in a convoy of three station wagons, two Mercurys, and a Buick.

Mrs. Soames T. Browne, who was wearing a wide-brimmed hat and a flowing light blue silk dress briefly offered Matt Payne a hand covered in an elbow-length glove.

"Hello, Matthew. How nice to see you. Be sure to give my love to your mother and father."

"I'll do that, Mrs. Browne," Matt said. "Thank you."

She did not introduce him to the blonde with Daffy.

"Come along, girls," Mrs. Browne said, snatching back her hand and sweeping quickly through the vestibule into the church.

"I'm Matt Payne," Matt said to the blonde, "since Daffy apparently isn't going to introduce us."

"Sorry," Daffy said. "Amanda, Matt. Don't be nice to him; he's being a real prick."

"Who is Daffy Browne and why is she saying all those terrible things about me?"

"You know damn well why," Daffy said.

"Haven't the foggiest," Matt said.

"Well, for one thing, Matt, Amanda won't have a date for the cocktail party after the rehearsal."

"I thought I was going to be her date."

"Chad said you flatly refused," Daffy said.

"He must have been pulling your chain again," Matt said. "He has a strange sense of humor."

"He does not," Daffy said loyally.

"He was suspended from pool privileges at Rose Tree for a year for dropping Tootsie Rolls in the swimming pool," Matt said. "That isn't strange?"

It took Amanda a moment to form in her mind the mental image of Tootsie Rolls floating around a swimming pool, and then she bit her lip to keep from smiling.

"Is that true?" Amanda asked.

"Goddamn you, Matt!" Daffy said, making it clear it was true.

"The mother of the bride made one of her famous running dives into the pool," Matt went on. "Somewhere beneath the surface she opened her eyes and saw one of the Tootsie Rolls. She came out of the pool like a missile from a submarine."

Amanda laughed, a hearty, deep belly laugh. Matt liked it.

"My father wanted to award her a loving cup," Matt said, "inscribed 'to the first Rose Tree matron who has really walked on water,' but my mother wouldn't let him."

"I absolutely refuse to believe that," Daffy Browne said. "Matt, you're disgusting!"

Mrs. Soames T. Browne reappeared.

"Darling, the rector would like a word with you," she said, and led her into the church.

Amanda smiled at Matt Payne.

"You are going to the cocktail party?" she asked.

He nodded. "And the dinner. As a matter of fact, Amanda, whither thou goest, there also shall Payne go. That's from the Song of Solomon, in case you're a heathen and don't know your Bible."

She chuckled and put her hand on his arm. "I'm glad," she said.

"Pay close attention inside," Matt said. "You and I may well be going through some barbarian ritual like this ourselves in the very near future."

She met his eyes for a moment, appraisingly.

"Chad tells me that you've taken a job with the city," she said, smoothly changing the subject.

"Is that what he told you?" Matt asked dryly.

"Was he pulling my chain too?"

"No."

"What do you do?"

"Street cleaning."

"Street cleaning?"

"Right now I'm in training," Matt said. "Studying the theory and history, you see. But one day soon I hope to have my own broom and garbage can on wheels."

"City Sanitation, in other words? Aren't you ever serious?"

"I was serious a moment ago, when I said you should pay close attention to the barbaric ritual."

The only thing that hadn't been just fine with Amanda in the time since he'd met her in the vestibule at St. Mark's was that he hadn't been able to get her alone. There had always been other people around and no way to separate from the group.

He *had* managed to kiss her, twice. The night before last he had tried to kiss her at the Merion Cricket Club, before Madame Browne had hauled her off in the station wagon. She had turned her face at the last second and all he got was a cheek. A very nice cheek, to be sure, but just a cheek. Last night she had not turned her face as she prepared to enter what he thought of as the Barque of the Vestal Virgins to be hauled off from the Rose Tree Hunt Club to the Browne place in Merion.

It had not been a kiss that would go down in the history books to rank with the one Delilah gave Samson before she gave him the haircut, but it had been on the lips, and they were sweet lips indeed, and his heart had jumped startlingly.

Tonight they would be alone. The Brownes were entertaining, especially their out-of-town guests, at cocktails and dinner at the Union League in downtown Philadelphia. It was tacitly admitted to be an old-folks' affair, and the young people could leave after dinner. Amanda liked jazz, another character trait he found appealing. So, they would go listen to jazz. With a little luck the lights would be dim. She probably would let him hold her hand, and possibly permit even other manifestations of affection.

If the gods favored him, after they left the jazz joint she would accept his invitation to see his apartment. There, he wasn't sure what he would do. On one hand, he would cheerfully sacrifice one nut and both ears to get into Amanda's pants, but on the other, she was clearly not the sort of girl from whom one could expect a quick piece of tail. Amanda Spencer was the kind of girl one marched before an altar and promised to be faithful to until death did you part.

Matt Payne was very much aware that he could fuck up the whole relationship by making a crude pass at her. He didn't want to do that.

God only knows what that goddamn Daffy has told her about me. Going back to me talking her out of her pants when we were five.

The residence of Mr. and Mrs. Soames T. Browne in Merion was an adaptation, circa 1890, of an English manor house, circa 1600. The essential differences were that the interior dimensions were larger and there was inside plumbing. But everything else was there: a forest of chimneys, a cobblestone courtyard, enormous stone building blocks, turretlike protrusions, leaded windows, ancient oaks, formal gardens, and an entrance that always reminded Matt of a movie he'd seen starring Errol Flynn as Robin Hood. In the movie, when the heavy oak door had swung slowly open, Errol Flynn had run the door opener through with a sword.

The heavy oak door swung open and an elderly black man in a gray cotton jacket stood there.

"I'm very glad to see you, Matt," the Brownes' butler said.

"Why do you say that, Mr. Ward?" Matt asked. He had known the Brownes' butler, and his wife, all of his life.

"Because the consensus was that you wouldn't show and

I'd wind up driving Daffy's friend into town," Ward said. "They're all gone."

"This one's sort of special," Matt confessed.

"It was her and me against everybody else," Ward said. "She insisted on waiting for you."

"Really?" Matt replied, pleased.

"I'll go tell her you're here," Ward said. "There's a fresh pot of coffee in the kitchen, if that interests you."

"No thank you. I'll just wait."

He watched the elderly man slowly start to ascend the stairs. He had taken only four or five steps when Amanda appeared at the top and started down.

"See?" she said to the butler. "We were right." She looked at Matt. "I saw you drive up. I love the car, but you don't strike me as the Porsche type."

"I can get a gold chain and unbutton my shirt to the navel, if you like," Matt said.

She had come up to him by then.

"No thank you." She chuckled, then surprised him by kissing him on the lips.

"Hot damn!" he said.

"Draw no inferences," she said. "I'm just a naturally friendly person."

When he got behind the wheel and looked at Amanda as she got in beside him, he remembered too late that he had forgotten to hold the door for her.

"I should have held the door for you," he said. "Sorry. My mother says I have the manners of a cossack."

She laughed again, and all of a sudden it occurred to him that their faces were no more than six inches apart—and nothing ventured, nothing gained.

"God, that was nice!" he said a moment later.

"Drive," she said. "Has this thing got a vanity mirror?"

"A what?"

She pulled the visor down and found what she was looking for.

"That's a vanity mirror," she said, and replenished her lipstick. "You've probably got some lipstick on you."

"I will never wash again."

She handed him a tissue.

"Take it off," she ordered, and he complied.

"These are really nice wheels," she said a short while later. "But I bet all the girls tell you that."

"My graduation present," Matt said.

"You already dinged it," Amanda said.

"You mean the cracked turn-signal lens?" he asked, surprised that she had noticed it. "That's nothing. You should have seen what happened to my *first* Porsche. That was totaled."

"Are you putting me on?"

"Not at all. A guy in a van ran into the back and really clobbered it."

"I think I would have killed him."

"As a matter of fact, I did," Matt said. "Took out my trusty five-shooter and blew his brains out."

He heard her inhale. After a moment she said, "You mean six-shooter," and then added, "That wasn't funny. Sometimes, Matt, you don't know where to draw the line."

"Sorry."

"That was the pot calling the kettle black," she said. "I'm sorry, I had no right to say that to you."

"You have blanket authority to say anything you want to me."

He gave into the temptation and grabbed her hand. When she didn't object and withdraw it, he kissed it. Then she pulled it free.

"Am I going to have trouble with you tonight?"

"No," he said. "We do what you want to do, and nothing else."

"Funny, I thought you were going to offer to show me your etchings."

"I don't have any etchings," he said.

"But you do have an apartment, right?"

"You're supposed to wait until I ask you before you indignantly tell me you're not that kind of girl," Matt said.

She laughed, the genuine laugh Matt had come to like.

"Touché," she said.

"After we escape from this dinner, would you like to see my apartment?"

"I'm not that kind of girl."

"I was afraid of that," he said. "No, that's not true. I

knew that. You brought this whole thing up. I'm getting a bum rap."

"Daffy warned me about you," she said. "The best defense is a good offense. Haven't you ever heard that?"

"How did the kiss fit into that strategy?"

"How far is where we're going?" she said, cleverly changing the subject.

"Not far enough. In no more than twenty minutes we'll be there."

A Mercedes-Benz 380 SL convertible with its ragtop up drove onto the fourth floor of the Penn Services Parking Garage. The driver, a young woman, looked forward over the steering wheel, looking for a place to park.

She did not look toward where Charles was standing, behind a round concrete pole at the north end of the building, in a position that both gave him a view of the street down which Anthony J. DeZego would probably come—unless, of course, he sent Jowls the Bellboy to fetch the car—and also shielded him from the view of anyone who came out of the stairwell to get his car.

And she did not find a parking space, as Charles knew she would not; the fourth floor was full.

The Mercedes continued around and went up the vehicular ramp to the roof.

Charles looked out the window again and saw Anthony J. DeZego walking quickly down the street toward the Penn Services Parking Garage from the fourth-floor window. He was alone; there would have been a problem if he had had the blonde-without-a-bra with him.

He looked down at the street and saw Victor, or at least Victor's shoulder, where he was sitting in the Pontiac. It would have been better if he could have caught Victor's attention and signaled him that DeZego was coming; but where Victor was parked, the garage attendant could see him and probably would have remembered having seen some guy across the street in a Pontiac who kept looking up at the garage.

Victor was watching the exit; that was all that counted.

Charles took his pigskin gloves from his pocket and pulled them on. Then he picked up the carry-on bag and walked down the center of the vehicular path toward the stairwell. If another car came or someone walked out of the stairwell, he would be just one more customer leaving the garage.

No one came.

The stairwell was sort of a square of concrete blocks set aside the south side of the building. The door from it was maybe six feet from the wall. Management had generously provided a rubber wedge to keep the door open when necessary. When Charles decided the dame in the Benz had had time to park her car and go down the stairs, he opened the door and propped it open with the wedge.

He had considered doing the job in the stairwell itself but had decided that the stairwell probably would carry the sound of the Remington down to the attendant and make him curious. When he heard footsteps coming up the stairwell, he would kick the wedge loose and let the automatic door-closer do its thing.

Then, when DeZego came onto the fourth floor, and he was sure it was him, he would do the job. With the door closed, the noise would not be funneled downstairs.

He stepped into the shadow of the stairwell wall, unzipped the carry-on, removed the Remington, pushed the safety off, and checked to make sure the red on the little button was visible, that he hadn't by mistake put the safety on. Then he put the Remington under the Burberry trench coat. The pocket had a flap and a slit, so that you could get your hand inside the coat. He held the Remington by the pistol grip straight down against his leg.

He heard footsteps on the stairs.

He dislodged the rubber wedge with his toe, and the door started to close.

He put his ear to the concrete, not really expecting to hear anything. But he was surprised. The stairs were metal, and they sort of rang like a bell. He could hear DeZego coming closer and closer. He waited for the door to open.

It didn't.

There was a moment's silence, and Charles decided that DeZego had reached the landing. The door would open any second.

But then there came the unmistakable sound of footsteps on the metal stairs again.

What the fuck?

Lover Boy is going up to the roof. He's daydreaming, or stupid, or something, his Caddy is on *this* floor, not the fucking roof! In a moment he'll come back down.

But he did not.

Charles considered the situation very quickly.

No real problem. There or here. There's nobody on the roof, and if he sees me, he doesn't know me.

He pulled the door open and, as quietly as he could, quickly ran up the stairs to the roof. He pulled the stairwell door open.

Lover Boy was right there, leaning against the concrete blocks of the stairwell, like he was waiting for somebody.

"Long walk up here," Charles said, smiling at him.

"You said it," Anthony J. DeZego said.

Charles walked ten feet past Anthony J. DeZego, turned around suddenly, raised the shotgun to his shoulder, and blew off the top of Anthony J. DeZego's head.

DeZego fell backward against the concrete blocks of the stairwell and slumped to the ground.

There was a sound like a run-over dog.

Charles looked around the roof. In the middle of the vehicular passageway was a young woman, her eyes wide, both of her hands pressed against her mouth, making run-over-dog noises.

Charles raised the Remington and fired. She went down like a rock.

The goddamned broad in the goddamned Mercedes! She didn't go downstairs. She sat there and fixed her fucking hair or something!

Charles went to Anthony J. DeZego's corpse and took the Caddy keys from his pocket.

I better do her again, to make sure she's dead.

There was the sound of tires squealing. Another car was coming up.

And since there's no room on the fourth floor, he'll be coming up here! Damn!

Charles went into the stairwell and down to the fourth floor. He opened the door a crack, saw nothing, and then pushed it open wide enough to get through.

He went to DeZego's Cadillac, unlocked the door, put the Remington on the floor, and got behind the wheel. He started the engine and drove down the vehicular ramp. He stopped at the barrier, put the window down, handed the attendant a five-dollar bill and the claim check, waited for his change, and then for the barrier to be lifted.

Then he drove out onto the street and turned left. He looked in the rearview mirror and saw the Pontiac pull away from the curb and start to follow him.

"Damn, here we are already," Matt Payne said as he turned the Porsche into the Penn Services Parking Garage behind the Bellevue-Stratford Hotel in downtown Philadelphia.

"How time flies," Amanda said, mocking him gently.

He stopped to get a ticket from a dispensing machine and then drove inside. He drove slowly, hoping to find a space on a lower floor. There were none. He searched the second level, and then the third and fourth. They finally emerged on the roof.

Matt stepped hard on the brakes. The Porsche shuddered and skidded to a stop, throwing Amanda against the dashboard.

"My God!" she exclaimed.

"Stay here," Matt Payne ordered firmly.

"What is it?" Amanda asked.

He didn't answer. He got out of the Porsche and ran across the rooftop parking lot. Amanda saw him drop to one knee, and then for the first time saw that a girl was lying facedown, on the roadway between lines of parked cars.

She pushed open her door and got out and ran to him.

"What happened?" Amanda asked.

"I told you to stay in the fucking car!" he said furiously.

She looked at him, shocked as much by the tone of his voice as by the language, and then at the girl on the floor. For the first time she saw there was a pool of blood.

"What happened?" she asked, her voice weak.

"Will you please go get in the goddamned car?" Matt asked.

"Oh, my *God*!" Amanda wailed. "That's *Penny*!"

"You know her?"

"Penny Detweiler," Amanda said. "You must know her. She's one of the bridesmaids."

Matt looked at the girl on the floor. It *was* Penelope Detweiler, Precious Penny to Matt, to her intense annoyance, because that's what her father had once called her in Matt's hearing.

Why didn't I recognize her? I've known her all of my life!

"I'll be damned," he said softly.

"Matt, what *happened* to her?"

"She's been shot," Matt Payne said, and looked at Amanda.

You don't expect to find people you know, especially people like Precious Penny, lying in a pool of blood after somebody's shot them in a garage. Things like that aren't supposed to happen to people like Precious Penny.

He found his voice: "Now, for chrissake, will you go get in the goddamned car!" he ordered furiously.

Amanda looked at him with confusion and hurt in her eyes.

"This just happened," he explained more kindly. "Whoever did it may still be up here."

"Matt, let's get out of here. Let's go find a cop."

"I am a cop, Amanda," Matt Payne said. "Now, for the last fucking time, will you go get in the car? Stay there until I come for you. Lock the doors."

He stooped, bending one knee, and when he stood erect again, there was a snub-nosed revolver in his hand. Amanda ran back to the silver Porsche and locked the doors. When she looked for Matt, she couldn't see him at first, but then she did, and he was holding his gun at the ready, slowly making his way between the parked cars.

I don't believe this is happening. I don't believe Penny Detweiler is lying out there bleeding to death, and I don't believe that Matt Payne is out there with a gun in his hand, a cop looking for whoever shot Penny.

Oh, my God. What if he gets killed?

FOUR

With difficulty, for there is not much room in the passenger compartment of a Porsche 911 Carrera, Amanda Spencer crawled over from the passenger seat to the driver's and turned the ignition key.

There was a scream of tortured starter gears, for the engine was still running. She threw the gearshift lever into reverse, spun the wheels, and turned around, then drove as fast as she dared down the ramps of the parking garage to street level.

She slammed on the brakes and jumped out of the car and ran to the attendant's window.

"Call the police!" she said. "Call the police and get an ambulance."

"Hey, lady, what's going on?"

"Get on that phone and call the police and get an ambulance," Amanda ordered firmly. "Tell them there's been a shooting."

A red light began to flash on one of the control consoles in the radio room of the Philadelphia Police Department.

Foster H. Lewis, Jr., who was sitting slumped in a battered and sagging metal chair, a headset clamped to his head, threw a switch and spoke into his microphone. "Police Emergency," he said.

Foster H. Lewis, Jr., was twenty-three years old, weighed two hundred and twenty-seven pounds, stood six feet three inches tall, and was perhaps inevitably known as Tiny. For more than five years before he had entered the Police Academy, he had worked as a temporary employee in Police Emergency: five years of nights and weekends and during the summers answering calls from excited citizens in trouble and needing help had turned him into a skilled and experienced operator.

He had more or less quit when he entered the Police Academy and was working tonight as a favor to Lieutenant Jack Fitch, who had called him and said he had five people out with some kind of a virus and could he help out.

"This the police?" his caller asked.

"This is Police Emergency," Tiny Lewis said. "May I help you, sir?"

"I'm the attendant at the Penn Services Parking Garage on Fifteenth, behind the Bellevue-Stratford."

"How may I help you, sir?"

"I got a white lady here says there's been a shooting on the roof and somebody got shot and says to send an ambulance."

"Could you put her on the phone, please?"

"I'm in the booth, you know, can't get her in here."

"Please stay on the line, sir," Tiny said.

There are twenty-two police districts in Philadelphia. Without having to consult a map, Tiny Lewis knew that the parking garage behind the Bellevue-Stratford Hotel was in the 9th District, whose headquarters are at 22nd Street and Pennsylvania Avenue.

He checked his console display for the 9th District and saw that an indicator with 914 on it was lit up. The 9 made reference to the District; 14 was the number of a radio patrol car assigned to cover the City Hall area.

Tiny Lewis reached for a small black toggle switch on the console before him and held it down for a full two seconds. A long beep was broadcast on the Central Division radio frequency, alerting all cars in the Central Division, which includes the 9th District, that an important message is about to be broadcast.

"Fifteenth and Walnut, the Penn Services Parking Garage, report of a shooting and a hospital case," Tiny Lewis said into his microphone, and added, "914, 906, 9A."

There was an immediate response: "914 okay."

This was from Officer Archie Hellerman, who had just entered Rittenhouse Square from the west. He then put the microphone down, flipped on the siren and the flashing lights, and began to move as rapidly as he could through the heavy early-evening traffic on the narrow streets toward the Penn Services Parking Garage.

Tiny Lewis began to write the pertinent information on a three-by-five index card. At this stage the incident was officially an "investigation, shooting, and hospital case."

As he reached up to put the card between electrical contacts on a shelf above his console, which would interrupt the current lighting the small bulb behind the 914 block on the display console, three other radio calls came in.

"Radio, EPW 906 in."

"9A okay."

"Highway 4B in on that."

EPW 906 was an emergency patrol van, in this case a battered 1970 Ford, one of the two-man emergency patrol wagons assigned to the 9th District to transport the injured, prisoners, and otherwise assist in law enforcement. If this was not a bullshit call, 906 would carry whoever was shot to a hospital.

The district sergeant, 9A, was assigned to the eastern half of the 9th District.

Highway 4B was a radio patrol car of the Highway Patrol, an elite unit of the Philadelphia Police Department which the the Philadelphia *Ledger* had recently taken to calling Carlucci's Commandos.

As a police captain, the Honorable Jerome H. "Jerry" Carlucci, mayor of the City of Philadelphia, had commanded the Highway Patrol, which had begun, as its name implied, as a special organization to patrol the highways. Even before Captain Jerry Carlucci's reign, Highway Patrol had evolved into something more than motorcycle-mounted cops riding up and down Roosevelt Boulevard and the Schuylkill Expressway handing out speeding tickets. Carlucci, however, had presided over the ultimate transition of a traffic unit into an all-volunteer elite force. Highway had traded most of its motorcycles for two-man patrol cars and had citywide authority. Other Philadelphia police rode alone in patrol cars and patrolled specific areas in specific districts.

Highway Patrol had kept its motorcyclist's special uniforms (crushed crown cap, leather jacket, boots, and Sam Browne belts) and prided itself on being where the action was; in other words, in high-crime areas.

Highway Patrol was either "a highly trained, highly mobile anticrime task force of proven effectiveness" (Mayor Jerry Carlucci in a speech to the Sons of Italy) or "a jack-booted Gestapo" (an editorial in the Philadelphia *Ledger*).

Tiny Lewis had expected prompt responses to his call. EPWs generally were sent in on any call where an injury was reported, a supervisor responded to all major calls, and somebody from Highway Patrol (sometimes four or five cars) always went in on a "shooting and hospital case."

The door buzzer for the radio room went off. One of the uniformed officers on duty walked to it, opened it, smiled, and admitted a tall, immaculately uniformed lieutenant.

He was tall, nearly as tall as Tiny Lewis, but much leaner. He had very black skin and sharp Semitic features. He walked to Tiny Lewis's control console and said, somewhat menacingly, "I didn't expect to find you here. I went to your apartment and they told me where to find you."

"My apartment? Not my 'disgusting hovel'?"

"We have to talk," Lieutenant Lewis said.

"Not now, Pop," Tiny Lewis said. "I'm working a shooting and hospital case." And then he added, "In your district, come to think of it. On the roof of the Penn Services Parking Garage behind the Bellevue-Stratford. Civilian by phone, but I don't think it's bullshit."

"Can we have coffee when you get off?" Lieutenant Lewis asked. "I just heard you're going to Special Operations."

"Strange, I thought you arranged that," Tiny said.

"I told you, I just heard about it."

"Okay, Pop," Tiny said. "I'll meet you downstairs."

Lieutenant Lewis nodded, then walked very quickly out of the radio room.

Officer Archie Hellerman, driving RPC 914, couldn't count how many times he had been summoned to the Penn Services Parking Garage since it had been built seven years before. The attendant had been robbed at least once a month. One attendant, with more guts than brains, had even been shot at when he had refused to hand over the money.

Like most policemen who had been on the same job for years, Archie Hellerman had an encyclopedic knowledge of the buildings in his patrol area. He knew how the Penn Services Parking Garage operated. Incoming cars turned off South 15th Street into the entranceway. Ten yards inside, there was a wooden barrier across the roadway. Taking a ticket from an automatic ticket dispenser activated a mechanism that raised the barrier.

Departing cars left the building at the opposite end of the building, where an attendant in a small, allegedly robbery-proof booth collected the parking ticket, computed the charges, and, when they had been paid, raised another barrier, giving the customer access to the street.

Archie Hellerman in RPC 914 was the first police vehicle to arrive at the crime scene. As he approached the garage, he turned off his siren but left the flashing lights on. He pulled the nose of his Ford blue-and-white onto the exit ramp, which was blocked by a silver Porsche 911 Carrera, and jumped out of the car.

There was a civilian woman, a good-looking young blonde in a fancy dress, standing between the Porsche and the attendant's booth. She was obviously the complainant, the civilian who had reported the shooting.

Just seeing the blonde and her state of excitement was enough to convince Archie that the call was for real. Something serious had gone down.

"What's going on, miss?" Archie Hellerman asked.

"A girl has been shot on the roof. We need an ambulance."

The dying growl of a siren caught Archie's attention. He stepped back on the sidewalk and saw a radio patrol wagon, its warning lights still flashing, pulling up. There was another siren wailing, but that car, almost certainly the Highway car that had radioed in that it was going in on the call, was not yet in sight.

Archie signaled for the wagon to block the entrance ramp and then turned back to the good-looking blonde.

"You want to tell me what happened, please?"

"Well, we drove onto the roof, and my boyfriend saw her lying on the floor—"

"Your boyfriend? Where is he?"

I said "my boyfriend." Why did I say "my boyfriend"?

"He's up there," Amanda Spencer said. "He's a policeman."

"Your boyfriend is a cop?"

Amanda Spencer nodded her head.

Matt Payne is a cop. He really is a cop, as incredible as that seems. He had a gun, and he talked to me like a cop.

The driver of EPW 906, Officer Howard C. Sawyer, a very large twenty-six-year-old who had been dropped from a farm team of the Baltimore Orioles just before joining the Department sixteen months ago, pulled the Ford van onto the entrance ramp and started to get out.

He heard a siren die behind him, then growl again, and turned to look.

"Get that out of there!" the driver of Highway 4B shouted, his head out the window of the antenna-festooned but otherwise unmarked car.

Officer Sawyer backed the van up enough for the Highway Patrol car to get past him. The tires squealed as the car, in low gear, drove inside the building and started up the ramp to the upper floors. Sawyer saw that the driver was a sergeant; and, surprised, he noticed that the other cop was a regular cop, wearing a regular, as opposed to crushed-crown, uniform cap.

At precisely that moment the driver of Highway 4B, Sergeant Nick DeBenedito, who had been a policeman for ten years and a Highway Patrol sergeant for two, had a professional, if somewhat unkind, thought: *Shit, I'm riding with a rookie! And I got a gut feeling that whatever this job is, it's for real.*

Then, as he glanced over at Officer Jesus Martinez, he immediately modified that thought. Martinez, a slight, sharp-featured Latino kid of twenty-four, was, by the ordinary criteria, certainly a rookie. He had been on the job less than two years. But he'd gone right from the Police Academy to a plainclothes assignment with Narcotics.

He'd done very well at that, learning more in the year he'd spent on that assignment about the sordid underside of Philadelphia than a lot of cops learned in a lifetime. And then he'd topped that off helping to catch a scumbag named Gerald Vincent Gallagher, the junkie who had fatally shot Captain Richard F. "Dutch" Moffitt during a failed holdup of the Waikiki Diner on Roosevelt Boulevard.

Every cop in Philadelphia, all eight thousand of them, had been looking for Gerald Vincent Gallagher, especially every cop in Highway. Captain "Dutch" Moffitt had been the Highway commander. But Martinez and his partner, McFadden, had found him, by staking out where they thought he would show up. Martinez and Gallagher had both shown a lot of balls and unusual presence of mind under pressure by chasing the scumbag first through the crowded station and then down the elevated tracks of the subway. They'd had a chance to shoot Gallagher but hadn't fired because they were concerned about where his bullets might land.

McFadden had just about laid his hands on the son of a bitch when Gallagher had slipped and fried himself on the third rail and then gotten himself chopped up under the wheels of a subway train, but that didn't take one little thing away from the way Martinez and McFadden had handled themselves.

Around the bar of the FOP (Fraternal Order of Police), they said they ought to give them two citations, one for finding Gallagher and another for saving the city the cost of trying the son of a bitch.

Once they'd gotten their pictures in the newspapers, of course, that had ruined them for an undercover job in Narcotics. In most other big-city police departments, what they had done would have seen them promoted to detective. But in Philadelphia, all promotions are by examination, and Jesus Martinez had not yet taken it, and Charley McFadden hadn't been on the job long enough even to take it.

That didn't mean the department big shots weren't grateful. They also knew that most young cops who had worked in plainclothes regarded being ordered back into uniform as sort of a demotion, and they didn't want to do that to Martinez and McFadden. "They" included Chief Inspector Dennis V. Coughlin, arguably the most influential of all the chief inspectors.

And at about that time His Honor the Mayor had offered some more of his "suggestions" for the betterment of the Police Department, this one resulting in the establishment of a new division to be called Special Operations, under a young, hotshot staff inspector named Wohl, about whom little was known except some of the old-timers said that his father had been the mayor's rabbi when the mayor was a cop.

The mayor hadn't stopped with that, either. His other "suggestions" had pissed off just about everybody in Highway. He had "suggested" that a newly promoted captain named David Pekach, who had been assigned to Narcotics, be named the new commander of Highway, to replace Captain Dutch Moffitt. Everybody in Highway thought that Dutch Moffitt's deputy, Mike Sabara, who had been on the same captains' promotion list as Pekach, would get the job. Not only that, but Pekach was well-known within Highway as the guy who had bagged the only drug-dirty cop, a sergeant, Highway had ever had.

He had also "suggested" that Captain Sabara be named deputy commander of the new Special Operations Division. And finally, what had really pissed Highway off, he had "suggested" that Highway be placed under the new Special Operations Division. Highway, from its beginnings, had always been special and separate. Now it was going to be under some young clown whose only claim to fame was that he was well connected politically.

It had quickly become common knowledge in Highway that their new boss, Staff Inspector Peter Wohl, not only looked wet behind the ears but was. He was the youngest of the sixteen staff inspectors in the Department. He had spent very little time on the streets as a "real cop," but instead had spent most of his career as an investigator, most recently of corrupt politicians, of which Philadelphia, it was said, had more than its fair share. He had never worn a uniform as a lieutenant or a captain and had zero experience running a district or even a special unit, like Homicide, Intelligence, or even the K-9 Corps.

Five days before, Sergeant DeBenedito had been ordered to report to the commander of Special Operations in Special Operations' temporary headquarters at Bustleton and Bowler Streets in Northeast Philadelphia.

Captains Sabara and Pekach were in Staff Inspector Peter Wohl's office when he went in. Mike Sabara was wearing the uniform prescribed for captains not attached to Highway Patrol. It consisted of a white shirt with captain's bars on the collar and blue trousers. He carried a snub-nosed Smith & Wesson .38 Special revolver in a small holster on his belt. DeBenedito had heard that Wohl had told him, to make the point that Sabara was no longer in Highway, that he had his choice of either civilian clothing, or uniform without the distinguishing motorcyclist boots and Sam Browne belt with its row of shiny cartridges.

Captain Pekach was wearing the Highway uniform. The contrast between the two was significant.

Wohl, DeBenedito thought somewhat unkindly, did not even look like a cop. He was a tall, slim young man with light brown hair. He was wearing a blue blazer and gray flannel slacks, a white button-down shirt with a rep-striped necktie. He looked, DeBenedito thought, like some candy-ass lawyer or stockbroker from the Main Line.

He was sitting on a couch with his feet, shod in glistening loafers, resting on a coffee table. When his office had been Dutch Moffitt's office, there had been neither coffee table nor couch in it.

"Well, that was quick," Wohl said. "I just sent for you."

"I just came in, sir," DeBenedito said, shaking hands first with Mike Sabara and then with Pekach.

"Help yourself to coffee," Wohl said, gesturing toward a chrome thermos.

"No thank you, sir."

"Okay. Right to the point," Wohl had said. "Do you know Officers Jesus Martinez and Charles McFadden?"

"I've seen them around, sir."

"You know *about* them?"

"Yes, sir."

"I'm going to make them probationary Highway Patrolmen," Wohl said.

"I don't know what that means, sir," DeBenedito said.

"That's probably because I just made it up," Wohl confessed cheerfully, with a chuckle. To DeBenedito's surprise, Captain Sabara laughed.

"A probationary Highway Patrolman," Wohl went on, "is a young police officer who has done something outstanding in the course of his regular duties. On the recommendation of his captain, and if he volunteers, he will be temporarily assigned to Highway. For three months he will be paired with a supervisor—a sergeant such as yourself, DeBenedito. . . ."

DeBenedito became aware that Wohl was waiting for a response. "Yes, sir," he said.

"During that three months the probationers will ride either with their sergeant or with a *good* Highway cop. And I mean replacing the second cop in the car, not as excess baggage in the backseat."

"Yes, sir," DeBenedito said.

"And at the end of the three months the supervisor will recommend, in writing, that the probationer be taken into Highway; in other words, go through the Wheel School and the other training or not. With his reasons."

Sergeant DeBenedito did not like what he had heard. When it became apparent to him that Wohl was again waiting for a response, he blurted, "Can you do that, sir?"

"Do you mean, do I have the authority?"

"Yes, sir. I mean, the requirements for getting into Highway are pretty well established. We don't take people with less than four, five years—"

"Didn't," Wohl said, interrupting. "B.W."

" 'B.W.,' sir?"

"Before Wohl," Wohl explained. "And do I have the authority? I don't know. But until someone tells me in writing that I don't, I'm going to presume that I do."

"Yes, sir," DeBenedito said.

"I don't think length of service would be that important a criterion for getting into Highway," Wohl said. "I think doing an outstanding job should carry more weight."

"Sir," DeBenedito said, "with respect, Highway is different."

He saw in the look on Captain Sabara's face that that had been the wrong thing to say.

"Cutting this short," Wohl said, a hint of annoyance in his voice, "based on Captain Sabara's recommendation of you, Sergeant, you are herewith appointed probationary evaluation officer for Officers Jesus Martinez and Charles McFadden, whose probationary period begins today. If you run into any problems, let Captain Pekach know. That will be all. Thank you."

Captain Pekach had followed DeBenedito out of Wohl's office.

"I want to introduce you to Martinez and McFadden," Pekach said. "I told them to wait in the roll call room."

"I guess I said the wrong thing in there, huh?" DeBenedito had asked.

"You're going to have to learn to know what you're talking about before you open your mouth," Pekach had replied. "I don't think you would have told the inspector that Highway was different if you knew he was the youngest sergeant ever in Highway, would you?"

"Jesus, was he?"

"Yeah, he was. He was also the youngest captain the Department has ever had, *is* the youngest staff inspector the Department has ever had, and if he doesn't shoot himself in the foot with Special Operations, stands, I think, a damned good chance to be the youngest full inspector."

"Should I go back in there and apologize?"

"No. Let it go. Peter Wohl doesn't carry a grudge. But if you're looking for advice, don't start this evaluation business with Martinez and McFadden thinking it's a dumb idea it was your bad luck to get stuck with. Give it your best shot."

"Yes, sir," DeBenedito said. "They worked for you in Narcotics, didn't they, Captain?"

"Yeah. And they both did a good job for me. But if you're asking if this was my idea, the answer is no. And if you're asking whether I think either of them can cut the mustard, the answer is, I don't know."

Sergeant Nick DeBenedito, driving with great skill, drove up the ramps until he reached the fourth floor. Then he stopped by the stairwell.

"Martinez," he ordered calmly, "you go up the stairs. I don't think we're still going to find anybody up there, but you never know. If you hear somebody going down the stairs, go and yell down at the district guy." He pointed to the side of the parking garage, where a line of windows were open.

"Got it," Martinez said, then got out of the car and went to the stairwell. DeBenedito saw him take his revolver from his holster and carefully push the stairwell door open and go inside. Then DeBenedito stepped on the accelerator and started up the last ramp to the roof. As he drove, he drew his revolver.

Jesus Martinez listened carefully inside the stairwell for any noise and heard none. Then he went up the stairs, taking them two at a time, until he reached the door opening onto the roof.

He listened there for a moment, heard nothing, and then, standing clear of the door, pushed it open. He quickly glanced around. Sergeant DeBenedito was out of his car. He was holding his revolver in both hands, aiming at someone out of sight.

Christ, Jesus Martinez thought in admiration, *he's already got the son of a bitch on the ground!*

He trotted between the parked cars, staying out of what would be the line of fire if DeBenedito fired his revolver, until he could see who was on the ground.

There was the body of a girl in a fancy dress, lying in a pool of blood, and a man in a tuxedo, lying facedown.

"Put cuffs on him, Martinez," DeBenedito ordered.

The man lying facedown moved his head to look at Jesus Martinez.

"Hay-zus, tell him I'm a cop," Matt Payne said.

"Sergeant," Martinez said, "he's a cop."

DeBenedito looked at him, more for absolute confirmation than in surprise. He started to holster his gun.

"Sorry," he said.

Matt Payne got to his knees.

"Is there a wagon on the way?"

"Martinez, yell down for that wagon to get up here," DeBenedito ordered. Jesus ran to the edge of the roof and did so.

"There's a body, white male, head blown away, over by

the stairwell," Payne said, pointing. "I think the doer, doers, were long gone when I drove up here."

"You look familiar," DeBenedito said. "I know you?"

"My name is Payne," Matt said. "I work for Inspector Wohl."

Oh, shit! DeBenedito thought. And then he knew who this guy in the tuxedo was. He was the rookie who had blown the brains of the Northwest Philly serial rapist all over his van.

FIVE

"What the hell happened here?" Sergeant DeBenedito asked Matt Payne as he dropped to one knee to examine the woman on the floor.

She was unconscious but not dead. When he felt his fingers on her neck, feeling for a heartbeat, she moaned. DeBenedito looked impatiently over his shoulder for the wagon.

If we don't get her to a hospital soon, she will be dead.

"She was on the ground, the floor, when I drove up here," Matt said. "When I saw she was shot, I sent my date down to call it in. Then I found the dead guy."

"Any idea who they are?"

"Her name is Detweiler," Matt said. "Penny—Penelope—Detweiler. I guess she was up here with her car—"

"Brilliant," DeBenedito said sarcastically.

"She was going the same place we were," Matt said. "She's a bridesmaid—"

"A what?"

"A bridesmaid. There's a dinner at the Union League."

"Who is she?"

"I told you. Her name is Detweiler," Matt said, and then finally understood the question. "She lives in Chestnut Hill. Her father is president of Nesfoods."

"But you don't know the other victim?"

"No. I don't think he was with her. He's not wearing a dinner jacket."

"A what?"

"A tuxedo. The dinner is what they call 'black-tie.' "

RPW 902 came onto the roof.

Officer Howard C. Sawyer saw DeBenedito and the victim and quickly and skillfully turned the van around and backed up to them. Officer Thomas Collins, riding shotgun in 902, was out of the wagon before it stopped, first signaling to Sawyer when to stop and then quickly opening the rear door.

"This one's still alive," DeBenedito said. "There's a dead one—" He stopped, thinking, *I don't know if the other one is dead or not; all I have is this rookie's opinion that he's dead.*

"The other one *is* dead, right?" he asked, challenging Matt Payne.

"The top of his head is gone," Matt said.

DeBenedito looked at Officers Sawyer, Collins, Payne, and Martinez.

What I have here is four fucking rookies!

The victim moaned as Sawyer and Collins, as gently as they could, picked her up and slid her onto a stretcher.

The second officer in an RPW, the one said to be "riding shotgun," was officially designated as "the recorder"; he was responsible for handling all the paperwork. According to Department procedure, the recorder in an RPW would ride with the victim in the back of the wagon en route to the hospital to interview her, if possible, and possibly get a "dying declaration," what would be described in court as the last words of the deceased before dying. A dying declaration carried a lot of weight with jurors.

Sergeant DeBenedito didn't think Officer Collins looked bright enough to write down his own laundry list.

He made his decision.

"Take her to Hahneman, that's closest," he ordered, referring to Hahneman Hospital, on just the other side of City Hall on North Broad Street. "Martinez, you get in the back with the girl and see what you can find out. You know about 'dying declarations'?''

"Yeah," Martinez said.

"And you, Payne, take the stairs downstairs and seal off the building. Nobody in or out. Got it?"

"Got it," Matt said, and started for the stairwell.

DeBenedito started for his car, and then changed his mind. He still didn't know for sure if the second victim was really dead.

One look at the body confirmed what Payne had told him. The top of the head was gone. The face, its eyes open and distorted, registered surprise.

On closer inspection the victim looked familiar. After a moment Sergeant DeBenedito was almost positive that the second victim was Anthony J. DeZego, a young, not too bright, Mafia guy known as Tony the Zee.

Now he walked quickly to the Highway car and picked up the microphone.

"Highway 21."

"Highway 21," police radio responded.

"I got a 5292 on the roof of the Penn Services garage," DeBenedito reported. "Notify Homicide. The 9th District RPW is transporting a second victim, female Caucasian, to Hahneman."

DeBenedito glanced around the roof and saw an arrow indicating the location of a public telephone.

"Okay, 21," police radio responded.

DeBenedito tossed the microphone on the seat and trotted toward the telephone, searching his pockets for change.

He dialed a number from memory.

"Homicide."

"This is Sergeant DeBenedito, Highway. I got a 5292 on the roof of the Penn Services Parking Garage behind the Bellevue-Stratford. Top of his head blown off. I think he's a mob guy called Tony the Zee."

"Anthony J. DeZego," the Homicide detective responded. "Interesting."

"There was a second victim. Female Caucasian. Multiple wounds. Looks like a shotgun. Identified as Penelope Detweiler. Her father is president of Nesfoods."

"Jesus!"

"She's being transported to Hahneman."

"This is Lieutenant Natali, Sergeant. We got the 5292 from radio. A couple of detectives are on the way. When they get there, tell them I'm on my way. You're sure it's Tony the Zee?"

"Just about. And the ID on the girl is positive."

"I'm on my way," Lieutenant Natali said, and the phone went dead.

DeBenedito dialed another number.

"Highway, Corporal Ashe."

"Sergeant DeBenedito. Pass it to the lieutenant that I went in on shots fired at the parking garage behind the Bellevue. The dead man is a mob guy, Tony the Zee DeZego. Shotgun took the top of his head off. There's a second victim, white female, transported to Hahneman. Name is Detweiler. Her father is president of Nesfoods."

"I'll get it to Lieutenant Lucci right away, Sergeant," Corporal Ashe said.

Sergeant DeBenedito hung up without saying anything else and went back on the roof to have another look at Tony the Zee.

I wonder who blew this scumbag guinea gangster away? thought Sergeant Vincenzo Nicholas DeBenedito idly. The previous summer he had flown to Italy with his parents to meet most, but not all, of his Neapolitan kinfolk.

Then he thought: *Damn shame that girl had to get in between whatever happened here, on her way, all dressed up, to a party at the Union League.*

And then he had another discomfiting thought: Was *the nice little rich girl from Chestnut Hill just an innocent bystander? Or was she fucking around with Tony the Zee?*

Matt Payne pulled open the door to the stairwell and started down, taking the stairs two and three at a time.

He wanted to see what had happened to Amanda Spencer, and he also desperately needed to relieve his bladder. He had been startled to hear the scream of the tires on the Porsche when she had turned it around and driven off the roof. He had had several thoughts: that she was naturally frightened and logically was therefore getting the hell away from the scene; then he was surprised that she could drive the

Porsche, and he modified this last thought to *"drive the Porsche so well"* when he saw her make the turn, then head down the ramp as fast as she could.

Between the third and second floors he startled a very large florid-faced cop wearing the white cap cover of Traffic who was leaning against the cement-block wall. The Traffic cop pushed himself off the wall to block Matt's passage and looked as if he were about to draw his pistol.

"I'm a cop," Matt called. "Payne, Special Operations."

He fished in his pocket and came out with his badge.

"What the hell is going on up there?" the Traffic cop asked.

"A couple of people got shot. With a shotgun. One is dead, and the van is taking a woman to the hospital."

The Traffic cop got out of the way, and Matt ran down the stairs to ground level. He pushed open the door and found himself on 15th Street. Ten yards away, he saw the nose of his Porsche sticking out of the garage and onto the sidewalk. There were a half dozen police cars, marked and unmarked, clustered around the entrance and exit ramps, half up on the sidewalk. A Traffic sergeant was in the narrow street, directing traffic.

When he reached the exit ramp, Amanda was talking to a man with a detective's badge hanging out of the breast pocket of a remarkably ugly plaid sport coat. When she saw him, Amanda walked away from the detective and up to Matt.

"How is she?"

"She's alive," Matt said. "They're taking her to the hospital. We've got to move the Porsche."

As if on cue, the emergency patrol wagon pulled up behind the Porsche and Officer Howard C. Sawyer impatiently sounded the horn. Matt jumped behind the wheel and pulled the Porsche out of the way, onto the sidewalk.

The EPW came off the exit ramp, turned on its siren and flashing lamps, and when the Traffic sergeant, furiously blowing his whistle, stopped the flow of traffic, bounced onto 15th Street, turning left.

When Matt got out of the car, the detective was waiting for him.

"You're the boyfriend?" he asked, and then without waiting for a reply asked, "You found the victim? You're a cop? That's your car?"

Matt looked at Amanda when the detective said the word *boyfriend*. She shrugged her shoulders and looked uncomfortable.

"My name is Payne," Matt said. "Special Operations. That's my car. We saw one of the victims on the ground when we drove onto the roof."

"You're Payne? The guy who blew the rapist away?"

Matt nodded.

"There's a Highway sergeant up there," Matt said. "He sent me to seal the building."

"It's been sealed," the detective said, gesturing up and down the street. "I'm Joe D'Amata, Homicide," he said. "You have any idea what went down?"

"*Two* victims," Matt said. "I found a white male with his head blown off next to the stairwell. Looks like a shotgun." He looked at Amanda. "Did Miss Spencer tell you who the female is?"

"I was about to ask her," the detective said.

"She's Penny Detweiler," Amanda said.

"You know her? You were with her?"

"We know her. We weren't with her. Or not really."

"What the hell does that mean?"

"There's a dinner party. There's a wedding. She was supposed to be at it."

"A dinner party or a wedding?" D'Amata asked impatiently. "Which?"

"A wedding dinner party," Matt said, feeling foolish, and anticipated D'Amata's next question. "At the Union League."

D'Amata looked at Payne. Ordinary cops do not ordinarily go to dinner at the Union League. He remembered what he had heard about this kid. There had been a lot of talk around the Department about him. Rich kid. College boy from Wallingford. But it was also said that his father, a sergeant, had been killed on the job. And there was no question he'd blown away the serial rapist. There had been a picture of him in all the papers, with Mayor Carlucci's arm around him. The critter had tried to run him down with a van, and then the kid had blown the critter's brains out. The critter had had a woman, a naked woman, tied up in the back of the van when it happened. If the kid hadn't caught him when he did, the woman would have been another victim. The critter had tortured and mutilated his previous victim before he'd killed her. A real scumbag loony.

"The Union League," Detective D'Amata said as he wrote it down.

"Her parents are probably there now," Matt Payne said. "Somebody's going to have to tell them what happened."

"You mean, you want to?"

"I don't know how it's done," Matt confessed.

Detective D'Amata looked around, found what he was looking for, and raised his voice: "Lieutenant Lewis?"

Lieutenant Foster H. Lewis, Sr., of the 9th District, who had only moments before arrived at the crime scene, looked around to see who was calling him, and found D'Amata.

"See you a minute, Lieutenant?" D'Amata called.

Lieutenant Lewis walked over.

"Lieutenant, this is Officer Payne, of Special Operations. He and this young lady found the victims."

Lieutenant Lewis looked carefully at Officer Matthew Payne, who was wearing a dinner jacket Lieutenant Lewis would have bet good money was his and hadn't come from a rental agency. He knew a good deal about Officer Matthew W. Payne.

There was a vacancy for a lieutenant in the newly formed Special Operations Division. Lewis had thought—before he'd heard that Foster, Jr., was being assigned there—that it might be a good place for him to broaden his experience and enhance his career. So far all of his experience had been in one district or another.

An old friend of his, a Homicide detective named Jason Washington, had been transferred, over his objections, to Special Operations, and he'd had a long talk with Washington about Special Operations and its youthful commander, Staff Inspector Peter Wohl.

In the course of that conversation the well-publicized heroics of Wohl's special assistant had come up. To Lewis's surprise, Jason Washington had kind words for both men: "Peter Wohl's as smart as a whip and a straight arrow. A little ruthless about getting the job done, not to protect himself. And the kid's all right too. Denny Coughlin dumped him in Wohl's lap; he didn't ask for the job. I think he's got the making of a good cop; the last I heard, it wasn't illegal to be either rich or well connected.''

"I'm surprised, Officer Payne," Lieutenant Lewis said, "that Inspector Wohl hasn't told you that it is Departmental procedure for an officer in civilian clothing at a crime scene to display his badge in a prominent place."

Matt looked at him for a moment, then said, "Sorry, sir."

He took the folder holding his badge and photo identification card from his pocket and tried to shove it into the breast pocket of his dinner jacket. It didn't fit. He started to unpin the badge from the leather folder.

I wonder, Lieutenant Lewis thought, *how this young man's father feels about him becoming a policeman? He is probably at least as unenthusiastic about it as I am about that hardheaded, overgrown namesake of mine.*

It is a question of upward and downward social mobility. My son has thrown away a splendid chance at upward mobility, to become a doctor; to make, a few years out of medical school, more money than I will ever make in my lifetime. This young man is turning his back on God alone knows what. Certainly, a partnership in Mawson, Payne, Stockton, McAdoo and Lester. Very possibly a chance to become a senator or a governor. Certainly to make a great deal of money.

I am as baffled by this one as I am by Foster.

"Lieutenant," Detective D'Amata said, "Payne knows one of the victims. The woman." He consulted his notebook. "Her name is Penelope Detweiler. He says her parents are probably at the Union League—"

"Chestnut Hill?" Lieutenant Lewis asked, interrupting. "Those Detweilers, Payne?"

"Yes, sir."

Lieutenant Lewis also knew a good deal about the Detweilers of Chestnut Hill. Four generations ago George Detweiler had gone into partnership with Chadwick Thomas Nesbitt to found what was then called the Nesbitt Potted Meats and Preserved Vegetables Company. It was now Nesfoods International, listed just above the middle of the Fortune 500 companies and still tightly held. C. T. Nesbitt III was chairman of the Executive Committee and H. Richard Detweiler was President and Chief Executive Officer.

C. T. Nesbitt IV was to be married the day after tomorrow by the Episcopal Bishop of Philadelphia at St. Mark's Church. His Honor the Mayor and Mrs. Carlucci had been invited, and there had been a call from a mayor's officer to the 9th District commander, saying the mayor didn't want any problems with traffic or anything else.

Extra officers from the 9th District had been assigned to assist the Traffic Division in handling the flow of traffic. As a traffic problem it would be much like a very large funeral. A large number of people would arrive, more or less singly, at the church. Traffic flow would be impeded as each car (in many cases, a limousine) paused long enough to discharge its passengers and then moved on to find a parking place. After the wedding the problem would grow worse, as the four hundred odd guests left all at once to find their cars or limousines for the ride to the reception at the home of the bride's parents. Only the problem of forming a funeral convoy of cars would be missing.

Additionally there would be a number of plainclothes officers from Civil Affairs and the Detective Division mingling with the guests at the church and at the pre-wedding cocktail party for out-of-town guests in the Bellevue-Stratford Hotel.

Captain J. J. Maloney, the 9th District Commander, had ordered Lieutenant Foster H. Lewis, Sr., to take care of it.

"Has the family of the victim been informed?" Lieutenant Lewis asked.

"No, sir," D'Amata said.

"Sir, I thought maybe I could do that," Payne said.

Lieutenant Lewis thought that over carefully for a moment. It had to be done. Normally it would be the responsibility of the 9th District. But if Payne did it, it would probably be handled with greater tact than if he dispatched an RPC to do it. He considered for a moment going himself, or going with Payne, and decided against it. He also decided that he would not take it upon himself to notify the mayor, although he was sure Jerry Carlucci would want to hear about this. Let Captain J. J. Maloney tell the mayor, or one of the big brass. He would find a phone and call Maloney.

"Very well," Lieutenant Lewis said. "Do so. I don't think

I have to tell you to express the regret of the Police Department that something like this has happened, do I?''

"No, sir."

"As I understand the situation, we don't know what happened here, do we?''

"No, sir," Matt Payne said.

"I'm sure that you will not volunteer your opinions, will you, Payne?''

"No, sir."

"And then come back here," Lieutenant Lewis said. "I'm sure Detective D'Amata, and others, will have questions for you."

"Yes, sir."

Lieutenant Lewis turned to Amanda Spencer.

"I didn't get your name, miss," he said.

"Amanda Spencer."

"Are you from Philadelphia, Miss Spencer?''

"Scarsdale," Amanda said, adding, "New York."

"You're in town for the wedding?''

"That's right."

"Where are you staying here?''

"With the Brownes, the bride's family," Amanda answered. "In Merion."

That would be the Soames T. Brownes, Lieutenant Lewis recalled from an extraordinary memory. Soames T. Browne did not have a job. When his picture appeared, for example, in a listing of the board of directors of the Philadelphia Savings Fund Society, the caption under it read "Soames T. Browne, Investments." The Brownes—and for that matter, the Soames—had been investing, successfully, in Philadelphia businesses since Ben Franklin had been running the newspaper there.

There was going to be a lot of pressure on this job, Lewis thought. And a lot of publicity. People like the Nesbitts and the Brownes and the Detweilers took the term *public servant* literally, with emphasis on *servant*. They expected public servants, like the police and the courts, to do what they had been hired to do, and were not at all reluctant to point out where those public servants had failed to perform. When a Detweiler called the mayor, he took the call.

Lieutenant Lewis thought again that Jerry Carlucci had

been invited to the wedding and the reception and might even be at the Union League when the Payne kid walked in and told them that Penelope Detweiler had just been shot.

"Ordinarily, Miss Spencer, we'd ask you to come to the Roundhouse—"

"The what?" Amanda asked.

"To the Police Administration Building—"

"The whole building is curved, Amanda," Matt explained.

"—to be interviewed by a Homicide detective," Lieutenant Lewis went on, clearly displeased with Matt's interruption. "But since Officer Payne was with you, possibly Detective D'Amata would be willing to have you come there a little later."

"No problem with that, sir," D'Amata said.

And then, as if to document his prediction that the shooting was going to attract a good deal of attention from the press, an antenna-bedecked Buick Special turned out of the line of traffic and pulled into the exit ramp, and Mr. Michael J. O'Hara got out.

Mickey O'Hara wrote about crime for the Philadelphia *Bulletin*. He was very good at what he did and was regarded by most policemen, including Lieutenant Foster H. Lewis, Sr., as almost a member of the Department. If you told Mickey O'Hara that something was off the record, it stayed that way.

"Hey, Foster," Mickey O'Hara said, "that white shirt looks good on you."

That made reference to Lieutenant Foster's almost brand-new status as a lieutenant. Police supervisors, lieutenants and above, wore white uniform shirts. Sergeants and below wore blue.

"How are you, Mickey?" Lewis said, shaking O'Hara's hand. "Thank you."

"And what are you doing, Matt?" O'Hara said, offering his hand to Officer Payne. "Moonlighting as a waiter?"

"Hey, Mickey," Payne said.

"What's going on?"

"Hold it a second, Mickey," Lewis said. "Miss Spencer, you'll have to make a statement. Payne will tell you about

that. And you come back here, Payne, as soon as you do
what you have to do.''

"Yes, sir. See you, Mickey.''

O'Hara waited until Matt Payne had politely loaded
Amanda Spencer into the Porsche, gotten behind the wheel,
and was fed into the line of traffic by the Traffic sergeant
before speaking.

"Nice kid, that boy,'' he said.

"So I hear,'' Lieutenant Lewis said.

"What does he have to do before he comes back here?''

"Tell H. Richard Detweiler that his daughter was found
lying in a pool of blood on the roof of this place; somebody
popped her with a shotgun,'' Lewis said.

"No shit? Detweiler's daughter? Is she dead?''

"No. Not yet, anyway. They just took her to Hahneman.
There's another victim up there. White man. He got his head
blown off.''

"Robbery?'' Mickey O'Hara asked. "With a shotgun?
Who is he?''

"We don't know.''

"Can I go up there?'' Mickey asked.

"I'll go with you,'' Lewis said, and gestured toward the
stairwell.

Between the third and fourth floors of the Penn Services
Parking Garage, Lieutenant Lewis and Mr. O'Hara encountered Detective Lawrence Godofski of Homicide coming
down the stairs.

Godofski had a plastic bag in his hand. He extended it to
Lieutenant Lewis.

"Whaddayasay, Larry?'' Mickey O'Hara said.

"How goes it, Mickey?''

The plastic bag contained a leather wallet and a number of
cards, driver's license, and credit cards, which apparently had
been removed from the wallet.

Lieutenant Lewis examined the driver's license through the
clear plastic bag and then handed it to Mickey O'Hara. The
driver's license had been issued to Anthony J. DeZego, of a
Bouvier Street address in South Philadelphia, an area known
as Little Italy.

"I'll be damned,'' Mickey O'Hara said. "Tony the Zee.
He's the body?''

Detective Godofski nodded.

"This is pretty classy for Tony the Zee, getting himself blown away like this," O'Hara said. "The last I heard, he was driving a shrimp-and-oyster reefer truck up from the Gulf Coast."

"Godofski," Lieutenant Lewis said, "have you thought about bringing Organized Crime in on this?"

"Yes, sir. I was about to do just that."

"You find anything else interesting up there?"

Godofski produced another plastic bag, this one holding two fired shotshell cartridges.

"Number seven and a halfs," he said. "Rabbit shells."

"No gun?"

"No shotgun. Tony the Zee had a .38, a Smith and Wesson Undercover, in an ankle holster. I left it there for the lab guys. He never got a chance to use it."

"What the hell has H. Richard Detweiler's daughter got to do with a second-rate guinea gangster like Tony the Zee?" Mickey O'Hara asked rhetorically.

Lieutenant Lewis shrugged and then started up the stairs again.

The Union League of Philadelphia is a stone Victorian building—some say a remarkably ugly one—on the west side of South Broad Street, literally in the shadow of the statue of Billy Penn, which stands atop City Hall at the intersection of Broad and Market Streets.

South Broad Street, in front of the Union League, has been designated a NO PARKING AT ANY TIME TOW-AWAY ZONE. Several large signs on the sidewalk advertise this.

Traffic Officer P. J. Ward, who was directing traffic in the middle of South Broad Street, was thus both surprised and annoyed when he saw a silver Porsche 911 pull up in front of the Union League, turn off its lights, and stop. Then a young guy in a monkey suit got out and quickly walked around to the other side to open the door for his girlfriend.

Ward quickly strode over.

"Hey, you! What the hell do you think you're doing?"

The young guy in the monkey suit turned to face him.

"I won't be long," he said. "I'm on the job."

There was a silver-colored badge pinned to his jacket, but

Officer Ward decided he wasn't going to take that at what it looked like. There was a good chance, he decided, that when he got a good look at the badge, it would say PRIVATE INVESTIGATOR or OFFICIAL U.S. TAXPAYER, and that the young man in the monkey suit driving the Porsche would turn out to be a wiseass rich kid who thought he could get away with anything.

"Hold it a minute," he said, and trotted onto the sidewalk.

The badge was real. The next question was what was this rich kid driving a Porsche 911 doing with it?

"I'm Payne, Special Operations," the young guy said, and held out his photo ID. Ward saw at a glance that the ID was the real thing.

"What's going on?"

"I have to go in here a minute," Matt said. "I won't be long."

"Don't be," Officer Ward said.

Matt took Amanda's arm and they walked up the stairs to the front door. As they reached the revolving door to the entrance foyer, it was put into motion for them. Matt saw that just inside was a large man, who smelled of retired cop and was functioning more as a genteel bouncer than a doorman.

He had seen the two young people all nicely dressed up and decided they had legitimate business inside.

"Good evening," he said, then saw the badge on the young man's lapel, and surprise registered on his face.

"The Browne dinner?" Matt asked.

"Up the stairs, sir, and to your right," the man at the door said, pointing.

Matt and Amanda started up the stairs. Matt unpinned his badge and put it in his pocket. He would need it again when he went back to the garage, but he didn't want to put it on display here. Then he thought of something else.

"Here," he said, handing the Porsche keys to Amanda.

"What's this for?" she asked.

"Well, I sort of hoped you'd park it for me until I can catch up with you," Matt said. "I really can't leave it parked out in front."

"When are you going to 'catch up with me'?"

"As soon as I can. Sometime tonight you're going to have to make a statement at Homicide."

"I already told that detective everything I know."

"You know that," Matt said. "He doesn't."

She took the keys from him.

"I was about to say," she said, a touch of wonder in her voice, " 'You're not going to just leave me here like this, are you?' But of course you have to, don't you? You're *really* a policeman."

"I'm sorry," Matt said.

"Don't be absurd," Amanda said. "Why should you be sorry? It's just that—you don't look like a cop, I guess."

"What does a cop look like?"

"I didn't mean that the way it came out," she said.

She took his arm and they went the rest of the way up the stairway.

"Wait here, please," Matt said when they came to the double doors leading to the dining room. He stepped inside.

"May I have your invitation, sir?"

"I won't be staying," Matt said as he spotted the head table, and Mr. and Mrs. H. Richard Detweiler, and started for it.

"Hey!" the man who'd asked for the invitation said sharply, and started after him.

Mr. H. Richard Detweiler, who obviously had had a couple of drinks, was engaged in animated conversation with a youthful, trim, freckle-faced woman sitting at his right side. She was considerably older than she looked, Matt knew, for she was Mrs. Brewster Cortland Payne II, and she was his mother.

She smiled at him with her eyes when she saw him approaching the table, then returned her attention to Mr. Detweiler.

"Mr. Detweiler?" Matt said. "Excuse me?"

"Matt, you're interrupting," Patricia Payne said.

The man who had followed Matt across the room came up. "Excuse me, sir, I'll have to see your invitation," he said.

H. Richard Detweiler first focused his eyes on Matt, and then at the man demanding an invitation.

"It's all right," he said. "He's invited. He'd forget his head if it wasn't nailed on."

"Mr. Detweiler, may I see you a moment, please, sir?"

"Matt, for God's sake, can't you see that I'm talking to your mother?"

"Sir, this is important. I'm sorry to interrupt."

"Well, all right, what is it?"

"May I speak to you alone, please?"

"Goddammit, Matt!"

"Matt, what is it?" Patricia Payne asked.

"Mother, please!"

H. Richard Detweiler got to his feet. In the process he knocked over his whiskey glass, swore under his breath, and glowered at Matt.

Matt led him out of the room.

"Now what the devil is going on, Matt?" Detweiler asked impatiently, and then saw Amanda. "How are you, darling?"

"Mr. Detweiler," Matt said, "there's been an incident—"

"Incident? Incident? What kind of an *incident*?"

Brewster C. Payne II came out of the room.

"Penny's been hurt, Mr. Detweiler," Matt said. "She's been taken to Hahneman Hospital."

In a split second H. Richard Detweiler was absolutely sober.

"What, precisely, has happened, Matt?" he asked icily.

"I think it would be a good idea if you went to the hospital, Mr. Detweiler," Matt said.

Detweiler grabbed Matt by the shoulders.

"I asked you a question, Matt," he said. "Answer me, dammit!"

"Penny appears to have been shot, Mr. Detweiler," Matt said.

"Shot?" Detweiler asked incredulously. *"Shot?"*

"Yes, sir. With a shotgun."

"I don't believe this," Detweiler said. "Is she seriously injured?"

"Yes, sir, I think she is."

"How did it happen? Where?"

"On the roof of the parking garage behind the Bellevue," Matt said. "That's about all we know."

" 'All we know'? What about the police?"

"I'm a policeman, Mr. Detweiler," Matt said. "We just don't know yet what happened."

"That's right," Detweiler said, dazed. "Your dad told me you were a policeman—and then there was all the business in the newspapers. My God, Matt, what happened?"

"I don't know, sir."

"Dick, you'd better go to the hospital," Brewster C. Payne said. "I'll get Grace and bring her over there."

"My God, this is unbelievable!" Detweiler said.

"It would probably be quicker if you caught a cab out front," Matt said.

H. Richard Detweiler looked at Matt intently for a moment, then ran down the stairs.

"How did you get involved in this, Matt?" Brewster C. Payne II asked.

"Amanda and I found her— Excuse me. Dad, this is Amanda Spencer. Amanda, this is my father."

"Hello," Amanda said.

"We drove onto the roof of the garage and found her," Matt said. "Amanda called it in. They took her to Hahneman in a wagon."

"How badly is she injured?"

"It was a shotgun, Dad," Matt said.

"Oh, my God! A robbery?"

"We don't know yet," Matt said. "I have to get back over there." He looked at Amanda. "I'll see you . . . later."

"Okay," Amanda said.

Matt ran down the stairs, taking his badge from his pocket and pinning it to his lapel again. The Traffic cop would probably be waiting for him. He reached the door, stopped, and then trotted into the gentlemen's lounge. Concentrating on the business at hand, he didn't notice the young gentleman at the adjoining urinal until he spoke.

"What the *hell* have you pinned to your lapel, Payne?"

Matt turned and saw Kellogg Shaw, who had been a year ahead of him at Episcopal Academy and then had gone on to Princeton.

"What's that sore on the head of your dick, Kellogg?" Matt replied, and then ran out of the men's room, zipping his fly on the run. He glanced over his shoulder and saw Kellogg Shaw exposing himself to the mirror over the sinks.

SIX

Victor, checking his rearview mirror to make sure that Charles was still behind him, flicked on his right-turn signal and turned into the short-term parking lot at Philadelphia International Airport.

He took a ticket from the dispensing machine, then drove around the lot until he found two empty parking spaces. A moment after he stopped, Charles pulled the Cadillac in beside him.

Charles got out of the Cadillac, glanced around the parking lot to make sure that no one had an idle interest in what they were doing, and then opened the door of the Pontiac. Quickly he shifted the Remington Model 1100 from the floor of the Cadillac to the floor of the Pontiac. Victor helped him put it out of sight under the seat.

Charles then took his carry-on from the Cadillac and walked toward the terminal building. Victor waited until Charles was almost out of sight, then got out of the Pontiac. He put the keys on top of the left rear tire, then took his carry-on from the backseat, slammed the doors, checked to make sure they were locked, and then walked to the terminal.

Victor checked in with TWA, then went to the cocktail lounge. Charles was at the bar. Victor touched his shoulder and Charles turned.

"Well, look who's here," Charles said.

"Nice to see you. Everything going all right?"

"No problems at all."

"Can I buy you a drink?"

"A quick one. I'm on United 404 in fifteen minutes."

"Lucky you. I've got to hang around here for an hour and a half."

Fifteen minutes later Charles boarded United Airlines Flight 404 for Chicago. An hour and fifteen minutes after that, Victor boarded TWA Flight 332 for Los Angeles, with an intermediate stop in St. Louis.

At the entrance to the Penn Services Parking Garage there was a crowd of citizens, almost all of them well dressed and almost all of them indignant, even furious.

They had been told, or were being told, by uniformed police officers and detectives that the entire Penn Services Parking Garage had been designated a crime scene and they could not reclaim their cars, or even go to them, until the investigation of the scene had been completed. And they had been told, truthfully, that no one could even estimate how long the investigation of the crime scene would take.

Matt felt sorry for the cops charged with keeping the civilians out. The necessity to go over the garage with a fine-tooth comb was something understood by everyone who had ever watched a cops-and-robbers television show. But that was different.

"I'm a law-abiding citizen, and not a holdup man or a murderer or whatever the hell went on in there. I didn't do anything, and all I want to do is get in my own goddamn car and go home. It's a goddamn outrage to treat law-abiding citizens like this! How the hell am I supposed to get home?"

When he got to the entrance ramp, Matt saw that it was crowded with police cars. They had moved off the street, he realized, to do what they could about getting traffic flowing smoothly again. He decided that the mobile crime lab, and the other technical vehicles, had gone up to the roof.

"Detective D'Amata?" Matt asked the district cop standing in front of the stairwell door.

"On the roof."

Matt went up the stairs two at a time and was a little winded when he finally emerged on the roof. There was a district cop just outside the door, and he took a good look at Matt and his badge but didn't say anything to him.

The mobile crime lab was there, doors open, and three other special vehicles. CRIME SCENE—DO NOT CROSS tape had been strung around the area, the entire half of the roof, and a photographer armed with a 35-mm camera as well as a revolver was shooting pictures of the bloody pool left when the van cops had loaded Penelope Detweiler into their van and hauled her off to Hahneman.

Matt looked around for Detective D'Amata. Before he found him, Lieutenant Foster H. Lewis came up unnoticed behind Matt and touched his arm.

"They want you in homicide, Payne," he said. "Right now."

"Yes, sir," Matt said.

"You know where it is?"

All too well, Matt thought. *When I was questioned by Homicide detectives after I killed the rapist, it had been only after three hours of questioning and a twenty-seven-page statement that someone finally told me it had been a "good" shooting.*

"Yes, sir."

Matt turned and started toward the stairwell. The body of the man who had had half his head blown off was still where Matt had first seen it, slumped against the concrete block wall of the stairwell.

It was horrible, and Matt felt a sense of nausea. He pushed open the stairwell door and started down them. The urge to vomit passed.

And I didn't faint, Matt thought, not without a sense of satisfaction. *When I saw the mutilated body of Miss Elizabeth Woodham, 33, of 300 East Mermaid Lane, Roxborough, I went out like a light and looked like an ass in front of Detective Washington.*

Detective Jason Washington, acknowledged to be the best Homicide detective in the department, had been transferred, over his bitter objections, to the newly formed Special Operations Division. When the state police had found a body in Bucks County meeting the description of Elizabeth Woodham, who had been seen as she was forced into a van, Washington had gone to the country to have a look at it and had taken Matt with him. Not as a fellow police officer, to help with the investigation, but as an errand boy, a gofer. And Matt hadn't even been able to do that; one look at the body and he'd fainted.

Washington, a gentleman (he perfectly met Matt's father's definition of a gentleman: He was never seen in public unshaven, in his undershirt, or with run-down heels; and he never unintentionally said something rude or unkind), hadn't told anyone that Matt had passed out and had gone much further than he had to, trying to make Matt feel better about it.

But the humiliation still burned.

When Matt reached the street, at the entrance ramp a taxi was discharging a passenger with a distracted, I'm-in-a-hurry look on his face. Matt ran to the cab and got in, thinking that if the man getting out had parked his car in the garage, he was about to find something he could talk about when he got home.

"You're not going to believe this, Myrtle, but when I went to get the car from the garage, the goddamn cops wouldn't let me have it. They had some kind of crime in there, and they acted as if I had something to do with it. Can you imagine that? I had to come home in a cab, and I don't have any idea when I can get the car back."

"The Roundhouse," Matt told the cabdriver.

"Where?"

"The Police Department Administration Building at 8th and Race," Matt answered.

"You a cop?" the driver asked doubtfully.

"Yeah."

"I saw the badge," the driver said. "What's going on in there?"

"Nothing much," Matt said.

"I come through here twenty minutes ago, and there was cop cars all over the street."

"It's over now," Matt said.

The cab dropped him at the rear of the administration building. There is a front entrance, overlooking Metropolitan Hospital, but it is normally locked.

At the rear of the building a door opens onto a small foyer. Once inside, a visitor faces a uniformed police officer sitting behind a heavy plate-glass window.

To the right is the central cell room, in effect a holding prison, to which prisoners are brought from the various districts to be booked and to face a magistrate, who sets (or denies) bail. Those prisoners for whom bail is denied, or who can't make it, are moved, males to the Detention Center, females to the House of Correction.

The magistrate's court is a small, somewhat narrow room separated from the corridor leading to the gallery where the public can view arraignment proceedings. This, a dead-end corridor, is walled by large sections of Plexiglas, long fogged by scratches received over the years from family, friends, and lovers, pressing against it to try to get closer to the accused as they are being arraigned.

The arraignment court, as you look down on it from the gallery, has a bench on the left-hand side where the magistrate sits; tables in front of the bench where an assistant district attorney and a public defender sit; and across from them are two police officers, who process the volumes of paperwork that accompanies any arrest. The prisoners are brought up from the basement detention unit via a stairway shaft, which winds around an elevator. All the doors leading into the arraignment court are locked to prevent escape.

To the left is the door leading to the main foyer of the Police Department Administration Building. The door has a solenoid-equipped lock, operated by the police officer behind the window.

Matt went to the door, put his hand on it, and then turned so the cop on duty could see his badge. The lock buzzed, and Matt pushed open the door.

He went inside and walked toward the elevators. On one wall is a display of photographs and police badges of police officers who have been killed in the line of duty. One of the photographs is of Sergeant John Xavier Moffitt, who had been shot down in a West Philadelphia gas station while answering a silent burglar alarm. He had left a wife, six months pregnant with their first child.

Thirteen months after Sergeant Moffitt's death, his widow, Patricia, who had found work as a secretary-trainee with a law firm, met the son of the senior partner as they walked their small children near the Philadelphia Museum on a pleasant Sunday afternoon.

He told her that his wife had been killed eight months before in a traffic accident while returning from their lake house in the Pocono Mountains. Mrs. Patricia Moffitt became the second Mrs. Brewster Cortland Payne II two months after she met Mr. Payne and his children. Shortly thereafter Mr. Payne formally adopted Matthew Mark Moffitt as his son and led his wife through a similar process for his children by his first wife.

"Can I help you?" the cop on duty called to Matt Payne as Matt walked toward the elevators. It was not every day that a young man with a police officer's badge pinned to the silk lapel of a tuxedo walked across the lobby.

"I'm going to Homicide," Matt called back.

"Second floor," the cop said.

Matt nodded and got on the elevator.

The Homicide Division of the Philadelphia Police Department occupies a suite of second-floor rear offices.

Matt pushed the door open and stepped inside. There were half a dozen detectives in the room, all sitting at rather battered desks. None of them looked familiar. There was an office with a frosted glass door, with a sign, CAPTAIN HENRY C. QUAIRE, above it. Matt had met Captain Quaire, but the office was empty.

He walked toward the far end of the room, where there were two men standing beside a single desk that faced the others. Sitting at the desk was a dapper, well-dressed man in civilian clothing whom Matt surmised was the watch officer, the lieutenant in charge.

As he walked across the room he noticed that one of the two "interview rooms" on the corridor side of the room was occupied; a large, blondheaded man in a sleeveless T-shirt was sitting in a metal chair, his left wrist encircled by a handcuff. The other handcuff was fastened to a hole in the chair. The chair itself was bolted to the floor.

He saw Matt looking at him and gave him a look of utter contempt.

As Matt approached the desk at the end of the room the mustached, dark-skinned man sitting at it saw him coming and moved his head slightly. The other two men turned to look at him. Matt saw a brass nameplate on the desk, LIEU-TENANT LOUIS NATALI, whom Matt surmised was the lieutenant in charge.

"My name is Payne, Lieutenant," Matt said as he reached the desk. "I was told to report here."

No one responded, and Matt was made uncomfortable by the unabashed examination he'd been given by all three men. The examination, he decided, was because of the dinner jacket, but there was something else in the air too.

"He's all yours," Lieutenant Natali said finally.

"Let's find someplace to talk," the smaller of the two detectives said, and gestured vaguely down the room.

There was an unoccupied desk, and Matt headed for it.

"Let's use this," the detective called. Matt stopped and turned and saw that the detective was pointing to the second, empty interview room. That seemed a little odd, but he walked through the door, anyway.

The two detectives followed him inside. One closed the door after them. The other, the one who had suggested the use of the interview room, signaled for Matt to sit in the interviewee's chair.

Matt looked at it with unease. There was a set of handcuffs lying on it, one of the cuffs locked through a hole in the chair.

"Go on, sit down," the detective said, adding, "Payne, my name is Dolan. Sergeant Dolan."

Matt offered his hand. Sergeant Dolan ignored it. Neither did he introduce the other detective.

"Where's your car, Payne?" Sergeant Dolan asked. "Outside? You mind if we have a look in it?"

"What?"

"I asked if you mind if we have a look in your car."

"I don't know where my car is right now," Matt replied. "Sorry. Why are you interested in my car?"

"What do you mean, you don't know where your car is?"

"I mean, I don't know where it is. I loaned it to somebody."

"Somebody? Does somebody have a name?"

"You want to tell me what this is all about?"

"This is an interview. You're a police officer. You should know what an interview is."

"Hey, all I did was find the injured girl and the dead guy."

"What I want to know is two things. What were you doing up there, and where's your car? *Three* things: Why were you so anxious to get your car away from the Penn Services Parking Garage?"

"And I'd like to know why you're asking me all these questions."

"Don't try to hotdog me, Payne, just answer me."

Matt looked at Sergeant Dolan and decided he didn't like him. He remembered two things: that his mother was absolutely right when she said he too often let his mouth run away with him when he was angry or didn't like somebody; and that he was a police officer, and this overbearing son of a bitch was a police *sergeant*. It would be very unwise indeed to tell him to go fuck himself.

"Sorry," Matt said. "Okay, Sergeant. From the top. I went to the top of the garage because I wanted to park my car and there were no empty spots on the lower floors. When I got there, I found Miss Detweiler lying on the floor. Injured. The lady with me—"

"How did you know the Detweiler girl's name? You know her?"

"Yes, I know her."

"Who was the lady with you?"

"Her name is Amanda Spencer."

"And she knows the Detweiler girl too?"

"Yes. I don't know how well."

"How about Anthony J. DeZego? You know him?"

"No. Is that the dead man's name?"

"You sure you don't know him?"

"Absolutely."

Lieutenant Louis Natali had watched as the two Narcotics detectives led Payne into the interview room and closed the door. He opened a desk drawer and took a long, thin cigar from a box and very carefully lit it. He examined the glowing coal for a moment and then made up his mind. Whatever the hell was going on smelled, and he could not just sit there and ignore it.

He stood up, walked down the room, and entered the room next to the interview room. It was equipped with a two-way mirror and a loudspeaker that permitted watching and listening to interviews being conducted in the interview room.

The mirror fooled no one; any interviewee with more brains than a retarded gnat knew what it was. But it did serve several practical purposes, not the least of which was that it intimidated, to some degree, the interviewees. They didn't know whether or not somebody else was watching. That tended to make them uncomfortable, and that often was valuable.

But the primary value, as Natali saw it, of the two-way mirror and loudspeaker was that it provided the means by which other detectives or Narcotics officers could watch an interview. They could form their own opinion of the responses the interviewee made to the questions, and of his reaction to them. Sometimes a question that should have been asked but had not occurred to them, and they could summon one of the interviewers out of the room and suggest that he go back in and ask it.

And finally, as was happening now, the two-way mirror afforded supervisors the means to watch an interview when they were either curious or did not have absolute faith in the interviewers to conduct the interview, keeping in mind Departmental regulations and the interviewees' rights.

While Lieutenant Natali was happy to cooperate with the Narcotics Division, as he was now, he had no intention of letting Narcotics do anything in a Homicide interview room that he would not permit a Homicide detective to do. And there was something about this guy Dolan that Natali did not like.

"So if you had to guess, Payne, where would say your car is now?" Sergeant Dolan asked.

"Another parking lot somewhere. I just don't know."

"And your girlfriend?"

"I suppose she's back at the Union League having dinner."

"Why don't we go get her?"

"Why can't we wait until the party is over? Detective D'Amata, who was there when Lieutenant Lewis sent me to tell the Detweilers what happened, didn't say anything about getting her over here right away."

"Detective D'Amata has nothing to do with this investigation," Dolan said. "He's Homicide. I'm Narcotics. Let's go get your girlfriend, Payne."

"What the hell is this all about?" Payne asked. Natali saw that he was genuinely surprised and confused to hear that Dolan was from Narcotics. Surprised and confused but not at all alarmed.

"Come on, let's go," Dolan said.

Lieutenant Natali walked out of the small room as the other Narcotics detective came out of the interview room, followed by Payne and then Sergeant Dolan.

Dolan looked at Natali, and it was clear to Natali that he knew he had been watching the interview, and was surprised and annoyed that he had.

"Thank you for your cooperation, Lieutenant," Sergeant Dolan said. "We're going to see if we can find Officer Payne's lady friend and his car, and finish this at Narcotics. I'll see that the both of them get back over here."

Natali nodded but didn't say anything.

He watched as they left the office and then went into Captain Henry C. Quaire's office and closed the door after him. He had called Quaire at home before going to the Penn Services Parking Garage, and Quaire had shown up there ten minutes after he had, and sent him back to the Roundhouse.

He went to the desk and, standing up, dialed a number from memory.

"Radio," Foster H. Lewis, Jr., answered.

"This is Lieutenant Natali, Homicide. Can you get word to W-William One to call me at 555-3343?"

"Hold One, Lieutenant," Foster H. Lewis, Jr., said, and then activated his microphone and threw the switch that would broadcast what he said over the command band.

W-William One was the radio call sign of the commanding officer, Special Operations Division. The private official telephone number of the commanding officer of the Homicide Division was 555-3343.

There were some official considerations—and some ethical and political ones—in what Lieutenant Natali was doing. Viewed in the worst light, Natali was violating Departmental policy by advising the commanding officer of the Special Operations Division that one of his officers was being interviewed by Narcotics officers. That was technically the business of the commanding officer of the Narcotics Division, who would probably confer with Internal Affairs before notifying him.

Ethically he was violating the unspoken rule that a member of one division or bureau kept his nose out of an investigation being conducted by officers of another division or bureau.

Politically he knew he was risking the wrath of the commanding officer of the Narcotics Division, who almost certainly would learn—or guess, which was just as bad—what he was about to do. And it was entirely possible that the commanding officer of the Special Operations Division, who was about as straight a cop as they came, would, rather than being grateful, decide that Natali had no right to break either the official or unofficial rules of conduct.

On the other hand, if he had to make a choice between angering the commanding officer of the Narcotics Division or the commanding officer of Special Operations, it was no contest. For one thing, the commanding officer of Special Operations outranked the Narcotics commanding officer. For another, so far as influence went, the commanding officer of Special Operations won that hands down too. He held his present assignment because the word to give it to him had come straight from Mayor Jerry Carlucci. And he was very well connected through the Department.

Peter Wohl's father was Chief Inspector August Wohl (retired). Despite a lot of sour-grapes gossip, that wasn't the reason Peter Wohl had once been the youngest sergeant in Highway, and was now the youngest staff inspector in the Department, but it hadn't hurt any, either.

But what had really made Louis Natali decide to telephone Staff Inspector Peter Wohl was his realization that not only did he really like him but thought the reverse was true. Peter Wohl would decide he had called as a friend, which happened to be true.

"Sorry, Lieutenant," Foster H. Lewis, Jr., reported, "W-William One doesn't respond. Shall I keep trying?"

"No. Thanks, anyway," Natali said, and hung up.

He left Captain Quaire's office and walked back to his desk and searched through it until he found Peter Wohl's home telephone number. He started to go back to Quaire's office for the privacy it would give him and then decided to hell with it. He sat down and dialed the number.

On the fourth ring there was a click. "This is 555-8251," Wohl's recorded voice announced. "When this thing beeps, you can leave a message."

Natali raised his wrist to look at his watch and waited for the beep.

"Inspector, this is Lieutenant Natali of Homicide. It's five minutes after nine. If you get this message within the next forty-five—"

"I'm here, Lou," Peter Wohl said, interrupting. "What can I do for you?"

"Sorry to bother you at home, Inspector."

"No problem. I'm sitting here trying to decide if I want to go out for a pizza or go to bed hungry."

"Inspector, did you hear about Tony the Zee?"

"No. You are talking about Anthony J. DeZego?"

"Yes, sir. He got himself blown away about an hour and a half ago. Shotgun. On the roof of the Penn Services Parking Garage behind the Bellevue-Stratford. There's some suggestion it's narcotics-related."

"Those who live by the needle die by the needle," Wohl said, mockingly sonorous. "You got the doer?"

"No, sir. Not a clue so far."

"Am I missing something, Lou?" Wohl asked.

"Inspector, Narcotics is interviewing one of your men. He found the body and—"

"They think he's connected. Got a name?"

"Payne," Natali said.

"Payne?" Wohl parroted disbelievingly. "Matthew Payne?"

"Yes, sir. I thought you would like to know."

"Why do they think he was involved?"

"There was another victim, Inspector. A girl. Penelope Detweiler. A 9th District wagon carried her to Hahneman.

Payne knew her. And he removed his car from the crime scene right afterward. I think that's what made them suspicious.''

There was a moment's silence on the line.

''Where do they have him?''

''They had him here, but they just left. Sergeant Dolan?''

''Don't know him.''

''And another guy. Plainclothes or a detective. I don't know him. Dolan said they were going to get Payne's girlfriend and his car—she has the car—and finish the interview at Narcotics.''

''Thank you, Lou. I owe you one. How many does that make now?''

Staff Inspector Peter Wohl hung up without waiting for a reply.

Peter Wohl put the telephone back in its cradle and stood up. He had been sprawled, in a light blue cotton bathrobe, on the white leather couch in his living room, dividing his attention between television (a mindless situation comedy but one that featured an actress with a spectacular bosom and a penchant for low-necked blouses) and a well-worn copy of a paperbound book entitled *Wiring Scheme, Jaguar 1950 XK120 Drophead Coupe*.

Above the couch (which came with two matching armchairs and a plate-glass and chrome coffee table) was a very large oil painting of a voluptuous and, by current standards, somewhat plump, nude lady that had once hung behind the bar of a now defunct men's club in downtown Philadelphia. The service bar of the same club, heavy 1880s mahogany, was installed across the room from the leather furniture and the portrait of the naked, reclining, shyly smiling lady.

The decor clashed, as Peter Wohl ultimately had, with the interior designer who had gotten him the leather, glass, and chrome furniture at her professional discount when she had considered becoming Mrs. Peter Wohl. Dorothea was now a Swarthmore wife, young mother, and fading memory, but he often thought that the white leather had become a permanent part of his life. Not that he liked it. He had found out that the resale value of high-fashion furniture was only a small fraction of its acquisition cost, even if that cost had reflected a forty-percent professional discount.

He turned the television off and went into his bedroom. His apartment had once been the chauffeur's quarters, an apartment built over the slate-roofed, four-car garage behind a turn-of-the-century mansion on Norwood Street in Chestnut Hill. The mansion itself had been converted into luxury apartments.

He went to his closet, hung the bathrobe neatly on a hanger, and took a yellow polo shirt, sky-blue trousers, and a seersucker jacket from the closet. He put the shirt and trousers on, and then a shoulder holster that held a Smith & Wesson .38-caliber Chief's Special five-shot revolver.

Still barefoot, he sat down on his bed and pulled the telephone on the bedside table to him.

"Special Operations, Lieutenant Lucci."

"Peter Wohl, Tony," Wohl said. Lieutenant Lucci was actually the watch officer for the four-to-midnight shift of the Highway Patrol. When Special Operations had been formed, it had moved into the Highway Patrol headquarters at Bustleton and Bowler Streets in Northeast Philadelphia. For the time being at least, with Special Operations having nowhere near its authorized strength, Wohl had decided that there was no way (for that matter, no reason) to have the line squad supervisor on duty for the four-to-midnight and midnight-to-eight shift. The Highway watch officer could take those calls.

"Good evening, sir," Lucci said. Two weeks before, Lucci had been a sergeant, assigned as Mayor Jerry Carlucci's driver. Before that he had been a Highway sergeant. Wohl thought he was a nice guy and a good cop, even if his closeness to the mayor was more than a little worrisome.

"What do you know about DeZego getting himself shot, Tony?"

"Blown away, Inspector," Lucci said. "With a shotgun. On the roof of that parking garage behind the Bellevue-Stratford. Nick DeBenedito went in on the call. We were just talking about it."

"Is he there?"

"I think so. You want to talk to him?"

"Please."

Sergeant Nick DeBenedito came on the line thirty seconds later. "Sergeant DeBenedito, sir."

"Tell me what happened with Tony the Zee, DeBenedito."

"Well, I was downtown, and there was a 'shots-fired,' so I went in on it. It was on the roof of the parking garage behind the Bellevue. Inspector, I didn't know he was a cop."

"That who was a cop?"

"Payne. I mean, he was wearing a tuxedo and he had a gun, so I put him down on the floor. As soon as Martinez told me he was a cop, I let him up and said I was sorry."

Peter Wohl smiled at the mental image of Matt Payne lying on the concrete floor of the parking garage in his formal clothes.

"What went down on the roof?"

"Well, the way I understand it, Payne went up there in his car with his girlfriend, saw the first victim—the girl. She was wounded. So he sent his girl downstairs to the attendant's booth to call it in, tried to help the girl, and then he found Tony the Zee. The doer—doers—had a shotgun. They practically took Tony the Zee's head off. Anyway, then we got there. The doers were long gone. I sent Martinez with the wagon to see if he could get a dying declaration—"

"Did she die?"

"No, sir. But Martinez said she was never conscious, either."

"Okay."

"So I hung around until Lieutenant Lewis from the 9th, and then the Homicide detectives, showed up, and then I went to the hospital and got Martinez and we resumed patrol."

"Do you have any reason to think that Payne was involved?"

"Lieutenant," DeBenedito said uncomfortably, "what I saw was a civilian with a gun at a crime scene. How was I supposed to know he was a cop?"

"You did exactly the right thing, Sergeant," Wohl said. "Thank you. Put Lieutenant Lucci back on, will you?"

"Yes, sir?"

"Where's Captain Pekach?"

"Probably at home, sir. He said either he'd be there or in Chestnut Hill. I got the numbers. You want them?"

"No thank you, Tony, it's not that important. I'm going to Narcotics. If I go someplace else, I'll call in."

"Are we involved in this, Inspector?"

"No. But Narcotics is interviewing a very suspicious character they think is involved. I want to find out what they think they have."

"No kidding? Anybody we know?"

"Officer Payne." Wohl chuckled and hung up.

Captain David Pekach, the recently appointed Highway commander, previously had been assigned to the Narcotics Division. If he had happened to be either at Bustleton and Bowler or on the streets, Wohl would have asked him to meet him at Narcotics, which was located in a onetime public-health center at 4th Street and Girard Avenue, sharing the building with Organized Crime.

But he wasn't working. That meant he was almost certainly in Chestnut Hill with his lady friend, Miss Martha Peebles. Dave Pekach was thirty-two or thirty-three, and Martha Peebles a couple of years older. It was the first romance either had had, and Wohl decided that the problem with Narcotics was not serious enough to interfere with true love.

Lieutenant Anthony Lucci, who knew that Pekach, his immediate superior, had come to Highway from Narcotics, did not know of Pekach's relationship with Miss Martha Peebles. All he knew was that his orders from Captain Pekach had been to keep him informed of anything out of the ordinary.

So far as he was concerned, when Wohl, who was Captain Pekach's immediate superior, announced he was going to Narcotics, to see what they had on Officer Matthew Payne, who, it was common knowledge, had a very powerful rabbi, Chief Inspector Dennis V. Coughlin, and in whom the mayor himself, after the kid had taken down the Northwest Philly serial rapist, had a personal interest, that was something out of the ordinary.

He dialed Pekach's home number and, when there was no answer, dialed the number in Chestnut Hill Pekach had provided.

A very pleasant female voice answered and, when Lucci asked for Captain Pekach, said, "Just one moment, please."

Less clearly, Lieutenant Lucci heard her continue. "It's for you, Precious."

SEVEN

When Officer Robert F. Wise saw the Jaguar pull into the Narcotics Division Building parking lot, and into the spot reserved for inspectors, he went quickly from inside the building and intercepted the driver as he was leaving his car.

Officer Wise, who was twenty-five, slightly built, and five feet eight inches tall, had been on the job not quite three years. He had hoped, when just over a year ago he was transferred to Narcotics, he would be able to work his way out of his present duties—which could best be described as making himself useful (and visible in uniform) around the building—and into a job as a plainclothes investigator.

But that hadn't happened. One of the sergeants had been kind enough to tell him that he didn't think it would ever happen. He was too nice a guy, the sergeant said, which Wise understood to mean that he could never pass himself off as a drug peddler. A month before, Wise had applied for transfer to the newly formed Special Operations Division. He hadn't heard anything about the request. In the meantime he was doing the best job he knew how to do.

He had been told to keep his eye on the parking lot behind the building. There had been complaints from various inspectors that when they had come to visit Narcotics, the parking space reserved for visiting inspectors had been occupied by various civilian cars, most of them junks, which they knew damned well were not being driven by inspectors.

The Jaguar that had just pulled up with its nose against the INSPECTORS sign in the parking lot certainly could not be called a junk, but Officer Robert F. Wise doubted that the civilian in the nice, but sporty, clothes was an inspector. Inspectors tended to be fifty years old and wore conservative business suits, not yellow polo shirts, sky-blue pants, and plaid hats.

"Excuse me, sir," Officer Robert F. Wise said, "but you're not allowed to park there."

"Why not?" the young man in the plaid hat asked pleasantly enough.

"Sir, this is a Police Department parking lot."

"You could have fooled me," the young man said, smiling, and gestured toward the other cars in the lot. A good deal of Narcotics work requires that investigators look like people involved in the drug trade. The undercover cars they used, many of them confiscated, reflected this; they were either pimpmobiles or junkers.

"Sir, those are police cars."

"I'm a 369," the young man said.

A police officer in civilian clothes who wishes to identify himself as a cop without producing his badge or identity card says "I'm a 369."

"Well, then," Officer Wise said, "you should know better than to park in an inspector's spot. Move it out of there."

"I'm Inspector Wohl," the young man said, smiling. "Keep up the good work." He started toward the rear door of the Roundhouse.

Two things bothered Officer Wise. For one thing, there were three different kinds of inspectors in the Philadelphia Police Department. There were chief inspectors, who ranked immediately below deputy commissioners. These officers were generally referred to as, and called themselves, Chief. When in uniform, they wore a silver eagle, identical to Army and Marine Corps colonels' eagles, as their insignia of rank.

Next down in the rank hierarchy were inspectors, who, in uniform, wore the same silver oak leaf as Army and Marine Corps lieutenant colonels. And at the bottom were staff inspectors, who wore a golden oak leaf as their insignia. There were not very many staff inspectors (Wise could not remember ever having seen one), but he understood they were sort of super-detectives and handled difficult or delicate investigations.

The guy in the sky-blue pants didn't look to Wise much like a cop, much less a senior officer. He was more than likely a cop, but a wise guy, and no more a chief inspector and/or division chief, and thus entitled to park where he had parked, than Wise was.

"Excuse me, sir, would you mind showing me some identification?"

An unmarked car came into the parking lot at that moment and drove up to them quickly. Wise saw first that it was an unmarked Highway Patrol car. For one thing, it was equipped with more shortwave antennae than ordinary police cars, marked or unmarked, normally carried; and for another, the driver was wearing the crush-crowned uniform cap peculiar to Highway.

Then he saw that the driver was wearing a white shirt, which identified him as at least a lieutenant, and then, when he stopped the car and got out, Wise saw his rank insignia, the twin silver bars of a captain, and then he recognized him. It was Captain David Pekach.

The young guy in the sky-blue pants smiled and said, "You just happened to be in the neighborhood, right? And thought you'd drop by?"

"Lucci called me," Pekach said. "Don't blame him. I told him to call me when something out of the ordinary happened."

"I didn't want to interfere with your love life, Dave. I had visions of you sipping fine wine by candlelight as Miss What's-her-name whispered sweet nothings in your ear," Wohl said.

"What's going on here?" Pekach said. He did not like being teased about Miss Martha Peebles. "Lucci said something about young Payne?"

"Narcotics brought him and his girlfriend here. I don't know why," Wohl said. "That's why I'm here."

"Give me a minute to park the car, Inspector," Captain Pekach said, "and I'll come with you. Or would I be in the way?"

"I didn't send for you, Dave, but I'm glad to see you," Wohl said.

He held out his badge and photo identification to Officer Wise.

"Oh, that's all right, Inspector," Officer Wise said, waving it away. "Sorry to bother you."

Officer Wise decided that his chances of being transferred to Special Operations had just dropped from slim to zero. He had put this encounter all together now. The young guy in the silly cap and sky-blue pants was Peter Wohl, who although "only" a staff inspector, was the Special Operations division commander.

"No bother," Wohl said as Pekach got back in his car and drove it toward a work shed near the gasoline pump.

"Inspector, I'm sorry about this," Officer Wise said.

"Never be sorry for doing your job," Wohl said. "And don't worry, you're not the only one who doesn't think I look like a cop. I get that from my father all the time."

A moment later Captain Pekach walked up to them again.

"They're searching a silver Porsche back there," he said, pointing to the work shed.

"Are they really?" Wohl said. "Dave, while I go ask what they're looking for, why don't you go inside and nose around."

"You going to come in, or should I come back when I find out?"

"I'll come in," Wohl said, and walked to the work shed.

Both doors of the Porsche, and the hoods over the rear engine compartment and the in-front trunk, were open when Wohl walked up to the car. Two Narcotics officers in plainclothes looked up at Wohl. He flashed his badge.

"What are you looking for?" Wohl asked.

"Sergeant Dolan brought it in. He says they probably got rid of it by now but to check, anyway."

"Got rid of what?"

"Probably cocaine," one of the Narcotics cops said.

"You've got a search warrant?"

"No. The owner's a cop. We have permission."

"What makes you think it's dirty?" Wohl asked.

"Sergeant Dolan thinks he—and it—is," the cop replied. "How else would a cop get the dough for a car like this?"

"Maybe he's lucky at cards," Wohl said. "You find anything?"

The cop shook his head no, then said, "Dolan said we probably wouldn't."

Wohl smiled at them and then walked to the Narcotics Building.

He found Officer Matthew Payne, his black bow tie untied and his top collar button open, sitting on one of a row of folding chairs in a room on the first floor.

Payne stood up when he saw Wohl, but Wohl waved him back into his seat and walked down the room to a door marked NO ADMITTANCE and pushed it open.

Captain Pekach and a tall, very thin, bald-headed man in his fifties were inside.

"Inspector," Pekach said, "you know Lieutenant Mikkles, don't you?"

"Sure do," Wohl said. "How are you, Mick?"

Mikkles shook Wohl's hand but didn't say anything.

"Sergeant Dolan's not here," Pekach went on. "He went to the medical examiner's office. They found a plastic bag full of a white crystalline powder on DeZego. He went to check it out."

"Where's the girl?" Wohl asked.

Lieutenant Mikkles pointed to a steel door with INTERVIEW ROOM painted on it.

"You charging her with anything, Mick? Or Officer Payne?"

"We don't have enough to charge either one of them," Mikkles said.

"Just Sergeant Dolan's *feeling* that they're dirty, right?"

"I really don't know much about this, Inspector," Mikkles said.

"They want Officer Payne and the girl at Homicide to make a statement. Would it be all right with you if I took them there?"

"I don't see any problem with that," Lieutenant Mikkles said.

"What about if I asked Captain Pekach to meet with Sergeant Dolan to ask him what he thinks he's got going here? Would you have any problem with that?"

"Sure. Why not?"

Wohl walked to the interview-room door, opened it, went inside, and closed it after him.

Amanda Spencer, sitting in a steel chair that was bolted to the floor, looked at him warily.

He smiled at her.

"Well, *I* don't think you did it," he said.

She smiled, a little hesitantly.

"My name is Peter Wohl," he said. "I'm Matt's boss."

"Hello," she said.

"The people who work in Narcotics spend their lives surrounded by the scum of the earth," Wohl said. "Sometimes—and I suppose it's understandable—they seem to forget that there are some nice people left in the world. What I'm trying to say is that I'm sorry about this, but I understand why it happened."

"They were just doing their jobs, I suppose," Amanda said. "I mean, there was a shooting—"

"Well, I'm relieved that you understand."

"Can I go now?"

"There's bad news and good news about that," Wohl said. "The bad news is that you still have to make a statement at Homicide. That's in the Police Department Administration Building. I'll get you through that as quickly as possible, but it has to be done."

"That's the good news?" she asked almost lightheartedly.

"No. The good news is that you get to ride down there in my car. I drive a Jaguar XK-120. It's a *much* nicer car than that piece of German junk your boyfriend drives."

"I have this strange feeling you're not kidding," Amanda said.

"Do I look like a kidder?"

"Yes, you do," Amanda said, laughing. "What kind of a cop are you, anyway?"

"Depending on who you ask, you can get a very wide range of responses to that question. Are you ready to go?"

"That's the understatement of the year," she said.

He held the door open for her, and she walked out of the interview room.

"Just a moment, please," he said, and walked to Lieutenant Mikkles.

"Your men tell me they found nothing in Officer Payne's car. Is there any reason he can't have it back?"

"No, I don't suppose there is."

"Try 'No, sir,' Mikkles," Captain Pekach said, flaring.

"No, sir," Mikkles said.

"Do you think it would be a good idea, Lieutenant, if you went with Officer Payne to reclaim his car?" Wohl asked evenly.

"Yes, sir. I'll do that."

"Ask him to meet me in Homicide, please. Tell him I'm driving the young lady."

"Yes, sir," Mikkles repeated.

Wohl waited until Mikkles had left the room before speaking to Pekach.

"Run down Sergeant Dolan and find out what he thinks he has," Wohl said. "And then meet us at Homicide. When you're in your car, get word to Lucci where I am."

"Yes, sir."

"And before I forget: On your way out, if that young cop is still out there, talk to him and see if you think he'd be useful to us in Special Operations. He struck me as pretty bright."

It was quarter after eleven before Homicide had finished taking the statements of Officer Matthew Payne and Miss Amanda Spencer, and Captain Pekach had not yet returned from meeting with Sergeant Dolan.

Wohl, who was ninety-five percent convinced that what had happened was that Dolan, for any number of reasons—ranging from a fight with his wife to resentment about a cop wearing formal clothes and driving a Porsche to plain stupidity—had gone off the deep end, but he was reluctant to turn Payne and, for that matter, the girl, loose until he heard from Pekach.

He walked to where they were sitting, on folding chairs against the interior wall.

"Am I the only undernourished person in the room? Did you two get dinner?"

"I'm not especially hungry," Payne said.

"I'm starved," Amanda said. "I haven't had a thing to eat since lunch."

"They serve marvelous hoagies at the 12th Street Market this time of night," Wohl said.

"I just got hungry," Matt Payne said.

"I'd like to know how Penny is," Amanda said.

"I checked a little while ago," Wohl said. "She's listed as 'critical but stable.' "

"What does that mean?"

"That she's hanging on," Wohl said.

"You know where I mean, Matt?" Wohl asked. "In the 12th Street Market?" Matt nodded. "Take Amanda there. I'll meet you. I want to get word to Pekach where we'll be."

In the elevator Amanda said, "He's very nice."

"What was that business about you riding in his car?" Matt asked.

"You're jealous!"

"Oh, bullshit!"

"You are!" she insisted.

"The hell I am."

She smiled at him triumphantly.

"Whatever you say, Officer Payne," she said.

"Thanks for getting us out of there," Matt Payne said to Peter Wohl.

They were sitting at a tiny table in the 12th Street Market, on fragile-looking bent-wire chairs. Three enormous hoagies on paper plates, a pitcher of beer, and three mugs left little room for anything else.

Peter Wohl finished chewing a large mouthful before replying.

"My pleasure," Wohl said.

"How'd you find out?" Matt asked.

"Lieutenant Natali called me. He thought I ought to know."

"Am I in trouble?" Matt Payne asked as he poured a mug half full of beer.

"Why did you take your car away from the crime scene without permission?"

"I didn't know I needed permission. It was blocking the exit ramp. I moved it out of the way of the wagon when they took Penny Detweiler to Hahneman. And then, when I went to the Union League to tell her parents what had happened, I just got in it and drove off. No one said I shouldn't."

"Who told *you* to notify her parents?"

"There was a 9th District lieutenant there. I didn't get his name. Great big black guy. I told him I knew her parents, where they were, and he said it was okay for me to tell them. He saw me get in the car, and he didn't say anything."

"Lewis? Lieutenant Lewis?"

"Yeah. I'm sure that's the name."

"Officer Lewis's father," Wohl said.

"Oh! Oh, yeah. I didn't put that together."

"Okay. Let's take it from the top."

"Jesus, again?"

"Don't be a wiseass with me, Matt. The last I heard, not only am I your commanding officer but also I'm one of the good guys."

"Sorry," Matt said sincerely. "That son of a bitch upset me. The whole thing upset me."

"From the top," Wohl repeated, reaching for the pitcher of beer.

Captain David Pekach walked up just as Matt finished, and a second pitcher of beer was delivered. He took one of the bent-wire chairs from an adjacent table and sat down on it.

"You want a glass? Good beer," Wohl said.

"No thanks. I'm cutting down. Oh, what the hell!"

He got up and went to the stand and returned with a mug.

"What did you find out?" Wohl asked.

Pekach looked at Payne and Amanda and then at Wohl, his raised eyebrows asking if Wohl wanted him to continue in front of them.

"Go on," Wohl said. "I'm convinced that neither Matt Payne nor Miss Spencer shot Tony the Zee or is into drugs."

"Dolan says the Detweiler girl was," Pekach said.

"My God!" Amanda exclaimed.

"What?" Matt asked incredulously. "That's absurd!"

"No, it's not. Dolan is a good cop," Pekach said, re-

sponding more to Peter Wohl's raised eyebrows than to Matt
Payne. "I believe him. He says that he was following her,
that he has reason to believe she went to the Penn Services
Parking Garage to make a buy, and that the shooting was tied
in with that. And Tony the Zee had a thousand dollars' worth
of Coke on him, in a plastic bag."

"Dolan was following her?" Wohl asked thoughtfully.
"Where was he during the actual shooting?"

"He said the first he heard of it, he was across the street,
watching the entrance and exit, and the other one, who I used
to think was a smart cop, was watching the fire exits in the
alley."

"Try that again, I'm confused," Wohl said.

"Okay. They followed her to the parking garage. Dolan
stayed across the street and watched the entrance and exit
ramps. Gerstner, the other Narcotics cop, watched the fire
exits on the alley. At least until he heard the sirens and went
out on the street to see what was happening. I guess that's
when the doers left the building, via the fire escape to the
alley."

"So where does Dolan figure Payne ties in?"

"He saw him drive in. Had no idea at first he was a cop
but recognized him as someone—him and Miss Spencer—he
had seen in the last couple of days. And then he saw him
drive his car away from the place later. And apparently figured that's where the drugs—according to him, the Detweiler
girl is into cocaine—were."

"That whole scenario is incredible," Matt said.

"No it's not," Wohl said. "If I were the cop on the street,
Dolan, that's pretty much how I would see it."

"You don't think I'm into drugs? Or that Amanda is?"

"I didn't say that," Wohl said carefully. "No. I don't think
either of you are. But if this Sergeant Dolan has good reason
to believe that the Detweiler girl was into drugs, I have no
reason to doubt him. And you didn't help matters any by
driving away from the crime scene with Miss Spencer."

Matt exhaled audibly.

"Payne went to the Union League," Wohl explained to
Pekach, "to tell the Detweiler girl's family what had happened. Lieutenant Lewis, who I suppose was the senior supervisor there then, told him it was okay."

"Dolan didn't mention Lewis," Pekach said.

"Is there a Captain Petcock or something here?" a loud voice interrupted. Matt stopped and turned to the voice. A tall, very skinny, long-haired man in white cook's clothing was holding up a telephone.

"Close." Wohl chuckled. "Go answer the phone, Captain Petcock."

"Yes, sir, Inspector Wall," Pekach said, and got up.

"Miss Spencer—" Wohl began.

"You were calling me Amanda," she said. "Does Miss Spencer mean I'm a suspect again?"

"*Amanda,* did you ever hear anything about the Detweiler girl being into drugs?"

She hesitated a moment before replying. Matt wondered if she was going to defend Penny Detweiler loyally.

"She took diet pills to stay awake to study sometimes," she said finally. "And I suppose she smokes grass—I *know* she smokes grass—I'm about the only one I know who doesn't. But I never heard anything about her and heroin or cocaine or anything else. *Hard* drugs."

"Just out of idle curiosity, why don't you smoke grass?" Wohl asked.

"I tried it once and it made me sick," Amanda said.

"Me too," Wohl said, smiling at the look of surprise on Matt Payne's face.

Captain David Pekach walked back up to the table.

"That was Lucci," he said. "There was just a radio call. M-Mary One wants H-Highway One and W-William One to meet him at Colombia and Clarion."

Curiosity overwhelmed Amanda Spender's normally good manners. "M-Mary One? W-William One? What in the world is that?"

"The mayor is M-Mary One," Wohl explained, somewhat impatiently. "Did Lucci say what the mayor is doing at Colombia and Clarion?"

"They found a 22nd District cop lying in the gutter," Pekach said. "Shot to death."

"Oh, my God!" Amanda said.

Wohl stood up, fished in his pockets, and came up with a set of keys. He handed them to Payne.

"I'll ride with Captain Pekach, Matt. The Jag's on 12th

Street. Right across from your car. You bring the Jag there. You know where it is?"

Matt shook his head no.

"Just before you get to Temple University on North Broad, turn right," Captain Pekach said. "Couple of blocks in from North Broad. Colombia and Clarion. You won't have any trouble finding it."

"Yes, sir," Matt said.

"Are you going to be able to get home by yourself all right, Amanda?" Wohl asked.

"Sure. Don't worry about me, I've got Matt's car."

Wohl and Pekach hurried away.

"Is it always like this?" Amanda asked.

"No," Matt said. "It isn't."

He went to the counter and paid the bill. When they got outside to 12th Street, he handed Amanda the keys to the Porsche.

"Wouldn't it be easier if I just got in a cab?" she asked. "Or, how long are you going to be?"

"God knows," he said. "I really don't want to leave the car here. Some street artist would draw his mother's picture with a key on the hood by the time I got back."

"Couldn't I leave it at your apartment, then?" she asked. "Aren't you going to need it?"

"Jesus, would you?" he asked.

"Sure."

"I live on Rittenhouse Square—"

"That's right by the church?"

"Yeah. I live on the top floor of the Delaware Cancer Society Building—"

"Where?" she asked, chuckling.

"You can't miss it. Anyway, there's a parking garage in the back. Just drive in. There's two parking spaces with my name on them. And there's a rent-a-cop on duty. He'll call you a cab."

He started to hand her money. She waved it away.

"Nice girls don't take cab fare," she said. "Haven't you ever heard of women's lib?"

"This has been one hell of a date, hasn't it?" he said.

"It lends an entirely new meaning to the word *memorable*," Amanda said.

"I'm sorry."

"Don't be an ass," she said, and stretched upward to kiss him.

Whatever her intentions, either to kiss his cheek or, chastely, his lips, it somehow didn't turn out that way. It was not a passionate embrace ending with Amanda semi-swooning in his arms, but when their lips broke contact, there seemed to be some sort of current flowing between them.

"Jesus!" Matt said softly.

She put her hand up and laid it for a moment on his cheek. Then she ran across the street and got in the Porsche.

Matt got in Wohl's Jaguar and drove north to Vine Street, then left to North Broad, and then turned right onto Broad Street. There was not much traffic, and understandably reasoning that he was not going to get ticketed for speeding while driving Inspector Wohl's car to a crime scene, he stepped hard on the gas.

A minute or two later there was the growl of a siren behind him, and he pulled toward the right. An Oldsmobile, its red lights flashing from their concealed position under the grill, raced past him. After a moment he realized that the car belonged to Chief Inspector Dennis V. Coughlin. He wondered if Denny Coughlin, or Sergeant Tom Lenihan, who was driving, had recognized him or Wohl's car or both.

Just south of Temple University he saw that Captain Pekach was right; he would have no trouble finding Colombia and Clarion. There were two RPCs, warning lights flashing, on Broad Street and Colombia, and two uniformed cops in the street.

When he signaled to turn right, one of them emphatically signaled for him to continue up Broad Street. Matt stopped.

"I'm Payne. Special Operations. I'm to meet Inspector Wohl here."

The cop looked at him doubtfully but waved him on.

Clarion is the second street in from Broad. There was barely room for Matt to make it past all the police cars, marked and unmarked, lining both sides of Colombia. There was a black Cadillac limousine nearly blocking the intersection of Clarion and Colombia. Matt had seen it before. It was the mayoral limousine.

Then he saw two familiar faces, Officer Jesus Martinez and

the Highway sergeant who had almost made him piss his pants on the roof of the Penn Services Parking Garage by suggesting that the price for moving a fucking muscle would be having his fucking brains blown out, and who had seemed wholly prepared to make good the threat.

They were directing traffic. The sergeant first began—impatiently, even angrily—to gesture for him to turn right, south, on Clarion, and then he apparently recognized Wohl's car, for he signaled him to park it on the sidewalk.

Matt got out of the car and looked around for Wohl. He was standing with Police Commissioner Thaddeus Czernich, Chief Inspector Dennis V. Coughlin, half a dozen uniformed senior supervisors, none of whom looked familiar, two other men in civilian clothing, and His Honor, Mayor Jerry Carlucci.

Twenty feet away, Matt saw Sergeant Tom Lenihan standing with three men Matt supposed were both policemen and probably drivers. He walked over to them.

And then he saw the body. It was in the gutter, facedown, curled up beside a 22nd District RPC. There were a half dozen detectives, or crime-lab technicians, around it, two of them on their hands and knees with powerful, square-bodied searchlights, one of them holding a measuring tape, the others doing something Matt didn't quite understand.

"Hello, Matt," Tom Lenihan said, offering his hand. "I thought that was you in Wohl's Jag."

"Sergeant," Matt said politely.

"This is Matt Payne, Special Operations—" Lenihan said, beginning the introductions, but he stopped when Mayor Carlucci's angry voice filled the street.

"I don't give a good goddamn if Matt Lowenstein, or anyone else, likes it or not," the mayor said. "The way it's going to *be*, Tad, is that Special Operations is going to take this job and get whatever sons of bitches shot this poor bastard in cold blood. And you're going to see personally that the Department gives Wohl everything he thinks he needs to get the job done. Clear?"

"Yes, sir," Commissioner Czernich said.

"And now, Commissioner, I think that you and I and Chief Coughlin should go express our condolences to Officer Magnella's family, don't you?"

"Yes, sir," Commissioner Czernich and Chief Coughlin said, almost in unison.

The mayor marched toward the small knot of drivers, heading for his limousine. He smiled absently, perhaps automatically, at them, and then spotted Matt Payne. The expression on his face changed. He walked up to Matt.

"Were you at the Union League tonight?"

"I didn't quite make it there, Mr. Mayor," Matt said.

"Yeah, and I know why," the mayor said. He turned to Commissioner Czernich. "And while I'm at it, Tad, I want you to assign Wohl to get to the bottom of what happened to Detweiler's daughter and that mafioso scumbag DeZego on the roof of the parking garage tonight."

Commissioner Czernich looked as if he were about to speak.

"You don't have anything to say about anyone not going to like that, do you, Commissioner?" the mayor asked icily.

"No, sir," Commissioner Czernich said.

"You hear that, Peter?" the mayor called.

"Yes, sir," Peter Wohl replied.

"Keep up the good work, Payne," the mayor said, then walked quickly to his limousine.

EIGHT

Staff Inspector Peter Wohl walked to where Officer Payne was standing. Matt saw Captain Pekach step out of the shadows and follow him.

"What did the mayor say to you?" Wohl asked.

"He asked me if I'd been at the Union League," Matt replied, "and then he turned and told the Commissioner he wanted us to handle what happened at the Penn Services Parking Garage."

Wohl shook his head.

"I had a strange feeling I should have driven myself up here," Wohl said to Pekach. "Jesus Christ!"

Matt added, chuckling, "And then he told me to keep up the good work."

"I'm beginning to wonder if I can afford you and all your good work, hotshot," Wohl said, and then he saw the look on Matt's face. "Relax. Only kidding."

"You think he might think it over and change his mind?" Captain Pekach asked.

"No. That would mean he made a mistake. We all know the mayor never makes a mistake. Where's Mike?"

"At home."

"And Jason Washington? You know where he is?"

"At the shore. He's got a place outside Atlantic City."

"When's he coming back?"

"Day after tomorrow."

"Get on the radio, Dave. Get word to Mike Sabara to meet me here. And get me a number on Washington. He'll have to come back tomorrow. What about Tony Harris?"

"He's probably at home this time of night."

"Get him over here—now," Wohl ordered. "Have Lucci tell him he and Washington have this job."

"Yes, sir," David Pekach said.

"Where's my car?" Wohl asked Matt.

Matt pointed.

"You might as well go home," Wohl said.

"I don't mind staying," Matt said.

"Go home," Wohl repeated. "I'm going to have enough trouble with Chief Lowenstein the way things are. I don't need his pungent observations about a cop in a tuxedo."

"You're going to stay here?"

"Until Lowenstein shows up and can vent his spleen at me," Wohl said, and then added, "Speaking of the devil . . ."

Everybody followed his glance down Colombia Street, where a black, antenna-festooned car was approaching.

"I think that's Mickey O'Hara, Inspector," Pekach said. "He's driving a Buick these days."

"Yeah, so it is," Wohl said. "But if our Mickey is here, can Chief Lowenstein be far behind?" He looked around the area, then turned to Pekach. "There's enough district cars here. Do we need Sergeant—What's-his-name?—anymore?"

Pekach found what Wohl had seen.

"DeBenedito, Inspector. No."

"Sergeant DeBenedito!" Wohl called.

DeBenedito trotted over.

"Yes, sir?"

"There's no point in you hanging around here, Sergeant," Wohl said. "Take Officer Payne home, and then take it to the barn."

"Yes, sir."

Matt looked at his watch. It was a quarter past one. DeBenedito and Martinez had already worked more than an hour past the end of their shift.

"I can catch the subway, Inspector," he said.

"If the mayor heard that a guy in a dinner jacket got propositioned on the subway, Officer Payne, he would almost certainly give the investigation of that affront to law and order to Special Operations too. Go with the sergeant."

Pekach laughed.

"Good night, Matt," Wohl said. "See you in the morning. Early in the morning."

"Good night, Inspector," Matt said. "Captain."

"Good night, Payne."

Matt got in the back of the Highway RPC.

"Where do you live, Payne?"

"Rittenhouse Square," Officer Jesus Martinez answered for Matt. "In the Delaware Valley Cancer Society Building."

"Yeah, that's right. You guys know each other, don't you?"

Matt knelt on the floor and put his elbows on the top of the front seat.

"What the hell happened here tonight?" he asked as they drove down Colombia to North Broad and then turned left toward downtown.

"A very nice young cop named Joe Magnella got himself shot," DeBenedito said.

"You knew him?" Matt asked.

"He was a second cousin once removed, or a first cousin twice removed, something like that. My mother's sister, Blanche, is married to his uncle. I didn't know him good, but I seen him at weddings and funerals, feast days, like that. Nice kid. Just come back from Veet-Nam. I don't think he was on the job six months. He was about to get married. *Son of a bitch!*"

"What happened?" Matt asked softly.

"Nobody seems to know. He was working an RPC out of the 22nd. He didn't call in or anything, from what I hear. There was a call to Police Emergency, saying there was a cop shot on Clarion Street. Fucker didn't give his name, of course. Martinez and I were on Roosevelt Boulevard, not close, but it was a cop, so we went in on it. By the time we got there, the place was crawling with cops, so we found ourselves directing traffic. Anyway, the kid was in the gutter, dead. Shot at least twice. The door to his car was open, but he hadn't taken his gun out or anything. And he hadn't called in to say he was doing anything out of the ordinary. Some son of a bitch who didn't like cops or whatever just shot him.''

''Jesus Christ!'' Matt said.

''What was that shit going on between the mayor and them other big shots?'' Sergeant DeBenedito asked.

''The mayor assigned the investigation to Special Operations,'' Matt said.

''Can you guys handle something like that? This is a fucking homicide, isn't it? Pure and simple?''

''When we were looking for the Northwest rapist,'' Matt said, ''Inspector Wohl had two Homicide detectives transferred in. The best. Jason Washington and Tony Harris. If anybody can find the man who shot . . . what was his name . . . ?''

''Magnella, Joseph Magnella,'' DeBenedito furnished.

''. . . Officer Magnella, those two can.''

''Washington is that great big black guy?''

''Yeah.''

''I seen him around,'' DeBenedito said. ''And I heard about him.''

''He's really good,'' Matt said. ''I had the chance to be around him—''

''You're the guy who put down the rapist, ain't you?'' DeBenedito asked, and then went on without waiting for an answer. ''Martinez told me about that after I put you on the ground in the parking garage. I'm sorry about that. You didn't look like a cop.''

''Forget it,'' Matt said.

''Talk about looking like a cop!'' Martinez said. ''Did you see the baby-blue pants and the hat on Inspector Wohl? It looked like he was going to play fucking golf or something! Jesus H. Christ!''

''Is he as good as they say he is?'' DeBenedito asked, ''or does he just have a lot of pull?''

''Both, I'd say,'' Matt said. His knees hurt. He pushed himself back onto the seat as DeBenedito drove around City Hall and then up Market Street.

The Highway Patrol pulled to the curb on the south side

of Rittenhouse Square as a foot-patrol officer made his way down the sidewalk. He looked on curiously as the cop in the passenger seat jumped out and opened the rear door so that a civilian in a tuxedo could get out. (The inside handles on RPCs are often removed so that people put in the back can't get out before they're suppose to.)

"Good night, Hay-zus," Matt said, and raising his voice, called, "Thanks for the ride, Sergeant."

"Stay off parking garage roofs, Payne," Sergeant De-Benedito called back as Jesus Martinez got back in and slammed the door.

"Good morning," Matt said to the foot-patrol cop.

"Yeah," the cop responded, and then he watched as Matt let himself into the Delaware Valley Cancer Society Building. It was a renovated, turn-of-the-century brownstone. Renovations for a long-term lease as office space to the Cancer Society had been just about completed when the architect told the owner he had found enough space in what had been the attic to make a small apartment.

Matt had found the apartment through his father's secretary and moved in when he'd gone on the job. A month ago he had learned that his father owned the building.

The elevator ended on the floor below the attic. He got out of the elevator, thinking it was a good thing Amanda had been willing to park his car for him before catching a cab to Merion; he would need his car tomorrow, for sure, and then walked up the narrow flight of stairs to the attic apartment.

The lights were on. He didn't remember leaving them on, but that wasn't at all unusual.

He walked to the fireplace, raised his left leg, and detached the Velcro fasteners that held his ankle holster in place on the inside of his leg and took it off. He took the pistol, a five-shot .38 caliber Smith & Wesson Chief's Special from it. He laid the holster on the fireplace mantel and then wiped off the pistol with a silicone-impregnated cloth.

Jason Washington had told him about doing that; that anytime you touched the metal of a pistol, the body left minute traces of acidic fluid on it. Eventually it would eat away the bluing. Habitually wiping it once a day would preserve the bluing.

He laid the pistol on the mantel and, starting to take off his dinner jacket, turned away from the fireplace.

Amanda Spencer was standing by the elbow-high bookcase that separated the "dining area" from the "kitchen." Both, in Matt's opinion, were too small to be thought of without quotation marks.

"Welcome home," Amanda said.

Matt dismissed the first thought that came to his mind: that Amanda was here because she wanted to make the beast with two backs as wishful-to-the-nth-degree thinking.

"No rent-a-cop downstairs?" he asked. "I should have told you to look in the outer lobby. They can usually be found there, asleep."

"He was there. He let me in," Amanda said.

"I don't understand," Matt said.

"Either do I," she said. "What happened where you went with Peter Wohl?"

"There was a dead cop," Matt said. "A young one. Now that I think about it, I saw him around the academy. Somebody shot him."

"Why?"

"No one seems to know," Matt said. "Somebody called it in, a dead cop in the gutter. When they got there, there he was."

"How terrible."

"He had been to Vietnam. He was about to get married. He was a relative of Sergeant DeBenedito."

"Who?"

"He was at the garage," Matt said. "And then he was at Colombia and Clarion—where the dead cop was. Wohl had him drive me home."

"Oh."

"Amanda, I'll take you out to Merion. But first, would you mind if I made myself a drink?"

"I helped myself," she said. "I hope that's all right."

"Don't be silly."

He started for the kitchen. As he approached her, Amanda stepped out of the way, making it clear, he thought, that she didn't want to be embraced, or even patted, in the most friendly, big-brotherly manner.

In the kitchen he saw that she had found where he kept his

liquor, in a cabinet over the refrigerator; a squat bottle of twenty-four-year-old Scotch, a gift from his father, was on the sink.

He found a glass and put ice in it, and then Scotch, and then tap water. He was stirring it with his finger when Amanda came up behind him and wrapped her arms around him.

"I wanted to be with you tonight," she said softly, her head against his back. "I suppose that makes me sound like a slut."

"Not unless you announce those kind of urges more than, say, twice a week," he said.

Oh, shit, he thought, *you and your fucking runaway mouth! What the* hell *is the matter with you?*

Her arms dropped away from him and he sensed that she had stepped back. He turned around.

"I suppose I deserved that," she said.

"I'm sorry," Matt said. "Jesus Christ, Amanda, I can't tell you how sorry I am I said that."

She looked into his eyes for a long time.

"You'll be the second, all right? I was engaged," she said.

"I know," he said.

"You do?"

"I mean, I know you're not a slut. I have a runaway mouth."

"Yes, you do," she agreed. "We'll have to work on that."

She put her hand to his cheek. He turned his head and kissed it.

When he met her eyes again, she said, "I knew you were going to be trouble for me the first time I laid eyes on you."

"I'm not going to be trouble for you, I promise."

She laughed.

"Oh, yes you are," she said. "So now what, Matthew? You want to show me your etchings now or what?"

"They're in my sleeping-accommodations suite," he said. "That's the small closet to your immediate rear."

"I know," she said. "I looked. Lucky for you I didn't find any hairpins or forgotten lingerie in there."

"You'll be the first," he said.

"You mean in *there*," she said, and when she saw the uncomfortable look on his face, she stood on her toes and kissed him gently on the lips. Then she took his hand and led him into his bedroom.

When Sergeant Nick DeBenedito and Officer Jesus Martinez walked into Highway Patrol headquarters at Bustleton and Bowler, Officer Charley McFadden was sitting on one of the folding metal chairs in the corridor.

Martinez was surprised to see him. He knew that McFadden had spent his four-to-midnight tour riding with a veteran Highway Patrolman named Jack Wyatt. Since he and DeBenedito were more than an hour late coming off shift, he had presumed that Charley would be long gone.

McFadden, a large, pleasant-faced young man of twenty-three, had already changed out of his uniform. He was wearing a knit sport shirt, a cotton jacket with a zipper closing, and blue jeans. When McFadden stood up, the jacket fell open, exposing, on his right, his badge, pinned over his belt, and his revolver. Charley carried his off-duty weapon, a .38-caliber five-shot Smith & Wesson Undercover Special revolver in a "high-rise pancake," a holster reportedly invented by a special agent of the U.S. Secret Service, which suspended the revolver under his right arm, *above* the belt, almost as high as a shoulder holster would have placed it.

Jesus thought Charley looked, except that his hair was combed and he was shaved and the clothes were clean, as he had looked when the two of them were working undercover in Narcotics.

"You still here, McFadden?" Sergeant DeBenedito asked in greeting.

"I thought maybe Hay-zus would want to go to the FOP bar and hoist one," Charley said.

Charley had taken to using the Spanish pronunciation of Martinez's Christian name because of his mother, a devout Irish Catholic who had been made distinctly uncomfortable by having to refer to her son's partner as Jesus.

"Yeah, why not?" Martinez replied. Actually he did not want to go to the FOP bar with Charley at all. But he didn't see how he could say no after Charley had hung around the station for more than an hour waiting for him. "Give me a minute to change."

He consoled himself with the thought that it was only the

decent thing to do. Charley had, after all, volunteered to drive him to work when he learned that Jesus's Ford was (again) in the muffler shop for squeaking brakes, and then he'd hung around for more than an hour waiting to drive him home. If he wanted to have a beer, they'd go get a beer.

Five minutes later he emerged from the locker room in civilian clothing. He wore a dark blue shirt, even darker blue trousers, and a light brown leather jacket. There was a fourteen-karat gold-plated chain around his neck, and what the guy in the jewelry store had said was an Inca sun medallion hanging from that. His badge was in his pocket, and although he, too, carried an Undercover Special, he did so in a shoulder holster. He had tried the pancake and it hadn't worked. His hips weren't wide enough or something. It always felt like it was about to fall off.

Despite the early-morning hour, the parking lot of the FOP Building, just off North Broad Street in Central Philadelphia, was almost full. About a quarter of the Police Department had come off shift at midnight with a thirst. Cops are happiest in the company of other cops, and attracting more customers to the bar at the FOP has never posed a problem for the officers of the FOP.

Jesus followed Charley down the stairs from the street to the basement bar and was surprised when Charley took a table against the wall. Charley usually liked to sit at the bar, which gave him, he said, a better look at the activity, by which he meant the women.

"Hold the table," Charley ordered, and went to the bar. He returned with two bottles of Ortlieb's and a huge bowl of popcorn. A year or so before, Jesus Martinez had become interested in nutrition, and was convinced that popcorn, and most of what else Charley put in his mouth, was not good for you.

"You're going to eat the whole damned bowl?"

"You can have some," Charley said. "I read in the paper that they just found out that popcorn is just as good for you as wheat germ."

"Really?" Jesus said, and then realized his chain was being pulled.

"Yeah, the article said that they found out that popcorn is

almost as good for you as french fries *without* catsup. No match, of course, for french fries *with* catsup.''

"Bullshit!''

"Had you going, didn't I?'' Charley asked, pleased with himself.

"Laugh at me all you want. All that garbage you keep putting in your mouth is going to catch up with you sooner or later.''

"Tell me about Payne,'' McFadden said abruptly.

"You heard about that, huh?'' Jesus said, chuckling.

"Yeah, I heard about it,'' McFadden said, on the edge of unpleasantness.

"Well, it was really sort of funny—''

"Funny?'' McFadden asked. "You think it's funny?''

"Yeah, Charley, I do. It was sort of funny.''

"Well, I think it was shitty, pal!''

"What the hell are you talking about?''

"What are *you* talking about?''

"I'm talking about DeBenedito putting Payne down on the roof of the parking garage in his fancy clothes.''

"I didn't hear about that,'' McFadden said.

"Well, DeBenedito and I went in on the shooting on the roof of the Penn Services Parking Garage. He put me out of the car one floor down, and I went up the stairs. When I got there, he's got your pal Payne down on the floor. *'Tell him I'm a cop, Martinez!'* Payne yells when he sees me. So I did, and DeBenedito let him up. I thought it was funny. If you don't, go fuck yourself.''

"I didn't hear about that,'' Charley repeated, sounding a little confused. "I was talking about *your* pal, Sergeant Dolan, taking Payne and his girlfriend over to Narcotics and searching his car.''

"I don't know anything about that,'' Jesus said.

"Bullshit!''

"I don't. You sure about your facts?''

"Yeah, I'm sure about my facts.''

"Well, all I know is that Payne was at the scene, where the cop got shot. He came there driving Inspector Wohl's Jaguar, and then Wohl made us take him home. That's one of the reasons we was an hour late. If Dolan had him over at Narcotics, two things: One, I didn't know about it; and two, he would now be in Central Lockup. Dolan doesn't make mistakes.''

''Yeah, I know you think he walks on water.''

''He's a goddamned good cop,'' Martinez said flatly. ''Where'd you hear he had something going with Payne?''

''Wyatt and I went by Bustleton and Bowler about ten-thirty, and somebody told him, and he told me.''

''You sure he wasn't pulling your chain?''

''Yeah. It was no joke. Dolan had Payne, his girlfriend, and his car, over at Narcotics.''

''Then Dolan had something,'' Martinez said.

''Something he got from you, maybe?'' McFadden asked.

''I told you, I never heard about this,'' Martinez said, and then the implication of what McFadden had said sank in.

''Fuck you, Charley!'' he said, flaring, and he stood up so quickly that he bumped against the table, knocking over the beer bottles. ''Jesus Christ, what a shitty thing to say!''

''If you didn't do it, then I'm sorry,'' McFadden said after a moment.

''That's not good enough. Fuck you!''

''You cut off his tire valves!'' McFadden said. ''Tell me that wasn't a shitty thing to do.''

''The son of a bitch was sound asleep on a stakeout,'' Martinez said. ''He deserved that.''

''No he didn't. A pal would have woke him up.''

''Rich Boy is not my pal,'' Martinez said. ''He doesn't take me riding around in his Porsche like some people I know. All he's doing is *playing* cop.''

''He put down the Northwest rapist. That's *playing* cop?''

''You know, and I know, that he just stumbled on that scumbag,'' Martinez said.

''He put him down! Jesus Christ, Hay-zus!''

''Okay, so he put him down,'' Martinez admitted grudgingly. ''But it wouldn't surprise me at all to find he's stuffing shit up his nose.''

''You've got no right to say something like that!''

''You had no right to say what you did about me fingering him to Dolan.''

''I said I was sorry.''

''Yeah, you said you were sorry,'' Martinez said. ''I'm going home. I've had enough of your bullshit for one night.''

"Oh, sit down and drink your beer."

"Fuck you."

"Sit down, Hay-zus."

"Or what?"

"Or I'll sit on *you*."

Martinez glowered at him angrily for a moment and then smiled.

"You would, too, you fucking, overgrown Mick."

"You bet your ass I would," McFadden said.

Matt woke up and opened his eyes and saw that Amanda was supporting her head on her hand and looking down at him.

"Hi," she said, and bent her head and kissed him.

"Christ, and some people have alarm clocks!"

She laughed.

He looked up at the ceiling, where his bedside clock, a housewarming gift from his sister Amy, projected the time on the ceiling. It was a quarter past five.

"What were you thinking?" he asked.

"Wondering, actually."

"Okay. What were you wondering?"

"Two things."

"What two things?"

"Whether there is anything in your refrigerator besides a jar of olives."

"No," he said. "I haven't been shopping in a week. And what else were you wondering?"

"Whether I'm pregnant," Amanda said.

"Jesus! You're not on the pill?"

"I stopped taking the pill when I broke my engagement. And something like this wasn't supposed to be on the agenda."

"I would be delighted to make an honest woman of you," Matt said.

"Maybe I'll be lucky."

"Not at all, my pleasure."

"That's not what I meant." She giggled and jerked one of the hairs curling around his nipple out.

"Ouch," he said, and reached out for her and pulled her down to him so that she was lying with her face on his chest and her leg thrown over him.

"This is probably not a very smart thing for us to do," she said.

"I disagree absolutely," he said.

"What are the Brownes going to think?" she asked.

"We could tell them we had car trouble. Do you really care what the Brownes think?"

"No," she said, after a moment. "Okay. We'll tell them we had car trouble and not give a damn whether or not they believe us."

He chuckled and tightened his arm around her.

"Are you going to feed me, or what?" she asked.

"I'd rather 'or what,' " he said.

"You're boasting," she said. "Idle promises."

"See for yourself," Matt said.

She raised her head an inch off his chest.

"I'll be damned," she said. "Isn't that amazing?"

There were two Highway cops sitting at the counter of the small restaurant in the Marriott Motel on City Line Avenue when Matt and Amanda walked in.

He didn't recognize either of them and saw nothing like recognition in their eyes, either. Both looked carefully at Amanda and him, however, something Matt ascribed to Amanda's good looks, her low-cut evening dress, and the disparity between that and the tweed sport coat and slacks he had put on to go to work; or all of the above.

He was wrong. As soon as they had sat down in one of the booths, he saw alarm in Amanda's eyes and looked over his shoulder to see what had caused it. Both Highway cops were marching to the booth.

And they were, Matt thought, in their breeches and boots, their Sam Browne belts and leather jackets, intimidating.

"Seen the papers, Payne?" the larger of the two asked.

"No."

"Thought maybe not," the cop said.

How the hell am I going to introduce these guys to Amanda? That's obviously what they want, and I have absolutely no idea what either of their names are.

He was wrong about that too. The second Highway cop carefully laid slightly mussed copies of the *Bulletin*, the

Ledger, and the *Daily News* on the table and then nodded to Amanda.

"Ma'am," he said. By then the first cop was halfway to the door.

"Hey!" Matt called. Both cops looked at him. "Thank you."

Both waved and then left the diner.

"For a moment there I thought we were going to be arrested again," Amanda said.

"We weren't."

"Call it what you like," she said. "Are they all like that?"

"Like what?"

"So, what's a word? Those two looked like an American version of the Gestapo."

"They're Highway," Matt said. "They're sort of special. Sort of the elite."

"That's what they said about the Gestapo," Amanda said.

"Hey, they're the good guys," Matt said.

"How is it they knew you?"

"I guess they know I work for Inspector Wohl."

"What does Peter Wohl have to do with them?"

"He's their boss, one step removed. He commands Special Operations. Highway is under Special Operations."

A waitress appeared with menus.

"Isn't that awful?" she said, pointing at the front page of the *Daily News*.

Matt looked at it for the first time. Above the headline there was a half-page photo of Anthony J. DeZego slumped against the concrete blocks of the stairwell at the Penn Services Parking Garage.

MAFIA FIGURE MURDERED SOCIALITE WOUNDED IN CENTER CITY SHOOTING

"Let me see," Amanda said, and he slid the tabloid across the table to her and turned to the *Ledger*. The story was at the lower right corner of the front page, under a two-column picture of Miss Penelope Detweiler:

NESFOODS HEIRESS SHOT
IN CENTER CITY
POLICE BAFFLED
BY EARLY EVE SHOOTING

By Charles E. Whaley,
Ledger Staff Writer

Phila—Miss Penelope Detweiler, 23, of Chestnut Hill, was seriously wounded, apparently by a shotgun blast, in the Penn Services Parking Garage, on South 15th Street early last evening. She was taken to Hahneman Hospital where she is reported by a hospital spokesperson to be in "serious but stable" condition.

Miss Detweiler, whose father, H. Richard Detweiler, is president of Nesfoods International, was en route to the Union League Club on South Broad Street for a social event when the shooting occurred. A family spokesperson theorized that Miss Detweiler had just parked her car when she found herself in the middle of a "gangland shootout."

Police Captain Henry Quaire refused to comment on the shooting, saying the case is under investigation, but he did confirm that Miss Detweiler had been found lying on the floor of the roof of the garage by Miss Amanda

Chase Spencer, of Scarsdale, N.Y., and her escort, as they parked their car. The couple were also guests of Mr. and Mrs. Chadwick T. Nesbitt III at the Union League dinner to honor out-of-town guests for the wedding (tonight) of Miss Daphne Browne of Merion and Lieutenant C. T. Nesbitt IV, USMCR.

"It is absurd to think that Miss Detweiler was anything more than an innocent bystander," the Detweiler family spokesperson said. "It is a sad commentary on life in Philadelphia that something like this could happen."

Matt slid the *Ledger* across the table to Amanda and then became aware that the waitress was still standing there.

"Amanda, would you like to order?"

"I think I lost my appetite," she said.

"You have to eat."

"Can I get a breakfast steak?" she asked.

"Honey, anything your heart desires, we got it," the waitress said.

"They're running a special on me," Matt said. "I'm specially marked down for the occasion."

"Breakfast steak, medium-rare, eggs sunny-side up, toast, tomato juice, and coffee," Amanda said.

"Twice," Matt said. "Thank you."

Matt turned to the *Bulletin*. It used two photographs on the front, placed side by side. One was the same photo the *Ledger* had used of Amanda. The other was of Anthony J. DeZego scowling at the camera from above a board that read PHILA POLICE DEPT and carried his name and the date. Under these the caption gave their names and read, "shooting victims."

MAFIOSO KILLED: SOCIALITE WOUNDED IN CENTER CITY POLICE SEEKING CLUES IN EARLY EVENING SHOOTING

By Michael J. O'Hara

A shotgun blast to the head killed Anthony J. "Tony the Zee" DeZego, a Philadelphia underworld figure, and a second blast critically wounded Penelope Detweiler, socialite daughter of H. Richard Detweiler, president of Nesfoods International, shortly after seven last night on the roof level of the Penn Services Parking Garage on South 15th Street in downtown Philadelphia.

Miss Detweiler is in "critical but stable" condition at Hahneman Hospital. She was struck by "many" pellets from a shotgun shell, according to a hospital spokesman.

Off-duty Police Officer Matthew M. Payne discovered first Miss Detweiler, lying in a pool of blood, and then DeZego's body when he went to park his car. Payne, who is special assistant to Staff Inspector Peter Wohl, commanding officer of the Police Department's Special Operations Division, last month shot to death Warren K. Fletcher, 31, of Germantown, ending what Mayor Jerry Carlucci termed "the reign of terror of the Northwest serial rapist."

Miss Detweiler, Payne, and Miss Amanda Spencer, of Scarsdale, N.Y., who was with Payne in his silver Porsche, were en route to the Union League Club on South Broad Street to attend a dinner being given for out-of-town wedding guests by C. T. Nesbitt III, Nesfoods International chairman of the board, whose son is to marry Daphne Browne of Merion at seven-thirty tonight at St. Mark's Church, near the site of the shooting.

According to senior police officials, it is most likely that Miss Detweiler was an innocent bystander caught in the middle of a mob exchange of gunfire, but this reporter has learned that police are quietly investigating the possibility that Miss Detweiler knew De-Zego, and possibly may have gone to the parking garage to meet him.

In a surprise development last night, Police Commissioner Thaddeus Czernich announced that responsibility for the investigation of the shooting had been assigned to Staff Inspector Peter Wohl and the Special Operations Division.

Such an investigation would normally be conducted by the Homicide Division.

Commissioner Czernich also assigned to Wohl the investigation of the murder of Police Officer Joseph Magnella, who was shot to death last night in North Philadelphia. (See related story, Page 3A.) One theory advanced for this unusual move was the reassignment of ace Homicide Detectives Jason Washington and Anthony J. Harris to Special Operations during the search for the North Philadelphia serial rapist.

"They've got my name in here," Amanda said, "but not yours."

"The *Ledger* never mentions a cop's name unless they can say something nasty about him," Matt said.

"Really?" Amanda said, not sure if he was serious or not. She put her hand on the *Bulletin*. "What does that one say?"

"About the same thing," Matt said.

"Through?" Amanda asked, and slid the *Bulletin* away from Matt's side of the table.

He saw her eyes widen when she got to the place in the story about him. She glanced at him, then finished the story.

"You never told me about that," she said.

"Yes I did," Matt said. "You said if you had a car like mine and somebody dinged it, you'd kill him. And I said somebody did and I had."

The waitress appeared with a stainless-steel coffee pot. Amanda waited until she had poured the coffee and left.

"I thought you were just being a wiseass," she said.

"You should have seen what he did to my car," Matt said. "He was lucky I didn't get really mad."

"Matt, *stop*!"

"Sorry," he said after a moment.

And a moment after that Amanda reached out and caught his hand. They sat that way, holding hands and looking into each other's eyes, until the waitress delivered breakfast.

NINE

There was a fence around the Browne place in Merion, field-stone posts every twenty-five feet or so with wrought-iron bars between them. The bars were topped with spear points, and as a boy of six or seven Matt had spent all of one afternoon trying to hammer one loose so that he would have a spear to take home.

There was also a gate and a gate house, but the gate had never in Matt's memory been closed, and the gate house had always been locked and off-limits.

When he turned off the road, the gate was closed, and he had to jump on the brakes to avoid hitting it. And the door to the gate house was open. A burly man in a dark suit came out of it and walked to the gate.

A rent-a-cop, Matt decided. *Had he been hired because the Princess of the Castle was getting married? Or did it have something to do with what had happened at the parking garage?*

The rent-a-cop opened the left portion of the gate wide enough to get through and came out to the Porsche.

"May I help you, sir?"

"Would you open the gate, please? Miss Spencer is a guest here."

The rent-a-cop looked carefully at both of them, then smiled, said, "Certainly, sir," and went to the gate and swung both sides open.

Matt saw that a red-and-white-striped tent, large enough for a two-ring circus, had been set up on the lawn in front of the house. There were three large caterer's trucks parked in the driveway. A human chain had been formed to unload folding chairs from one of them and set them up in the tent, and he saw cardboard boxes being unloaded in the same way from a second.

Soames T. Browne, in his shirt sleeves, and the bride-to-be, in shorts and a tattered gray University of Pennsylvania sweatshirt that belonged, Matt decided, to Chad Nesbitt, were standing outside the castle portal when Matt drove up. The rent-a-cop had almost certainly telephoned the house. Matt saw another large man in a business suit standing just inside the open oak door.

"I'll see you later," Matt said, waving at the Brownes with his left hand and touching Amanda's wrist with his right.

Amanda kissed his cheek and opened her door.

Soames T. Browne came around to Matt's side. Matt rolled the window down.

"Morning."

"Daffy said Amanda was probably with you," Browne said. "You should have called, Matt."

"Matt had to work—" Amanda said.

"*Sure* he did," Daffy snorted.

"—and I waited for him."

"Come in and have some coffee, Matt," Soames T. Browne ordered. "I want a word with you."

"I can't stay long, Mr. Browne."

"It won't take long," Browne said.

Matt turned the ignition off and got out of the car. There was a breakfast room in the house, on the ground floor of one of the turrets, with French windows opening onto the formal garden behind the house. Soames Browne led Matt to it, and then through it to the kitchen, where Mrs. Soames T.

Browne, in a flowing negligee, was perched on a stool under a rack of pots and pans with a china mug in her hand.

"Good morning," Matt said.

She looked over him to Amanda.

"We were worried about you, honey," she said.

"I was with Matt," Amanda said.

"That's what we thought; that's why she was worried," Daffy said.

"We should have called. I'm sorry," Matt said.

"We were just going to do something about breakfast," Mrs. Browne said. "Have you eaten?"

"We just had breakfast, thank you," Amanda said.

"I didn't know Matt could cook," Daffy said sweetly.

"Coffee, then?" Mrs. Browne asked.

"Please," Amanda said.

"Do you know how Penny is, Matt?" Soames T. Browne asked.

"As of midnight she was reported to be 'critical but stable,' " Matt said.

"How do you know that?"

"My boss told us," Matt said.

"That was seven hours ago," Soames T. Browne said.

"Would you like me to call and see if there's been any change?"

"Could you?"

"I can try," Matt said. He looked up the number of Hahneman Hospital in the telephone book and then called.

"I'm sorry, sir, we're not permitted to give out that information at this time."

"This is Officer Payne, of the police."

"One moment, please, sir."

The next voice, very deep, precise, that came on-line surprised Matt: "Detective Washington."

"This is Matt Payne, Mr. Washington."

"What can I do for you, Matt?"

"I'm trying to find out how Penelope Detweiler is. They put me through to you."

"For Wohl?"

"For me. She's a friend of mine."

"I heard that. I'll want to talk to you about that later. At six o'clock they changed her from 'critical' to 'serious.' "

"That's better?"

Washington chuckled.

"One step up," he said.

"Thank you," Matt said.

"You at Bustleton and Bowler?"

"No. But I'm headed there."

"When you get there, don't leave until we talk."

"Yes, sir."

"Don't call me sir, Matt. I've told you that."

The phone went dead. Matt hung it up and turned to face the people waiting for him to report.

"As of six this morning they upgraded her condition from 'critical' to 'serious,' " he said.

"Thank God," Soames T. Browne said.

"Mother, I'm sure Penny would want us to go through with the wedding," Daphne Browne said.

"Why did this have to happen *now*?" Mrs. Soames T. Browne said.

Matt started to say, *Damned inconsiderate of old Precious Penny, what?* but stopped himself in time to convert what came out of his mouth to "Damned shame."

Even that got him a dirty look from Amanda.

"What do you think, Matt?" Soames T. Browne said.

"It's none of my business," Matt said.

"Yes it is, you're Chad's best man."

"Chad's on his way to Okinawa," Matt said. "It's not as if you could postpone it for a month or so."

"Right," Daffy Browne said. "I hadn't thought about that. We *can't* postpone it."

"I think Matt is absolutely right, Soames," Mrs. Browne said.

"That's a first," Matt quipped.

"What did you say, Matthew?" Mrs. Browne asked icily.

"I said, you're going to have to excuse me, please. I have to go to work."

"You will be there tonight?" Daffy asked.

"As far as I know."

"I wanted to ask you, Matt, what happened last night," Soames T. Browne said.

"I don't really know, Mr. Browne," Matt said.

And then he walked out of the kitchen. Amanda's eyes found his and for a moment held them.

Peter Wohl leaned forward, pushed the flashing button on one of the two telephones on his office coffee table, picked it up, said "Inspector Wohl" into it and leaned back into a sprawling position on the couch, tucking the phone under his ear.

"Tony Harris, Inspector," his caller said. "You wanted to talk to me?"

"First things first," Wohl said. "You got anything?"

"Not a goddamn thing."

"You need anything?"

"How are you fixed for crystal balls?"

"How many do you want?"

Harris chuckled. "I really can't think of anything special right now, Inspector. This one is going to take a lot of door-bell ringing."

"Well, I can get you the ringers. I had Dave Pekach offer overtime to anybody who wants it."

"I don't have lead fucking one," Harris said.

"You'll find something," Wohl said. "The other reason I asked you to call is that I have sort of a problem."

"How's that?"

"You know a lieutenant named Lewis? Just made it? Used to be a sergeant in the 9th?"

"Black guy? Stiff-backed?"

"That's him."

"Yeah, I know him."

"He has a son. Just got out of the Police Academy."

"Is that so?" Harris said, suspicion evident in his voice.

"He worked his way through college in the radio room," Wohl said.

"You don't say?"

"The commissioner assigned him to Special Operations," Wohl said.

"You want to drop the other shoe, Inspector?"

"I thought he might be useful to you," Wohl said.

"How?"

"Running errands, maybe. He knows his way around the Department."

"Is that it? Or don't you know what else to do with him?"

"Frankly, Tony, a little of both. But I won't force him on you if you don't want him."

Harris hesitated, then said, "If he's going to run errands for me, he'd need wheels."

"Wheels or a car?" Wohl asked innocently.

Harris chuckled. "Wheels" was how Highway referred to their motorcycles.

"I forgot you're now the head wheelman," he said. "A *car*."

"That can be arranged."

"How does he feel about overtime?"

"I think he'd like all you want to give him."

"Plainclothes too," Harris said. "Okay?"

"Okay."

"When do I get him?"

"He's supposed to report here right about now. You get him as soon as I can get him a car and into plainclothes."

"Okay."

"Thanks, Tony."

"Yeah," Harris said, and hung up.

Detective Jason Washington was one of the very few detectives in the Philadelphia Police Department who was not indignant or outraged that the murders of both Officer Joseph Magnella and Tony the Zee DeZego had been taken away from Homicide and given to Special Operations.

While he was not a vain man, neither was Jason Washington plagued with modesty. He knew that it was said that he was the best Homicide detective in the department (and this really meant something, since Homicide detectives were the crème de la crème, so to speak, of the profession, the best detectives, period) and he could not honestly fault this assessment of his ability.

Tony Harris was good, too, he recognized—nearly, but not quite as good as he was. There were also some people in Intelligence, Organized Crime, Internal Affairs, and even out in the detective districts and among the staff inspectors whom Washington acknowledged to be good detectives; that is to say, detectives at his level. For example, before he had been given Special Operations, Staff Inspector Peter Wohl had earned Washington's approval for his work by putting a series of especially slippery politicians and bureaucrats behind bars.

Jason Washington had, however, been something less than enthusiastic when Wohl had arranged for him (and Tony Harris) to be transferred from Homicide to Special Operations. He had not only let Wohl know that he didn't want the transfer, but also had actually come as close as he ever had to pleading not to be transferred.

There had been several reasons for his reluctance to leave Homicide. For one thing, he liked Homicide. There was also the matter of prestige and money. In Special Operations he would be a Special Operations detective. Since Special Operations hadn't been around long enough to acquire a reputation, that meant it had no reputation at all, and that meant, as opposed to his being a Homicide detective, he would be an ordinary detective. And ordinary detectives, like corporals, were only one step up from the bottom in the police hierarchy.

As far as pay was concerned, Washington's take-home pay in Homicide, because of overtime, was as much as a chief inspector took to the bank every two weeks.

Washington and his wife of twenty-two years had only one child, a girl, who had married young and, to Washington's genuine surprise, well. As a Temple freshman Ellen had caught the eye of a graduate student in mathematics and eloped with him, under the correct assumption that her father would have a really spectacular fit if she announced that she wanted to get married at eighteen. Ellen's husband was now working for Bell Labs, across the river in Jersey, and making more money than Washington would have believed possible for a twenty-six-year-old. Recently they had made him and Martha grandparents.

Mrs. Martha Washington (she often observed that she had nearly not married Jason because of what her name would be once he put the ring on her finger) had worked, from the time Ellen entered first grade, as a commercial artist for an advertising agency. With their two paychecks and Ellen gone, they lived well, with an apartment in a high rise overlooking the Schuykill River, and another near Atlantic City, overlooking the ocean. Martha drove a Lincoln, and one of his perks as a Homicide detective was an unmarked car of his own, and nothing said about his driving it home every night.

Wohl, who had once been a young detective in Homicide, understood Washington's (and Tony Harris's) concern that a transfer to Special Operations would mean the loss of their Homicide Division perks, perhaps especially the overtime pay. He had assured them that they could have all the overtime they wanted, and their own cars, and would answer only to him and Captain Mike Sabara, his deputy. He had been as good as his word. Better. The cars they had been given were brand-new, instead of the year-old hand-me-downs from inspectors they had had at Homicide.

They had been transferred to Special Operations after the mayor had "suggested" that Special Operations be given responsibility to catch the Northwest Philly serial rapist. After the kid, Matt Payne, had stumbled on that scumbag and put him down, Washington had gone to Wohl and asked about getting transferred back to Homicide.

Wohl had said, "Not yet. Maybe later," explaining that he didn't have any idea what the mayor, or for that matter, Commissioner Thad Czernich, had in mind for Special Operations.

"If the mayor has another of his inspirations for Special Operations, or if Czernich has one, I want you and Tony already here," Wohl had said. "I don't want to have to go through another hassle with Chief Lowenstein over transferring you back again."

Chief Inspector Matt Lowenstein headed the Detective Bureau, which included all the detective divisions, as well as Homicide, Intelligence, Major Crimes, and Juvenile Aid. He was an influential man with a reputation for jealously guarding his preserve.

"What are we going to do, Inspector," Washington had argued, "recover stolen vehicles?"

Wohl had laughed. Department policy required that a detective be assigned to examine any vehicle that had been stolen and then recovered. There were generally two types of recovered stolen vehicles: They were recovered intact, after having been taken for a joyride; or they were recovered as an empty shell, from which all resalable parts had been removed. In either case there was almost never anything that would connect the recovered vehicle with the thief. Investigating recovered vehicles was an exercise in futility and thus ordinarily assigned to the newest, or dumbest, detective in a squad.

"For the time being, I'll talk with Quaire, and see if he'd like you to work on some of the jobs you left behind at Homicide. But I have a gut feeling, Jason, that there will be enough jobs for you here to keep you from getting bored."

And Wohl had been right about that too. Police Commissioner Czernich (Washington had heard even before leaving Atlantic City for Philadelphia where the decision had come from) had decided to give Special Operations the two murder jobs.

And there was no wheel in Special Operations. In Homicide, as in the seven detective divisions, detectives were assigned jobs on a rotational basis as they came in. It was actually a sheet of paper, on which the names of the detectives were listed, but it was called the wheel.

If the mayor hadn't given Wohl the two murders and they had gone instead to Homicide, it was possible, even likely, that the wheel would have seen the jobs given to somebody else. He and Harris, because of the kind of jobs they were, would probably have been called in to "assist," but the jobs probably would have gone to other Homicide detectives. In Special Operations it was a foregone conclusion that these two murder jobs would be assigned to Detectives Washington and Harris.

And they were good jobs. Solving the murder of an on-the-job police officer gave the detective, or detectives, who did so greater satisfaction than any other. And right behind that was being able to get a murder-one indictment against one mafioso for blowing away another.

Jason Washington was beginning to think that his transfer to Special Operations might turn out to be less of a disaster than it had first appeared to be.

He was not surprised when he pulled into the parking lot at Bustleton and Bowler Streets to see Peter Wohl's nearly identical Ford in the COMMANDING OFFICER's reserved parking space, although it was only a quarter to eight.

When he walked into the building, the administrative corporal called to him, "The inspector said he wanted to see you the minute you came in."

He smiled and waved and went to Wohl's office.

"Good morning, Inspector," Washington said.

"Morning, Jason," Wohl replied. "Sorry to have to call you back here."

"How am I going to get a tan if you keep me from laying on the beach?" Washington said dryly.

"Get one of those reflector things," Wohl replied, straight-faced, "and sit in the parking lot during your lunch hour. Now that you mention it, you do look a little pale."

Jason Washington's skin was jet black.

They smiled at each other for a moment, and then Wohl said, "Harris was at Colombia Street—"

"I talked to Tony this morning," Washington said, interrupting him.

"Okay," Wohl said. "Did I mention last night that a Narcotics sergeant named Dolan thought Matt Payne was involved at the parking garage?"

"Tony told me," Washington said.

Then that, Wohl thought a little angrily, must be all over the Department.

"Well, I don't think he's dirty, but he did find the girl, and DeZego's body. If you want to talk to him, he should be here any minute."

"He called the hospital while I was there," Washington said. "I told him I'd see him here."

"You were at the hospital?" Wohl asked.

Washington nodded.

"I don't know why I got out of bed so early to talk to you," Wohl said.

"Early to bed, early to rise, et cetera, et cetera," Washington said. "You going to need Payne this morning, Inspector?"

"Not if you want him for anything. If I have to say this, Jason, just tell me what you think you need."

"I thought I'd take him to Hahneman and then to the parking garage," Washington said. "I didn't get in to see the girl. That needed permission of a doctor who won't be in until eight."

Wohl's eyebrows rose questioningly.

"They're giving me the runaround," Washington went on. "I didn't push it. Incidentally, they've got a couple of Wachenhut Security guys down there guarding her room. One of them is a retired sergeant from Northwest detectives."

"I'm not surprised. The victim, according to the paper—have you seen the papers?"

Washington nodded.

"Is the Nesfoods Heiress," Wohl concluded.

"Which is something I should keep in mind, right?" Washington laughed.

"Right," Wohl said. "There's coffee, Jason, while you're waiting for Payne."

"Thank you," Washington said, and went to the coffee-brewing machine.

Wohl picked up one of the telephones on his desk.

"When Officer Payne comes in, don't let him get away," he said, and then, "Okay. Tell him to wait." He turned to Washington. "Payne's outside."

"I think he might get some answers I couldn't," Washington said. "Is that all right with you?"

There was a just perceptible hesitation before Wohl replied, "Like I said, whatever you want, Jason."

"You know what I'm asking," Washington said.

"Yeah. I think we have to give him the benefit of the doubt until proven otherwise. I think he knows he's a cop."

"Yeah, so do I. And I really think he might be useful. I don't have a hell of a lot of experience with Nesfood Heiresses."

"Don't let them worry you," Wohl said. "Dave Pekach seems to do very well with heiresses."

"How about that?" Washington laughed. "Is that as serious as I hear?"

"Take a look at his watch," Wohl said. "He had a birthday."

"What's he got?"

"A gold Omega with about nine dials," Wohl said. "It does everything but chime. Maybe it does that too."

"Well, good for him," Washington said. He put down his coffee cup and stood up and shot his cuffs.

"I'll keep you up-to-date," he said. "Thanks for the coffee."

"Let me know if I can help," Wohl said.

"I will. Count on it," Washington said.

He walked out of Peter Wohl's office. Matt Payne was leaning over the desk of Wohl's administrative sergeant.

"Still have your driver's license, Matthew?" Washington said.

"Yes, sir."

"The next time you say 'Yes, sir' to me, I will spill something greasy on that very nice sport coat," Washington said. "Come on, hotshot, take me for a drive." He saw the look on Matt's face and added, "I fixed it with the boss."

"Frankly," H. Russell Dotson, M.D., a short, plump man in a faintly striped dark blue suit that Jason Washington thought was very nice, indeed, said, "I'm very reluctant to permit you to see Miss Detweiler—"

"I understand your concern, Doctor," Washington said. "May I say two things?"

Dotson nodded impatiently.

"Time is often critically important in cases like this—"

"I know why you think you should see her," Dr. Dotson interrupted. If the interruption annoyed Washington, it didn't show on his face or in his voice.

"And we really do understand your concern about unduly upsetting your patient, and with that in mind I arranged for Officer Payne to come with me and actually speak with Miss Detweiler. Officer Payne is a close friend—"

"So that *is* who you are! Matt Payne, right? Brewster Payne's boy?"

"Yes, sir," Matt said politely.

"I thought I recognized you. And you're a policeman?"

"Yes, sir."

"That's a new one on me," Dr. Dotson said. "Since when?"

"Since right after graduation, Dr. Dotson," Matt said.

"Well, you understand my concern, Matt. I don't want anything to upset Penny. She's been severely traumatized. Physically and psychologically. For a while there, frankly, I thought we might lose her."

"She's going to be all right now?"

"Well, I don't think she's going to die," Dr. Dotson said.

"But she's still very weak. We had her in the operating room for over two hours."

"I understand, sir," Matt said.

"I'm going in there with you," Dr. Dotson said. "And I want you to keep looking at me. When I indicate that I want you to leave the room, I want you to leave right then. Understood? Agreed?"

"Yes, of course, sir."

"Very well, then."

If it had been Dr. Dotson's intention to discreetly keep Jason Washington out of Penelope Detweiler's room, he failed. By the time the doctor turned to close the door, Washington was inside the room, already leaning against the wall, as if to signal that while he had no intention of intruding, neither did he intend to leave.

Penny Detweiler's appearance shocked Matt Payne. The head of her bed was raised slightly, so that she could watch television. Her face and throat and what he could see of her chest were, where the skin was not covered with bandages and exposed sutures, black and blue, as if she had been severely beaten. Patches of hair had been been shaved from the front of her head, and there were bandages and exposed sutures there too. Transparent tubing fed liquid into her right arm from two bottles suspended at the head of the bed.

"Now that the beauticians are through with you, are you ready for the photographer?" Matt asked.

"I made them give me a mirror," she said. "Aren't I ghastly?"

"I cannot tell a lie. You look like hell," Matt said. "How do you feel?"

"As bad as I look," she said, and then, "Matt, what are *you* doing here? And how did you get in?"

"I'm a cop, Penny."

"Oh, that's right. I heard that. I don't really believe it. Why did you do something like that?"

"I didn't want to be a lawyer," Matt said. He saw that Dr. Dotson, who had been tense, had now relaxed somewhat.

She laughed and winced.

"It hurts," she said. "Don't make me laugh."

"What the hell happened, Penny?"

"I don't know," she said. "I was walking to the stairwell. You know where this happened to me?"

"We found you. Amanda Spencer and me. When we drove on the roof, you were on the floor. Amanda called the cops."

"You did? I don't remember seeing you."

"You were unconscious," Matt said.

"I guess I won't be able to make it to the wedding, will I?" she asked, and then added, "What are they going to do about the wedding?"

"I saw Daffy—and the Brownes—before I came here. They asked me what I thought about that, and since it was none of my business, I told them."

She giggled, then winced again.

"I told you, don't make me laugh," she said. "Every time I move my—chest—it hurts."

"Sorry."

"What did you tell them?"

"That Chad is in the Marines and that they couldn't postpone it."

"And?"

"I don't know, but I think everything's going ahead as planned."

"Just because this happened to me is no reason to ruin everybody else's fun," Penny said.

"I still don't know what happened to you," Matt said.

"I don't really know," Penny said.

"You don't remember anything?"

"I remember getting out of my car and walking toward the stairwell. And then the roof fell in on me. I remember, sort of, being in a truck—not an ambulance, a truck—and I think there was a cop in there with me. But that's all."

"There's no roof over the roof," Matt said.

"You know what I mean. It was like something ran into me. Hit me hard."

"You didn't see anyone up there?"

"No."

"Nothing at all?"

"There was nobody up there but me," she said firmly.

"Does the name Tony DeZego mean anything to you?"

"No. Who?"

"Tony. Tony DeZego."

"No," she said, "should it?"

"No reason it should."

"Who is he?"

"A guinea gangster," Matt said.

"A what?"

"An Italian-American with alleged ties to organized crime," Matt said dryly.

"Why are you asking me about him?"

"Well, he was up there too," Matt said. "On the roof of the garage. Somebody blew the top of his head off with a shotgun."

"My God!"

"No great loss to society," Matt said. "He wasn't even a good gangster. Just a cheap thug with ambition. A small-time drug dealer, from what I hear."

"I think that's about enough of a visit, Matt," Dr. Dotson said. "Penny needs rest. And her parents are on their way."

Matt touched her arm.

"I'll bring you a piece of the wedding cake," he said. "Try to behave yourself."

"I don't have any choice, do I?" she said.

In the corridor outside, Dr. Dotson laid a hand on Matt's arm.

"I can't imagine why you told her about that gangster," he said.

"I thought she'd be interested," Matt said.

"Thank you very much, Dr. Dotson," Jason Washington said. "I very much appreciate your cooperation."

"She's lying," Matt said when Washington got in the passenger seat beside him.

"She is? About what?"

"About knowing DeZego."

"Really? What makes you think so?"

"Jesus, didn't you see her eyes when I called him a 'guinea gangster'?"

"You're a regular little Sherlock Holmes, aren't you?" Washington asked.

Matt looked at him, the hurt showing in his eyes.

"If I did that wrong in there, I'm sorry," he said. "If you

didn't think I could handle it, you should have told me what to ask and how to ask it. I did the best I could."

"As a matter of fact, hotshot," Washington said, "I couldn't have done it any better myself. I would have phrased the questions a little differently, probably, because I don't know the lady as well as you do, but that wasn't at all bad. One of the most difficult calls to make in an interview like that, with a subject like that, is when to let them know you know they're lying. That wasn't the time."

"I didn't think so, either," Matt said, and then smiled, almost shyly, at Washington.

"Let's go to the parking garage," Washington said.

As they drove around City Hall, Matt said, "I'd like to know for sure if she's taking dope. Do you suppose they took blood when she got to the hospital? That could be tested?"

"I'm sure they did," Washington said. "But as a matter of law, not to mention ethics, the hospital could not make the results of that test known to the police. It would be considered, in essence, an illegal search or seizure, as well as a violation of the patient's privacy. Her rights against compulsory incrimination would also be involved."

"Oh," Matt said.

"Your friend is a habitual user of cocaine," Washington went on, "using it in quantities that make it probable that she is on the edges of addiction to it."

Matt looked at him in surprise.

"One of the most important assets a detective can have, Officer Payne," Washington replied dryly, "is the acquaintance of a number of people who feel in his debt. Apropos of nothing whatever, I once spoke to a judge prior to his sentencing of a young man for vehicular theft. I told the judge that I thought probation would probably suffice to keep the malefactor on the straight and narrow, and that I was acquainted with his mother, a decent, divorced woman who worked as a registered nurse at Hahneman Hospital."

"Nice," Matt said.

"I suppose you know the difference between ignorance, and stupidity?"

"I think so." Matt chuckled.

"A good detective never forgets he's ignorant. He knows

very, very little about what's going on. So that means a good detective is always looking for something, or someone, that can reduce the totality of his ignorance.''

"Okay," Matt said with another chuckle. "So where does that leave us, now that we know she's using cocaine and knew DeZego?''

"I don't have a clue—witticism intended—why either of them got shot," Washington said. "There's a lot of homicide involved with narcotics, but what it usually boils down to is simple armed robbery. Somebody wants either the drugs or the money and uses a gun to take them. The Detweiler girl had nearly seven hundred dollars in her purse; Tony the Zee had a quantity of coke—say five hundred dollars worth, at least. Since they still had the money and the drugs, I think we can reasonably presume that robbery wasn't the basic cause of the shooting.''

They were at the Penn Services Parking Garage. When Matt started to pull onto the entrance ramp, Washington told him to park on the street. Just in time Matt stopped himself from protesting that there was no parking on 15th Street.

Washington did not enter the building. He walked to the alley at one end, then circled the building as far as he could, until he encountered a chain-link fence. He stood looking at the fence and up at the building for a moment, then he retraced his steps to the front and walked onto the entrance ramp. Then he walked up the ramp to the first floor.

Three quarters of the way down the parking area, Matt saw a uniformed cop, and a moment later yellow CRIME SCENE—DO NOT CROSS tape surrounding a Dodge sedan.

"What's that?" he asked, curiosity overwhelming his solemn, silent vow to keep his eyes open and his mouth shut.

"It was a hit on the NCIC when they ran the plates," Washington said. "Reported stolen in Drexel Hill."

The National Crime Information Center was an FBI-run computer system. Detectives (at one time there had been sixteen Homicide detectives in the Penn Services garage) had fed the computer the license numbers of every car in the garage at the time of the shooting. NCIC had returned every bit of information it had on any of them. The Dodge had been entered into the computer as stolen.

"Good morning," Washington said to the uniformed cop. "The lab get to this yet?"

"They were here real early this morning," the cop said. "I think there's still a couple of them upstairs."

Washington nodded. He walked around the car and then looked into the front and backseats. Then he started up the ramp to the upper floors.

"It'll probably turn out the Dodge has nothing to do with the shooting," he said to Matt. "But we'll check it out, just to be sure."

The ramp to the roof was blocked by another uniformed cop and a cross of crime-scene tape, but when Matt and Washington walked on it, Matt saw there was only a Police Lab truck and three cars—a Mercedes convertible, roof up; a blue-and-white; and an unmarked car—on the whole floor.

He could see a body form outlined in white, where Penny Detweiler had been when he had driven on the roof and where he had found the body of Anthony J. DeZego. It seemed pretty clear that the Mercedes was Penny's car.

But where was DeZego's?

A hollow-eyed man came out of the unmarked car, smiled at Washington, and offered his hand.

"You are your usually natty self this morning, Jason, I see," he said.

"Is that a touch of jealousy I detect, Lieutenant?" Washington replied. "You know Matt Payne? Matt, this is Lieutenant Jack Potter, the mad genius of Forensics."

"No. But what do they say? 'He is preceded by his reputation'? How are you, Payne?"

"How do you do, sir?"

"Anything?" Washington asked.

"Not much. We picked up some shotshell pellets and two wads, either from off the floor or picked out of the concrete. No more shell casings. Which means that the shooter knew what he was doing; or that he had only two shells, which suggests it was double-barrel, as opposed to an autoloader; or all of the above."

"Anything in the girl's car?"

"Uh-uh. No bags of anything," Lieutenant Potter replied. "Haven't had a chance either to run the prints or analyze what the vacuum cleaner picked up."

"I'd love to find a clear print of Mr. DeZego inside the Mercedes," Washington said.

"If there's a match, you'll be the first to know," Potter said.

"Can you release the Mercedes?" Washington asked. Potter's eyebrows rose in question. "I thought it might be a nice gesture on our part if Officer Payne and I returned the car to the Detweiler home."

"Why not?" Potter replied. "What about the Dodge? There was nothing out of the ordinary there."

"You've got the name and address of the owner?"

Potter nodded.

"Let me have it. I'll have someone check him out. I think we can take the tape down, anyway."

Potter grunted.

"Which raises the question, of course, of Mr. DeZego's car," Washington said. "Do you suppose he walked up here?"

"Or he came up here with the shooter and they left without him," Potter said.

"Or his car is parked on the street," Washington said. "Or *was* parked on the street and may be in the impound yard now."

"I'll check on that for you, if you like," Potter said.

"Matt," Washington said, "find a phone. Call Organized Crime and see if they know what kind of a car Anthony J. DeZego drove. Then call Traffic and see if they impounded a car like that and, if so, where they impounded it. Maybe we'll get lucky."

"Right," Matt replied.

"And if that doesn't work, call Police Radio and have them see if they can locate the car and get back to me, if they can."

"Right," Matt said.

Washington turned to Potter.

"You have any idea where the shooter was standing?"

"Let me show you," Potter said as Matt walked to the telephone.

TEN

Mrs. Charles McFadden, Sr., a plump, gray-haired woman of forty-five, was watching television in the living room of her home, a row house on Fitzgerald Street not far from Methodist Hospital in South Philadelphia when the telephone rang.

Not without effort, and sighing, she pushed herself out of the upholstered chair and went to the telephone, which had been installed on a small shelf mounted on the wall in the corridor leading from the front door past the stairs to the kitchen.

"Hello?"

"Can I reach Officer McFadden on this number?" a male voice inquired.

"You can," she said. "But he's got his own phone. Did you try that?"

"Yes, ma'am. There was no answer."

Come to think of it, Agnes McFadden thought, *I didn't hear it ring.*

"Just a minute," she said, and then: "Who did you say is calling?"

"This is Sergeant Henderson, ma'am, of the Highway Patrol. Is this Mrs. McFadden?"

"Senior," she said. "I'm his mother."

"Yes, ma'am."

"I'll get him," she said. "Just a moment."

She put the handset carefully beside the base and then went upstairs. Charley's room was at the rear. When he had first gone on the job—working Narcotics undercover, which had pleased his mother not at all, the way he went around looking like a bum and working all hours at night—he had had his own telephone line installed.

Then, as happy as a kid with a new toy train, he had found a little black box in Radio Shack that permitted the switching on and off of the telephone ringer. It was a great idea, but what happened was that after he turned off the ringer, he forgot to turn it back on, which meant that either he didn't get calls at all, or the caller, as now, had the number of the phone downstairs, and she or his father had to climb the stairs and tell him he had a call.

She knocked at his door and, when there was no answer, pushed it open. Charley was lying facedown on the bed in his Jockey shorts, his arms and legs spread, snoring softly. That told her that he'd stopped off for a couple (to judge by the sour smell, a whole hell of a lot more than a couple) of beers when he got off work last night.

She called his name and touched his shoulder. Then she put both hands on his shoulders and bounced him up and down. He slept like the dead. Always had.

Finally he half turned and raised his head.

"What the hell, Ma!" Charley said.

"Don't you swear at me!"

"What do you want, Ma?"

"There's some sergeant on the phone."

Still half asleep, Charley found his telephone, picked it up, heard the dial tone, and looked at her in confusion.

"Downstairs," she said. "You and your telephone switch!"

He got out of bed with surprising alacrity and ran down

the corridor. She heard the thumping and creaking of the stairs as he took them two at a time.

"McFadden," he said to the telephone.

"Sergeant Henderson, out at Bustleton and Bowler."

"Yes, sir?"

"You heard about Officer Magnella being shot last night?"

"Yeah."

"We're trying to put as many men on it as we can. Any reason you can't do some overtime? Specifically, any reason you can't come in at noon instead of four?"

"I'll be there."

Sergeant Henderson hung up.

Charley had two immediate thoughts as he put the phone in its cradle: *Jesus, what time is it?* and, an instant later, *Jesus, I feel like death warmed over. I've got to start cutting it short at the FOP.*

"What was that all about?" his mother asked from the foot of the stairs, and then, without waiting for a reply, "Put some clothes on. This isn't a nudist colony."

"I gotta go to work. You hear about the cop who got shot?"

"It was on the TV. What's that got to do with you?"

"They're still trying to catch who did it."

Mrs. Agnes McFadden had been the only person in the neighborhood who had not been thrilled when her son had been called a police hero for his role in putting the killer of Captain Dutch Moffitt of the Highway Patrol out of circulation. She reasoned that if Gerald Vincent Gallagher was indeed a murderer, then obviously he could have done harm to her only son.

"I thought you were in training to be a Highway Patrolman."

Charley McFadden had done nothing to correct his mother's misperception that Highway Patrol was primarily charged with removing speeding and/or drunk drivers from the streets.

"I am," he said. "It's overtime. I gotta go."

"I'll make you something to eat," she said.

"No time, Ma. Thanks, anyway."

"You have to eat."

"I'll get something after I report in."

He went up the stairs and to his bedroom and found his watch. It was quarter to ten. He had declined breakfast because he knew it would be accompanied by comments about his drinking, his late hours, and probably, since she had heard about Magnella getting himself shot, by reopening the subject of his being a cop at all.

But since he had announced he had to leave right away, he would have to leave right away, and even if he took his time getting something to eat and going by the dry cleaners to drop off and pick up a uniform, he still would have an hour or more to kill before he could sign in.

He took his time taking a shower, steeling himself several times for the shock turning off the hot water would mean, hoping that the cold would clear his mind, and then he shaved with care.

He didn't need a haircut, although getting one would have killed some time.

Fuck it, he decided finally. *I'll just go get something to eat and go out to Bustleton and Bowler and just hang around until noon.*

His mother was standing by the door when he came down the stairs, demanding her ritual kiss and delivering her ritual order for him to be careful.

He noticed two things when he got to the street: first, that the right front wheel of his Volkswagen was on the curb, which confirmed he had had a couple of beers more than he probably should have had at the FOP; and, second, that the redhead with the cute little ass he had noticed several times around the neighborhood was coming out of the McCarthys', across the street and two houses down.

He smiled at her shyly and, when she smiled back, equally shyly, gave her a little wave. She didn't wave back. Just smiled. But that was a step in the right direction, he decided. Tomorrow morning he would ask around and see who she was. He could not ask his mother. She would know, of course; she knew when anybody in the neighborhood burped, but if he asked her about the girl, the next thing he knew, she would be trying to pair him off with her.

Charley knew that his mother devoutly believed that what he needed in his life was a nice, decent Catholic girl. If the redhead with the cute little ass had anything to do with the McCarthys, she met that definition. Mrs. McCarthy was a

Mass-every-morning Catholic, and Mr. McCarthy was a big deal in the Knights of Columbus.

Still, it was worth looking into.

He got into the Volkswagen, started it up, and drove around the block, eventually turning onto South Broad Street, heading north. And there was the redhead, obviously waiting for a bus.

Impulsively he pulled to the curb and stopped. First he started to lean across the seat and roll the window down, and then he decided it would be better to get out of the car. He did so, and leaned on the roof and smiled at her. He was suddenly absolutely sure that he was about to make a real horse's ass out of himself.

"You looking for a ride?" he blurted.

"I'm waiting for a bus," the redhead said.

"I didn't mean that the way it sounded," Charley said.

"How did you mean it?" the redhead said.

"Look," he said somewhat desperately, "I'm Charley McFadden—"

"I know who you are," she said. "My Uncle Bob and your father are friends."

"Yeah," he said.

"You don't remember me, do you?" she said.

"Yeah, sure I do."

"No you don't." She laughed. "I used to come here when I was a kid."

His mind was blank. "Look, I'm headed across town. Can I give you a ride?"

"I'm going to Temple," she said. "You going anywhere near there?"

"Right past it," he said.

"Then yes, thank you, I would like a ride," she said.

"Great," Charley said.

She walked to the car and got in. When he got behind the wheel and glanced at her, she had her hand out.

"Margaret McCarthy," she said. "Bob McCarthy is my uncle, my father's brother."

"I'm pleased to meet you," Charley said.

He turned the key, which resulted in a grinding of the starter gears, as the engine was already running. He winced.

"So what are you doing at Temple?" he asked a moment or so later.

"Going for my B.S. in nursing."

"Your what?"

"I'm already an RN," she said. "So I came here to get a degree. Bachelor of Science, in Nursing. I live in Baltimore."

"Oh," Charley said, digesting that. "How long will that take?"

"About eighteen months," she said. "I'm carrying a heavy load."

"Oh."

What the hell did she mean by that?

"I'm a cop," he said.

She giggled.

"I would never have guessed," she said.

"Oh, Christ!" he said.

"Uncle Bob sent us the clippings from the newspaper," Margaret McCarthy said, "when you caught that murderer."

"Really?"

"My father said he thought you would wind up on the other side of the bars," she said, laughing. And then she added, "Oh, I shouldn't have said that."

"It's all right," he said.

"You put a golf ball through his windshield," she said. "Do you remember that? Playing stickball?"

"Yeah," Charley said, remembering. "My old man beat hell out of me."

"So, do you like being a policeman?"

"I liked it better when I was plainclothes," he said. "But, yeah, I like it all right."

"I don't know what that means," she said.

"I used to work undercover Narcotics," Charley said. "Sort of like a detective."

"That was in the newspapers," she said.

"Yeah, well, after that, getting your picture in the newspapers, the drug people knew who I was. So that was the end of Narcotics for me."

"You liked that?"

"I liked Narcotics, yeah," Charley said.

"What are you doing now?"

"What I want to do is be a detective," Charley said. "So what I'm really doing now is killing time until I can take the examination."

"How are you 'killing time'?"

"Well, they transferred us, me and my partner, Hay-zus Martinez—"

"Hay-zus?"

"That's the way the Latin people say Jesus," Charley explained.

"Oh," she said.

"They transferred us to Special Operations," Charley said, "which is new. And then they made us probationary Highway Patrolmen. Which means if we don't screw up, after six months we get to be Highway Patrolmen."

"Is that something special?"

"They think it is. Like I said, I'd rather be a detective."

"I should think that after what you did, they'd want to make you a detective," Margaret McCarthy said.

"It don't work that way. You have to take the examination."

"Oh," she said.

I'm going to ask her if she wants to go to a movie or something. Maybe dinner and a movie.

He had difficulty framing in his mind the right way to pose the question, the result of that being that they rode in silence almost to the Temple campus without his saying a word.

Then he was surprised to hear himself say, "Right in there, two blocks down, is where Magnella got himself shot."

"You mean the police officer who was murdered?" Margaret asked, and when Charley nodded, she went on. "My Uncle Bob and his father are friends. They're in the Knights of Columbus together."

"Yeah. That's why I'm going to work now. They called up and asked me to come in early to work on that."

"Like a detective, you mean?"

"Yeah, well, sort of."

"That should be very rewarding," Margaret McCarthy said. "Working on something like that."

"Yeah," he said. "Look, you want to catch a movie, have dinner or something?"

"A movie or dinner sounds nice," she said. "I'm not so sure about something."

"I'll call you," he said. "Okay?"

"Sure," she said. "I'd like that. I get out at the next corner."

"How about in the morning?" Charley asked.

"You want to go to the movies in the morning?"

"Christ, I'm on the four-to-twelve," he said. "How are we going to . . ."

"We could have coffee or something in the mornings," she said. "My first classes aren't until eleven."

He pulled to the curb and smiled at her. She smiled back. A horn blew impatiently behind him.

Charley, at the last moment, did not shout, "Blow it out your ass, asshole!" at the horn blower. Instead he got out of the Volkswagen and stood on the curb with Margaret McCarthy for a moment.

"I have to go, Charley," she said. "I'll be late."

"Yeah," he said. "I'll call you."

"Call me," she said.

They shook hands. Margaret walked onto the campus.

Charley glowered at the horn blower, who was now smiling nervously, and then got in the Volkswagen and drove off. He remembered that he had not dropped off his dirty uniform at the dry cleaner. It didn't seem to matter. He felt better right now than he could remember feeling in a long time.

Things were looking up. Even things at work were looking up. It didn't make sense that they would call him, and probably Hay-zus, too, to go through that probationary bullshit and pay them overtime. The odds were that Captain Pekach was going to put them back on the street, doing what he knew they already knew how to do: grabbing scumbags.

"Is Inspector Wohl in his office?" the heavyset, balding man with a black, six-inch-long handmade long filler Costa Rican cigar clamped between his teeth demanded.

"I believe he is, sir," Sergeant Edward Frizell said politely as he picked up his telephone. "I'll see if he's free, sir."

By the time he had the telephone to his ear, Chief Inspector Matt Lowenstein was inside Staff Inspector Peter Wohl's office at the headquarters of the Special Operations Division at Bustleton and Bowler Streets.

Peter Wohl was not at his desk. He was sitting on his couch, his feet up on his coffee table. When he saw Lowenstein come through the door, he started to get up.

"Good morning, Chief," he said.

Lowenstein closed the door.

"I came to apologize," he said. "For what I said last night."

"No apology necessary, Chief."

"I didn't mean what I said, Peter, I was just pissed off."

"You had a right to be," Wohl said. "I would have been."

"At the dago I did. Do. Not at you. God*damn* him! If he wanted to run the Police Department, why didn't he just stay as commissioner?"

"Because when he was commissioner, the mayor could tell him how to run the Department. Now he answers only to God and the voters."

"I'm not so sure how much input he'd take from God," Lowenstein said. "The last I heard, God was never a captain in Highway."

Wohl chuckled. "Would you like some coffee?" he asked.

"Yes, I would, thank you," Lowenstein said.

When Wohl handed him the cup, Lowenstein said, "I want you to know that before I came out here, I called Homicide and Organized Crime and Narcotics and told them that I completely agreed with Czernich's decision and that they were to give cooperation with you their highest priority. Goddamn lie, of course, about me agreeing, but it wasn't your fault, and I want the people who shot that young cop. As far as the DeZego job goes, frankly you're welcome to that one. I don't want the Detweilers mad at me."

"Thanks a lot, Chief," Wohl said.

"What's this I hear that one of your guys is dirty?"

"No. I don't think so. The Narcotics sergeant went off the deep end."

"Is that so?"

"The cop he suspected of being dirty is Matt Payne."

"Dutch Moffitt's nephew? I thought that he was working for you."

"He is. Payne drove into the parking lot shortly after the

Detweiler girl. The Narcotics sergeant was watching her. Right afterward Payne drove away, which the sergeant thought was suspicious. Payne drives a Porsche, which is the kind of a car a successful drug dealer would drive. And then, when the Narcotics guy found out Payne was a cop, he really put his nose in high gear.''

"But he's clean?"

"Payne parked his car there because he was also headed for the Union League, and the reason he drove the car away was because the 9th District lieutenant, Foster Lewis . . . ?"

"I know him. Just made lieutenant. Good cop."

". . . on the scene sent him to tell the Detweiler family, at the Union League."

"Payne drives a Porsche?"

Wohl nodded.

"Nice to have a rich father."

"Obviously."

"I heard Denny Coughlin put him in your lap."

"Chief Coughlin and the gentleman with an interest in the Police Department we were discussing earlier," Wohl said. "After Payne shot the rapist the mayor told the newspapers that Payne is my special assistant, so I decided Payne *is* my special assistant."

"Good thinking," Lowenstein said, chuckling.

"I also got Foster H. Lewis, Jr., this morning," Wohl said.

"Lewis's son is a cop?"

"Just got out of the Academy."

"Why did they sent him here?"

"Just a routine assignment of a new police officer that the mayor just happened to announce in a speech at the First Abyssinian Baptist Church."

"Oh, I see." Lowenstein grunted. "The Afro-American voters. There's two sides to being the mayor's fair-haired boy, aren't there?"

"Chief," Wohl said solemnly, "I have no idea what you're talking about."

"The hell you don't," Lowenstein growled. "What are you going to do with the Lewis boy?"

"I gave him to Tony Harris, as a gofer. Harris has Lewis, and Jason Washington just borrowed Payne."

"To do what?"

"Whatever Jason tells him to. I think Washington likes him. I think they may have the same tailor."

"Well, you better hope Harris and Washington get lucky," Lowenstein said. "Your salami is on the chopping block with these two jobs, Peter."

"Chief, that thought *has* run through my mind," Wohl said.

Chief Lowenstein, who had not finished delivering his assessment of the situation, glowered at Peter Wohl for cutting him short and then went on.

"When the Payne kid got lucky and put down the serial rapist, that only made Arthur Nelson and his goddamn *Ledger* pause for breath. It did not shut him up. Now he's got two things: drug-related gang warfare in the center city with a nice little rich girl lying in a pool of blood as a result of it; and a cop shot down in cold blood, the cops not having a clue who did it. Nelson would make a case against the Department, and Carlucci, if the doers were already in Central Lockup. With the doers still running around loose—"

"I know," Wohl said.

"I don't think you do, Peter," Lowenstein said as he hauled himself to his feet. "I was sitting at my kitchen table this morning wondering if I had the balls to come out here and apologize to you when Carlucci made up my mind for me."

"I'm sorry?" Wohl asked, confused.

Chief Lowenstein examined the glowing end of his cigar for a moment and then met Wohl's eyes.

"The dago called me at the house," he said. "He said he wanted me to come out here this morning and see how things were going. He said that he'd told Lucci to call him at least once a day, but that 'too much was at stake here to leave something like this to someone like Lucci.' "

"Jesus Christ!" Wohl said bitterly. "If he didn't think I could do the job, why did he give it to me?"

"Because if you do the job, *he* looks good. And if you don't, *you* look bad. They call that smart politics, Peter."

"Yeah," Wohl said.

"I think I can expect at least a daily call from the dago, Peter, asking me how I think you're handling this. I wouldn't worry about that. I don't want these jobs back, so all he's going to get from me is an expression of confidence in you, and the way you're doing things. On the other hand, whatever else I may think of him, your Lieutenant Lucci *is* smart enough to know which side of the bread has the butter—no telling what he's liable to tell the dago.''

''Christ, my father warned me about crap like this. I didn't believe him.''

''Give my regards to your dad, Peter,'' Lowenstein said. ''I always have admired him.''

Wohl stared at the phone on his coffee table for a moment. When he finally raised his eyes, Lowenstein was gone.

Lieutenant Foster H. Lewis, Sr., who was wearing a light blue cotton bathrobe over his underwear, had just offered, aloud, although he was alone in the apartment, his somewhat less than flattering opinion of morning television programming and the even more appallingly stupid people who watched it, himself included, when the chimes sounded.

He went to the door and opened it.

''Good morning, sir,'' the uniformed policeman standing there said, ''would you like to take a raffle ticket on a slightly used 1948 Buick?''

''What did you do, Foster, lose your key?''

He looks good in that uniform, even if I wish he weren't wearing it.

''So that I wouldn't lose it, I put it somewhere safe,'' Tiny Lewis said. ''One of these days I'll remember where.''

''I just made some coffee. You want some?''

''Please, Dad.''

''What are you doing here?''

''I've got to get a suit,'' Tiny said. ''Mom said she put them in a cedar bag.''

''Probably in your room,'' Foster Lewis, Sr., said. ''Am I permitted to ask why you need a suit?''

''Certainly,'' Tiny said. He followed his father into the kitchen and took a china mug from a cabinet.

''Well?'' Foster Lewis asked.

''Well, what? Oh, do you want to know why I need a suit?''

''I asked. Where were you when I asked?''

"You asked if you were permitted to ask, and I said, 'Certainly,' but you didn't actually ask."

"Wiseass." His father chuckled. "There's a piece of cake in the refrigerator."

"Thank you," Tiny said, and helped himself to the cake.

"You know a Homicide—ex-Homicide—detective named Harris? Tony Harris?"

"Yeah. Not well. But he's supposed to be good."

"You are now looking, sir, at his official errand runner," Tiny said.

"What does that mean?"

"I suppose it means that if he says 'Go fetch,' I go fetch, happily wagging my tail."

"If you're being clever, stop it," his father said. "Tell me what's going on."

"Well, I was told to report to a Captain Sabara at Highway. When I got there, he wasn't, but Inspector Wohl called me into his office—"

"You saw him?" Foster Lewis, Sr., asked.

"Yeah. Nice guy. *Sharp* dude. *Nice* threads."

I was on the job, Lieutenant Foster H. Lewis thought, *for two or three years before I ever saw an inspector up close.*

"Go on."

"Well, he said that Harris has the Magnella job, and that he needed a second pair of hands. He said it would involve a lot of overtime, and if I had any problem with that to say so; he didn't want any complaints later. So I told him the more overtime the better, and I asked him what I would be doing. He said—that's where I got that—that if Harris said 'Go fetch,' I was to wag my tail and go fetch. He said the detail would last only until Harris got whoever shot Magnella, but it would be good experience for me."

"That's it?"

"Well, he gave me a speech about what not to do with the car—"

"What car?"

"A '71 Ford. Good shape."

"You have a Department car?"

"Yeah. Unmarked, naturally," Tiny said just a little smugly.

"My God!"

"What's wrong?"

Lieutenant Foster H. Lewis, Sr., thought, *When I got out of the Academy, I was assigned to the 26th District. A pot-bellied Polack sergeant named Grotski went out of his way to make it plain he didn't think there was any place in the Department for niggers and then handed me over to Bromley T. Wesley, a South Carolina redneck who had come north to work in the shipyards during the Second World War and had joined the cops because he didn't want to go back home to Tobacco Road.*

I walked a beat with Bromley for a year. When he went into a candy store for a Coke or something, he made me wait outside. For six months he never used my name. I was either "Hey, You!" or worse, "Hey, Boy!" I was told that if I turned out okay, maybe after a year or so, I could work my way up to a wagon. The son of a bitch made it plain he thought all black people were born retarded.

Bromley T. Wesley was an ignorant bigot with a sixth-grade education, but he was a cop. He knew the streets and he knew people, and he taught me about them. Between Wesley and what I learned on the wagon, when I went out in an RPC by myself for the first time I was a cop.

What the hell is Peter Wohl thinking of, putting this rookie in civilian clothes instead of in a wagon, at least?

"Nothing, I suppose," Lieutenant Lewis said. "It's a little unusual, that's all. Eat your cake."

ELEVEN

The normally open gate of the Detweiler estate in Chestnut
Hill, like the gate at the Browne place in Merion, was now
both closed and guarded by rent-a-cops.

When Matt pulled the nose of Penelope Detweiler's Mercedes against the gate, one of them, a burly man in a blue
suit, came through a small gate within the gate and looked
down at Matt.

"May I help you, sir?"

"We're returning Miss Detweiler's car," Matt said.

" 'We,' sir?"

"I'm a cop," Matt said, and jerked his thumb toward Jason Washington, who was following him in the unmarked
Ford. "And so is he."

"You expected?"

"No."

"I'll have to call, sir."

"Tell them it's Matt Payne."

The rent-a-cop looked at him strangely and then said,
"Matt Payne. Yes, sir."

He went back through the small gate, entered the gate house, and emerged a moment later to swing the left half of the double gate open. He waved Matt through.

H. Richard Detweiler, himself, answered the door. He had a drink in his hand.

"Boy, that was quick!" he said. "Come in, Matt."

"Sir?"

"I just this second got off the phone with Czernich," Detweiler said. "Penny was worried about her car, so I called him and asked about it, and he said he'd have it sent out here."

"I think we probably were on our way when you called him, Mr. Detweiler," Matt said. "Mr. Detweiler, this is Detective Washington."

"I was just talking about you too," Detweiler said, offering Washington his hand. "Thad Czernich told me you're the best detective in the Department."

"Far be it from me to question the commissioner's judgment," Washington said. "How do you do, Mr. Detweiler?"

Detweiler chuckled. "Oh, about as well as any father would be after just seeing a daughter who looks like the star of a horror movie."

"We saw Miss Detweiler earlier this morning," Washington said.

"So she said. That was kind of you, Matt. And you, too, Mr. Washington."

"I think you'll be surprised to see how quickly that discoloration goes away, Mr. Detweiler," Washington said.

"I hope," Detweiler said. "I needed a drink when I got back here. I'd offer you one, but I know—"

"That would be very nice, thank you," Washington said.

"Oh, you can take a drink on duty?" Detweiler asked. "Fine. I always feel depraved drinking alone. Let's go in the bar."

He led them to a small room off the kitchen.

"This is supposed to be the serving pantry," he said, motioning them to take stools set against a narrow counter under and above the glass-fronted cupboards. The cupboards held canned goods, and there was an array of bottles on the counter.

"I'm not exactly sure what a butler's pantry is supposed to

be for,'' Detweiler went on, reaching for a bottle of gin. "My grandfather copied this place from a house in England, so it came with a butler's pantry. Anyway, what *we* serve here is liquor. Help yourself."

"Matt, if you would splash a little of that Johnny Walker Black in a glass, and a *little* water, and *one* ice cube?" Washington said.

"You sound like a man who appreciates good Scotch and knows how to drink it," Detweiler said.

"I try," Washington said.

Matt made two drinks to Washington's specifications, handed him one, and raised his own.

"To Penny's recovery," he said.

"Hear, hear," Washington said.

"Penny," Detweiler said, his voice breaking. "God*damn* whoever did that to her!"

"I'm sure He will," Washington said, "but we would like to get our licks in on him before he gets to the Pearly Gates."

Detweiler looked at him, smiling.

"Good thinking," he said.

The telephone on the counter buzzed; one of the four lights on it lit up. Detweiler made no move to answer it.

"Have you found out anything, Mr. Washington? What's going on?"

"Well, frankly, Mr. Detweiler, we don't have much to go on. The theory I'm working under is that Miss Detweiler was simply in the wrong place at the wrong time—"

"Is there another theory? Theories?"

"Well, I've been doing this long enough to know the hazards of reaching premature conclusions—" Washington said.

"Goddamn," Detweiler said, angrily grabbing for the phone, which had continued to buzz, "we keep six in help here, and whenever the phone rings, they *all* disappear." He put the handset to his ear and snarled, "Yes?"

There was a pause.

"This is Dick Detweiler, Commissioner. I wish I could get people as efficient as yours. No sooner had I put down the phone than Matt Payne and Detective Washington drove up with my daughter's car. I'm impressed with the service."

There was an inaudible reply to this, then Detweiler said,

"Thank you very much, Commissioner." He extended the phone to Washington. "He wants to talk to you."

"Yes, sir."

"Watch yourself out there, Washington. And when you leave, call me and let me know how it went."

The phone went dead in Washington's ear.

"Yes, of course, Commissioner," Washington said after a pause that sounded longer than it was. "Thank you very much, sir. Good-bye, sir."

He handed the telephone to Detweiler.

"The commissioner asked me to impress upon you, Mr. Detweiler, that the Department is doing everything humanly possible to get to the bottom of this, to find whoever did this to your daughter. He said that I was to regard this case as my first priority."

"Thank you," Detweiler said. "That's very good of him."

"We were talking, a moment ago, about other theories," Washington said. "I think one of the possibilities we should consider is robbery."

"Robbery?"

Washington nodded.

"Ranging from a simple, that is to say, unplanned, mugging, some thug lurking in the parking garage for whoever might come his way to someone who knew about the dinner party in the Union League—"

"How would someone know about that?" Detweiler said, interrupting.

"I'm sure it was in the society columns of the newspapers," Washington went on. "That might explain the shotgun."

"Excuse me?"

"Muggers are rarely armed with anything more than a knife. A *professional* thief, for lack of a better word, who went to the Penn Services Parking Garage knowing that there would be a number of well-to-do people using it at that time, would be more likely to take a shotgun with him. Not intending to shoot anyone but for its psychological effect."

"Yes," Detweiler said.

"And his plans could have gone astray, and he found himself having to use it."

"Yes, I see," Detweiler said.

"Was your daughter wearing any valuable jewelry, Mr. Detweiler?"

"I don't think so," Detweiler said. "She doesn't have any. Some pearls. All girls have pearls. But nothing really valuable." He looked at Matt and grinned. "Matt hasn't seen fit to offer her an engagement ring yet. . . ."

"A brooch? A pin of some sort?" Washington said, pursuing the matter.

"She has a pin, a brooch"—he gestured at his chest to show where a female would wear such an ornament—"from my wife's mother. She could have been wearing that. It has some rubies or whatever, in a band of—what do they call those little diamonds?—chips?"

"I believe so," Washington said.

"She could have been wearing that," Detweiler said.

"There was no such pin in her personal effects," Washington said. "Do you happen to know where she kept it?"

"In her room, I suppose," Detweiler said. "Do you think we should check to see if it's there?"

"I think we should," Washington said.

Detweiler led them up a narrow flight of stairs from the serving pantry to the second floor and then into Penelope's bedroom. There was a Moroccan leather jewelry case, sort of a miniature chest of drawers, on a vanity table. Detweiler went to it and searched through it and found nothing.

"It's not here," he said. "But let me check with my wife. She needed a lay-down when we came back from the hospital."

Washington nodded sympathetically.

"I hate to disturb her," he said.

"Nonsense, she'd want to help," Detweiler said, and walked out of the room.

Washington immediately picked up a wastebasket beside the vanity table and dumped the contents on the floor. He squatted and flicked through with his fingers, picking up a couple of items and putting them in his pocket. Then, very quickly, he was erect again.

"Fix that," he ordered, and moved toward a double mirrored-door closet. Matt set the wastebasket upright and began to replace what Washington had dumped on the floor. When he was finished, he turned to see what Washington was doing. He was methodically patting down the clothing hanging in the closet, dipping his hands in every pocket. Matt saw him stuffing small items—including what, at quick glance, appeared to be some sort of plastic vial—in his pocket.

And then Mrs. H. Richard Detweiler appeared in the doorway, just a moment after Washington had slid closed the mirrored door.

"I think this is what you were looking for," she said, holding up a gold brooch.

"Hello, Mrs. Detweiler," Matt said. "Mrs. Detweiler, this is Detective Washington."

"I'm Grace Detweiler. How do you do?" she said, flashing a quick smile. Then she turned to Matt. "I don't know what to think about you. It's natural to see you here, under these absolutely horrible circumstances, but not as a policeman. I really don't quite know what to make of that."

"We're trying to find out what happened to Penny," Matt said.

"You're driving your mother to distraction, you know," she said. "I can't fathom your behavior."

"Grace," H. Richard Detweiler said, "that's none of your business."

"Yes it is," she snapped. "Patricia is one of my dearest friends, and I've known Matt since he was in diapers."

"Matt's no longer a child," Detweiler said. "He can make his own decisions about what he wants to do with his life."

"Why am I not surprised you'd say something like that?" she replied. "Well, all right then, Mr. Policeman, what do you think happened to Penny?"

"Right now we think she was just in the wrong place at the wrong time," Matt said.

"How can parking your car in a public garage be the wrong place?" she snapped.

"We think she was probably an innocent bystander," Matt said.

"*Probably?* What do you mean, 'probably'? What other explanation could there possibly be?"

"Ma'am, we try to check out everything," Washington said. "That's why we were interested in the jewelry."

"Penny doesn't have any good jewelry," she said.

"They didn't know that until they asked," Detweiler said. "Ease off, Grace."

Washington gave him a grateful look.

"Mrs. Detweiler, what about money?" Washington asked.

"What about it?"

"Did Miss Detweiler habitually carry large amounts of cash?"

"No," she said, "she didn't. It's not safe to carry cash, or anything else of value, in your purse these days."

"Yes, ma'am, I'm afraid you're right about that," Washington agreed. "You would say, then, that it's probable she didn't have more than a hundred dollars in her purse?"

"I would be very surprised if she had more than—actually, as much as—fifty dollars. She had credit cards, of course."

"There were seven or eight of those in her purse," Washington said. "They weren't stolen."

"Well, this pretty much shoots down your professional-thief theory then, doesn't it, Mr. Washington?" H. Richard Detweiler said.

"Yes, sir. It certainly looks that way, doesn't it? We're back to Matt's theory that Miss Detweiler was an innocent bystander."

"Does that mean that whoever did this to my daughter is going to get away with it?" Grace Detweiler asked unpleasantly.

"No, ma'am," Washington said. "I think we'll find whoever did it."

"I called Jeanne Browne, Matt," Grace Detweiler said, "and told her that there is absolutely no reason to let what happened to Penny interfere with Daffy and Chad's wedding."

"I was out there this morning," Matt replied. "They were worried about it. What to do, I mean."

"Well, as I say, Mr. Detweiler and I have agreed that this should not interfere with the wedding in any way. Are we going to see you there?"

"I'll be holding Chad up," Matt said.

"Nice to have met you, Mr. Washington," she said, and marched out of the room.

"She didn't mean to jump on you that way, Matt," H. Richard Detweiler said. "She's naturally upset."

"Yes, sir," Matt said.

"Thank you very much for your cooperation, Mr. Detweiler," Washington said.

"Thank you, Mr. Washington," Detweiler said. "And you, too, Matt."

In the car Washington asked, even before they'd passed through the gate, "What's going on this afternoon? With the wedding party?"

"I don't know what you're asking," Matt confessed.

"If you weren't out Sherlock Holmesing with me, where would you be?"

Pushing a typewriter outside Wohl's office, Matt thought, then, *That's not what he's asking.*

"With Chad Nesbitt," Matt said.

"The bridegroom?"

"Yeah."

"That's what I hoped," Washington said. "Where's that gorgeous new car of yours?"

"Bustleton and Bowler."

Washington reached for the microphone, then flicked a switch.

"W-William Three," he said into the mike. "I need a Highway car to meet me at City Line and Monument."

"W-William Three, this is Highway Twenty. I'm westbound on the Schuylkill Expressway at City Line."

"Highway Twenty, meet me at City Line and Monument."

"Twenty, 'kay."

Washington put down the microphone and turned to Matt. "They'll give you a ride to get your car," he said. "What I'm hoping is that your peers will not be struck dumb when they remember you're a cop. You just might pick up something. Go through the whole business. What is that again?"

"Not much. Just the wedding itself and the reception."

"The bachelor party was last night?"

"Yeah. I missed it."

"Pity. It might have been interesting."

Washington shifted around on the seat, taking out the stuff he had removed from Penelope Detweiler's wastebasket and clothing pockets and handing it to Matt. There were half a dozen matchbooks, several crumpled pieces of paper, several tissues with what could have been spots of dried blood on them, and the small plastic vial.

"What do you think is in the vial?"

"I wouldn't be surprised if what was in the vial was cocaine," Washington said. "I'll drop it by the lab and find out. The tissues indicate she might have been injecting heroin."

Washington saw the look of mingled surprise and confusion on Matt's face and went on: "Heroin users will often dab the needle mark with tissues. Thus the blood spots. Cocaine is usually snorted or smoked, but some experienced junkies sometimes mix cocaine with their heroin and then inject it. They call it a speedball. The cocaine provides an immediate euphoria, a rush, lasting maybe fifteen, twenty, twenty-five minutes. Then the heroin kicks in, as a depressant, and brings the user down from the high into a mellow low lasting for several hours. Very powerful, very dangerous."

"Jesus," Matt said, visibly upset. Then he asked, "Is it evidence? I mean, we didn't have a search warrant or probable cause."

"No. Moot point. No Assistant DA in his right mind is going to try to indict Penelope Detweiler for simple possession."

"Her mother said she probably didn't have fifty dollars in cash; she really had seven hundred and change."

"Her mother told us the truth, as far as she knew it. I don't think she knows that her daughter is doing cocaine. But that does suggest, since Penelope uses coke and didn't have any but had a lot of money, that she was shopping for some, doesn't it?"

"From DeZego?"

"We don't know that, but—"

"Somebody was trying to rip DeZego off, and/or his customer?"

"But why the shotgun? Why kill him?" Washington replied. "Any of that stuff ring a bell?"

"Gin-mill matchbooks," Matt said. "From saloons where Penny and her kind drink."

"They all familiar?"

"This one's new to me," Matt said, holding up a large matchbook with a flocked purple cover and the legend IN-DULGENCES stamped in silver.

Washington glanced at it.

"New to me too," he said. "Is there an address?"

"Not outside," Matt said. He opened it. "There's a phone number, printed inside."

"I'll check that out," Washington said. "Anything else?"

Matt examined the other matchbooks.

"Phone number in this one, handwritten."

Matt unfolded the crumpled pieces of paper.

"This one has a printed number: four eight two. Looks like something from the factory. There's another phone number in one of the others, and the last one is the same as the first."

"Call in to Special Operations every hour or so. When I get addresses, I'll pass them on to you. If you come up with something, pass it on. Leave a phone number, so if something interesting turns up I think you should know, I can call you." He paused and smiled. "I'll say I'm the Porsche service department."

"Clever," Matt said, chuckling.

"Yes, I sometimes think so," Washington said. "The evidence is overwhelming."

A Highway Patrol car was waiting at City Line and Monument when Jason Washington and Matt Payne got there. Washington stopped on the pedestrian crosswalk and Matt got out. Matt walked to the Highway car, opened the back door, and got in.

"Hi," he said. "I need a ride to Bustleton and Bowler."

"What the hell are we supposed to be, a fucking taxi?" asked the driver, a burly cop with an acne-scarred face.

"I thought you were *supposed* to be the Gestapo," Matt said.

Oh, shit, there goes the automatic, out-of-control mouth again.

The Highway cop in the passenger seat, a lean, sharp-featured man with cold blue eyes, turned and put his arm on the back of the seat and looked at Matt. Then he smiled. It did not make him look much warmer.

"He can't be in the Gestapo, Payne," he said. "You have to be able to read and write to be in the Gestapo."

"Fuck you too," the driver said.

"You in a hurry or what?" the other one asked. "We was about to get coffee when we got the call."

"Coffee sounds like a fine idea," Matt said.

"Why don't we go to the Marriott on City Line?" he said to the driver, and then turned back to Matt. "Is that Washington as good as people say?"

"I was just thinking about that," Matt said. "Yeah. He's good. Very good. He not only knows what questions to ask, but how to ask them. A master psychologist."

"He better be a master something," the driver said. "They don't have shit on who shot the cop, much less the mob guy."

"Instead of going off shift," the cop with the cold blue eyes said, "we're doing four hours of overtime."

"I heard about that," Matt said. Peter Wohl had told him how it worked: While detectives rang doorbells and talked to people—conducted "neighborhood interviews"—Highway cops would cover the area, stopping people on the street and in cars, both looking for information and hoping to find someone with contraband—drugs, for example, or stolen property. If they did, the people caught would be given a chance to cooperate, in other words provide information. If they did, the contraband might get lost down the gutter or even dropped on the sidewalk where it could be recovered.

If they didn't have any information to offer, they would be arrested for the violation. By the time their trial came up, they might work hard on coming up with something the police could use, knowing that if they did and the Highway cops told one of the ADAs (assistant district attorneys) of their cooperation, he would be inclined to drop the charges.

Anyone caught in the area with an unlicensed pistol would be taken into Homicide for further questioning.

They pulled into the parking lot of the Marriott on City Line Avenue and went into the restaurant and sat at the counter. Matt sensed that they immediately had become the center of attention—much, if not most, of it nervous.

He remembered Amanda's reaction to the Highway cops in the diner at breakfast.

There is something menacing about the Highway Patrol. Is that bad? Any cop in uniform is a symbol of authority; that's why there is a badge, which, if you think about it, is descended from the coat of arms of a feudal lord and means about the same thing: I am in the service of authority. The badge says, "I am here to enforce the law, the purpose of which is to protect you. If you are obeying the law, you have nothing to fear from me. But, malefactor, watch out!"

Given that, isn't the very presence of these two, in their leather jackets and boots and rows of shiny cartridges, a deterrent to crime and thus of benefit to society? No stickup man in his right mind would try to rob this place with these two in here.

On the other hand, if some third-rate amateur came in here and saw only Officer Matthew Payne, in plainclothes, with his pistol cleverly concealed and his badge in his pocket, he would figure it was safe to help himself to what's in the cash register, using what force he considered necessary and appropriate.

A little fear of law enforcers, ergo sum, is not necessarily a bad thing.

There was almost immediate substantiation of Officer Payne's philosophic ruminations. The proprietor, wrapped in a grease-spotted white apron, came out from the kitchen smiling. He shook hands with both Highway Patrolmen.

"How about a cheese steak?" he asked. "I just finished slicing—"

"No thanks," the Highway cop with the cold blue eyes said. "Just coffee."

The driver said, "Thanks, anyway. Next time."

The proprietor, Matt saw, was genuinely disappointed.

He's genuinely pleased to see the Gestapo and sorry he can't show his appreciation for what they do for him; allow him, so to speak, his constitutional right to the pursuit of happiness.

"You hungry, Payne?" the blue-eyed cop asked, then saw the look of surprise in the proprietor's eyes and added, "He might not look it, but he's a cop."

"Actually," the driver said, "he's a pretty good cop. Dave, say hello to Matt Payne. He's the guy who took down the Northwest Philly rapist."

"No *shit*?" the proprietor said, and grabbed Matt's hand. "I'm really happy to meet you. Jesus Christ, I . . . can't I get you something more than a lousy cup of coffee?"

"Coffee's fine, thank you," Matt said.

"Well, then, you got to promise to come back when you have an appetite, for chrissake. My pleasure."

"Thank you, I will," Matt said.

I'm sorry he brought that up, Matt thought. And then, *Don't be a hypocrite. No, you're not. You love it.*

There was a good deal of resentment in Highway about Staff Inspector Peter Wohl's having named Officers Jesus Martinez and Charles McFadden as "probationary Highway Patrolmen."

It was not directed toward Martinez or McFadden. It wasn't their fault. But it was almost universally perceived as a diminution of what being Highway meant. An absolute minimum of three years, most often four or five or even longer, in a district before transfer to Highway. Then Wheel School, where motorcycling skills were taught, and then a year or so patrolling I-95 and the Schuykill Expressway, and only then, finally, being assigned to a Highway RPC and sent out to high-crime areas citywide.

Martinez had been on the job less than two years, and McFadden even less, and here they were riding around with Sergeant DeBenedito on probation, and unless he could really find something wrong with them, when they finished, they would go to Wheel School and be in Highway.

The resentment was directed primarily at Inspector Wohl, but some went toward Captain Sabara (who really should have told Wohl what a dumb idea it was, and talked him out of it) and Captain Pekach (ditto, but what can you expect from a guy who used to wear a pigtail when he was in Narcotics?).

A problem arose when Officers Martinez and McFadden reported, four hours early, for overtime duty in connection with the investigation of the murder of Officer Magnella. Written instructions, later updated, had come down from Captain Pekach's office concerning the probationary periods of Officers McFadden and Martinez. Among other things, they stated, in writing, that the probationary officers would ride with either Sergeant DeBenedito or with Highway officers on a list attached and with no one else.

Captain Pekach, who, it was suspected, was not overly enthusiastic about Inspector Wohl's brainstorm, was nevertheless determined to see that it was carried out as well as it could be. He was not going to see Martinez and McFadden turned into passengers in Highway RPCs. He spread the word that it was to be a learning experience for them, watching the best Highway cops on the job.

The list of officers who would take the probationers with them had been drawn up by Sergeant DeBenedito, approved by Captain Pekach and then by Captain Sabara. The officers on it were experienced, intelligent, and a cut above their peers.

The same qualities that had gotten them on the probationary officer supervisor's list were the qualities that had seen them assigned to ring doorbells and otherwise assist Detective Tony Harris in the investigation of the murder of Officer Magnella.

When Officers Martinez and McFadden reported, four hours early, for overtime work, Sergeant DeBenedito was not around. Inspector Wohl had learned that DeBenedito was related to Officer Magnella, had relieved him of his regular duties, and told him to do what he could for Magnella's family, both personally and as the official representative of Highway and Special Operations.

Neither was anyone on the list of Highway cops authorized to supervise the probationers available.

So what to do with Martinez and McFadden?

The first thought of Sergeant William "Big Bill" Henderson was to find something useful for them to do around Bustleton and Bowler. There was always paperwork to catch up with, and housekeeping chores. They could take care of that while *real* Highway cops went about their normal duties. He proposed this to Lieutenant Lucci.

Lieutenant Lucci had been a Highway sergeant under Mike Sabara before he had gone off to be the mayor's driver. He clearly remembered, from painful personal experience, that when Mike Sabara said something, he grew very annoyed when later he learned that only the letter, and not the spirit, of his orders had been followed. And he had been present when Captain Sabara had said, "I don't want these two riding around as passengers or shoved off somewhere in a corner."

The problem was presented to Captain David Pekach. It annoyed him. For one thing, it struck him as the sort of question that a sergeant should be able to decide on his own, without involving his lieutenant and the commanding officer. For another, Officers Martinez and McFadden had worked for him in Narcotics, and it was his judgment that they were pretty good cops who had learned more working undercover about what it takes to be a good cop in their brief careers than most cops, including some in Highway, learned in ten years.

"For chrissake, Luke!" he said, his Polish temper bubbling over slightly. "If you really need me to make this momentous decision, I will. Put them in a goddamn car and have them hand out goddamn speeding tickets on the goddamn Schuykill Expressway!"

Almost immediately, after Lucci had fled his office, he regretted having lost his temper. What he should have done, he realized—what really would have been the most efficient utilization of available manpower resources—was to order the two of them back into civilian clothes and given them to Tony Harris. And if that had offended the prima donnas of Highway, fuck them.

But it was too late for that now that he had lost his temper and ordered the first thing that came into his mind. A commanding officer who is always changing his orders is correctly perceived by his subordinates to be someone who isn't sure what he's doing.

Lieutenant Lucci relayed the commanding officer's decision vis-à-vis Officers Martinez and McFadden to Sergeant Big Bill Henderson, who relayed it, via a ten-minute pep talk, to Martinez and McFadden.

Following a review of the applicable motor vehicle codes of the Commonwealth of Pennsylvania and the City and County of Philadelphia, he explained, in some detail, the intricacies of filling out the citation form.

Then he turned philosophical, trying to make them understand that because of the personnel shortage caused by the murder of Officer Magnella, they were being given a special opportunity to show their stuff. He could not remember, he told them (honestly) any other time when two untrained officers had been sent out by themselves in a Highway car. If they performed well, he told them, it certainly would reflect well on the report Sergeant DeBenedito would ultimately write on them. And he made the point that they should feel no embarrassment, or reluctance, to call for assistance or advice anytime they encountered a situation they weren't quite sure how to handle.

Officers Martinez and McFadden heard him out politely, then left the building and got in the Highway RPC.

"Do you believe that shit?" Jesus Martinez said.

"If I'd have known they were going to have us handing out speeding tickets, I'd have told them to stick their overtime up their ass," Charley McFadden said.

TWELVE

Matt dropped change into the pay phone at the gas station where he parked his car near Special Operations, got a dial tone, and dialed a number from memory.

"Hello?"

The voice of the bridegroom-to-be did not seem to be bubbling over with joyous anticipation or anything else.

"It's not too late to change your mind," Matt said. "I believe that's known as leaving the bride at the altar."

"Where the fuck have you been? Where are you?"

"I just got off work," Matt said. "I'm at Bustleton and Bowler."

"I was getting worried."

"I can't imagine why."

"Can you get a couple of suitcases in that car of yours?"

"Sure."

"Then come get me," Chad Nesbitt ordered. "You can take me by Daffy's with my bags and then to the hotel."

"Oh, thank you! Thank you!" Matt said emotionally, but he said it to a dead telephone. Chad Nesbitt had hung up.

Second Lieutenant Chadwick T. Nesbitt IV, USMCR, was waiting under the fieldstone portico of the Nesbitt mansion in Bala-Cynwyd when Matt got there. He was in uniform, freshly shaved, and sitting astride a life-size stone lion. Two identical canvas suitcases with his name, rank, and serial number stenciled on them sat beside the lion. A transparent bag held a Marine dress uniform, and there was a box that presumably held the brimmed uniform cap, and another that obviously held Chad's Marine officer's sword.

He held a stemmed glass filled with red liquid in his hand. Another glass, topped with a paper napkin, was balanced on one of the suitcases.

"It took you long enough," he greeted Matt when Matt got out of the car and walked up to him.

"Fuck you."

"Well, fuck you too. Now you don't get no Bloody Mary."

"Is that what that is?" Matt replied, picking up the glass. "Thank you, I don't mind if I do."

They smiled at each other.

"You must have had a good time last night," Matt said. "You look like the finest example of the mortician's art."

"Speaking of that, where the hell were you?"

"Fighting crime, where do you think?"

" 'Fighting crime'? Is that what you call it? Daffy said you were shacked up with What's-her-name Stevens."

"Her name is Amanda and we weren't shacked up."

"Methinks thou dost protest too much," Chad said. "Madame Browne is, of course, morally outraged at you."

"So what else is new?"

"I think I'll have another of these to give me courage to face the traffic, and then you can take us over there, and then to the hotel."

"I thought you weren't supposed to see the bride before the wedding."

"All I'm going to do is drop my bags off. Then we go to the hotel and get a little something to quiet my nerves."

"You're already—or maybe still—bombed," Matt said. "I don't want to have to carry you into the church."

"You have always been something of a prig, Payne. Have I ever told you that?"

"Often," Matt said, putting the Bloody Mary down and

picking up the suitcases. "Jesus, what the hell have you got in here?"

"Just the chains and whips and handcuffs and other stuff one takes on one's bridal trip," Chad said. "Plus, of course, what every Marine second lieutenant takes with him when going off to battle the forces of Communism in far-off Okinawa."

"The sword and dress blues too?"

"I'll change into the blues at the hotel, and then out of them at Daffy's after the wedding. We don't use swords no more, you know, to battle the forces of Communism."

Matt set the suitcases on the cobblestone driveway and opened the hatch.

"Get in," he said, then, "What are your travel plans, by the way?"

"We're going into New York tonight and flying to the West Coast tomorrow."

"You're not coming back here?"

"I hope to come back, of course, but if you were asking 'after the wedding and before going overseas,' no."

He swung his leg off the stone lion, picked up Matt's Bloody Mary glass, and walked to the car.

"If you were to open the door for me, I think I could get in without spilling any of this on your pristine upholstery," he said.

Matt closed the hatch and opened the door for him. He took his Bloody Mary from him, drained it, and set the glass on the step.

When he straightened, Mrs. Chadwick T. Nesbitt III was standing there.

"I'm not at all sure that's a very good idea, Matt," she said, and then walked around him to the car.

"He insisted, Mother," Chad said. "He said he didn't think he could get through the ceremony without the assistance of a little belt."

"Well, don't let him give you any more," she said. "Have you got everything?"

"Yes, Mother."

"You're sure?"

"Yes, Mother."

"Well, then, I guess we'll see you at St. Mark's."

"God willing, and if the creek don't rise," Chad said, and slammed his door shut.

Matt walked around to the driver's side of the Porsche.

"Matt . . ." Chad's mother said.

"Yes, ma'am."

"Just . . . behave, the two of you."

"We will," Matt said.

He got behind the wheel, made a U-turn, and started down the drive to the gate.

Mrs. Nesbitt waved. Chad waved back.

"Mother, I think, is aware that she may be watching her firstborn leave the family manse for the last time," Chad said. "That somewhat discomfiting thought has occurred to me."

Matt didn't know what to say.

"If I asked you politely, would you give me a straight answer to a straight question?" Chad asked.

Matt sensed that Chad was serious. "Sure," he said.

"What does it feel like to kill somebody?"

"Jesus!"

"At the moment your experience in that area exceeds mine," Chad said, "although, to be sure, I am sure the Marine Corps plans to correct that situation as quickly as possible."

"I haven't had nightmares or done a lot of soul-searching about it," Matt said. "Nothing like that. The man I shot was a certified scumbag—"

"Interesting word," Chad said, interrupting. "Meaning, I take it, someone who has as much value as a used rubber?"

"I really don't know what it means. It's . . . cop talk. A very unpleasant individual. The same day I shot him, earlier that day I saw what he did to a woman he abducted. He raped her, tortured her, mutilated her, and then killed her. I suppose that's part of the equation. I knew that he was no fucking good."

"In other words, you were pleased that you had killed him?"

"When I saw him, he tried to run me over. He totaled my car. The only emotion I had was fear and anger. He was trying to kill me. I had a gun, so I killed him."

"Courage is defined as presence of mind under stress," Chad said.

"Then, *ergo sum*, courage was not involved in what I did," Matt said. "He had a woman in the van, another one he had abducted. It was just blind fucking luck that I didn't hit her when I was shooting at him. If I had had *'presence of mind,'* I wouldn't have shot at him at all."

"The newspapers made quite a hero of you," Chad said thoughtfully. "The Old Man sent them all to me."

"That was all bullshit," Matt said.

"Fuck you. *I'm* impressed."

"You never were very smart."

"So tell me, Sherlock, who popped Penny Detweiler?"

"We're still looking," Matt said.

"Let me give you a clue," Chad said. "Daffy said Penny knew that Eye-talian."

"Daffy told you that?"

"Surprised?"

"No," Matt said. "She tell you anything else?"

"No. Just that she knew Penny had been seeing him."

" 'Seeing,' as opposed to 'buying cocaine from'?"

"Penny's into cocaine?"

"A small voice just told me I shouldn't be talking to you about this."

"Just between thee, me, and this empty Bloody Mary glass?"

"To go absolutely no further than that, Chad, yeah. Penny has a problem with cocaine. But she doesn't know that we know, and I want to keep it that way."

"What she said was 'seeing,' " Chad said, "as in getting fucked by. She didn't say anything about dope. Are you sure about that? *Penny Detweiler?*"

"Yeah, we're sure, Chad."

" *'We're* sure,' huh? I think I liked things better when 'we' meant you and me and Daffy and Penny, and the cops were . . . well, the goddamn cops."

"I'm sorry we got into this," Matt said. "Do you suppose you could forget we did?"

"Consider it forgotten," Chad said. "But one more question?"

"You can *ask* it."

"You ever take any of that shit?"

"No."

"You never even smoked grass?"

"No."

"Me, either. But I'm beginning to suspect that it's us two Boy Scouts alone in the world."

Soames T. Browne, whom they found wandering around among the catering staff on his lawn, insisted they have a little nip with him, which turned into three before they could get away.

"You know, I really think he likes me," Chad said when they were finally back in the Porsche.

"You're taking Daffy off his hands," Matt said. "He should be overwhelmed with gratitude."

"Fuck you, Matt."

"He will be considerably less fond of you, of course, if you show up at the church shit-faced."

"Don't worry about me, buddy," Chad said confidently.

Matt dropped Chad and his sword and dress blues and uniform cap box off at the Bellevue-Stratford Hotel on South Broad Street, then drove to his apartment on Rittenhouse Square, several blocks away. The idea was that he would pick up his tails and carry them to the hotel and change there in the suite of rooms the Nesbitts had taken for Chad's out-of-town ushers.

But he decided that he would rather not do that, as it would really be easier to change in his apartment. He called Special Operations on the rent-a-cop's telephone. Jason Washington was not there, so he left word for him that he had confirmation that Penelope Detweiler knew Anthony J. DeZego and that he would be, for the next couple of hours, at the Bellevue-Stratford.

Then he walked back to the Bellevue-Stratford Hotel.

The Nesbitts had rented two large adjoining suites on the seventh floor for Chad's out-of-town guests. The Brownes had done the same thing for Daffy's friends, putting the girls up in a series of rooms on the fifth floor. It was inevitable that they should find each other, and there was a party just getting started when he got there. The official pre-wedding party, in a ballroom on the mezzanine floor, would not start for an hour.

He had been in the room less than five minutes when one of Chad's Marine Corps buddies answered the telephone, then stood on a coffee table, holding up the phone, and bellowed, *"At ease!"*

When he had everyone's attention, some of it shocked, he politely inquired, "Is there a Mr. Matthew Payne in the house?"

"Here," Matt said, and went and took the phone, certain that it would be Jason Washington. It was not.

"Matt, if he comes to the church drunk," Daffy Browne said, "I'll never speak to you again as long as I live."

"Would you be willing to put that in writing?"

"Oh, Matt, *please!*"

"I'll do my best, Daffy," Matt said.

"Try to remember this is the most important day in our *lives*," Daffy said.

"Right."

"He listens to you, Matt, you know he does."

He was looking at Chad Nesbitt. Chad had a Bloody Mary in his hand.

Bullshit, he listens to me!

"Relax, Daphne," he said. "I'll get him to the church on time."

Daffy was not amused. She hung up. Matt put the telephone down and walked over to Chad.

"That was the bride-to-be," he said. "She wants you sober for the wedding."

"Well, one doesn't always get what one wishes, does one?"

"Come on, Chad. You get pissed and I'm the villain."

"Who's going to get pissed?"

Matt decided he was wasting his breath.

If he wants to drink, he will drink. He does not listen to me. If he gets pissed, Daffy will be pissed off with me, and that means that I will not be able to get her alone and ask her, between old pals, what she knows about Penny and Tony the Zee. Shit!

A gentle hand brushed his back.

"I thought maybe you'd be here," Amanda said.

She was so close that he could smell her perfume. She was wearing a skirt and a crisp white blouse.

Jesus, she's beautiful!

"Hi," he said.

"I understand that this disreputable character has been keeping you out all night," Chad said to Amanda.

Amanda walked away without replying, or even showing that she had heard him. Matt walked after her. She headed for the door; he caught up with her there.

"Where are you going?" he asked.

"If you're having a good time," she said, "by all means stay."

He followed her into the corridor and to the elevator.

"I heard all that," she said. "You did everything you could be expected to do."

"Tell Daffy," he said.

"I intend to," Amanda said.

That pleased him very much.

"There's a couple of bars right here in the hotel," he said as they stepped onto the elevator.

"No bars, thank you," she said.

"Okay. Then how about Professor Payne's famous walking tour of downtown Philadelphia until it's time for the cocktail party?"

"No cocktail party for me, thank you just the same."

"Then where would you like to go? What would you like to do?"

She looked up at him with mischief, and something else, in her eyes.

"Really?" he asked after a moment.

"Really," she said.

Somehow their hands touched and then grasped, and holding hands, they walked out of the elevator and through the lobby and then to the apartment over the Delaware Valley Cancer Society on Rittenhouse Square.

At five minutes to five Lieutenant Tony Lucci knocked at Staff Inspector Peter Wohl's office door, waited to be told to come in, and then announced, "Everyone's here, Inspector."

"Ask them to come in, please, Tony," Wohl said. He was sitting on the front edge of his desk. Chief Inspector Dennis V.

Coughlin and his driver, Sergeant Tom Lenihan, who had come to Bustleton and Bowler ten minutes before, were sitting on the couch.

"Harris has the Lewis kid with him, Inspector. Him too?"

"Why not?"

I recognize your dilemma, Tony, my boy. His Honor the Mayor has told you to keep your eye on things, or words to that effect. And now, with, so to speak, a conference at the highest levels of this little fiefdom about to take place behind a closed door without you, you don't quite know how to handle it. Are you going to ask if I want you in here? If you do that, it would be tantamount to admitting that you are functioning as the mayor's little birdie. Or are you going, so to speak, to put your ear to the keyhole? Desperately hoping, of course, that I won't catch you at it.

"Yes, sir," Lucci said.

Captains Mike Sabara and David Pekach, Detectives Jason Washington and Tony Harris, and Officer Foster H. Lewis, Jr., filed into the office.

Lieutenant Lucci stood in the open door, almost visibly hoping that he would be told to come in.

"Chief," Wohl said, "do you know Officer Lewis?"

"How are you?" Coughlin said, offering his hand. "I know your dad."

Wohl looked at Lucci in the door, his eyebrows raised in question. Lucci quickly closed the door.

"For reasons I can't imagine, Officer Lewis is known as Tiny," Wohl said. "He's been helping Tony."

There were chuckles and Coughlin said, "Good experience for you, son."

"Tiny, would you ask Lucci to come in here?" Wohl said.

Coughlin looked at Wohl curiously as Tiny went to the door.

Lucci appeared in a moment.

"Tony, get yourself a pad and sit in on this, please," Wohl said. Lucci disappeared for a moment, then returned with a stenographer's notebook and three pencils in his hand.

"Tony, I want you to make note of anything you think the mayor would like to know. I know he's interested in what we're doing, and you're obviously the best person to tell him.

From now on I want you to stay in close touch with him, so that he's up-to-date on what's happening."

"Yes, sir," Lucci said, now very confused.

Coughlin's and Wohl's eyes met for a moment; Wohl thought he saw both amusement and approval in Coughlin's eyes.

This is either proof of my general, all-around brilliance in How to Deal with the Honorable Jerry Carlucci, or one more proof of the adage that when rape is inevitable, the thing to do is relax and enjoy it.

"From now until we can clear these jobs—Officer Magnella, Anthony J. DeZego, and Penelope Detweiler," Wohl began, "I think we should have a meeting like this every day. At this time of day, probably, but that can be changed if need be. And I think we should start by hearing what Tony has."

"I've got zilch," Tony Harris said.

"That's encouraging," Coughlin said sarcastically.

"Officer Magnella, on routine patrol in the 22nd District," Harris said, "was shot by the side of his RPC near the intersection of Colombia and Clarion between eleven-ten and eleven twenty-five. We know the time because he met with his sergeant at eleven-ten, and the call from the civilian that a cop had been shot came at eleven twenty-five. The medical examiner has determined that the cause of death is trauma caused by five .22-caliber—.22 Long Rifle, specifically—lead bullets, four in the chest, and one in the upper left leg.

"Officer Magnella did not, *did not*, get on the radio to report that he was doing anything at all. When he met with his sergeant, he did not indicate to him that anything at all was out of the ordinary. In fact, he commented that it had been an unusually quiet night. Neither his sergeant, nor his lieutenant, was aware of him taking any kind of a special interest in anything in his patrol area. *Nobody* in the 22nd had any idea that he was on to something special. There have been no reports of any special animosity toward him specifically, or the 22nd generally.

"There are *no* known witnesses, except, of course, the civilian who called Emergency and reported him down. That civilian is not identified and has not come forward. Obviously he—the tape suggests it was a male, probably white and probably around forty—doesn't want to get involved.

"No one in the neighborhood heard anything unusual, including shots. A .22 doesn't make a hell of a lot of noise.

"Everything I have been able to turn up suggests that Magnella was a straight arrow. He didn't gamble; he hardly drank; he was about to get married to a girl from his neighborhood; he was a churchgoer; he didn't drink—I said that, didn't I? Anyway, there's nothing to suggest that the shooting was connected to anything in his personal life—"

"What's your gut feeling, Tony?" Chief Coughlin asked, interrupting.

"Chief, what I think is he saw something, a couple of kids, a drunk, a hooker, nothing he considered really threatening. And he stopped the car and got out and they—or maybe even *she*—shot him."

"Why?" Coughlin asked.

Harris shrugged and held his hands up in a gesture of helplessness.

"So where are you now, Tony?" Coughlin asked.

"Going over it all again. There are some people in the neighborhood we haven't talked to yet. We're going to talk to people who work in the neighborhood. We're going to check everybody Magnella ever arrested. We're going to talk to his family again, and people in his neighborhood—"

"You need anything?" Coughlin asked.

That's my question, Wohl thought. *But Coughlin wanted to ask it so that when Tony says, "Can't think of anything," he can say, "Well, if there's anything at all you need, speak up." And Lucci will report that to the mayor, that Chief Coughlin is staying on top of things.*

"Can't think of anything, Chief," Tony Harris said.

"Well, if there's anything you need, anything at all, speak up," Coughlin said.

"You getting everything you need from Homicide?" Wohl asked.

"Yeah, sure," Harris said. "Lou Natali even called me up and asked if there was anything he could do. Said Chief Lowenstein told him to."

"I'm sure that it's just a matter of time, Tony," Coughlin said.

"Jason?" Wohl asked.

"Nothing. Well, not quite nothing. We found out the

Detweiler girl uses cocaine, and we found out she kne~ DeZego, so that's where we're headed.''

"You're sure about that?'' Coughlin asked. "Detweiler's daughter is using cocaine?''

"I'm sure about that,'' Washington said evenly.

"Jesus!'' Coughlin said. "And she knew DeZego?''

"I got that just a couple of minutes ago when I came in,'' Washington said. "Matt Payne left a message.''

"I thought he was working with you. I mean, why isn't he here?'' Coughlin asked.

"He's at the wedding. I thought he might hear something. He did. I wouldn't be surprised if he heard a little more at the reception.''

"I thought you were working on the scenario that the Detweiler girl was just an innocent bystander,'' Coughlin said.

"That was before we found out she's using cocaine and knew DeZego.''

"Any other explanation could turn into a can of worms, Jason,'' Coughlin said.

"I'm getting a gut feeling, Chief, that what happened on the roof was that somebody wanted to pop DeZego. I have no idea why. But if that holds up, if DeZego getting popped wasn't connected, in other words, with cocaine or robbery— but had something to do with the mob is what I'm trying to say—then the Detweiler girl could very easily really be an innocent bystander.''

"Yeah,'' Coughlin said thoughtfully, adding, "It could very well be something like that.''

You'd like that, wouldn't you, Chief? Wohl thought, somewhat unpleasantly. *That would eliminate that can of worms you're talking about.*

"I'm going to see Jim Osgood when I leave here,'' Washington said. "Maybe he'll have something.''

Lieutenant James H. Osgood, of the Organized Crime Division, was the department expert on the internal workings of the mob (actually, *mobs*) and the personal lives of their members.

"You waited until now to get into that?'' Coughlin asked. It was a reprimand.

"I was over there at eight this morning, Chief,'' Washington said, "before I went to Hahneman to see the girl. Osgood was in New York. He got back, was supposed to get back, at five.''

"If anyone would have a line on something like that, it would be Osgood," Chief Coughlin said somewhat lamely.

"Chief," Wohl asked, "am I under any sort of budgetary restrictions about overtime?"

"Absolutely not!" Coughlin said emphatically. "You spend whatever you think is necessary, Peter, on overtime or anything else."

I hope you wrote that down, Lucci. I'm sure that Chief Coughlin really wants that on the record, for the mayor to know that he personally authorized me to spend whatever I think is necessary on overtime or anything else. The son of a bitch is covering his ass while he hangs me out in the wind.

"Anybody else got anything?" Wohl asked.

Heads shook. "No."

"Chief, have you got anything else?" Wohl asked.

"No. I'm going to get out of here and let you and your people get on with it," Coughlin said.

He got out of the couch, shook hands with everyone in the room, and left.

"I think this is where, as your commanding officer, I am expected to say something inspiring," Wohl said.

They all looked at him.

" 'Something inspiring,' " Wohl said. "Get the hell out of here. I'll see you tomorrow."

When they had all gone, Wohl closed the door after them and then sat on the edge of his desk again and pulled the phone to him.

"Yes?" a gruff voice asked.

"Buy you a beer?"

"Come to supper."

"I don't want to, Dad," Wohl said.

"Oh," Chief Inspector August Wohl (retired), said. "Downey's, Front and South, in half an hour?"

"Fine. Thanks."

THIRTEEN

Captain David Pekach was relieved when the meeting in Wohl's office broke up so quickly. Under the circumstances it could have gone on for hours.

Both he and Mike Sabara followed Lieutenant Lucci to his desk, where Sabara told Lucci he would either be at home or at St. Sebastian's Church; Lucci had both numbers. Pekach told him that he would be at either of the two numbers he had given Lucci, and from half past seven at the Ristorante Alfredo downtown. He wrote the number down and gave it to Lucci.

Lucci and Sabara exchanged smiles.

"Big date, Dave, huh?" Sabara asked.

"I'm taking a lady friend to dinner, all right?" Pekach snapped. "Is there anything wrong with that?"

"Wow!" Sabara said. "What did I do? Strike a raw nerve?"

Pekach glared at him, then walked toward the door to the parking lot.

"*Nice* watch, Dave," Sabara called after him.

Pekach turned and gave him the finger, then stormed out of the building. Sabara and Lucci grinned at each other.

"What was that about the watch?" Lucci asked.

"His *'lady friend'* gave him a watch for his birthday," Sabara said. "An Omega. Gold. With all the dials. What do you call it, a chronometer?"

"Chrono*graph*," Lucci said. "Gold, huh?"

"Gold," Sabara confirmed.

"Why's he so sensitive about her?" Lucci asked, deciding at the last moment not to tell Captain Sabara that he had heard Captain Pekach's lady friend call him Precious when he had called him at her house.

"I don't know," Sabara replied. "I've seen her. She's not at all bad-looking. Nothing for him to be ashamed of."

She was Miss Martha Ellen Peebles, a female Caucasian thirty-four years and six months old, weighing 121 pounds and standing five feet four inches tall.

Miss Peebles resided alone, in a turn-of-the-century mansion at 606 Glengarry Lane in Chestnut Hill. There was a live-in couple—a chauffeur-butler-majordomo and a housekeeper-cook—who were in turn helped by a constantly changing staff of maids and groundskeepers, most often nieces and nephews of the live-in couple, who kept the place up.

The house had been built by Alexander F. Peebles, who owned, among other things, what the *Wall Street Journal* estimated was eleven percent of the nation's anthracite coal reserves. Mr. Peebles had one son, Alexander, Jr., who in turn had two children, Martha, and her brother Stephen, four years younger.

Mrs. Alexander Peebles, Jr., had died of cancer when Martha was twelve and Stephen eight. Alexander Peebles decided on the night that God finally put his wife out of her misery that his daughter was an extraordinarily good creature. Martha, who was entitled to being comforted by him on the loss of her mother, had instead come to him, in his gun-room sanctuary, where he was wallowing in Scotch-soaked self-pity, and comforted him. He was not to worry, Martha had told him; she would take care of him from now on.

Mr. Peebles never remarried and devoted the remaining eighteen years of his life to his quest for grouse in Scotland, big game in Africa, trophy sheep in the Rocky Mountains, and his collection of pre-1900 American firearms.

Since Martha truly believed she was taking care of him, her father didn't think it right to leave her at home in the company of a governess or some other domestic, so he engaged a tutor-companion for her and took her along on his hunting trips.

Their adoration was mutual. Martha thought her father was perfect in all respects. He thought she embodied all the desirable feminine traits of beauty and gentility. Her reaction to learning, while they were shooting Cape Buffalo in what was then still the Belgian Congo, that Miss Douglass, her tutor-companion, was sharing his cot was, he thought, simply splendid. One simply didn't expect that sort of sympathetic, sophisticated understanding from a sixteen-year-old girl. And by then she was as good a shot as most men he knew. What more could a father expect of a daughter?

Alexander Peebles, Jr.'s, relationship with his son was nowhere near so idyllic. The boy had always been delicate. That was probably genetic, he decided, inherited from his mother's side of the family. Her father had died young, he recalled, and her two brothers looked like librarians.

The several times he had tried to include Stephen, when he turned sixteen, in hunting trips had been disasters. When Stephen had finally managed to hit a deer-for-the-safari-pot in Tanganyika, he had looked down at the carcass and wept. The next year, after an absolutely splendid day of shooting driven pheasant on the Gladstone estate in Scotland, when their host had asked him what he thought of pheasant shooting, Stephen had replied, "Frankly I think it's disgusting slaughter."

When Alex Peebles had told his son that his remark had embarrassed him and Martha, Stephen had replied, "Tit for tat, Father. *I* am grossly embarrassed having a father who brings a whore along on a trip with his children."

Alex Peebles, furious at his defiant attitude and at his characterization of Karen Cayworth (who really had had several roles in motion pictures before giving up her acting career to become his secretary) as a whore, had slapped his son, intending only that, not a dislocated jaw.

Predictably, Martha had stood by her father and gone with

Stephen to the hospital and then ridden with him on the train to London and put him on the plane home. She had then returned to Scotland. But the damage had been done, of course. Lord Gladstone was polite but distant, and Alex Peebles knew that it would be a long time before he was asked to shoot the estate again.

Five months after that, a month before he was to graduate, Stephen was expelled from Groton for what the headmaster called "the practice of unnatural vice."

From then on, until his death of a heart attack in the Rockies at fifty-six, Alex Peebles had as little to do with his son as possible. He put him on an allowance and gave him to understand that he was not welcome in the house on Glengarry Lane when his father was at home.

Martha, predictably, urged him to forgive and forget, but he could not find it in himself to do so. He relented to the point of offering, via Martha, to arrange for whatever psychiatric treatment was necessary to cure him of his sexual deviance. Stephen, as predictably, refused, and so far as Alex Peebles was concerned, that was that.

Alex Peebles's last will and testament was a very brief document. It left all of his worldly possessions, of whatever kind and wherever located, to his beloved daughter, Martha, of whom he was as proud as he was ashamed of his son, to whom, consequently, he was leaving nothing.

It did occur to Alex Peebles that Martha, being the warm-hearted, generous, indeed Christian young woman that she was, would certainly continue to provide some sort of financial support for her brother. Stephen would not end up in the gutter.

It never entered Alex Peebles's mind that Martha, once the to-be-expected grief passed, would have trouble getting on with her own life. She was not at all bad-looking, and a damn good companion, and he was, after all, leaving her both a great deal of money and a law firm, Mawson, Payne, Stockton, McAdoo & Lester, which he felt sure would manage her affairs as well, and as honestly, as they could.

Equally important—perhaps even more so—Martha was highly intelligent, well read, and levelheaded. Somewhere down the pike a man would enter her life. It was not unreasonable to hope that she would name her firstborn son after her father, Alexander Peebles Whatever.

He erred. Matha Peebles was devastated by the death of her father, and her perception of herself as a thirty-year-old woman literally all alone in the world, rather than passing, grew worse.

A self-appointed delegation of her mother's family pressed her soon after the will was probated to share her inheritance with her brother. Stephen's "peculiarities," they argued, were not his fault and probably should be laid at his father's feet. His treatment of his son, they said, was barbaric.

When she refused to do that, deciding it would constitute disobedience, literally, of her father's last will and testament, she understood that she was more than likely closing the door on any relationship she might have developed with them. That prediction soon proved to be true.

She came to understand that while she had a large number of acquaintances, she had very few, almost no, friends. There were overtures of friendship, to be sure. Some of them were genuine, but she quickly understood that she had virtually nothing in common with other well-to-do women in Philadelphia except money. She hadn't been in any school long enough to make a lifelong best friend, and felt that it was too late to try to do so now.

There was some attention from men, but she suspected that much of it was because they knew (from a rather nasty lawsuit Stephen had undertaken and lost, to break his father's will) that she alone owned Tamaqua Mining and everything else. And none of the suitors, if that word fit, really interested her.

The hunting was gone too. It was not the sort of thing a single woman could do by herself, even if she had wanted to, and without her father she had no interest in going.

She forced herself to take an interest in the business, going so far as to spend three months in Tamaqua and Hazleton, and taking courses in both mineralogy and finance at the University of Pennsylvania. Taking the courses became an end in itself. It passed the time, got her out of the house every day, and posed a challenge to her when an essay was required or an examination was to be taken.

Three years after their father died, she allowed Stephen to

move back into the house. Or didn't throw him out when he moved back in without asking. She didn't want to fight with him, the court suit had been a terrible experience, she was lonely, and they could at least take some meals together.

But that didn't work, either. Stephen's young friends proved to be difficult. They didn't like him; she saw that. They were selling themselves to him. There wasn't much difference, she came to think, between her father's "secretaries" and Stephen's young men. While there probably was not an actual cash payment in either case, there were gifts and surprises that amounted to the same thing.

And when the gifts and surprises were not judged to be adequate by Stephen's young men, there were either terrible scenes or the theft of things they saw in the house. That came to a head with a handsome young man named William Walton, who said he was an actor.

She went to Stephen and told him she was sure that his friend, William Walton, was stealing things, and Stephen told her, almost hysterically, that she didn't know what she was talking about. When she insisted that she knew precisely what she was talking about, he said some very cruel things to her. She told Stephen that the next time something turned up missing, she was going to the police.

It did and she did, and the police came and did nothing. When Stephen heard about her calling the police, there was another scene, ending when she told him he had two days to find someplace else to live.

Stephen had moved out the next day. She had come down the stairs as he was putting his suitcases out and he had seen her.

"I'm sorry it's come to this, Stephen," she said.

He had looked up at her with hate in his eyes.

"Get fucked!" he had shouted. "You crazy goddamn bitch, get fucked! That's what you need, a good fuck!"

He's beside himself, she decided, *because I told him to get out and because he knows that I was right, that his William Walton doesn't really like him for himself and really is stealing things. As long as he could pretend he wasn't stealing things, he could pretend that William Walton liked him for himself.*

She had turned and gone back upstairs and into the gun

room and wept. The gun room had been her father's favorite place, and now it was hers.

What Stephen had said, "Get fucked," now bothered her. Not the words but what they meant.

Why haven't I been fucked? I am probably the only thirty-four-year-old virgin in the world, with the possible exception of cloistered nuns. The most likely possibility is that I am not so attractive to men so as to make them really try to overcome what is my quite natural maidenly reticence. Another possibility, of course, is that my natural maidenly reticence has been reinforced by the fact that I have encountered very few (unmarried) men who I thought I would like to have do that to me. Or is it "with" me?

And there is another possibility, rather disgusting to think of, and that is that I am really like Stephen, a deviate, a latent Lesbian. Otherwise, wouldn't I have had by now some of that overwhelming hunger, to be fucked, so to speak, that all the heroines in the novels are always experiencing? Or, come to think of it, some women I know have practically boasted about? Why don't my pants get wet when some man touches my arm—or paws my breast?

Realizing that she was slipping into depression, which, of late, had meant that she would drink more than was good for her, she resolved to fight it.

She took out a bottle of the port her father had liked so much and taught her to appreciate, and drank two glasses of it, and not a drop more, and then left the gun room, carefully locking it after her.

In the next two days there were more thefts of bric-a-brac and other valuables, and she called the police again, and again they did nothing.

So she got in her car and drove downtown to see Colonel J. Dunlop Mawson, one of the senior partners in the law firm of Mawson, Payne, Stockton, McAdoo & Lester in the Philadelphia Savings Fund Society Building. Colonel Mawson wasn't there, but another senior partner, Brewster C. Payne, of whom, she remembered, her father had spoken admiringly, saw her.

She told him what was going on, of the thefts and the break-ins, and how the police had been absolutely useless. He tried to talk her into moving out of the house until the police could get to the bottom of what was happening. She told him she had no intention of being run out of her own house.

He told her that Colonel Mawson and Police Commissioner Czernich were great friends, and that as soon as Colonel Mawson returned to the office, he would tell him of their conversation and that he felt sure Colonel Mawson would get some action from the police.

The very same day, late in the afternoon, Harriet Evans, the gentle black woman who—with her husband—had been helping them run the house as long as Martha could remember, came upstairs and said, "Miss Martha, there's another policeman to see you. This one's a captain."

Miss Martha Peebles received Captain David Pekach, commanding officer of the Highway Patrol, in the upstairs sitting room. She explained the problem all over again to him, including her suspicion that Stephen's "actor" friend was the culprit. He assured her that the entire resources of the Highway Patrol would from that moment guarantee the inviolability of her property.

Somehow in conversation it came out that Captain Pekach was not a married man. And she mentioned her father's weapons, and he expressed interest, and, somewhat reluctantly, she took him to the gun room.

When he showed particular interest in one piece, she identified it for him: "That is a U.S. rifle, that is to say, a military rifle, Model of 1819—"

"With a J. H. Hall action," Captain Pekach interrupted.

"Oh, do you know weapons?"

"And stamped with the initials of the proving inspector," he went on. "Z. E. H."

"Zachary Ellsworth—" Martha began to explain.

"Hampden," Captain Pekach concluded as their eyes met. "Captain, Ordnance Corps, later Deputy Chief of Ordnance."

"He was born in Allentown, you know," Martha said.

"No. I didn't know."

"There are some other pieces you might find interesting, Captain," Martha said, "if I'm not taking you away from something more important."

He looked at his watch.

"I'm running late now," he said.

"I understand," she said.

"But perhaps some other time?"

"If you like."

He gestured around the gun room.

"I could happily spend the next two years in here," he said.

He means that. He does want to come back!

"Well, perhaps when you get off duty," she said.

He looked pained.

"Miss Peebles, I'm commanding officer of the Highway Patrol. We're trying very hard to find the man the newspapers are calling the Northwest Philadelphia serial rapist."

"Yes, I read the papers."

"I want to speak to the men coming off their shifts, to see if they may have come up with something. That will keep me busy, I'm afraid, until twelve-thirty or so."

"I understand," she said. Then she heard herself say, actually shamelessly and brazenly lie, "Captain, I'm a night person. I rarely go to bed until the wee hours. I'm sure if you drove past here at one, or even two, there would be lights on."

"Well, I had planned to check on your property before going home," he said. "I've stationed officers nearby."

"Well, then, by all means, if you see a light, come in. I'll give you a cup of coffee."

After five minutes past one that morning Martha Peebles could no longer think of herself as the world's oldest virgin, except for cloistered nuns, perhaps.

And her father, she thought, would have approved of David, once he had gotten to know him. They were very much alike in many ways. Not superficially. Inside.

Martha knew from the very beginning, which she placed as the moment, postcoitus, that he had reached out to her and rolled her over onto him, so that she lay with her face against the hair on his chest, listening to the beat of his heart, feeling the firm muscles of his leg against hers, that David was the man she had been waiting for—without of course knowing it—all her life.

Captain David Pekach drove directly from the meeting in Staff Inspector Peter Wohl's office at Bustleton and Bowler to

606 Glengarry Lane in Chestnut Hill. He parked his un-marked car in one of the four garage stalls in what had been the carriage house behind the house, then walked back down the drive to the entrance portico.

The door opened as he got there.

"Good evening, Captain," Evans, the black guy, greeted him. He was wearing a gray cotton jacket and a black bow tie.

"What do you say, Evans?"

"Miss Martha said to say that if you would like to change, she will be with you in a moment."

"We're going to dinner," Pekach said.

"So I understand, sir. Can I get you a drink, Captain? Or a glass of beer?"

"A beer would be fine, thank you," Pekach said.

"I'll bring it right up, sir," Evans said, smiling.

Martha had told David that Evans "adores you, and so does Harriet," and Evans was always pleasant enough, but there was something about him—and about his wife—living in the house and knowing about him and Martha that made Pekach uncomfortable.

Pekach climbed the wide curving stairs and went down the corridor to "his room." That was a little game they were playing. The story was that because he lived to hell-and-gone on the other side of Philadelphia, he sometimes "stayed over." When he "stayed over," he stayed in a guest room, which just happened to have a connecting door to Martha's bedroom.

Everytime he "stayed over," which was more the rule than the exception, either he or Martha carefully mussed the sheets on the bed in the guest room, sometimes by even bouncing up and down on them. And every morning either Harriet or one of the nieces made up the guest-room bed and everyone pretended that was where he had slept.

When he went in the guest room, there was clothing, not his, on what—because he didn't know the proper term—he called the clotheshorse. It was a mahogany device designed to hold a jacket and trousers. There was a narrow shelf be-hind the jacket hanger, intended, he supposed, to hold your wallet and change and watch. He had never seen any clothing on it and had never used it. He hung his uniforms and clothes in an enormous wardrobe.

When he opened the wardrobe to change into civilian clothing, there was another surprise. He had expected to find his dark blue suit and his new gray flannel suit (Martha bought it for him at Brooks Brothers, and he hated to remember what it had cost). The wardrobe was now nearly full of men's clothing, but neither his dark blue suit nor his new gray flannel suit was among them.

"What the hell?" he muttered, confused. He turned from the wardrobe. Both Evans (bearing a tray with a bottle of beer and a pilsner glass) and Martha were entering the room.

Martha was wearing a black dress and a double string of pearls long enough to reach her bosom.

My God, she's good-looking!

"Oh, damn, you haven't tried it on yet!" Martha said.

"Tried what on?"

"That, of course, silly," she said, and pointed at the clothing on the clotheshorse.

"That's not mine," he said.

"Yes and no, Precious," Martha said. "Try it on."

She took the coat—he saw now that it was a blue blazer with brass buttons.

"Honey," he said, "I told you I don't want you buying me any more clothes."

"And I haven't," she said. "Have I, Evans?"

"No, Captain, she hasn't."

There was nothing to do but put the jacket on. It was double-breasted and it fit.

"Perfect," Evans said.

"Look at the buttons," Martha said. He looked. The brass buttons were the official brass buttons of the Police Department of the City of Philadelphia.

"Thank Evans for that," Martha said. "You have no idea how much trouble he had getting his hands on those."

"Where did the coat come from?"

"Tiller and Whyde, I think," Martha said.

"That's right, Miss Martha," Evans confirmed.

"What the hell is that?"

"Daddy's tailor—one of them—in London," Martha said. "Precious, you look wonderful in it!"

"This is your father's?" he asked. The notion made him slightly uncomfortable, quite aside from considerations of Martha getting him clothes.

"No, it's yours. *Now* it's yours."

"I suggested to Miss Martha, Captain," Evans said, "that you and Mr. Alex were just about the same size, and all his clothes were here, just waiting to feed the moths."

"So we checked, and Evans was right, and all we had to do was take the trousers in a half inch, and an inch off the jacket sleeves, and of course find your policeman's buttons. Evans knows this marvelous Italian tailor on Chestnut Street, so all you have to do is say 'Thank you, Evans.' "

"*All* of those clothes?" Pekach said, pointing to the wardrobe.

"Mr. Alex always dressed very well," Evans said.

Captain David Pekach came very close to saying *Oh, shit, I don't want your father's goddamn clothes.*

But he didn't. He saw a look of genuine pleasure at having done something nice on Evans's face, and then he looked at Martha and saw how happy her eyes were.

"Thank you, Evans," Captain Pekach said.

"My pleasure, Captain. I'm just glad the sizes worked out; that you were just a little smaller than Mr. Alex, rather than the other way around."

"It worked out fine, thank you, Evans."

Evans smiled and left the room.

"I don't know what I'm going to do with you," Pekach said to Martha.

She met his eyes and smiled. "Oh, you'll think of something."

Martha walked to where Evans had left the beer, poured some skillfully in the glass, and handed it to Pekach.

"I love it when I can do something nice for you, my Precious," she said.

He kissed her gently, tasting her lipstick.

"I better take a shower," he said.

She came into the bathroom, as she often did, and watched him shave. She had told him she liked to do that, to feel his cheeks when he had just finished shaving.

When they went downstairs, Evans had brought her Mercedes coupe around to the portico from the garage, and was holding the door open for her. Pekach got behind the wheel and glanced at her to make sure she had her seat belt fastened. There was a flash of thigh and of the lace at the hem of her black slip.

For a woman who didn't know the first fucking thing about sex, he thought for perhaps the fiftieth time, *she really knows how to pick underwear that turns me on.*

He put the Mercedes in gear, drove down the drive to Glengarry Lane, and idly decided that the best route downtown would be the Schuylkill Expressway.

Just north of the Zoological Gardens, Martha asked if they had caught whoever had shot the policeman.

"No. And we don't have a clue," Pekach said. "Just before I came . . . to your place"—he'd almost said "home"—"we had a meeting, and Tony Harris, who's running the job, and is a damn good cop, said all he knows to do is go back over what he already has."

"You almost said 'home,' " Martha said, "didn't you?"

He looked at her and was surprised to find they were holding hands.

"Slip of the tongue," he said.

"Nice slip, I like it."

"You too."

"I beg your pardon?"

"I like your slip," he said.

"Oh," she said. "Thank you."

She raised his hand to her mouth and kissed it.

There was the howl of a siren. He looked in the rearview mirror and saw a Highway car behind him and dropped his eyes to the large round speedometer of the Mercedes. The indicator was pointing just beyond seventy.

"Shit," he said, freed his hand, and moved into the right lane.

The Highway car pulled up beside him. The police officer in the passenger seat gestured imperiously for him to pull to the curb, the gesture turning into a friendly wave as Officer Jesus Martinez, a stricken look on his face, recognized the commanding officer of the Highway Patrol. The Highway car suddenly slowed and fell behind.

"I hate that," Pekach said. "Getting caught by my own men."

"Then you shouldn't speed, Precious." Martha laughed. "You should see your face!"

"It's this damn car," Pekach said. "They don't know it. If we were in my car, that wouldn't have happened."

"Then you should drive this car more, so they get to know it."

"I couldn't drive your car to work," he said.

"Why not?"

"Because it's yours."

"Let me give it to you, then."

"Martha, Goddammit, stop!"

"We've been over this before," she said. "It makes me happy to give you things."

"It's not right," he said.

"I love you and I can easily afford it, so what's wrong with it?"

"It's not right," he repeated.

"Sorry," Martha said.

"Honey, you always giving me things . . ." He searched for the words. "It makes me feel less than a man."

"That's absurd," she said. "Look at yourself! As young as you are, being a captain. Commanding Officer of Highway. You're worried about being a man?"

He didn't reply.

"And that's not the only manly thing you do very well," Martha said. She leaned over and put her tongue in his ear and groped him.

"Jesus, honey!"

"You must be getting tired of me," Martha teased. "I remember when you used to like that."

"I'm not tired of you, baby," he said. "I could never get tired of you."

"So then let me give you the car."

"Will you ever quit?"

"Probably not," she said, and caught his hand and held it against her cheek. Then she asked, "Where are we going? Not that it matters."

"Ristorante Alfredo," he said, trying to pronounce it in Italian.

"I hear that's very nice."

"Peter Wohl says it is," Pekach said. "I asked him for a

good place to go, and he said Ristorante Alfredo is very nice.''

''You like him, don't you?''

''He's a good boss. He doesn't *act* much like a cop, but from his reputation and from what I've seen, he's a hell of a cop.''

What Peter Wohl had said specifically were that there were two nice things about Ristorante Alfredo. First, that the food and atmosphere were first-class; and second, that the management had the charming habit of picking up the tab.

''The Mob owns it, I guess you know,'' Wohl had said. ''They get some sort of perverse pleasure out of buying captains and up their meals. You're a captain now, Dave. Enjoy. Rank hath its privileges. I try to make them happy at least once a month.''

Dave Pekach had made reservations for dinner at Ristorante Alfredo because of what Wohl had said about the food and atmosphere. He wasn't sure that Wohl wasn't pulling his leg about having the check grabbed. If that happened, fine, but he wasn't counting on it. He even sort of hoped they wouldn't. It was important somehow that he take Martha someplace that she would enjoy, preferably expensive.

There was a young Italian guy (a *real* Italian, to judge by the way he mangled the language) in a tuxedo behind a sort of stand-up desk in the lobby of Ristorante Alfredo. When Pekach said his name was Pekach and that he had made reservations, the guy almost pissed his pants unlatching a velvet rope and bowing them past it to a table in a far corner of the room.

Dave saw other diners in the elegantly furnished room looking at Martha in her black dress and pearls, and the way she walked, and he was proud of her.

The Italian guy in the tuxedo held Martha's chair for her and said he hoped the table was satisfactory, and then he snapped his fingers and two other guys appeared, a busboy and a guy in a short red jacket with what looked like a silver spoon on a gold chain around his neck. The busboy had a bottle wrapped in a towel in a silver bucket on legs.

The guy with the spoon around his neck unwrapped the towel so that Dave could see that what he had was a bottle of French champagne.

"Compliments of the house, Captain Pekach," the Italian guy said. "I hope is satisfactory."

"Oh, Moet is always satisfactory," Martha said, smiling.

"You permit?" the Italian guy said, and unwrapped the wire, popped the cork, and poured about a quarter of an inch in Pekach's glass.

I'm supposed to sip that, to make sure it's not sour or something, Dave remembered, and did so.

"Very nice," he said.

"I am so happy," the Italian guy said, and poured Martha and then Pekach each a glassful.

"I leave you to enjoy wine," the Italian guy said. "In time I will recommend."

"To us," Martha said, raising her glass.

"Yeah," Dave Pekach said.

A waiter appeared a minute or so later and delivered menus.

And a minute or so after that the Italian guy came back.

"Captain Pekach, you will excuse. Mr. Baltazari would be so happy to have a minute of your time," he said, and gestured across the room to the far corner where two men sat at a corner table. When they saw him looking, they both gave a little wave.

Dave Pekach decided the younger one, a swarthy-skinned man with hair elaborately combed forward to conceal male pattern baldness, must be Baltazari, whom he had never heard of. The other man, older, in a gray suit, he knew by sight. On a cork bulletin board in the Intelligence Division, his photograph was pinned to the top of the Organized Crime organizational chart. The Philadelphia *Daily News* ritually referred to him as "Mob Boss Vincenzo Savarese."

Jesus Christ, what's all this? What's he want to do, say hello?

The Italian guy was already tugging at Dave Pekach's chair.

"Excuse me, honey?"

"Of course," Martha said.

Dave walked across the room.

"Good evening, Captain Pekach," Baltazari said. "Welcome to Ristorante Alfredo. Please sit down."

He waved his hand and a waiter appeared. He turned over

a champagne glass and poured and then disappeared. Then Baltazari got up and disappeared.

"I won't take you long from the company of that charming lady," Vincenzo Savarese said. "But when I heard you were in the restaurant, I didn't want to miss the opportunity to thank you."

"Excuse me?"

"You were exceedingly understanding and gracious to my granddaughter, Captain, and I wanted you to know how grateful I am."

"I don't know what you're talking about," Dave Pekach said honestly.

"Last June—defying, I have to say, the orders of her parents—my granddaughter went out with a very foolish young man and found herself in the hands of the police."

Pekach shook his head, signifying that he was still in the dark as he searched his memory.

"It was very late at night in North Philadelphia, where Old York Road cuts into North Broad?"

Pekach continued to shake his head no.

"There was a chase by the police. The boy wrecked the car?" Savarese continued.

Dave suddenly remembered. He had been on the way home from his Cousin Stanley's wedding in Bethlehem. He had passed the scene of a wreck and had seen a Narcotics team and their car and, curious, stopped. What it was, was a minor incident, a carful of kids who had bought some marijuana, been caught at it, and had run.

There had been four kids, the driver and another boy, and two girls, both of them clean-cut, nice-looking, both scared out of their minds, in the back of a district RPC, which was about to transport them to Central Lockup. He had felt sorry for the girls and didn't want to subject them to the horrors of going through Central Lockup. So, after making sure the district cops had their names, he had turned them loose, sending them home in a cab.

"I remember," he said.

"My granddaughter said that you were gracious and understanding," Savarese said. "Far more, I suspect, than were her mother and father. I don't think she will be doing anything like that ever again."

"She seemed to be a very nice young woman," Pekach said. "We all stub our toes from time to time."

"I simply wanted to say that I will never forget your kindness and am very grateful," Savarese said, and then stood up and put out his hand. "If there is ever anything I can do for you, Captain . . ."

"Forget it. I was just doing my job."

Savarese smiled at him and walked across the restaurant to the door. The Italian in the tuxedo stood there waiting for him, holding his hat and coat.

Pekach shrugged and started back toward Martha.

Baltazari intercepted him.

"I think you dropped these, Captain," he said, and handed Pekach a book of matches.

"No, I don't think so," Pekach said.

"I'm sure you did," Baltazari said.

Pekach examined the matchbook. It was a Ristorante Alfredo matchbook. It was open, and a name and address was written inside it. The name didn't ring a bell.

"Mr. Savarese's friends are always grateful when someone does him, or his family, a courtesy, Captain Pekach," Baltazari said. "Now go and enjoy your meal."

Pekach put the matches in his pocket.

The young Italian was at his table.

"If I may suggest—"

"What was that all about?"

Dave shrugged. He smiled at her. "You may suggest," he said to the young Italian.

Martha's knee found Dave's under the table.

"I think you like our Tournedos Alfredo very much," the young Italian said.

"I love tournedos," Martha said.

Dave Pekach had no idea what a tournedo was.

"Sounds fine," he said.

Martha's knee pressed a little harder against his.

"And before, some clams with Sauce Venezia?"

"Fine," Dave said.

FOURTEEN

Certain enforcement and investigation jobs in Narcotics, Vice, and elsewhere require the use, in plainclothes, of young policemen who don't look like policemen, or even act like policemen, and whose faces are unknown to the criminals they are after. The only source of such personnel is the pool of young police officers fresh out of the Police Academy.

There are certain drawbacks to the assignment of such young and, by definition, inexperienced officers to undercover jobs. While they are working undercover, they require as much supervision as they can be given, because of their inexperience. But the very nature of undercover work makes close supervision difficult at best, and often impossible. Most of the time an undercover cop is on his own, literally responsible for his own fate.

Some young undercover cops can't handle the stress and ask to be relieved. Some are relieved because of their inability to do what is asked of them, either because of a psychological inability to act as anything but what they are—nice young men—or, along the same line, their inability to learn to think like the criminals they are after.

But some rookies fresh from the Academy take to under-cover work like ducks to water. The work is sometimes what they dreamed it would be like—conditioned by cops-and-robbers movies and television series—when they got to be cops: putting the collar on really bad guys, often accompanied by some sort of sanctioned violence, knocking down doors, or apprehending the suspect by running the son of a bitch down and slamming his scumbag ass against a wall.

There are rarely—although this is changing—either the gun battles or high-speed chases of movies and television, but there *is* danger and the excitement that comes with that, plus a genuine feeling of accomplishment when the assistant district attorney reviews their investigation and their arrest and decides it is worth the taxpayers' money and his time to bring the accused before the bar of justice, and, with a little luck, see the scumbag son of a bitch sent away for, say, twenty to life.

Officers Charles McFadden and Jesus Martinez had been good, perhaps even very good, undercover police officers working in the area of narcotics. Officer McFadden, very soon after he went to work, learned that he had a rather uncanny ability to get purveyors of controlled substances to trust him. Officer Martinez, who shared with Officer McFadden a set of values imparted by loving parents and the teachings of the Roman Catholic church, took great pride in his work.

He had a Latin temperament, which had at first caused him to grow excited or angry—or both—during an arrest. He had noticed early on that when he was excited or angry or both, more often than not the scumbags they had against the wall somewhere seemed far more afraid of him than they did of Officer McFadden, although Charley was six inches taller and outweighed him by nearly ninety pounds.

As Charley had honed the skills that caused the bad guys to trust him and help dig their own graves, Hay-zus worked on what he thought of as his practice of psychological warfare against the criminal element. During the last nine months or year of his undercover Narcotics assignment, he was seldom nearly as excited or angry as those he was arresting thought he was. And he had picked up certain little theatrical embellishments, for example, sticking the barrel of his revolver up an arrestee's nose or excitedly encouraging Charley, knowing that he was incapable of such a thing, to "Shoot the cocksucker, Charley. We can plant a gun on him."

Either or both techniques, and some others that he had learned, often produced a degree of cooperation from those arrested that was often very helpful in securing convictions and in implicating others involved in criminal activities.

Both Martinez and McFadden knew they had been good, perhaps even very good, undercover cops, and they both knew they had not been relieved of their undercover Narcotics assignments because of anything *wrong* they had done, but quite the reverse: They had bagged the junkie scumbag who had shot Captain Dutch Moffitt of Highway. That had gotten their pictures in the newspapers and destroyed their effectiveness on the street.

They would have happily forgone their celebrity if they had been allowed to keep working undercover Narcotics, but that, of course, was impossible.

A grateful Police Department hierarchy had sent them to Highway Patrol, where they were offered, presuming satisfactory probationary performance, appointment as *real* Highway Patrolmen much earlier on in their police careers than they could have normally expected.

Big fucking deal!

Maybe that shit about getting to wear boots and a Sam Browne belt and a cap with the top crushed down would appeal to some asshole who had spent four years in a district, keeping the neighborhood kids from getting run over on the way home from school, and turning off fire hydrants in the summer, and getting fucking cats out of fucking trees, and that kind of shit, but it did not seem so to either Hay-zus or Charley.

They had gone one-on-one (or two-on-two) with some really nasty critters in some very difficult situations, had come out on top, and thought themselves, not entirely without justification, to be just as experienced, just as good *real* cops, as anybody they'd met in Highway.

They were smart enough, of course, to smile and sound grateful for the opportunity they had been offered. While Highway wasn't undercover Narcotics, neither was it a district, where they would have spent their time breaking up major hubcap-theft rings, settling domestic arguments, and watching the weeds grow.

There was soon going be another examination for detective, and they were both determined to pass it. Once they were detectives, they had agreed, they could apply for—and more important probably get, because they had caught Gerald Vincent Gallagher, Esquire—something interesting, Major Crimes, maybe, but if not Major Crimes, then maybe Intelligence or even Homicide.

In the meantime they understood that the smart thing for them to do was keep smiling, keep their noses clean, keep studying for the detective exam, do what they were told to do, and act like they liked it.

As their first tour enforcing the Motor Vehicle Code on the Schuykill Expressway very slowly passed, however, they found this harder and harder to do.

Only two interesting things had happened since they began their patrol. First, of course, was making asses of themselves by turning the lights and the siren on and then pulling alongside Captain Pekach and that rich broad from Chestnut Hill he was fucking and signaling him to pull over.

Captain Pekach probably wouldn't say anything. He was a good guy, and before he made captain they had worked for him when he was a lieutenant in Narcotics, but that sure hadn't made them look smart.

And an hour after that a northbound Buick had clipped a Ford Pinto in the ass, spinning him around and over into the southbound lane, where he got hit by a Dodge station wagon, which spun him back into his original lane. Nobody got hurt bad, but there wasn't much left of the Pinto, and the Buick had a smashed-in grille from hitting the Pinto and a smashed-in quarter-panel where the Pinto had been knocked back into it by the Dodge. The insurance companies were going to have a hard time sorting out who had done what to whom on that one. It had been forty-five minutes before they'd gotten that straightened out, before the ambulance had carried the guy in the Pinto and his girlfriend off to the hospital and the wreckers had hauled the wrecked cars off.

Sergeant William "Big Bill" Henderson had shown up at the crash site about five minutes after they'd called it in, even before the ambulance got there. He clearly got his rocks off working accidents.

First he called for another Highway car, and then he took over from Charley McFadden, who by then had a bandage on the forehead of the guy in the Pinto where he'd whacked his head on the door and had him and his girlfriend calmed down and sitting in the back of the RPC.

He sent Charley down the expressway to help Hay-zus direct traffic around the wreck. And then once the other Highway car and then the ambulance and the wreckers showed up, he really started to supervise. He told the ambulance guys to put the guy in the Pinto in the ambulance, which wasn't really all that hard to figure out, since he was the only one bleeding. Then he told the wrecker guys how to haul away the Pinto and the Buick. He even got his whistle out and directed traffic while that was going on.

Sergeant Henderson, in other words, confirmed the opinion (asshole, blowhard) Officers McFadden and Martinez had formed of him when he delivered his little pep talk at Bustleton and Bowler before sending them on patrol.

Neither Charley nor Hay-zus had liked standing in the middle of the expressway, directing traffic. They had especially disliked it after the southbound lane had been cleared, and four hundred and twenty assholes had passed them going fifty miles an hour two feet away while gawking at the crumpled Pinto and the other cars.

It had to be done, of course; otherwise the assholes would have tried to drive right over the Dodge before they got that out of the way. Both privately wondered if the Highway guys got used to having two tons of automobile whiz past them—*whoosh, whoosh, whoosh, whoosh*—two feet away at fifty miles an hour, or if they were scared by it.

But directing traffic did temper their enthusiasm to enforce rigidly the Motor Vehicle Code insofar as it applied to permitted vehicular speeds. There were several things wrong with stopping a guy who was going five or ten miles over the posted speed limit but doing nothing else wrong.

First, there was something not quite right about handing a guy a ticket for doing something you knew you had done yourself. Then there was the fine; and there were a lot of points against your record in Harrisburg for a moving violation and so many points and you lost your license. And finally, the goddamn insurance companies found out you had a speeding ticket and they raised your premiums.

If a guy was going maybe seventy where the limit was fifty-five, or he was weaving in and out of traffic or tailgating some guy so close that he couldn't stop, that was something else: Ticket the son of a bitch and get him off the road before he hurt somebody.

That made the other things wrong with handing out tickets worthwhile. You never knew, when you pulled some guy to the side of the road to write him a ticket, what you were going to find. Ninety times out of a hundred it would be some guy who would be extra polite, admit he was going a little over the limit, and maybe mention he had a cousin who was an associate member of the FOP and hope you would just warn him.

Four times out of a hundred it would be some asshole who denied doing what you had caught him doing; said he was a personal friend of the mayor (and maybe was); or that kind of crap. And maybe one time in a hundred, one time in two hundred, when you pulled a car to the side and walked up to it, it was stolen, and the driver tried to back over you; or the driver was drunk and belligerent and would hit you with a tire iron when you leaned over and asked to see his license and registration. Or the driver was carrying something he shouldn't be carrying, something that would send him away for a long time, unless he could either bribe, or shoot, the cop who had stopped him.

And one hundred times out of one hundred, when you pulled a guy over on the Schuylkill Expressway, when you bent over and asked him for his license and registration, two-ton automobiles went fifty-five miles per hour two feet off your ass—*whoosh, whoosh, whoosh, whoosh*.

At five minutes past nine, heading north on the Schuylkill Expressway, Officers McFadden and Martinez spotted a motorist in distress, pulled to the side of the southbound lane.

"The time of day, prevailing weather conditions, the traffic flow, and other considerations will determine how much assistance you may render to a motorist in distress," Sergeant Big Bill Henderson had lectured them, "your primary consideration to be the removal or reduction of a hazard to the public, and secondly to maintain an unimpaired flow of traffic."

"In other words, Sergeant," McFadden had replied, "we don't have to change a tire for some guy unless it looks as if he's going to get his ass run over changing it himself?"

Officer Charles McFadden had a pleasant, youthfully innocent face, which caused Sergeant Henderson to decide, after glowering at him for a moment, that he wasn't being a wiseass.

"Yeah, that's about it," Sergeant Henderson said.

Officer Martinez, who was then driving, slowed so as to give them a better look at the motorist in distress. It was a two-year-old Cadillac Sedan de Ville. Apparently it had suffered a flat tire.

The motorist in distress was in the act of tightening the wheel bolts when he saw the Highway Patrol car. He stood up, quickly threw the other tire and wheel in the trunk, and finally the hubcap.

"Marvin just fixed his flat in time," Officer McFadden said. "Otherwise we would have had to help the son of a bitch."

Marvin P. Lanier, a short, stocky, thirty-five-year-old black male, was known to Officers Martinez and McFadden from their assignment to Narcotics. He made his living as a professional gambler. He wasn't very good at that, however, and was often forced to augment his professional gambler's income, or lack of it, in other ways. He worked as a model's agent sometimes, arranging to provide lonely businessmen with the company of a model in their hotel rooms.

And sometimes, when business was really bad, he went into the messenger business, driving to New York or Washington, D.C., to pick up small packages for business acquaintances of his in Philadelphia.

Narcotics had been turned on to Marvin P. Lanier by Vice, which said they had reason to believe Marvin was running coke from New York to North Philly.

Officers McFadden and Martinez had placed the suspect under surveillance and determined the rough schedule and route of his messenger service. At four o'clock one Tuesday morning, sixty seconds after he came off the Tacony-Palmyra Bridge, which is not on the most direct route from New York

City to North Philadelphia, they stopped his car and searched it and found one plastic-wrapped package of a white substance they believed to be cocaine, weighing approximately two pounds and known in the trade as a Key (from kilogram).

The search and seizure, conducted as it was without a warrant—which they couldn't get because they didn't have enough to convince a judge that there was "reasonable cause to suspect" Mr. Lanier of any wrongdoing—was, of course, illegal. Any evidence so seized would not be admissible in a court of law. Both Officers Martinez and McFadden and Mr. Lanier knew this.

On the other hand, if the excited and angry Hispanic Narcotics officer who had jammed the barrel of his revolver up Mr. Lanier's nostril and called him a "slimy nigger cocksucker" went through with his suggestion to "just pour that fucking shit down the sewer," Mr. Lanier knew that he would be in great difficulty with the business associates who had engaged him to run a little errand for them.

If he had been arrested, the cocaine, illegally seized or not, would be forfeited. It would be regarded as a routine cost of doing business. But if the fucking spick slit it open and poured it down the sewer, his business associates were very likely to believe that he had diverted at least twenty thousand dollars worth of their property to his own purposes, and that the Narcs putting it down the sewer was a bullshit story. Who would throw twenty big ones worth of coke down a sewer? That was as much as a fucking cop made in a fucking year!

A deal was struck. Mr. Lanier was permitted to go on his way with the Key, it being understood that within the next two weeks Mr. Lanier would come up with information that would lead Officers Martinez and McFadden to at least twice that much coke, and those in possession of it.

Mr. Lanier thought of himself as an honorable man and lived up to his end of the bargain. Officers Martinez and McFadden rationalized the somewhat questionable legality of turning Mr. Lanier and the Key of coke lose because it ultimately resulted in both the confiscation of three Keys and the arrest and conviction of three dopers who they otherwise wouldn't have known about. Plus, of course, they had scared the shit out of Marvin P. Lanier. It would be some time before he worked up the balls to go back into the messenger business.

They had not, in the three months after their encounter with Mr. Lanier, before they had been transferred from Narcotics, unduly pressed him for additional information. They viewed him as a long-term asset, and asking too much of him would have been like killing the goose who laid the golden egg. It would not have been to their advantage if Mr. Lanier had become suspected by those in the drug trade and removed from circulation.

"Do you think he spotted us?" Hay-zus asked. By then he had brought the RPC almost to a halt, and was looking for a spot in the flow of southbound traffic into which he could make a U-turn.

"He spotted the Highway car," McFadden replied. "But he was so busy shagging ass out of there, I don't think he saw it was you and me."

Hay-zus found a spot and, tires screaming, moved into it.

"Why do you think Marvin was so nervous?" Charley asked excitedly. "Shit, stop!"

"What for?" Hay-zus asked, slowing, although he was afraid he would lose Marvin in traffic.

"Marvin forgot his jack," Charley said. "Somebody's liable to run into it. And besides, I think we should give it back to him."

Hay-zus saw the large Cadillac jack where Marvin had left it. He turned on the flashing lights and, checking the rearview mirror first, slammed on the brakes.

Charley was out of the car and back in it, clutching the jack, in ten seconds.

"Marvin will probably be very grateful to get his jack back," he said as Hay-zus wound up the RPC. "And besides, if Big Bill wants to know how come we left the expressway, we can tell him we were trying to return a citizen's property to him."

"We got no probable cause," Hay-zus said.

"All we're going to ask him is what he heard about Officer Magnella. And/or that guinea gangster, what's his name?"

"DeZego," Hay-zus furnished.

"I guess he spotted us," Charley McFadden said. The proof of that was that Marvin's Cadillac was in the left lane, traveling at no more than forty-six miles per hour in a fifty-mile-per-hour zone.''

"What do we do?" Hay-zus asked.

"Get right on his ass and stay there. Let the cocksucker sweat a little. We can stop him when he gets off the expressway.''

Mr. Lanier left the Schuylkill Expressway via the Zoological Gardens exit ramp.

"Pull him over now?"

"Let's see where he's going," Charley said. "If he's dirty, he'll try to lose us. If he's not, he'll probably go home. He lives on 48th near Haverford, and he's headed that way.''

"Why follow the fucker home?"

"So we can let his neighbors see how friendly he is with the Highway Patrol," Charley said. "That ought to raise his standing in the community.''

"You can be a real prick sometimes, Charley," Hay-zus said admiringly.

Scrupulously obeying all traffic regulations, and driving with all the care of a school-bus driver, Mr. Lanier drove to his residence just off Haverford Avenue on North 48th Street. As the RPC turned onto 48th, Charley bumped the siren and turned the flashing lights on.

Mr. Lanier got out of his car and smiled uneasily at the RPC, which pulled in behind him.

"He didn't run," Hay-zus said.

"He's nervous," Charley said as he retrieved the jack and opened the door. "Hello there, Marvin," he called cheerfully and loudly. "You forgot your jack, Marvin.''

Marvin P. Lanier looked at McFadden and Martinez, finally recognizing them, and then suspiciously at the jack.

Charley thrust it into his hands.

"I guess I did," Marvin said. "Thanks a lot.''

No one moved for a full sixty seconds, although Mr. Lanier did glance nervously several times at the spick Narc who had once shoved the barrel of his revolver up his nostril.

"How come you guys are in uniform?" Mr. Lanier finally asked.

"What's that to you, shitface?" Officer Martinez said with a snarl.

"Aren't you going to put your jack in the trunk, Marvin?" Officer McFadden asked, ignoring him.

Mr. Lanier put his hand on the rear door of his Cadillac.

"I'm running a little late," he said. "I think I'll just put it in the backseat for now."

"You don't want to do that, Marvin," Officer McFadden said. "You'd get grease and shit all over the carpet. Why don't you put it in the trunk?"

"I don't think I want to do that," Mr. Lanier said.

"Who gives a flying fuck what you want, asshole?" Officer Martinez inquired.

"Why are you guys on my ass?" Mr. Lanier inquired.

"You know fucking well why!" Officer Martinez, now visibly angry, flared. "Now open the fucking trunk!"

Mr. Lanier opened the trunk of his vehicle, Officers Martinez and McFadden standing on either side of him as he did so.

"Well, what have we here?" Officer McFadden asked, leaning over and picking up a Remington Model 870 12-gauge pump-action shotgun with a short barrel.

"Marvin must be a deer hunter," Officer Martinez said. "You a deer hunter, Marvin?" he asked.

"Yeah," Mr. Lanier said without much conviction.

"You got a license for this, of course?" Officer McFadden asked, although he was fully aware that not only was such a license not required; there was no such thing as a license to possess a shotgun, as there was for possession of a pistol. Neither did it violate any laws for a citizen like Mr. Lanier, who had not been convicted of a felony and was not, at the moment, under indictment or a fugitive from justice to transport such a weapon unloaded and not immediately available, such as in a locked trunk.

"No," Mr. Lanier said resignedly, confirming Officer McFadden's suspicion that Mr. Lanier was not fully conversant with the applicable law.

"Goddamn, Marvin, what are we going to do with you?" Officer McFadden asked almost sadly.

"What're you doing with the shotgun, Marvin?" Officer Martinez snarled again.

"I just had it, you know?"

"You been picking up coke in Harlem again, Marvin?"

Officer McFadden asked sadly, as if he were very disappointed. "And the shotgun was a little protection?"

"Maybe," Officer Martinez said, getting a little excited, "if we wasn't right on your ass all the time so you couldn't get to that shotgun, you would have used it on us? Is that what you were doing with that fucking shotgun, you slimy nigger asshole?"

"No!" Mr. Lanier stated emphatically.

"You used that shotgun on Tony the Zee DeZego, didn't you, Marvin?" Officer McFadden suddenly accused.

"No!" Mr. Lanier proclaimed. "Honest to God! Some other guinea shot that motherfucker!"

"Bullshit!" Officer Martinez said, spinning Mr. Lanier around, pushing him against his Cadillac, kicking his feet apart and patting him down.

"I was in Baltimore with my sister when that happened," Mr. Lanier said. "I drove my mother down. My sister had another kid."

Officer Martinez held up a small plastic bag full of red-and-yellow capsules.

"Look what Marvin had in his pocket," he said.

"You got a prescription for these, Marvin?" Officer McFadden asked. "I'd hate to think you were using these without a prescription."

"You're not going to bust me for a couple of lousy uppers," Mr. Lanier said without much conviction.

"We're going to arrest you for the murder of Tony the Zee," McFadden said. "You have the right to remain silent—"

"I told you, I didn't have nothing to do with that. Some *guinea* shot him!"

"Which guinea?" Officer McFadden asked.

"I don't know his name," Mr. Lanier said.

Officers McFadden and Martinez exchanged glances.

They had worked together long enough that their minds ran in similar channels. Both had independently decided that Marvin had probably not shot Tony the Zee. There was no connection, and if there had been, the detectives or somebody would have picked up on it by now. It was possible, however, that Marvin had heard something in his social circles, concerning who had blown away Tony the Zee, that had not yet come to the attention of the detectives.

They knew they had nothing on Mr. Lanier. He had broken no law by having an unloaded shotgun in his trunk. The search of his person that had come up with the bag of uppers had been illegal.

"Maybe he's telling the truth," Officer McFadden said.

"This shit wouldn't know the truth if it hit him in the ass," Officer Martinez replied. "Let's take the son of a bitch down to the Roundhouse and let Homicide work him over."

"I swear to Christ, I was in Baltimore with my mother when that motherfucker got himself shot!"

"Who told you some guinea did it?" McFadden asked.

"I don't remember," Mr. Lanier said.

"Yeah, you don't remember because you just made that up!" Officer Martinez said.

There followed a full sixty seconds of silence.

"Marvin, if we turn you loose on the shotgun and the uppers, do you think you could remember who told you a guinea shot Tony the Zee?" Officer McFadden finally asked. "Or get me the name of the guinea he said shot him?"

"You are not going to turn this cocksucker loose?" Officer Martinez asked incredulously.

"He ain't lied to us so far," Officer McFadden replied.

"That's right," Mr. Lanier said righteously. "I been straight with you guys."

"I think we ought to give Marvin the benefit of the doubt," Officer McFadden said.

Officer Martinez snorted.

"But if we do, what about the shotgun and the uppers?" McFadden asked.

"What uppers?" Mr. Lanier said. "What shotgun?"

"What are you saying, Marvin?" Officer McFadden asked.

"Suppose the uppers just went down the sewer?" Mr. Lanier asked.

"And the shotgun? What are we supposed to do with the shotgun?"

"You mean that shotgun we just found laying in the gutter? That shotgun? I never saw it before. I guess you would do what you ordinarily do when you find a shotgun someplace. Turn it in to lost and found or whatever."

"What do you think, Hay-zus?" Officer McFadden asked.

"I think we ought to run the son of a bitch in, is what I think," Officer Martinez said, and then added, "But I owe you one, Charley. If you want to trust the son of a bitch, I'll go along."

Officer McFadden hesitated a moment and then said, "Okay, Marvin. You got it. You paid your phone bill? Still got the same number?"

"Yes."

"Be home at four tomorrow afternoon. Have something to tell me when I call you."

"I'll try."

"You better do more than try, you cocksucker. You better have something!" Officer Martinez said.

He picked up the shotgun and walked to the RPC and put it under the front seat.

"Marvin, I'm trusting you," McFadden said seriously. "Don't let me down."

Then he walked to the RPC and got in.

"We didn't ask him about Magnella," Hay-zus said as he turned right on Haverford Avenue and headed back toward the Schuykill Expressway.

"I think he was telling the truth," Charley said. "About what he heard, I mean, about some guinea popping Tony the Zee. I wanted to stay with that."

"I think his sister had a baby too," Hay-zus said. "But we should have asked him about Magnella, anyway."

"So we didn't," Charley said. "So what do we do with what we got?"

"You mean the shotgun?"

"I mean, who do we tell what he said about who shot DeZego?"

"Shit, I didn't even think about that. Big Bill will have a shit fit and have our ass if we tell him what we done."

Sergeant Big Bill Henderson, in his little pep talk, had made it clear that, except in cases of hot pursuit, or in responding to an officer-needs-assistance call, they were not to leave their assigned patrol route; in other words, since they were not *real* Highway Patrolmen, they could not, as *real* Highway cops could, respond to any call that sounded interesting, or head for any area of their choosing where things might be interesting.

"Well, we can't just sit on it," Charley said.

"Captain Pekach," Hay-zus said thoughtfully after a moment.

"He's not on duty and he's not at home. We saw him and the rich lady, remember?"

"In the morning," Hay-zus said. "We'll ask to see him first thing in the morning."

"He's liable to be pissed. You think about that?"

"Well, you said it, we can't just sit on what Marvin told us."

"Maybe we could just tell Washington."

"And he tells somebody what we told him, like Big Bill, or even the inspector? It's gotta be Captain Pekach."

Charley's silence meant agreement.

A moment later Charley asked, "What about the shotgun?"

"We run it through the NCIC computer to see if it's hot."

"And if it is?"

"Then we turn it in."

"And burn Marvin? Which means we have to explain how we got it."

"Maybe it ain't hot."

"Then what?"

"Then I'll flip you for it," Hay-zus said. "I always wanted a shotgun like that."

FIFTEEN

Amanda Spencer was a little drunk. Matt Payne's usual re-action to drunken—even half-drunk—women was that they had all the appeal of a run-over dog, but again, Amanda was proving herself to be the exception to the rule. He thought she was sort of cute. Her eyes were bright, and she was very intent.

And, Jesus Christ, she was beautiful!

She was still wearing the off-the-shoulder blue gown she and Daffy's other bridesmaids had worn at Saint Mark's. He found the curvature of the exposed portion of her upper bosom absolutely fascinating. During the ceremony his mind had wandered from what the bishop of Philadelphia was saying about the institution of marriage to recalling in some detail the other absolutely fascinating aspects of Amanda's anat-omy, in particular the delightful formation of her tail.

The ceremony had gone off without a hitch. Although Chad Nesbitt had been as tight as a tick, his condition hadn't been all that apparent, and except for one burp and one incident of flatulence that had caused some smiles and a titter or two, the exchange of vows had been appropriately solemn and even rather touching: Matt had happened to glance at Daffy while the bishop was asking her if she was willing to forsake all others until death did them part, and she actually had tears in her eyes as she looked at Chad.

Outside Saint Mark's afterward, however, his plans to kiss Amanda tenderly and as quickly as possible were sent awry by Lieutenant Foster H. Lewis, Sr., of the 9th District, who had been outside the church, seen Matt, and beckoned him over.

"Excuse me, please, Amanda," he said, and touched her arm, and she had smiled at him, and he'd walked over to Lieutenant Lewis.

"Yes, sir?"

"Are you on duty, Payne?"

"No, sir."

Lieutenant Lewis had examined him for a moment, nodded his head, and walked away.

By then Amanda had been shepherded into one of the limousines and driven off to the Browne estate in Merion. He had known that it was highly unlikely that Amanda would have gone back to his apartment with him before they went to the house for the reception, but it had not been entirely beyond the realm of possibility.

Matt had to drive out to the Brownes' place by himself.

But once there he had found her right away, by one of the bars, with a champagne glass in her hand that she, with what he thought was entirely delightful intimacy, had held up to his lips.

Chad had searched him out, by then more visibly pissed, and extracted a solemn vow that if something happened to him in the service, Matt would look after Daffy.

There had been an enormous wedding cake. Chad had used his Marine officer's sword to cut it. From the way he withdrew it from the scabbard and nearly stabbed his new bride in the belly with it, Matt suspected that it was no more than the third time the sword had been out of its scabbard.

An hour after that the bride and groom, through a hail of rice and bird seed, had gotten in a limousine and driven off.

And now, an hour after that, he and Amanda were dancing.

The vertical manifestation of a horizontal desire, he thought, delightfully aware of the pressure of Amanda's bosom against his abdomen, the brushing of his thighs against hers.

"I watched you during the wedding," Amanda said against his chest.

He pulled back and looked down at her and smiled.

"I saw your gun," she said.

"How could you do that?" he asked, surprised. "It's in an ankle holster."

"Figuratively speaking," she said, pronouncing the words very carefully.

"Oh," he said with a chuckle.

"Shipboard romance," she said.

"I beg your pardon?"

"You know about shipboard romances, presumably?" Amanda asked.

"No," he said.

"People fall in love on a ship very quickly," she said.

"Okay," he said.

"Because they are in a strange environment and there is an element of danger," Amanda said.

"You have made a study of this, I gather?"

"The romance fades when the ship docks," Amanda said, "and people see things as they really are."

"So we won't get on a ship," Matt said. "A small sailboat, maybe. But no ship. Or if we do, we'll just never make port. Like the *Flying Dutchman*."

"They grow up, so to speak," Amanda went on. "See things for what they really are."

"You said that," he said.

"*Or,*" she said significantly, "one of them does."

"Meaning what?" There was something in what was going on that made him uncomfortable.

"When are you going to stop playing policeman and get on with your life is what I'm wondering," she said, putting her face against his shirt again.

"I don't think I'm 'playing' policeman," he said.

"You don't *know* that you're playing policeman," she said. "That's what I meant when I said *one* of them grows up."

"I don't think I like this conversation," Matt said. "Why

don't we talk about something pleasant, like what are we going to do next weekend?''

"I'm *serious*, Matt."

"So'm I. So what's your point?"

"I know why you became a policeman," she said.

"You do?"

"Because you couldn't get in the Marines with Chad and had to prove you were a man."

"You have been talking to Daffy, I see," he said.

"Well, now you've done that. You became a cop and you shot a man. You have nothing else to prove. So why are you still a cop?"

"I like being a cop."

"*That's* what I mean," she said.

She stopped dancing, freed herself from his arms, and looked up at him.

"The ship has docked," she said.

"Meaning what?"

"Meaning I'm sorry I started this conversation," she said, "but I *had* to."

"I don't know what the hell you're talking about!"

"Yes you do!" she said, and Matt saw that she was on the edge of tears.

"What's wrong with me being a cop?" Matt asked softly.

"If you don't know, I certainly can't tell you."

"Jesus!"

"I'm tired," she said. "And a little drunk. I'm going to bed."

"It's early," he protested.

She walked away with a little wave.

"Call you in the morning before you go?"

There was no reply to that, either.

"Shit," Matt said aloud.

Thirty minutes later, just as Matt had decided she wasn't coming back out of the house, and as he had indicated to the bartender that he would like another Scotch and soda, easy on the soda, his father touched his arm and announced, "I've been looking for you."

I am about to get hell, Matt decided. *The party is just about over, and I have not danced with my mother. Actually I haven't done much about my mother at all except wave at her. And to judge by the look on his face, he is really pissed. Or disappointed in me, which is even worse than his being pissed at me.*

"My bad manners are showing again, are they?" Matt asked.

"Are you sober?" Brewster C. Payne asked evenly enough.

"So far," Matt said.

"Come with me, please, Matt," his father said. "There's no putting this off, I'm afraid."

"No putting what off?"

"Leave your drink," his father said. "You won't be needing it."

They walked out of the tent and around it and up the lawn to the house. His father led him into the butler's pantry, where he had been early that morning with Soames T. Browne.

H. Richard Detweiler was sitting on one of the high stools. When he saw Matt, he got off it and looked at Matt with both hurt and anger in his eyes.

"Would you like a drink, Matt?" Detweiler asked.

"He's already had enough to drink," Brewster C. Payne answered for him, and then turned to Matt. "Matt, you are quoted as saying that Penny has a problem with drugs, specifically cocaine."

"Quoted by whom?" Matt said.

"Did you say that? Something like that?" his father pursued.

"Jesus Christ!" Matt said.

"Yes, or no, for God's sake, Matt!" H. Richard Detweiler said angrily.

"Goddamn him!" Matt said.

"So it's true," Detweiler said. "What right did you think you had to say something filthy like that about Penny?"

"Mr. Detweiler, I'm a policeman," Matt said.

"Until about an hour ago I was under the impression that you were a friend of Penny's first, and a policeman incidentally," he said.

"Oh, Matt," Matt's father said.

"I think of myself as a friend of Penny's, Mr. Detweiler," Matt said. "We're trying very hard to find out who shot her and why."

"And the way to do that is spread . . . something like this around?"

"I didn't spread it around, Mr. Detweiler. I talked to Chad about Penny—"

"Obviously," Detweiler said icily.

"And in confidence I told him what we had learned about Penny—about Penny and cocaine."

"Not thinking, of course, that Chad would tell Daffy, and Daffy would tell her mother, and that it would soon be common gossip?" Brewster Payne said coldly.

"And that's all it is, isn't it?" H. Richard Detweiler said angrily, disgustedly. "Gossip? Filthy supposition with nothing to support it but your wild imagination? What were you trying to do, Matt, impress Chad with all the inside knowledge you have, now that you're a cop?"

"Where did you hear this, Matt? From that detective? The black man?" his father asked.

"Mr. Detweiler," Matt said, "I can't tell you how sorry I am you learned it the way you have, but the truth is that Penny is into cocaine. From what I understand, she is on the edge of being addicted to it."

"That's utter nonsense!" Detweiler flared. "Don't you think her mother and I would know if she had a problem along those lines?"

"No, sir, I don't think you would. You *don't*, Mr. Detweiler."

"I asked you the source of your information, Matt," his father said.

"I'm sorry, I can't tell you that," Matt said. "But the source is absolutely reliable."

"You mean you *won't* tell us," Detweiler said. "Did it occur to you that if there was any semblance of truth to this that Dr. Dotson would have been aware of it and brought it to my attention?"

"I can't believe that Dr. Dotson is not aware of it," Matt said. "Mr. Detweiler, I don't pretend to know anything about medical ethics—"

"Medical ethics or any other kind, obviously," Detweiler snapped.

"But Penny is twenty-one, an adult, and it seems to me that Penny wouldn't want you to know."

"Russell Dotson has been our family doctor for—for all of Penny's life and then some. Good God, Matt, he's a friend. He's outside right now. If he knew, *suspected*, something like that, he would tell me."

"I can't speak for Dr. Dotson, Mr. Detweiler," Matt said.

"Maybe we should ask him to come in here," Detweiler said. "I think I will. Let the two of you look each other in the eye."

"I wish you wouldn't do that, Mr. Detweiler," Matt said.

"I'll bet you do!"

"Dick, Matt may have a point," Brewster C. Payne said. "There is the question of doctor-patient confidentiality."

"Whose side are you on?" Detweiler snapped.

"Yours. Penny's. Matt's," Brewster C. Payne said.

Detweiler glowered at him for a moment, then turned to Matt. "How long did you say you have been aware of this situation?"

"Since I saw Penny in the hospital this morning," Matt said after having to think a moment.

Christ, was that only this morning?

"In other words, when you and that detective came to the house, you knew, or thought you knew, that Penny was a drug addict?"

"Yes, sir."

"In other words, then, when I allowed you, because I thought you were trying to find out who shot Penny, to paw through her drawers, you and that black detective were actually looking for evidence to support your notion that Penny's taking drugs?"

"No, sir," Matt said. "That's not so."

"Yes, it is, goddamn you! You took advantage of our friendship! That's despicable!"

"Dick, take it easy!" Brewster C. Payne said.

"You better get him out of here before I beat him up," H. Richard Detweiler said.

"Mr. Detweiler—" Matt said.

"Get out of my sight, goddamn you! I never want to see your face again!"

"You can believe this or not, Mr. Detweiler, but we're trying to help Penny," Matt said.

Detweiler stepped menacingly toward Matt.

"God*damn* you!"

Oh, Christ, I don't want to hit him! Matt thought.

His father stepped between them and kept them apart. He motioned with his head for Matt to leave.

Matt felt sick to his stomach. He fled the house and after some difficulty found his car. It was blocked in by several limousines, and he had to find their chauffeurs and get them to move them.

As he started down the drive he saw his father, obviously waiting for him. There was a temptation to pretend he didn't see him, but at the last moment he braked sharply and stopped and rolled down the window.

"You had better be sure of your facts," Brewster C. Payne said, leaning down to the window. "Dick Detweiler is looking for Dr. Dotson right now."

"And if Dotson won't tell him, then what?"

"All I'm saying is that you had better be sure of your facts," his father said.

"There seems to be some doubt in your mind, Dad," Matt said.

"I know that you don't have very much experience as a policeman," his father said. "If you had, you wouldn't have run off at the mouth about any of this to Chad. A lot of damage has been done."

"To whom, Dad?" Matt's mouth ran away with him. "To Penny? Or to your cozy relationship with Nesfoods International?"

"That," Brewster C. Payne said calmly, "was a despicable thing for you to say."

"You think so?" Matt said, his mouth now completely out of control. "Then try this on for size: Our information, as we cops are prone to say, is that Penny Detweiler was not only a coke junkie but was fucking that guinea gangster who got himself blown away. Nice girl, our precious Penny."

Brewster C. Payne looked at Matt intently for a moment, then straightened, turned, and started to walk back to the house.

Matt drove down the driveway and, after one of the rent-a-cops had carefully examined him and the car, was passed out the gate.

A hundred yards down the road he pulled the car to the

curb, got out, and took several deep breaths. The technique, alleged to constrain the urge to become nauseous, didn't work.

Matt took Lancaster Avenue, which is U.S. Highway 30, into Philadelphia, driving slowly, trying to think of some way he could explain, in the morning, his runaway mouth to Jason Washington. Then it occurred to him that he had to tell Peter Wohl, not Washington, and he had to tell him tonight, not wait until morning.

The worst possible, and thus the most likely, scenario was that the trouble I am going to cause for having confided, like a fourteen-year-old—which, it may be reasonably argued, I am, intellectually speaking—in Chad Nesbitt is going to start tonight. Mr. Detweiler will find Dr. Dotson. Dr. Dotson will either deny outright, or downplay, Penny's coke problem. Mr. Detweiler will then naturally construe Brewster C. Payne's best legal advice, to cool it, as being based on Brewster C. Payne's paternal loyalty to his son, Boy Cop, Ye Olde Blabbermouth. He will then express his displeasure, his outrage, to the nearest official ear he can find. Which will be that of His Honor Mayor Jerry Carlucci, last seen in the striped tent on his lawn.

There was a cheese-steak joint at 49th and Lancaster. He pulled the Porsche to the curb and walked across Lancaster to it. There was a 19th District RPC at the curb, and two cops at the counter drinking coffee.

The cops looked at him with unabashed curiosity, reminding him that he was wearing formal evening wear.

Be not concerned, Officers. While my unbelievable stupidity has just brought down upon the Police Department generally, and on two of its best, who have been both holding my hand to keep me out of trouble, and have so foolishly placed an entirely unjustified faith in my common sense, the completely justified wrath of a very powerful man, what you have here is not some rich kid in a monkey suit who will disturb the peace of this establishment, but, incroyable, one of you, a police officer, complete to gun, badge, and out in the Porsche, handcuffs and everything.

Matt walked to a pay phone mounted on the wall and fished change from his pocket. He had just received a dial tone when his eye fell on a stack on newspapers, apparently just delivered, on the counter. It was the *Ledger*. At first glance there seemed to be a three-column photograph of His Honor Mayor Jerry Carlucci just about in the act of either punching or choking someone.

Curiosity overwhelmed Matt. He hung the phone up and went to the counter. On closer examination the photograph on the front page of the *Philadelphia Ledger* was indeed of the mayor, and he did indeed look as if he were about to either choke someone or punch him out. The caption, simply "The Honorable Jerry Carlucci, mayor of the City of Philadelphia," provided no explanation.

The explanation came in the story below the picture.

SOCIALITES MARRY UNDER HEAVY POLICE GUARD: HEIRESS' SHOOTING CONTINUES TO BAFFLE POLICE

By Charles E. Whaley,
Ledger Staff Writer

Phila—The wedding of socialites Daphne Elizabeth Brown and Chadwick T. Nesbitt IV went on as scheduled at 7:30 P.M. at St. Mark's Church last evening, minus one bridesmaid, and with a heavy force of police and private security personnel evident at the church.

Penelope Detweiler, 23, whose father, H. Richard Detweiler, is president of Nesfoods International and who was to have been a bridesmaid, instead laid in Hahneman Hospital after having suffered multiple shotgun wounds at the hands of an unknown assailant in a downtown parking garage the previous day.

As the Right Reverend Wesley Framingham Kerr, Protestant Episcopal Bishop of Philadelphia, united in marriage the daughter of financier Soames T. Browne and the son of Nesfoods International Chairman, C.T. Nesbitt III, police and private detectives scattered among the socially prominent guests in the church nervously scanned them and the church itself in a manner that reminded this reporter of Secret Service agents guarding the president.

It was reported that the police were present at the orders of Philadelphia Mayor Jerry Carlucci, himself a guest, who is reported to be grossly embarrassed both that Miss Detweiler was shot in what appears to have been a Mafia-connected incident, and that the Special Operations Division of the Philadelphia Police Department, which was organized with his enthusiastic support, and which he personally charged with solving the crime, has been so far unable to identify any suspects in the shooting. The presence of private detectives at the church, reportedly from Wachenhut Security, Inc., was taken by some as an indication that the Browne and Nesbitt families had little faith in the Philadelphia Police Department to protect them and their guests.

Mayor Carlucci, outside the church, refused to discuss that issue with this reporter, and a scuffle ensued during which a *Ledger* photographer was knocked to the ground and his camera damaged.

(See related stories, "No Clues" and "Gangland War Victim," p.3a.)

"Oh, Jesus!" Matt said aloud.

His Honor must know about this. That's going to have put him in a lovely frame of mind so that when Mr. Detweiler says, "Jerry, old pal, let me tell you about this blabbermouth cop of yours," he will be understanding and forgiving.

He turned to page 3a and read the other stories.

"NO CLUES" SAY POLICE IN POLICEMAN'S MURDER; FUNERAL OF SLAIN OFFICER SCHEDULED FOR TODAY

By Mary Ann Wiggins
Ledger Staff Writer

Police Officer Joseph Magnella will be buried at three this afternoon, following a Mass of Requiem to be celebrated by John Cardinal McQuire, Archbishop of Philadelphia, at Saint Dominic's Church. Internment will be in the church cemetery, traditional last resting place for Roman Catholic police officers slain in the line of duty.

Officer Magnella, 24, of a Warden Street address in South Philadelphia, was found shot to death beside his 23rd Police District patrol car near Colombia and Clarion Streets just before midnight two nights ago.

A Vietnam veteran, he was unmarried and made his home with his parents. He had been on the police force less than a year and was engaged to be married.

Police Captain Michael J. Sabara, deputy commander of the Special Operations Division of the Police Department, which has been charged by Mayor Jerry Carlucci with solving his murder, admitted that so far the police "don't have a clue" as to who shot Magnella or why.

Mayor Jerry Carlucci, who was interviewed briefly as he left the Stanley Rocco & Sons Funeral Home, where he had gone to pay his respects, seemed visibly embarrassed at the inability of the police to quickly solve what he called "the brutal, cold-blooded murder of a fine young officer." He refused to discuss with this reporter the murder of Anthony J. DeZego, an alleged organized crime figure, and the wounding of socialite Penelope Detweiler, which occurred the same night Officer Magnella was shot to death.

Several thousand police officers, both fellow Philadelphia officers and police from as far away as New York City and Washington, D.C., are expected to participate in the final rites for Officer Magnella.

GANGLAND WAR VICTIM WAS "GOOD SON, HUSBAND AND FATHER" SAYS MOTHER OF ANTHONY J. DEZEGO

By Tony Schuyler, Ledger Staff Writer

Anthony J. DeZego, who met his death on the roof of the Penn Services Parking Garage two nights ago, his head shattered by a shotgun blast, was described on the eve of his funeral as a "good son, husband and father" by his mother, Mrs. Christiana DeZego.

DeZego, 34, was a truck driver for Gulf Sea Food Transport at the time of his death in what police suspect was a gangland killing. Police Captain Michael J. Sabara, Deputy Commander of Special Operations, which is investigating the early-evening murder, refused to comment on DeZego's alleged ties to organized crime but said the shooting was "not unlike a Mafia assassination." He said that DeZego had a criminal record dating back to his teens and had only recently been released from probation.

His most recent brush with the law, according to Captain Sabara, had been a conviction for "possession with intent to distribute controlled substances."

DeZego had recently purchased for his family (a wife and two sons) a home four doors down from that of his mother in South Philadelphia. His late-model Cadillac, found abandoned by police at Philadelphia International Airport the morning after the shooting, was returned to his family yesterday.

Salvatore B. Mariano, DeZego's brother-in-law and president of Gulf Sea Food Transport, said that DeZego was "a reliable employee and would be missed at work." He refused to speculate on how DeZego could afford a new home and a Cadillac on ordinary truck driver's wages and dismissed as "nonsense" that DeZego had ties to organized crime.

DeZego will be buried at three P.M. this afternoon, following a Requiem Mass at St. Teresa of Avalone Roman Catholic Church.

The investigation into his murder is "proceeding well," according to Captain Sabara, who declined to offer any further details. He confirmed that the investigation is being conducted by ace homicide detective Jason Washington.

"Nothing would please us more than to see Mr. De-Zego's murderer face the full penalty of the law," Sabara said.

"You want to *buy* that newspaper, Mac? Or did you think you was in a library?" a counterman with sideburns down to his chin line demanded.

"I want to buy it," Matt said. "Sorry."

He laid a dollar bill on the counter and turned back to the telephone and dialed Peter Wohl's home number.

After the fourth ring there was a click. "This is 555-8251," Wohl's recorded voice announced. "When this thing beeps, you can leave a message."

"Inspector, this is Matt Payne. I have to talk to you just as soon as possible—"

"This soon enough?" Wohl's cheerful voice interrupted.

Matt was startled.

"Have you seen the papers? The *Ledger*?"

"No. But I'll bet you called me to tell me about them," Wohl said dryly.

"There's a picture of the mayor on the front page. About to punch a photographer. And several bullshit stories putting him and us down."

"I'd like to see them," Wohl said. "Is *that* why you called me at quarter to one?"

"No, sir. Sir, I've fucked up."

"Another run-in with Sergeant Dolan?"

"No, sir. It's something else."

"Where are you?"

"At 49th and Lancaster. At a pay phone."

"If you don't think—which, *ergo sum,* you've called, so you don't—this will wait until morning, come over here. Bring the *Ledger* with you."

"Yes, sir, I'll be right there."

When he went outside, one of the two cops who had been at the counter was on the sidewalk. The other one was across the street, by the Porsche. Matt walked back across Lancaster Avenue.

"Nice car," the cop said.

"Thank you."

"You been drinking?"

"I had a couple of drinks," Matt said.

"Wedding, huh?"

"Yes, sir."

"Well, you always take a couple of drinks at a wedding, don't you? And you made it across the street in a straight line," the cop said.

"Yes, sir."

"You open to a little friendly advice?"

"Sure."

"Dressed up like that, driving a car like this, this time of night, with a couple of drinks in you, maybe stopping in a neighborhood like this isn't such a good idea. You know what I mean?"

"I think so," Matt said. "Yes. I know what you mean."

"Good night, sir," the cop said. "Drive careful."

He walked back across Lancaster Avenue, got in the 19th District RPC, and drove off.

He had no idea I'm cop. Obviously I don't look like a cop. Or act like one. But I know that, don't I, that I don't act like a cop?

As Matt swung wide to turn off Norwood Street in Chestnut Hill and to enter into the driveway that led to Peter Wohl's apartment, the Porsche's headlights swept across a massive chestnut tree and he thought he could see a faint scarring of the bark.

He thought: *I killed a man there.*

Warren K. Fletcher, 34, of Germantown, his brain already turned to pulp by a 168-grain round-nosed lead bullet fired from Officer Matt Payne's .38-caliber Chief's Special snub-nosed revolver, a naked civilian tied up with lamp cord under a tarpaulin in the back of his van, had crashed the van into that chestnut tree, ending what Michael J. O'Hara had called, in the *Philadelphia Bulletin*, "The Northwest Philadelphia Serial Rapist's Reign of Terror."

Matt recalled Chad asking him what it was like to have killed a man. And he remembered what he had replied: "I haven't had nightmares or done a lot of soul-searching about it. Nothing like that."

It was true, of course, but he suddenly understood why he had said that: It hadn't bothered him because it was unreal. It hadn't happened. Or it had happened to somebody else. Or in a movie. It was beyond credibility that Matthew M. Payne, of Wallingford and Episcopal Academy, former treasurer of Delta Phi Omicron at, and graduate of, the University of Pennsylvania, had been given a badge and a gun by the City of Philadelphia and had actually taken that gun from its holster and killed somebody with it.

He drove down the driveway. There was a Buick Limited parked in front of one of Peter Wohl's two garages. There was nothing on the car to suggest that it was a Department car, and he wondered who it belonged to.

He got out of the Porsche and climbed the stairs to Wohl's door and knocked.

A silver-haired, stocky man in his sixties, jacketless, his tie pulled down, wearing braces, opened the door.

"You must be Matt Payne," he said, offering one hand. The other held a squat whiskey glass. "I'm Augie Wohl. Peter's taking a leak. Come on in."

Matt knew that Peter Wohl's father was Chief Inspector August Wohl, retired, but he had never met him. He was an imposing man, Matt thought, just starting to show the signs of age. He was also, Matt realized, half in the bag.

"How do you do, sir?" Matt said.

"Let me fix you a little something," Chief Wohl said. "What's your pleasure?"

"I'm not sure that I should," Matt said.

"Oh, hell, have one. You're among friends."

"A little Scotch then, please," Matt said.

He followed Wohl's father across the room to Wohl's bar.

It was covered with takeout buckets from a Chinese restaurant. Chief Wohl reached over the bar, came up with a fifth of Johnnie Walker and a glass, and poured the glass half full. He added ice cubes from a plastic freezer tray and handed it to him.

"Dilute it yourself," he said cheerfully. "There's soda and water."

"Thank you," Matt said.

Peter Wohl, in the act of closing his zipper, came out of his bedroom.

"What we have here is obviously the best-dressed newspaper boy in Philadelphia," he said. "Have you and Dad introduced yourselves?"

He's not feeling much pain, either, Matt decided.

"Yes, sir."

"And I see he's been plying you with booze," Wohl went on. "So let me see what *The Ledger* has to say, and then you can tell me how you fucked up."

Matt handed him the newspaper, which Wohl spread out on the bar, and then read, his father looking over his shoulder.

"It could be worse," Chief Wohl said. "I think Nelson is being very careful. Nesfoods takes a lot of tomato soup ads in his newspapers."

"So how did you fuck up, Matt?" Peter Wohl asked.

Matt told him about his confrontation with H. Richard Detweiler, fighting, he thought successfully, the temptation to offer any kind of an excuse for his inexcusable stupidity.

"You're sure, son," Chief Wohl asked, "that Detweiler's girl has a drug problem?"

"If Washington has the nurse in Hahneman, Dad—" Peter Wohl said.

"Yeah, sure," Chief Wohl said. "What about the girl's relationship with DeZego? How reliable do you think that information is?"

"It's secondhand," Matt said. "It could just be gossip."

"You didn't tell her father about that, anyhow, did you, Matt?" Peter Wohl asked.

"No, sir, I didn't," Matt said. But that triggered the memory of his having told his father. And, shamed again, he felt morally obliged to add that encounter to everything else.

"Well, fortunately for you," Chief Wohl said, looking at Matt, "Jerry tried to belt the photographer. Or did he belt him? Or just try?"

"The paper said 'a scuffle ensued,' " Peter Wohl said.

"It was more than that," Chief Wohl said, went to the bar and read, somewhat triumphantly from the newspaper story: ". . . 'a scuffle ensued during which a *Ledger* photographer was knocked to the ground and his camera damaged.' " Don't you watch television? A cop is supposed to *get the facts*."

" 'Just the facts, ma'am.' " Peter Wohl chuckled, mimicking Sergeant Friday on *Dragnet*.

"Carlucci is going to be far more upset about that picture being on every other breakfast table in Philadelphia, son," Chief Wohl said, "than about you telling Detweiler his daughter has a drug problem."

"That was pretty goddamn dumb," Peter Wohl said.

"Yes, sir, I know it was. And I'm sorry as hell," Matt said.

"He was talking about Jerry Carlucci," Chief Wohl said.

"But the shoe fits," Peter Wohl said, "so put it on."

Matt glanced at him. There was a smile on Peter Wohl's face.

He's not furious, or even contemptuous, Matt realized, very surprised. *He doesn't even seem very annoyed. It's as if he expected this sort of stupid behavior from a rookie. Or maybe from a college boy.*

"Jerry never learned when not to use his fists," Chief Wohl said, then chuckled. "My God, the gorilla suit!" He laughed. "You ever tell Matt about Carlucci and the gorilla suit?"

Wohl, chuckling, shook his head.

"You tell him," he said, and walked to the bar.

"Well, this was ten, maybe twelve years ago," Chief Wohl began. "Jerry had Highway. I had Uniformed Patrol. Highway was under Uniformed Patrol then. I kept getting these complaints from everybody, the DA's office, a couple of judges, Civil Liberties, everybody, that Highway was taking guys to Bustleton and Bowler and working them over before they took them to Central Lockup. So I called Jerry in and read the riot act to him. I was serious, and he knew I was serious. I told him that the first time I could prove that he, or anybody in Highway, was working people over at Bustleton and Bowler, he would be in Traffic the next morning, blowing a whistle at Broad and Market . . ." He paused, glancing over his shoulder. "If you're making one of those for Matt, my glass has a hole in it too."

"None for me, thanks," Matt said about two seconds before Peter Wohl handed him a fresh drink.

"Ssh," Peter Wohl said, "you're interrupting the old man."

"So he stopped for a while," Chief Wohl went on. "Maybe for a week. Then I started hearing about it again. So I went to the sergeant in Central Lockup. I was serious about this and told him the next time they got a prisoner from Highway that looked like he'd been worked over, I wanted to hear about it right then. So, sure enough, two or three nights later, about eleven o'clock at night, I get this call from Central Lockup."

Peter Wohl handed his father a drink.

He looked at it, and then at Matt.

"Don't worry about getting home, son," he said. "I'll drive you myself."

"The hell you will." Peter Wohl laughed. "He stays here and you're getting driven home. The one thing I don't need is either or both of you running into a bus."

"You're not suggesting that I'm drunk, are you?"

"It's not a suggestion at all," Wohl said. "It's one of those facts you were talking about before." He went to the telephone and dialed a number.

"This is Inspector Wohl," he said. "Would you put out the word to have the nearest Highway car meet me at my house, please?"

"I'm not sure I like that," Chief Wohl said.

"I would rather have you pissed at me than Mother, okay?" Wohl said. "Finish the gorilla story."

"Where was I?"

"You got a call from Central Lockup," Peter furnished.

"Yeah. Right. So what happened, Matt, was that I got in my car and went down there. They had a bum, a real wiseass, in one of the cells, and somebody in Highway had really worked him over. Swollen lips. Black eye. The works. And I knew Jerry Carlucci had been out at Bustleton and Bowler.

So I thought I had him. So I went into the cell with this guy and asked him what had happened. 'Nothing happened,' he said. So I asked him where he got the cut lip and the shiner. And he said, 'From a gorilla.' And I said 'Bullshit' and he said a gorilla beat him up, and if I didn't like it, go fuck myself. And I asked, where did the gorilla beat him up, and he said 'Bustleton and Bowler' and I said there weren't any gorillas at Bustleton and Bowler, and he said 'The hell there wasn't, one of them came into the detention cell there and kicked the shit out of me.' ''

Peter Wohl laughed out loud. "True story, Matt," he said.

"Well," Chief Wohl went on, "like I said, Matt, this guy was a real wiseass, and I knew I was wasting my breath. If Carlucci had beat him up, he wasn't going to tell me. So I went home. About a week later a piece of paper crossed my desk. It was a court order for the release of evidence in a truck heist before trial. You know what I mean, son?"

"Matt," Peter Wohl said, "sometimes a court will order the release of stolen property to its owners before the case comes to trial, if they can prove undue hardship, that sort of thing."

"Yes, sir," Matt said.

"The evidence was described as 'theatrical costumes and accessories.' Highway had the evidence. I didn't pay much attention to it at the time, but the same afternoon, I was out at Bustleton and Bowler, and I was a little curious. So I asked the sergeant where the theatrical costumes were—I was asking, in other words, if they had been returned to the owners yet. The sergeant said, 'Everything but the gorilla suit's out in the storeroom. Captain Carlucci's got the gorilla suit.' ''

He put his glass down and laughed so hard, his eyes watered.

"That goddamn Jerry Carlucci had actually put the gorilla suit on, gone into the holding cell, and worked the bum over. And the bum, who had his reputation to think of, was not going to go to court and complain he'd been assaulted by a guy in a gorilla suit. Oh, Jesus, Jerry was one hell of a cop!"

There were the sounds of footsteps on the stairs outside, and then a rap at the door. Wohl went to it and opened it. Sergeant Big Bill Henderson stood there.

"Not that I'm not glad to see you, Sergeant," Wohl said, "but I guess I should have asked for a two-man car."

"What's the problem, Inspector?"

"There's no problem at all, Sergeant," Chief Wohl said. "My son has got the cockamamie idea that I'm too drunk to drive."

"Hello, Chief," Big Bill said. "Nice to see you again, sir."

"I was just telling Matt Payne about Jerry Carlucci and the gorilla suit," Chief Wohl said. "You ever hear that story?"

"No, sir," Big Bill said. "You can tell me on the way home. Inspector, I'll have a car pick up mine and meet me at the chief's house. Okay?"

"Fine," Wohl said. "Or we could wait for a two-man car."

"No, I'll take the chief. I want to hear about the gorilla suit." He winked at Peter Wohl.

Peter Wohl found his father's coat and helped him into it. Matt saw for the first time that Chief Wohl had a pistol.

I guess once a cop, always a cop.

"You tell Mother going to Groverman's Bar was your idea, Dad?" Peter said.

"I can handle your mother, don't you worry about that," Chief Wohl said. He walked over to Matt and shook his hand. "Nice to meet you, son. I probably shouldn't tell you this, but Peter thinks you're going to make a hell of a cop."

"I said 'in twenty years or so' is what I said," Peter Wohl said.

Chief Wohl and Sergeant Henderson left.

Wohl walked past Matt, into his bedroom, and returned in a moment carrying sheets and blankets and a pillow. He tossed them at Matt.

"Make up the couch. Go to bed. Do not snore. Leave quietly in the morning. You are still working with Jason?"

"Yes, sir. I'm to meet him at the Roundhouse at eight."

"Try not to breathe on him," Wohl said. "I would hate for him to get the idea that you've been out till all hours drinking."

"Yes, sir. Good night, sir."

At his bedroom door Peter Wohl turned. "When you hear

the gorilla suit story again, and you will, remember that the first time you heard it, you heard it from the source," he said.

"Yes, sir."

"Good night, Matt," Wohl said, and closed the door.

Matt undressed to his underwear. The last thing he took off was his ankle holster. He laid it on the table beside his tuxedo trousers.

My gun, he thought. *The tool of the policeman's trade. Chief Wohl still carries his. And Chief Wohl thinks I'm a cop. A rookie, maybe, but a cop. He wouldn't have told that story to a civilian, about the mayor when he was a cop, putting on a gorilla suit and knocking some wiseass around. I wouldn't tell it to my father; he's a civilian and wouldn't understand. And Chief Wohl wasn't kidding when he said that Inspector Wohl told him he thought I could make a good cop.*

Matt Payne went to sleep feeling much happier than when he had walked in the door.

SIXTEEN

Matt Payne's bladder woke him with a call to immediate action at half past five. It posed something of a problem. There was only one toilet in Peter Wohl's apartment, off his bedroom. It was either try to use that without waking Wohl or going outside and relieving himself against the wall of the garage, something that struck him as disgusting to do, but he knew he could not make it to the nearest open diner or hamburger joint.

When he stood up, the decision-making process resolved itself. A sharp pain told him he could not wait until he got outside.

On tiptoe he marched past Wohl, who was sleeping on his stomach with his head under a pillow. He carefully closed the door to the bathroom, raised the lid, and tried to accomplish what had to be done as quietly as possible. He had just congratulated himself on his skill doing that and begun to hope that he could tiptoe back out of Wohl's room undiscovered when the toilet, having been flushed, began to refill the tank. It sounded like Niagara Falls.

Finally it stopped, with a groan like a wounded elephant. Matt opened the door and looked. Wohl did not appear to have moved. Matt tiptoed past the foot of Wohl's bed and made it almost to the door.

"Good *morning*, Officer Payne," Wohl said from under his pillow. "You're up with the goddamn roosters, I see."

"Sorry," Matt said.

He closed Wohl's door, dressed quickly, left the apartment as quietly as he could, and drove to Rittenhouse Square. He went directly to the refrigerator, took out a half gallon of milk, and filled a large glass. It was sour.

Holding his nose, he poured it down the drain, then leaned against the sink.

The red light on his telephone answering machine was flashing.

"Why did you leave?" Amanda's voice inquired metallically. *Because, after telling me the cruise ship had docked, you went to bed.* "I hope I didn't run you off." *Perish the thought!* "Call me." *Now? It's quarter after six in the morning!*

This was followed by electronic beeping noises that indicated that half a dozen callers had declined Matt's recorded invitation to leave their number so he could get back to them. Then a familiar, deep, well-modulated voice: "This is Jason, Matt. I've got to do something first thing in the morning. Don't bother to come to the Roundhouse. I'll either see you at Bustleton and Bowler around nine, or I'll call you there."

Another series, five this time, of electronic beeping noises, indicating that many callers had not elected to leave a recorded message, and then Amanda's recorded voice, sounding as if she were torn between sorrow and indignation, demanded, "Where the hell are you? I've called you every half hour for hours. Call me!"

Matt looked at his watch.

It is now 6:18 A.M. I will shower and shave and see if I can eliminate the source of the rumbling in my belly, and then dress, and by then it will be close to 7:00 A.M., and I will call you then, because I really don't want to talk to Mrs. Soames T. Browne at 6:18 A.M.

At 7:02 A.M. Matt called the residence of Mr. and Mrs. Soames T. Browne and asked for Miss Spencer. Mrs. Soames T.

Browne came on the line. Mrs. Browne told him that five minutes before, Amanda had gotten into her car and driven home, and that if he wanted her opinion, his behavior in the last couple of days had been despicable. She said she had no idea what he'd said or done to Amanda to make her cry that way and didn't want to know, but obviously he was still as cavalier about other people's feelings as he had always been. She told him she had not been surprised that he had thought it amusing to try to get Chad drunk before the wedding, but she really had been surprised to learn that he had been spreading scurrilous stories about poor Penny Detweiler to one and all, with the poor girl lying at death's door in the hospital.

And then she terminated the conversation without the customary closing salutation.

"Oh, shit!" Matt said to a dead telephone.

He put on his necktie, slipped his revolver into his ankle holster, and left the apartment. He went to his favorite restaurant, Archie's, on 16th Street, where he had the *specialité de la maison*, a chili dog with onions and two bottles of root beer, for his breakfast.

Then he got in the Porsche and headed for Bustleton and Bowler. He was almost there when he noticed that a thumb-sized glob of chili had eluded the bun and come to rest on his necktie and shirt.

Jason Washington had been glad when the computer came along, not so much for all the myriad benefits it had brought to industry, academia, and general all-around record-keeping, but rather because it gave him something to sort of explain the workings of the brain.

He had been fascinated for years with the subconscious deductive capabilities of the brain, going way back to his freshman year in high school, where he found, to his delight, that he could solve simple algebraic equations in his head. He had often had no idea why he had written answers to certain examination questions, only that they had been the right answers. He had sailed through freshman algebra with an *A*. When he got to sophomore algebra, not having taken the time to memorize the various theories offered in freshman algebra, he got in trouble, but he never forgot the joy he had experienced the year before when the brain, without any effort at all on his part, had supplied the answers to problems he didn't really understand.

He had first theorized that the brain was something like a muscle; the more you flexed it, the better it worked. That seemed logical, and he carried that around a long time, even after he became a policeman. He had really wanted to become a detective and had studied hard to prepare for the detective's examination. When he took the examination, he remembered things he was surprised that he had ever learned. That tended to support the-brain-is-a-muscle theory, but he suspected that there was more to it than that.

He saw comptometers on various bureaucrats' desks, watched them in operation, and thought that possibly the brain was sort of a supercomptometer, but that (and its predecessor, the abacus) seemed too crude and too slow for a good comparison.

Then came the computer. Not only did the computer never forget anything it was told, but it had the capability to sort through all the data it had been fed, and do so with the speed of light. The computer was a brain, he concluded. More accurately the brain was a computer, a supercomputer, better than anything at MIT, capable of sorting through vast amounts of data and coming up with the answer you were looking for.

Some of its capabilities vis-à-vis police work were immediately apparent. If you fed everyone's license-plate number into it, and the other data about a car, and queried the computer, it would obligingly come up with absolutely correct listings of addresses, names, makes, anything you wanted to know.

Jason Washington had gone to an electronics store and bought a simple computer and, instead of watching television, had learned to program it in BASIC. He had written a program that allowed him to balance his checkbook. There had been a difference of a couple of pennies between what his computer said he had in his account and what the bank's computer said he had. He went over his program and then challenged the bank, not caring about the three cents but curious why two computers would disagree. He didn't get anywhere with the First Philadelphia Savings Fund Society, but a long-haired kid at the electronics store, a fellow customer, had taught him about anomalies.

As the kid explained it, it was a freak, where sometimes two and two added up to four point one, because something in either the data or the equation wasn't quite right.

By then Jason had been a detective for a long time, was already working in Homicide, and had learned that when you were working a tough job, what you looked for was something that didn't add up. An anomaly. That had a more professional ring to it than "something smells."

And he had learned something else, and that was that the brain never stopped working. It was always going through its data bank if you let it, sifting and sifting and sifting, looking through its data for anomalies. And he had learned that sometimes he could, so to speak, turn the computer on. If he went to sleep thinking about a problem, sometimes, even frequently, the brain would go on searching the data bank while he was asleep. When he woke up, rarely was there the solution to the problem. Far more often there was another question. There was no answer, the brain seemed to announce, because something is either missing or wrong. Then, wide awake, all you had to do was think about that and try to determine what was missing and/or what was wrong.

Jason Washington had gone to sleep watching the NBC evening news on television while he was going over in his mind the sequence of events leading to the death, at the hands of person or persons unknown, of Anthony J. DeZego.

Mr. DeZego had spent the day at work, at Gulf Seafood Transport, 2184 Delaware Avenue, which fact was substantiated not only by his brother-in-law, Mr. Salvatore B. Mariano, another guinea gangster scumbag, but by four of his coworkers whom Jason Washington believed were telling the truth.

Mr. DeZego had then driven to the Warwick Hotel in downtown Philadelphia in his nearly new Cadillac. That fact was substantiated by the doorman, whom Washington believed, who said that Mr. DeZego had handed him a ten spot and told him to take care of the car. The car had then been parked in the Penn Services Parking Garage, fourth floor, by Lewis T. Oppen, Jr., a bellboy, who had done the car parking, left the parking stub, as directed, on the dashboard, and then delivered the keys to Mr. DeZego in the hotel cocktail lounge.

Mr. DeZego had later walked to the Penn Services Parking Garage and gone to the roof, where someone had blown the top of his head off, before or after popping Miss Penelope Detweiler, who had more than likely gone there to meet Mr. DeZego.

There was additional confirmation of this sequence of events by Sergeant Dolan and Officer What's-his-name of Narcotics, who had staked out the Warwick. They even had photographs of Mr. DeZego arriving at the Warwick, in the bar at the Warwick, and walking to, and into, the Penn Services Parking Garage.

Mr. DeZego's car had been driven by somebody to the airport. Probably by the doer. Doers. Why?

"Wake up, Jason, dammit!" Mrs. Martha Washington had interrupted the data-sorting function of his subconscious brain. "You toss and turn all night if I let you sleep in that chair!"

"You act like I've done something wrong," Jason said indignantly.

His brain said, *There is an anomaly in what Dolan told me.*

"Run around the room or something," Martha Washington said. "Just don't lay there like a beached whale. When you snore, you sound like—I don't know what."

Jason went into the kitchen.

I will just go see Sergeant Dolan in the morning. But I can't take the kid with me. Dolan thinks Matt is dealing coke.

He poured coffee in a mug, then dialed Matt's number and told his answering machine not to meet him at the Roundhouse but to go to Bustleton and Bowler instead.

At nine-fifteen he went to bed, at the somewhat pointed suggestion of his wife.

He went to sleep feeding questions to the computer.

Where is the anomaly? I know it's there.

Officers Jesus Martinez and Charles McFadden, in uniform, came to their feet when Captain David Pekach walked into the building at Bustleton and Bowler.

"Good morning," Pekach said.

"Sir, can we talk to you?" McFadden asked.

I know what that's about, I'll bet, Pekach thought. *They were not thrilled by their twelve-hour tour yesterday riding up and down the Schuylkill Expressway. They want to do something important, be real cops, and they do not think handing out speeding tickets meets that criteria.*

Then he had an unpleasant thought: *Do they think that because they caught me speeding, they have an edge?*

"Is this important?" he asked somewhat coldly.

"I don't know," McFadden said. "Maybe not."

"Have you spoken to your sergeant about it?"

"We'd really like to talk to you, sir," Jesus Martinez said.

Pekach resisted the urge to tell them to go through their sergeant. They were good cops. They had done a good job for him. He owed them that much.

"I've got to see the inspector," he said. "Hang around, if you like. If I can find a minute, we'll talk."

"Yes, sir," Martinez said.

"Thank you," McFadden said.

Pekach walked to Peter Wohl's door. It was open, and Wohl saw him and waved him in.

"Good morning, Inspector," Pekach said.

"That's open to debate," Wohl said. "Have I ever told you the distilled essence of my police experience, Dave? Never drink with cops."

"You've been drinking with cops?"

"Two cops. My father and Payne."

Pekach chuckled. "What's that, the odd couple?"

"I went to cry on the old man's shoulder, and that led us first to Groverman's Bar and then to my place, and then Payne showed up to cry on my shoulder. I sent the old man home with Sergeant Henderson and made Payne sleep on my couch."

"What was Payne's problem?"

"He let his mouth run away with him, told the Nesbitt kid, the one who was married, the Marine . . . ?"

Pekach nodded.

". . . that we know the Detweiler girl was using coke. And he told the bride, and she told her mother, and her mother told H. Richard Detweiler, who is highly pissed that we could suspect his daughter of such a thing, and the last time Payne saw him, he was looking for the mayor to express his outrage.''

"Is he going to be trouble?"

"Probably," Wohl said, "but Payne looked so down in the mouth about it that I didn't have the heart to jump all over him. You may find this hard to believe, David, but when I was young, I ran off at the mouth once or twice myself.''

"No!" Pekach said in mock shock.

"True." Wohl chuckled. "How was your evening? How was Ristorante Alfredo? You go there?"

"Yeah. I want to talk to you about that," Pekach said, and handed Wohl the matchbook he had been given in the restaurant.

"There's a name inside. Marvin Lanier. Is that supposed to mean something to me?''

"I got that from Vincenzo Savarese," Dave replied.

Wohl looked at him with interest in his eyes.

"Not from Savarese himself," Pekach went on carefully, "but from the greaseball, Baltazari, who runs it for him. But he made it plain it had come from Savarese.''

"Ricco Baltazari gave you this?" Wohl asked.

There was a rap on the doorjamb.

"Busy?" Captain Mike Sabara asked when he had Wohl's attention.

"Come on in, Mike, I want you to hear this," Wohl said. As Sabara entered the office Wohl tossed the matchbook to him. "Dave got that from Vincenzo Savarese at the Ristorante Alfredo." When Sabara, after examining it, looked at him curiously, Wohl pointed to Pekach.

"Okay," Pekach said. "From the top. Almost as soon as we got in the place, the headwaiter came to the table and said Baltazari would like a word with me. He was sitting at a table across the room with Savarese.''

"They knew you were going to be there, didn't they?" Wohl said thoughtfully. "You made a reservation, right?"

"I had a reservation," Pekach said. "So I went to the table, and as soon as I got there, Baltazari left me alone with Savarese. Savarese told me he wanted to thank me for something I did for his granddaughter.''

"Huh?" Sabara asked.

"A couple of months ago, when I was still in Narcotics, I

was coming home late one night and stopped when I thought I saw a drug bust. Big bust. Four kids caught buying some marijuana. But they ran and there was a chase, and the kid wrecked his old man's car, so they were headed for Central Lockup. I looked at them, felt sorry for the girls, didn't want them to have to go through Central Lockup, and sent them home in a cab."

"And one of the girls was *Savarese's* granddaughter?" Sabara asked. "We got any unsolved broken arms, legs, and head assaults on the books? We could probably pin that on Savarese. You don't give grass to his granddaughter unless you've got a death wish."

Wohl chuckled. "He'd beat it. Temporary insanity."

"I didn't know who she was and had forgotten about it until Savarese brought it up."

Pekach nodded and went on. "He gave me some bullshit about my graciousness and understanding—"

"*I* always thought you were gracious and understanding, Dave," Wohl said.

"—and said he would never forget it, et cetera, and said if there was ever anything he could do for me—"

"And he probably meant it too," Sabara said. "Anybody you want knocked off, Dave? Your neighbors playing their TV too late at night, anything like that?"

"Shit, Mike!" Pekach exploded.

"Sorry," Sabara said, not sounding overwhelmed with remorse.

"What I thought he was doing was letting me know he'd grab the tab for dinner. But on my way back to the table Baltazari handed me that matchbook and said I dropped them, and I said no, and he said he was sure, so I kept them."

"You see the name inside?" Wohl asked.

"Yeah. It didn't mean anything to me. Baltazari gave me the same line of greaser bullshit, something about 'Mr. Savarese's friends always being grateful when somebody does him a favor.' What I think he said was 'him or his family a courtesy.' By then I was beginning to wish I'd tossed the little bitch in the can."

"No you didn't." Wohl chuckled. "You really are gracious and understanding, Dave."

Pekach glared at him.

"That wasn't a knife," Wohl said.

"So, anyway, when I got home, I called Records and got a make on this guy. Sort of a make. Black male. He's supposed to be a gambler, but what he really is, is a pimp. He runs an escort service."

"Marvin P. Lanier," Sabara said, reading the name inside the matchbook. "I never heard of him."

"Misterioso," Wohl said.

"I figured I better tell you about it," Pekach said.

"Yeah," Wohl said thoughtfully. "Neither of them gave any hint why they gave you this guy's name?"

"Nope," Pekach said.

One of the phones on Wohl's desk rang. Wohl was in his customary position, on the couch with his feet up on the coffee table. Pekach, who was leaning on Wohl's desk, looked at him questioningly. Wohl nodded. Pekach picked up the phone.

"Captain Pekach," he said, and listened, and then covered the mouthpiece with his hand. "There's a Homicide detective out there. Wants to see you, me, or Dave. You want me to take it?"

"Bring him in," Wohl said.

"Send him in, Sergeant," Pekach said to the phone, and put it back in its cradle. He went to the door and pulled it open.

Detective Joseph D'Amata walked in.

"Hey, D'Amata," Wohl called. "How are you?"

"Good morning, Inspector," D'Amata said. "Am I interrupting anything?"

"Captain Pekach was just telling Captain Sabara and me about his dinner last night," Wohl said. "What can we do for Homicide?"

"You hear about the pimp who got himself blown away last night?"

"I haven't read the overnights," Wohl said.

"Black guy," D'Amata said. "Lived on 48th near Haverford."

"His name wouldn't be Marvin P. Lanier, would it?" Wohl asked.

"Yes, sir, that's it," D'Amata said, obviously pleased. "I sort of hoped there'd be something for me here."

"I don't think I follow that," Wohl said.

"I got the idea, Inspector, that you—that is, Highway—knows something about this guy."

"Why would you think that?"

"You knew the name," D'Amata said, just a little defensively.

"That's all?"

"Sir, an hour before somebody shot this guy there was a Highway car in front of his house. With him. Outside the crime scene, I mean."

"You're sure about that?"

"Yes, sir. Half a dozen people in the neighborhood saw it."

"Dave?" Wohl asked.

Pekach threw up his hands in a helpless gesture, making it clear that he knew nothing about a Highway involvement.

"Fascinating," Wohl said. "More *misterioso*."

"Sir?" D'Amata asked, confused.

"Detective D'Amata," Wohl said, "why don't you help yourself to a cup of coffee and then have a chair while Captain Pekach goes and finds out what Highway had to do with Mr. Lanier last night?"

"Inspector, this is the first I've heard anything about this," Pekach said.

"So I gathered," Wohl said sarcastically.

Pekach left the office.

"How did Mr. Lanier meet his untimely demise, D'Amata?"

"Somebody popped him five times with a .38," D'Amata said. "In his bed."

"That would suggest that somebody didn't like him very much," Wohl said. "Any ideas who that might be?"

D'Amata shook his head.

"Have you learned anything that might suggest Mr. Lanier was connected with the mob?"

"He was a *pimp*, Inspector," D'Amata said.

"Then let me ask you this: Off the top of your head, would you say that Mr. Lanier was popped, in a crime of passion, so to speak, by one of his ladies, or by somebody who knew what he was doing?"

D'Amata thought that over briefly. "He took two in the head and three in the chest."

"Suggesting?"

"I don't know. Some of those whores are tough enough. A whore could have done it."

"Have you any particular lady in mind?"

"I asked Vice"—he paused and chuckled—"to round up the usual suspects. Actually for a list of girls who worked for him, or did."

Wohl chuckled and then asked, "Whose gun?"

"We don't have that yet," D'Amata said. "Those are interesting questions you're asking, Inspector."

"Just letting my mind wander," Wohl said. "Try this one: Can you think of any reason that Mr. Lanier's name would be known to Mr. Vincenzo Savarese?"

"Jesus!" D'Amata said. "Was it?"

"Let *your* mind wander," Wohl said.

"He could have owed the mob some money," D'Amata said. "He liked to pass himself off as a gambler. The mob likes to get paid."

"That would get him a broken leg, not five well-placed shots, and from someone with whom Mr. Savarese would be only faintly acquainted," Wohl said.

"Yeah," D'Amata said thoughtfully.

"What would that leave? Drugs?" Wohl asked.

There was not time for D'Amata to consider that, much less offer an answer. Pekach came back in the office.

"There's nothing in the records about a Highway car being anywhere near 48th and Haverford last night," he said.

"You sure?" D'Amata challenged, surprised.

"Yeah, I'm sure," Pekach said sharply. "Are you?"

"Captain," D'Amata said, "I got the same story from four different people. There was a Highway car there."

There was a knock at the door.

"Not now!" Wohl called.

There came another knock.

"Open the door, Dave," Wohl said coldly.

Pekach opened the door.

Officers Jesus Martinez and Charles McFadden stood there, looking more than a little uncomfortable.

"Didn't you hear me say not now?" Wohl said. "How many times do I have to—"

"Inspector," Charley McFadden blurted, "we heard Captain Pekach asking—"

"Goddammit, we're busy," Pekach flared. "The Inspector said not now. And whatever's on your mind, go through your sergeant!"

"That was us," Charley said. "At 48th and Haverford. With Marvin Lanier." He looked at Pekach. "That's what we wanted to see you about, Captain."

"Officer McFadden," Wohl said, "please come in, and bring Officer Martinez with you."

They came into the office.

"You have heard, I gather, that Mr. Lanier was shot to death last night?" Wohl asked.

"Just now, sir," Hay-zus said.

"Before we get started, this is Detective D'Amata of Homicide," Wohl said. "Joe, these two are Jesus Martinez and Charley McFadden, who before they became probationary Highway Patrolmen worked for Captain Pekach when they were all in Narcotics."

"I know who they are," D'Amata said.

"What is your connection with Mr. Lanier?" Wohl asked.

Charley McFadden looked at Hay-zus, then at Wohl, then at Pekach.

"What we wanted to tell Captain Pekach was that Marvin told us another guinea shot Tony the Zee," he blurted.

"Fascinating," Wohl said.

"What I want to know is what you were doing with Lanier when you were supposed to be patrolling the Schuylkill Expressway," Captain Pekach said.

"Isn't that fairly obvious, Dave?" Wohl said sarcastically. "Officers McFadden and Martinez decided that since no one else has any idea who shot Mr. DeZego and Miss Detweiler, it was clearly their duty to solve those crimes themselves, even if that meant leaving their assigned patrol area, which we, not having the proper respect for their ability as super-cops—they are, after all, former undercover Narcs—had so foolishly given them."

I said that, he thought, *because I'm pissed at what they did and wanted to both let them know I'm pissed, and to humiliate them. Having done that, I now realize that I am very likely to be humiliated myself. I have a gut feeling these two are at least going to be part of the solution.*

"I used to be a Homicide detective," Wohl said. "Let me see if I still remember how. McFadden—first of all, what was your relationship to Marvin Lanier?"

"He was one of our snitches. When we were in Narcotics."

"Then I think we'll start with that," Wohl said. "Let me begin this by telling you I want the truth, the whole truth, and nothing but the truth. Leave nothing out. You are already so deeply in trouble that nothing you admit can get you in any deeper. You understand that?"

The two mumbled "Yes, sir."

"Okay. Martinez, tell me how you turned Marvin Lanier into a snitch."

Wohl was convinced that the story was related truthfully and in whole. He didn't particularly like hearing that they had turned Lanier loose with a kilogram of cocaine—and could tell from the look on his face that Dave Pekach, who had been their lieutenant, was very embarrassed by it—but it convinced him both that McFadden and Martinez were going to tell the whole truth and that they had turned Lanier into a good snitch, defined as one that was more terrified of the cops who were using him than of the people on whom he was snitching.

He noticed, too, that neither Sabara, Pekach, or D'Amata had added their questions to his. On the part of D'Amata, that might have been the deference of a detective to a staff inspector—he didn't think so—but on the parts of Sabara and Pekach, who were not awed by his rank, it very well could be that they could think of nothing to ask that he hadn't asked.

Christ, maybe what I should have done was just stay in Homicide. I'm not all that bad at being a detective. And by now I probably would have made a pretty good Homicide detective. And all I would have to do is worry about bagging people, not about how pissed the mayor is going to be because one of my people ran off at the mouth.

"So when Marvin wanted to put his jack in the backseat instead of his trunk," Hay-zus said, "we knew there was something in the trunk he didn't want us to see. So there was. A shotgun.''

''A shotgun?'' Joe D'Amata asked. It was the first time he had spoken. ''A Remington 12 Model 1100, 12-gauge?''

''A Model 870,'' Martinez said. ''Not the 1100. A pump gun.''

''Is there an 1100 involved?'' Wohl asked.

''There was an 1100 under his bed,'' D'Amata said. ''I've got it out in my car.''

''And you say there was an 870 in his trunk?'' Wohl asked Martinez.

''Yes, sir.''

''Where is it?''

''Outside in my car.''

''You took it away from him? Why?''

''On what authority?'' Pekach demanded. Wohl made a calm-down sign to him with his hand.

''He didn't know it was legal,'' McFadden said.

''So you just decided to take it away from him? That's theft,'' Wohl said.

''We wanted something on him,'' McFadden protested. ''We was going to turn it in.''

Bullshit!

''That's when he told us another guinea shot Tony De-Zego,'' Hay-zus said. ''I don't know if that's so or not, but Marvin believed it.''

''He didn't offer a name?'' Wohl asked.

''We told him to come up with one by four this afternoon,'' McFadden said.

''And you think he would have come up with a name?''

''If he could have, he would have. Yes, sir.''

Wohl looked at Mike Sabara.

''Do you know where Washington is?''

''No, sir. But Payne's outside. They're working together, aren't they?''

''See if either of them is still there,'' Wohl ordered.

Pekach went to the door and a moment later returned with Matt Payne.

''Do you know where Washington is?''

''No, sir. He told me he would either see me here or phone.''

"Find him," Wohl ordered. "Tell him I want to see him as soon as I can."

"Yes, sir," Matt said, and left the room.

Wohl looked at Joe D'Amata.

"You know where this is going, don't you?" he asked.

"Sir, you're thinking there's a connection to the DeZego shooting?"

"Right. And since Special Operations has that job, I've got to call Chief Lowenstein and tell him I want the Lanier job—and that means you, too, Joe, of course—as part of that."

"He's not going to like that," Sabara said.

"If you're sure about that, Mike, you call him," Wohl said, and let Sabara wait ten seconds before he reached for the telephone himself.

To Peter Wohl's genuine surprise Chief Lowenstein agreed to have D'Amata work the Lanier job under Special Operations supervision with absolutely no argument.

"I don't believe that," he said when he hung up. "All he said was that you're a good man, D'Amata, and if there is anything else I need, all I have to do is ask for it."

"Well, how do you want me to handle it?" D'Amata asked.

"Very simply, ask Washington how *he* wants it handled. Aside from one wild one, I am about out of ideas."

"Wild idea?"

"I want to send the two shotguns to the lab. I have a wild idea that one of them is the one that popped DeZego."

"Yeah," D'Amata said thoughtfully, "could be."

"Do you two clowns think you could take the shotguns to the lab and tell them I need to know, as soon as possible, if the shells we have were ejected from either of them, without getting in any more trouble?"

"Yes, sir," Martinez and McFadden said in unison, and then McFadden asked, "You want us to come back here, sir?"

"No," Wohl said. "You're working four to twelve, right?"

"Yes, sir. Twelve to twelve with the overtime."

"I haven't made up my mind what to do with you," Wohl said. "Let your sergeant know where you're going to be, in case Washington or somebody wants to talk to you, and then report for duty at four. Maybe by then Captain Pekach can find somebody to sit on the both of you. Separately, I mean. Together you're dangerous.''

"Yes, sir," they chorused.

"Dave," Wohl said, turning to Pekach, "as soon as D'Amata gets Sherlock Holmes and his partner the shotgun, tell D'Amata what happened in the Ristorante Alfredo," Wohl ordered.

"Yes, sir."

The door opened. Matt Payne put his head in.

"Can't find Washington, sir. He doesn't answer the radio, and he's not at home.''

"What I told you to do, Payne, is find him. Not report that you can't. Get in a car and go look for him. The next time I hear from you, I want it to be when you tell me Detective Washington is on his way here.''

"Yes, sir," Matt said, and quickly closed the door again.

The telephone rang. Obviously his calls were being held. So the ring indicated that this call was too important to hold.

"Inspector Wohl," he said, answering it himself.

"Dennis Coughlin, Peter."

"Good morning, Chief."

"We're due in the mayor's office at 10:15. You, Matt Lowenstein, and me.''

"Yes, sir."

"He's mad, Peter. I guess you know.''

"Yes, sir."

The phone went dead.

Well, that explains Chief Lowenstein's inexplicable spirit of enthusiastic cooperation. He knew we were all going to have a little chat with the mayor. He can now go on in there and truthfully say that this very morning, when I asked for it, he gave one more of his brighter detectives and asked if there was anything else he could do for me.

SEVENTEEN

Detective Jason Washington did not like Sergeant Patrick J. Dolan, and he was reasonably convinced the reverse was true.

Specifically, as Washington drove his freshly waxed and polished, practically brand-new unmarked car into the parking lot behind the former district station house that was now the headquarters for both the Narcotics and Intelligence Divisions at 4th and Girard and parked it beside one of the dozen or more battered, ancient, and filthy Narcotics unmarked cars, he thought, *I will have to keep in mind that Dolan thinks I'm a slick nigger. It would be better for me if he thought I was a plain old, that is to say, mentally retarded nigger, but he is just smart enough to know that isn't so. He knows that Affirmative Action does not go so far as to put mentally retarded niggers to work as Homicide detectives.*

I will also have to remember that in his own way Dolan is a pretty good cop, that is to say, that a certain degree of intelligence does indeed flicker behind that profanely loud-mouthed mick exterior. He is not really as stupid as I would like to think he is, notwithstanding that really stupid business of hauling Matt Payne over here in the belief that he was dealing drugs.

Most important, I will have to remember that what Dolan hasn't told me—and there is something he hasn't told me—is because he doesn't even know he saw it. The dumb mick has tunnel vision. He was looking for a drug bust and saw two rich kids, one driving a Mercedes and one driving a Porsche, and he was so anxious to put them in the bag, what was important to him, a good drug bust, that he just didn't see Murder One going down.

Inside the building, Washington found Sergeant Patrick J. Dolan in the office of Lieutenant Mick Mikkles.

"Good morning, sir," Jason Washington said politely. "And thank you, Sergeant, for making yourself available."

"I'm due in court in an hour," Sergeant Dolan said. "What's on your mind, Washington?"

"I need a little help, Sergeant," Washington said. "I'm getting nowhere with the DeZego job."

"You probably won't," Dolan said. "You want to know what I think?"

"Yes, I really do."

"It was a mob hit. Pure and simple. DeZego broke the rules and they put him out of the game. It's just that simple. You're Homicide. You tell me how many mob hits ever wind up in court."

"Very, very few of them."

"Fucking right! You don't mind me telling you that you're spinning your wheels on this job, Washington?"

"Sergeant, I think you're absolutely right," Washington said. "But because of the Detweiler girl—"

"She's a junkie. I told you that."

"She's also H. Richard Detweiler's daughter," Washington said, "and so the mayor wants to know who did the shooting. If she wasn't involved—"

"I get the picture," Dolan interrupted. "So you go through the motions, right?"

"Exactly."

"So you came back here and *interviewed* me again. And I told you exactly the same thing I told you the first time, all right? So now we're finished, right?"

"I'd really like to go over it all again," Washington said.

"Jesus fucking Christ, Washington," Dolan said. He looked at his watch. "I *told* you, I'm due in fucking court in *fifty-five* minutes. I gotta go over my notes."

He really wants to get rid of me. And I don't think it has a damn thing to do with him being due in court.

"The mayor's on Inspector Wohl's back, so he's on mine. I really—"

"Fuck Inspector Wohl! That's your problem."

"Hey, Pat," Lieutenant Mikkles said, "take it easy!"

"You're thinking that if Wohl hadn't come here and turned his driver loose, you could have gotten something, right?"

"Yeah, that's exactly what I think."

"Well, then you know my problem with Wohl," Washington said.

"No, I don't know your problem with Wohl," Dolan said.

"You don't think I wanted to leave Homicide to go work for him, do you?"

Dolan considered that for a moment.

"Yeah, I heard about that. You and Tony Harris, right?"

"Right. Wohl's got a lot of clout, Sergeant. He generally gets what he wants."

That last remark was for you, Lieutenant Mikkles, to feed your understandable concern that if this doesn't go well, your face will be in the breeze when the shit hits the fan.

"Maybe from you," Dolan said.

"Pat," Lieutenant Mikkles said, "give him fifteen minutes. Go through the motions. You know how it is."

Dolan looked at Mikkles, his face indicating that he thought he had been betrayed. Mikkles nodded at him.

"Fifteen minutes," he said. "You'll still have time to make court."

"Okay," Sergeant Dolan said. "Fifteen minutes. Okay?"

"We'll just go through the motions," Washington said.

"Okay. Start."

"Those pictures you took handy?"

"What the hell do you need those for? I already showed them to you."

Why doesn't he want me to look at the pictures?

"Who knows? Maybe if we look at them again, we'll see something we missed."

"Like what?"

"I don't know."

"I don't know where the hell they are."

I am on to something!

"Maybe your partner has them?" Washington asked.

"Nah, they're probably in the goddamn file. I'll look," Dolan said, and left the room.

"Washington," Lieutenant Mikkles said, "Dolan is a good man."

"Yes, sir, I know."

"But he comes equipped with a standard Irish temper. I would consider it a favor if you could forget that 'Fuck Inspector Wohl' remark."

"I didn't hear anybody say anything like that, Lieutenant."

"I owe you one," Lieutenant Mikkles said.

"Forget it," Washington said.

Sergeant Dolan came back in the office with a handful of five-by-seven photographs.

"Here's the fucking photographs," he said, handing them to Washington. "What do you want to know?"

Washington looked through the photographs, then sorted them so they would be sequential.

They showed Anthony J. DeZego getting out of his car in front of the Hotel Warwick; handing the doorman money; walking toward the hotel cocktail lounge; inside the cocktail lounge (four shots, including one of the bellboy giving him the car keys); leaving the cocktail lounge; walking toward the garage; and, the last shot, entering the garage.

"This is in the right sequence? This all of them?" Washington asked, handing the stack of photographs to Dolan.

"What do you mean, is this all of them?" Dolan snapped. "Yeah, it's all of them." He flipped through them quickly and said, "Yeah, that's the order I took them in."

Anomaly! Anomaly! Anomaly!

"Sergeant, I'd like a set of these pictures for my report," Washington said. "The negatives, I guess, are in the photo lab?"

"The guy that runs the lab is a pal of mine," Dolan said. "I'll give him a ring and have him run you off a set."

"Thank you," Washington said. "Looking at them again, does anything new come to your mind?"

"Not a fucking thing," Dolan said firmly.

"Well, we tried," Washington said.

"Is that all?"

"Unless you can think of something."

"Not a fucking thing. If I think of something, I'll give you a call."

"I'd really appreciate that," Washington said.

"And like I said, I'll call my friend in the photo lab and have him run off a set of prints for you."

"Thank you," Washington said.

Jason Washington parked his unmarked car in the parking lot behind the Roundhouse at 7th and Race and walked purposefully toward the building.

There are four anomalies vis-à-vis Sergeant Dolan and his photographs.

One, Dolan had told me that he and his partner had been trailing the Detweiler girl and had trailed her to the parking garage. There were no photographs of Penelope Detweiler; they were all of Anthony J. DeZego. Why?

Two, there were no photographs of Matt Payne and his girlfriend in the Porsche. If he thought Matt was dealing drugs, there should have been.

Three, there were only thirteen photographs in the stack Dolan showed me. Thirty-five millimeter film comes in twenty-four- and thirty-six-exposure rolls. Ordinarily almost every frame on a roll of film is exposed, and ordinarily every exposed frame on a roll is printed. And since it is better to have too many photographs than too few, it seemed likely that Dolan would have taken far more than thirteen photographs during the time he had been watching DeZego. Probably a roll at the hotel, and then a fresh one, starting from the moment DeZego left the hotel. Probably a thirty-six-exposure roll, so he wouldn't run out at the wrong time. That's what I would have done.

Four, he suddenly turned obliging at the end. He would call a pal in the photo lab and have his pal make a set of prints and send them to me. Had he suddenly joined the Urban League and vowed to lean over backward in the interests of racial harmony and/or interdepartmental cooperation? Or did he want to control what pictures the lab sent me to include in my report?

Three guys were on duty in the photo lab. One of them seemed less than overjoyed to see Detective Jason Washington. Washington consequently headed straight for him.

"Morning!" he said cheerfully.

"I just this minute got off the phone," the lab guy, a corporal, said. "With Dolan, I mean."

"Good," Washington said. "Then you know why I'm here."

"I'll get to it as soon as I can," the corporal said. "You want to come by about two, or do you want I should send them to you?"

"I want them now," Washington heard himself say. "Didn't Sergeant Dolan tell you that?"

"What do you mean, 'now'?"

"Like, I'll wait," Washington said.

"It don't work that way, Washington, you know that. Other people are in line ahead of you."

"No," Washington said. "I'm at the head of line."

"The fuck you are!"

"Well, you can either take my word for that or we can call Inspector Wohl and he'll tell you I'm at the head of the line."

"Wohl don't run the photo lab," the corporal said.

This Irish bastard is sweating too. What the hell have I found here?

"Well, you tell him that."

"What I am going to do is find the lieutenant and ask him what to do about your coming in here like Jesus Christ Almighty. Who the fuck do you think you are, anyway?"

"Let's go see him together," Washington said.

"*I'll* go see him," the corporal said. "*You* read the fucking sign." He pointed to the sign: AUTHORIZED PERSONNEL ONLY IN THE LAB.

"I'm surprised," Jason Washington said as he ducked inside the counter, "that an experienced, well-educated police officer such as yourself hasn't learned that there is an exception to every rule."

"You lost your fucking mind or what, Washington?"

That's entirely possible. But the essence of my professional experience as a police officer is that there are times when you

*should go with a gut feeling. And this is one of those times.
I have a gut feeling that if I let you out of my sight, that roll,
or rolls, of film are going to turn up missing.*

What the hell are these two up to?

The corporal turned surprisingly docile when they were
actually standing before the lieutenant's desk. His indignation
vanished.

"Sir," he said, "Detective Washington has an unusual request that I thought you should handle."

"Hello, Jason," the lieutenant said. "Long time no see.
How are things out in the country? Do you miss the big city?"

"I would hate to think the lieutenant was making fun of
our happy home at Bustleton and Bowler," Washington said.
"Where the deer and the antelope play."

"Who, me?" the lieutenant chuckled. "What can we do
for you?"

"I'm working the DeZego job," Washington said.

"So I heard."

"Sergeant Dolan of Narcotics shot a roll of film. I need
prints this time yesterday."

"You got the negatives?" the lieutenant asked the corporal, who nodded. "You got it, Jason. Anything else?"

"I want to take the negatives with me."

After only a second's hesitation the lieutenant said, "Sign
a receipt and they're yours."

"And I may want some blown up specially," Washington
said. "Could I go in the darkroom with him?"

"Sure. That's it?"

*Since your face reflected a certain attitude of unease when
you heard that I want to go into the darkroom with you,
Corporal, and that I'm taking the negatives with me, I will
go into the darkroom with you and I will take the negatives
with me. What the hell is it with these photographs?*

"Yes, sir. Thank you very much."

"Anytime, Jason. That's what we're here for."

The corporal became the spirit of cooperation, to the point
of offering Washington a rubber apron once they entered the
darkroom.

*If I were a suspicious man, Washington thought, or a cynic,
I might think that he has considered the way the wind is blowing, and also that if anything is amiss, he didn't do it, or at*

least can't blamed for it, and has now decided that Dolan can swing in the wind all by himself.

There was only one roll of film, a thirty-six-exposure roll.

"Hold it up to the light," the corporal said. "Or, if you'd like, I can make you a contact sheet. Take only a minute."

"A what?"

"A print of every negative in negative size on a piece of eight-by-ten."

"Why don't you just feed the roll through the enlarger?" Washington asked.

Jason Washington was not exactly a stranger to the mysteries of a darkroom. Years before, he had even fooled around with souping and printing his own 35-mm black-and-white film. That had ended when Martha said the chemicals made the apartment smell like a sewage-treatment station and had to go. He had no trouble "reading" a negative projected through an enlarger, although the blacks came out white, and vice versa.

The first negative projected through the enlarger showed Anthony J. DeZego emerging from his Cadillac in front of the Warwick Hotel. The second showed him handing money to the doorman. The third showed him walking toward the door to the hotel cocktail lounge. The fourth showed him inside the cocktail lounge; the view partially blocked by a pedestrian, a neatly dressed man carrying an attaché case who was looking through the plate-glass window into the cocktail lounge. That photograph had not been in the stack of five-by-sevens Sergeant Dolan had shown him.

Next came an image of DeZego inside the bar, the pedestrian having moved on down the street. Then there were two images of DeZego's car as the bellboy walked toward it and got in it. The pedestrian was in one of the two, casually glancing at the car. He was not in the second photograph. Dolan had shown him a print of the bellman and the car, less the pedestrian.

What's with the pedestrian?

The next image was of DeZego's Cadillac making a left turn. And the one after that was of the pedestrian crossing the street in the same direction. Dolan's stack of prints hadn't included that one, either.

Is that guy following DeZego's car? Who the hell is he?

The next shot showed the chubby bellboy walking back to the hotel, apparently after having parked DeZego's Cadillac. Two frames later the pedestrian with the attaché case showed up again. Then came a shot of the bellboy giving DeZego his car keys, and then, no longer surprising Jason Washington, the pedestrian came walking down the sidewalk again.

"Go back toward the beginning of the roll, please," Jason Washington said. "The third or fourth frame, I think."

"Sure," the corporal said cooperatively.

The image of the well-dressed pedestrian with the attaché case looking into the Warwick Hotel cocktail lounge appeared.

"Print that one, please," Washington said.

"Five-by-seven all right?"

"Yeah, sure," Washington said, and then immediately changed his mind. "No, make it an eight-by-ten. And you better make three copies."

"Three eight-by-tens," the corporal said. "No problem."

Sergeant Patrick J. Dolan is an experienced investigator. If he didn't spot the guy with the attaché case, my name is Jerry Carlucci. Who the hell is he, and why didn't Dolan want me to see his picture?

Even in a well-equipped photographic laboratory with all the necessary equipment to print, develop, and then dry photographs, it takes some time to prepare thirty-six eight-by-ten enlargements. It was 10:10 when Detective Jason Washington, carrying three large manila envelopes each containing a set of the dozen photographs Sergeant Dolan had taken, but not either included in his report or shown to Washington, came out of the Police Administration Building.

He got in his car and drove the half dozen blocks to Philadelphia's City Hall, then parked his car in the inner courtyard with its nose against a sign reading RESERVED FOR INSPECTORS.

As he got out of the car he saw that he had parked beside a car familiar to him, that of Staff Inspector Peter Wohl. He checked the license plate to be sure. Wohl, obviously, was somewhere inside City Hall.

Peter will want to know about this, Jason Washington thought immediately. *But even if I could find him in here, what the hell could I tell him I have? It's probably a good thing I didn't bump into him.*

He then visited inside City Hall and began to prowl the cavernous corridors outside its many courtrooms, looking for Sergeant Patrick J. Dolan.

"You have your special assistant with you, Inspector?" Mayor Jerry Carlucci asked, by way of greeting, Staff Inspector Peter Wohl.

"No, sir," Peter Wohl replied.

"Where is he?"

"He's working with Detective Washington, sir."

"That's a shame," the mayor said. "I had hoped to see him."

"I didn't know that, sir."

"Didn't you, Inspector? Or were you thinking, maybe, 'He's a nice kid and I'll keep him out of the line of fire'?"

"I didn't know you wanted to see him, Mr. Mayor," Peter said.

"But now that you do, do you have any idea what I would have liked to have said to him, if given the opportunity?"

"I think he already heard that, Mr. Mayor, from me. Last night," Peter said.

"So you know he has diarrhea of the mouth?"

"I used those very words, Mr. Mayor, when I *counseled* him last night," Peter said.

Carlucci glowered at Wohl for a moment and then laughed. "You *counseled* him, did you, Peter?"

"Yes, sir."

"I don't know why the hell I'm laughing," the mayor said. "That was pretty goddamn embarrassing at the Browne place. Dick Detweiler was goddamn near hysterical. Christ, he *was* hysterical."

"Mr. Mayor," Chief Inspector Dennis V. Coughlin said, "I think any father naturally would be upset to learn that his daughter was involved with narcotics."

"Particularly if he heard it third hand, the way Detweiler did," the mayor said icily, "instead of, for example, from a senior police official directly."

"Yes, sir," Coughlin said.

His Honor the Mayor was not through.

"Maybe an *Irish* police official," Carlucci said. "The Irish are supposed to be good at politics. An Irishman could have told Detweiler about his daughter with a little Irish—what is it you call your bullshit, Denny, the kind you just tried to lay on me?—blarney."

"Sir," Wohl said, "it could have been worse."

"How the hell could it have been worse?" the mayor snapped. "Do you have any idea how much Detweiler contributed to my last campaign? Or phrased another way, how *little* he, and his friends, will contribute to my next campaign unless we put away, for a long time—and more importantly, soon—whoever popped his daughter?"

"We have information that Miss Detweiler was involved with Tony the Zee, Mr. Mayor. He may not know that. Payne didn't tell him."

The mayor looked him, his eyebrows raised in incredulity.

"Oh, *shit*!" he said. "How good is your information?"

"My source is Payne. He got it from the Nesbitt boy—the Marine?—who got it from the Browne girl," Wohl said.

"Then it's just a matter of time until Detweiler learns that too," the mayor said.

"Even if that's true, Mr. Mayor," Dennis Coughlin said, "I don't see how he could hold that against you."

The mayor snapped his head toward Coughlin and glowered at him a moment. "I hope that's more of your fucking blarney, Denny. I would hate to think that I have a chief inspector who is so fucking dumb, he believes what he just said."

"Jerry, for chrissake," Chief Inspector Matt Lowenstein said. It was the first time he had spoken. "Denny's on your side. We all are."

Carlucci glared at him, then looked as if he were going to say something but didn't.

"I really don't see, Jerry," Coughlin said reasonably, "how he could hold his daughter's problems against you."

"Okay," Carlucci said, his tone as reasonable, "I'll tell you how. We have a man who has just learned his daughter is into hard drugs. And, according to Peter, here, is about to learn that she has been running around with a guinea gangster. What's your information, Peter? What does 'involved with' mean? That she's been fucking him?"

"Yes, sir. Payne seemed pretty sure it was more than a casual acquaintance."

"Okay. So what we have here is a guy who is a pillar of the community. His *wife* is a pillar of the community. They have done everything they could for their precious daughter. They have sent her to the right schools and the right churches and seen that she associates with the right kind of people—like young Payne, for example. And all of a sudden she gets herself popped with a shotgun, and then it comes out that she's a junkie and fucking a guinea gangster. How can that be? It's certainly not *her* fault, and it's certainly not *their* fault. So it has to be society's fault. And who is responsible for society? Who is supposed to put gangsters and drug dealers in jail? Why, the *police* are. That's why we *have* police. If the *police* had done their job, there would be no drugs on the street, and if the *police* had done their job, that low-life guinea gangster would have been put in jail and would not have been getting in precious Penny's pants. That's what Detweiler called his daughter last night, by the way: 'precious Penny.' Is any of this getting through to you, Denny?"

"Yeah, sure," Coughlin said resignedly. "It's not fair, but that's the way it is."

"Nothing personal, Denny, but that's the first intelligent thing you've said so far this morning," the mayor said. He let that sink in a moment, then turned to Peter Wohl. "What I told Detweiler last night—not knowing, of course, that his precious Penny was fucking DeZego—was that we were close to finding the man who had shot her. How much more of an asshole is that going to make me look like, Peter?"

"We may be on to something," Wohl said carefully.

"Christ, I hope so. What?"

"Dave Pekach had dinner with his girlfriend—"

"The Peebles woman? That one?"

"Yes, sir."

"I'm going off on a tangent," the mayor said. "What about that? Is that going to embarrass the Department?"

"No. I don't think so," Wohl said. "Unless a police captain acting like a teenager in love for the first time is embarrassing."

The mayor was not amused. "She has friends in very high

places," he said coldly. "Do you think maybe you should drop a hint that he had better treat her right?"

"I don't think that's necessary, Mr. Mayor," Wohl said. "Dave Pekach is really a decent guy. And they're really in love."

The mayor considered that dubiously for a moment but finally said, "If you say so, Peter, okay. But what we don't need is any more rich people pissed off at the Department than we already have. Arthur J. Nelson and Dick Detweiler is enough already. So he had dinner with her . . ."

"At Ristorante Alfredo," Wohl went on. "He had made reservations. When he got there, Vincenzo Savarese was there. He gave him— I'm cutting corners here."

"You're doing fine," the mayor said.

"A little speech about being grateful for a favor Dave had done for him—nothing dirty there, just Dave being nice to a girl he didn't know was Savarese's granddaughter. You want to hear about that?"

"Not unless it's important."

"Savarese said thank you for the favor, and then Ricco Baltazari gave Dave a matchbook, said Dave dropped it. Inside was a name and address. Black guy named Marvin P. Lanier. Small-time. Says he's a gambler. Actually he's a pimp. And according to two of Dave's undercover cops—Martinez and McFadden, the two who caught the junkie who killed Dutch Moffitt—Lanier sometimes transports cocaine from Harlem."

"You've lost me," the mayor said. "What's a nigger pimp got to do with precious Penny Detweiler?"

"Last night Martinez and McFadden saw Lanier. They had been using him as a snitch. Lanier told them, quote, a guinea shot Tony the Zee, unquote."

"He had a name?" the mayor asked.

"He was supposed to come up with one by four o'clock this afternoon," Wohl said.

"You think he will?"

"Lanier got popped last night. Five shots with a .38," Wohl said. "Do you know Joe D'Amata of Homicide?"

"Yeah."

"He got the job. Because there was a Highway car seen at

the crime scene, he came out to Bustleton and Bowler first thing this morning to see what we had on Lanier.''

''Which was?''

''Nothing. Martinez and McFadden were in the car. Working on their own.''

''I'm having a little trouble following all this, Peter,'' the mayor said, almost apologetically.

''When McFadden and Martinez saw Lanier, they took a shotgun away from him. Joe D'Amata said Lanier had a shotgun under his bed. So I thought maybe there was a tie-in—''

''How?''

''Savarese pointed us to this guy. DeZego was popped with a shotgun. Lanier had two. Lanier gets killed.''

''What about the shotgun? Shotguns?''

''I sent them to the lab.''

''And?''

''I can call. They may not be through yet.''

''Call.''

Less than a minute later Wohl replaced one of the mayor's three telephones in its cradle.

''Forensics,'' Wohl announced, ''says that the shotgun-shell cases found on the roof of the Penn Services Parking Garage were almost certainly, based on the marks made by the ejector, fired from the Remington Model 1100 shotgun D'Amata found under Lanier's bed.''

''Bingo,'' Dennis V. Coughlin said.

''You're saying the pimp shot DeZego?'' the mayor asked.

''I think Savarese wants *us* to think Lanier shot DeZego,'' Matt Lowenstein said.

''Why?'' the mayor asked.

''Who the hell knows?'' Lowenstein said.

''Check with Organized Crime,'' the mayor said. ''See if they can come up with any reason the mob would want DeZego dead.''

''They're working on that, Jerry,'' Lowenstein said. ''I asked them the day after DeZego got popped; they said they'd already been asked to check by Jason Washington.''

If there was a rebuke in Lowenstein's reply, the mayor seemed not to have noticed.

''Washington working on this dead-pimp angle?'' Carlucci asked.

"No, sir," Wohl replied. "Chief Lowenstein loaned me D'Amata. I was going to have him work with Washington. But when I couldn't find him, I put Tony Harris on it."

"Why can't you find Washington?"

"I don't know where he is," Wohl said, and then heard his words. "I didn't mean that, sir, the way it came out. He's working on the street somewhere, and when I got the word to come here, he hadn't reported in yet. I've got Payne looking for him. For all I know, he's probably already found him."

"Tony Harris is working on the Officer Magnella job, right?" the mayor asked. "So you turn him off that to put him on this?"

"We're getting nowhere on the Magnella job, Mr. Mayor," Peter Wohl said. "That one's going to take time. I wanted a good Homicide detective at the Lanier scene while it was still hot."

"Meaning you don't think Joe D'Amata is a good Homicide detective?" Lowenstein snapped.

"If I didn't think Joe was as good as he is, I wouldn't have asked you for him, Chief," Wohl replied. "Maybe that was a bad choice of words. What I meant was that I wanted Harris and D'Amata, now that we know we're looking for something beside the doer of a pimp shooting, to take another look at the crime scene as soon as possible."

"I don't like that," the mayor said thoughtfully.

"Sir?" Peter asked.

"Shit, I didn't mean *that* the way it came out. I wouldn't tell you how to do your job, Peter. What I meant was what you said about the Magnella job, that it's going to take time. We can't afford that. You can't let people get away with shooting a cop. You have to catch him—them—quick. And in a good, tight, all-the-i's-dotted, all-the-t's-crossed arrest."

"Yes, sir, I know. But Harris told me all he knows how to do is go back to the beginning. There's nothing new to run down."

"Lowenstein giving you all the help you need?"

"Chief Lowenstein has been very helpful, sir. I couldn't ask for anything more," Wohl said.

"Denny, you paying attention?" the mayor asked.

"Sir?"

"Peter knows what's the right thing to say to make friends

and influence people. You ought to watch him, learn from him.''

"Oh, fuck you, Jerry," Coughlin said when he realized that the real target of Carlucci's barb was Wohl, and that he was being teased.

"Make that, 'oh, fuck you, Mr. Mayor,' sir," Carlucci said, chuckling. Then his voice grew serious. "Okay. Thanks for coming in. If it wasn't for what Peter said about the Magnella job, I'd say I feel a lot better than I felt before. Jesus, I'd like to hang the DeZego job on Savarese, or even on one of his scumbags."

Coughlin stood up and shook the mayor's hand when it was offered. Lowenstein followed him past the mayor's desk, and then past Wohl.

The mayor hung on to Wohl's hand, signaling that he wanted Wohl to remain behind.

"Yes, sir?"

"I spoke to your dad last night," the mayor said.

"Last night?" Peter asked, surprised.

"This morning. Very early this morning. He told me he had been talking to you and that you led him to believe your salami was on the chopping block with all this, and you thought that was unfair."

"I— We had a couple of drinks at Groverman's."

"So he said."

"I'm sorry he called you, Mr. Mayor."

"How could you have stopped him? What I told him, Peter, was that you were absolutely right. Your salami is on the chopping block, and it isn't fair. I also told him that if you come out of this smelling like a rose, you stand a good chance to be the youngest full inspector in the Department."

"Jesus," Wohl said.

"My salami's in jeopardy, Peter, not only yours. I'm going to look like a fucking fool if Special Operations drops the ball on all this. If I don't look like a fucking fool when this is all over, then you get taken care of. Take my meaning?"

"Yes, sir."

"Give my regards to your mother, Peter," Mayor Carlucci said, and walked Peter to his office door.

• • •

Charley McFadden was almost home before he realized there was a silver lining in the dark cloud of being on Inspector Wohl's shit list. And that was a dark cloud indeed. If Wohl was pissed at them, that meant Captains Sabara and Pekach were also pissed at them, and that meant that Sergeant Big Bill Henderson would conclude that hunting season was now open on him and Hay-zus. Christ only knew what *that* son of a bitch would do to them now.

There was a good possibility that he and Hay-zus would wind up in a district somewhere, maybe even in a goddamn wagon. McFadden really didn't want to be a Highway Patrolman, but he wanted to be an ordinary, turn-off-the-fire-hydrants, guard-a-school-crossing cop even less.

And if Wohl did send them to a district, it would probably go on their records that they had been Probationary Highway Patrolmen and flunked, or whatever it would be called. Busted probation. *Shit!*

The silver lining appeared when he turned onto his street and started looking for a place to park the Volkswagen. His eyes fell on the home of Mr. Robert McCarthy, and his mind's eye recalled the red hair and blue eyes and absolutely perfect little ass of Mr. McCarthy's niece, Margaret McCarthy, R.N.

And he had all fucking day off, until say, three, which would give him an hour to get back in uniform and drive out to Bustleton and Bowler.

He found a place to park—for once—almost right in front of his house and ran up the stairs and inside.

"What are you doing home?" his mother asked.

"Got something to do, Ma," he called as he went up the stairs.

He took his uniform off and hung it carefully in the closet. Then he dressed with great care: a new white shirt with buttons on the collar, like he had seen Matt Payne wear; a dark brown sport coat; slightly lighter brown slacks; black loafers with a flap and little tassels in front, also seen on Matt Payne; and a necktie with stripes like both Inspector Wohl and Payne wore. He was so concerned with his appearance that he forgot his gun and had to take the jacket off and put on his shoulder holster.

Then it occurred to him that although he had shaved before going out to Bustleton and Bowler, that was a couple of hours ago, and a little more after-shave wouldn't hurt anything; girls were supposed to like it, so he generously splashed *Brut* on his face and neck before leaving his room.

"Where are you going all dressed up?" his mother asked, and then sniffed suspiciously. "What's that I smell? Perfume?"

"It's after-shave lotion, Ma."

"I'd hate to tell you what it smells like," she said.

And then he was out the door.

He walked purposefully toward Broad Street until he was certain his mother, sure to be peering from behind the lace curtain on the door, couldn't see him anymore, and then he cut across the street and went back to the McCarthy house, where he quickly climbed the steps and rang the bell, hoping it would be answered before his mother made one of her regularly scheduled, every-five-minutes inspections of the neighborhood.

Mr. McCarthy, wearing a suit, opened the door.

"Hello, Charley, what can I do for you?"

"Is Margaret around?"

"We're going to pay our respects to the Magnellas," Mr. McCarthy said.

"Oh," Charley said.

"You been over there yet?"

"No."

"You want to go with us?"

"Yeah," Charley said.

"I thought maybe that's what you had in mind," Mr. McCarthy said. "You're all dressed up."

"Yeah," Charley said.

"Goddamn shame," Mr. McCarthy said.

"Hello, Charley," Margaret McCarthy said. "You going with us?"

She was wearing a suit with a white blouse and a little round hat.

Jesus Christ, that's a good-looking woman!

"I wanted to pay my respects," Charley said.

"You might as well ride with us," Mr. McCarthy said.

The ride to Stanley Rocco and Sons, Funeral Directors, was pleasant until they got there. That is to say, he got to ride in the backseat with Margaret and he could smell her— an entirely delightful sensation—even over his after-shave. He could even see the lace at the hem of her slip, which triggered his imagination.

But then, when Mr. McCarthy had parked the Ford and Margaret had climbed out and he had in a gentlemanly manner averted his eyes from the unintentional display of lower limbs and he got out, he saw that the place was crowded with cops, in uniform and out.

"Jesus, wait a minute," he said to Margaret.

He took out his wallet and sighed with relief when he found a narrow strip of black elasticized material. He had put it in there after the funeral of Captain Dutch Moffitt, intending to put it in a drawer when he got home.

Thank God I forgot!

"What is that?" Margaret asked.

"A mourning stripe," Charley said. "You cut up a hatband."

"Oh," she said, obviously not understanding.

"When there's a dead cop, you wear it across your badge," he explained as he worked the band across his. "I almost forgot."

He started to pin the badge to his lapel.

"You got it on crooked," Margaret said. "Let me."

He could see her scalp where her hair was parted as she pinned the badge on correctly.

She looked up at him and met his eyes and smiled, and his heart jumped.

"There," she said.

"Thanks," he said.

They caught up with Mr. and Mrs. McCarthy and walked to the funeral home.

There was a book for people to write their names in on a stand just inside the door. It was just about full.

He wrote "Officer Charles McFadden, Badge 8774, Special Operations" under the name of some captain he didn't know from the 3rd District.

Officer Joseph Magnella was in an open casket, surrounded by flowers. They were burying him in his uniform, Charley saw. There were two cops from his district, wearing white gloves, standing at each end of the casket, and there was an American flag on a pole behind each of them.

In his turn Charley followed Mr. and Mrs. McCarthy and

Margaret to the prie-dieu and dropped to his knees. He made
the sign of the cross and, with part of his mind, offered the
prayers a Roman Catholic does in such circumstances. They
came to him automatically, and although his lips moved, he
didn't hear them.

He was thinking, *Christ, they put face powder and lipstick
on him.*

*I wonder if they will take the badge off before they close
the casket, or whether they'll bury him with it.*

*The last time I saw him, he was still in the gutter with
somebody's coat over his face and shoulders.*

Holy Mary, Mother of God, don't let that happen to me!

*And the word is, they're not even close to finding the scum-
bags who did this to him!*

*I'd like to find those cocksuckers! They wouldn't look as
good in their coffins as this poor bastard does!*

As he had approached the coffin he had noticed the Magnella family, plus the girlfriend, sitting in the first row of
chairs. When he rose from the prie-dieu, they were all standing up. Mr. Magnella was embracing Mr. McCarthy, and
Mrs. McCarthy was patting Mrs. Magnella. The girlfriend
looked as if somebody had punched her in the stomach; Margaret was smiling at her uncomfortably.

"Al," Mr. McCarthy said when Charley approached, "this
is Charley McFadden, from the neighborhood."

"I'm real sorry this happened," Charley said as Mr. Magnella shook his hand.

"You knew my Joe?"

"No. I seen him around, though."

"It was nice of you to come."

"I wanted to pay my respects."

"This is Joe's mother."

"Mrs. Magnella, I'm real sorry for you."

"Thank you for coming."

"I was Joe's fiancée," the girlfriend said.

"I'm real sorry."

"We were going to get married in two months."

"I'm really sorry for you."

"Thank you for coming."

"I'm Joe's brother."

"I'm really sorry this happened."

"Thank you for coming."

"Bob," Mr. Magnella said to Mr. McCarthy, "go in the room on the other side and fix yourself and Officer McFadden a drink."

"Thank you, Al," Mr. McCarthy said. "I might just do that."

Margaret put her hand on Charley's arm, and they followed Mr. and Mrs. McCarthy across the room to a smaller room, where a knot of men were gathered around a table on which sat a dozen bottles of whiskey.

Margaret opened her purse and wiped her eyes with a handkerchief.

"Seagram's all right for you, Charley?" Mr. McCarthy asked.

"Fine," Charley said.

As he put the glass to his mouth the soft murmur of voices died out. Curious, he turned to see what was going on.

Mrs. Magnella had entered the room. She looked like she was headed right for him.

She was. Her son and husband were on her heels, looking worried.

"I know who you are," Mrs. Magnella said to Charley McFadden. "I seen your picture in the papers. You're the cop who caught the junkie and pushed him under the subway, right?"

That wasn't what happened. I was chasing the son of a bitch and he fell!

"Uh!" Charley said.

"I want you to find the people who did this to my Joseph and push them under the subway!"

"Mama," Officer Magnella's brother said. "Come on, Mama!"

"I want them dead! I want them dead!"

"Come on, Mama! Pop, where's Father Loretto?"

"I'm here," a silver-haired priest said. "Elena, what's the matter?"

"I want them dead! I want them dead!"

"It's going to be all right, Elena," the priest said. "Come with me, we'll talk."

"I'm sorry about this," Officer Magnella's brother said to

Officer McFadden as the priest led Officer Magnella's mother away.

"It's all right, don't worry about it," Charley said.

Margaret McCarthy looked at Charley McFadden and saw that it wasn't all right. Without thinking what she was doing, she put her hand out to his face, and when he looked at her, she stood on her tiptoes and kissed him.

EIGHTEEN

Officer Matthew Payne was feeling a little sorry for himself. He had been given an impossible task—how the hell was he supposed to find one man in a city the size of Philadelphia?—and Peter Wohl had made it plain that he expected him to accomplish it: No excuses, please. Just do it.

When he had tried looking for Jason Washington in all the places he could think, starting with his home, and then going to the Roundhouse and over to the parking garage and even to Hahneman Hospital, he went back to the Roundhouse, on the admittedly somewhat flimsy reasoning that Washington had told him to meet him in Homicide in the Roundhouse before he left word on the answering machine not to meet him there.

Washington was not in Homicide and had not been there.

It occurred to Matt that very possibly Washington had finished doing whatever he was doing and had gone, as he said he would, out to Bustleton and Bowler. If Washington *was* at Bustleton and Bowler, where he said he would be, and Officer

Payne was downtown at the Roundhouse looking for him, Officer Payne was going to look like a goddamn fool.

Which, in the final analysis, was probably a just evaluation.

He called Bustleton and Bowler.

"Special Operations, Sergeant Anderson."

"This is Payne, Sergeant. Is Detective Washington around there someplace?"

"No. He called in and wanted to talk to you. He said he told you to wait for him here."

"Did he say where he was?"

"No. He just said if I saw you, I was to sit on you."

"Okay."

"Wait a minute. He said that he would be at City Hall."

"Thank you very much," Matt said.

He hung up, rode the elevator down from Homicide, and ran out of the building into the parking lot, where a white-capped Traffic officer was in the process of putting an illegal-parking citation under the Porsche's windshield wiper.

"Could I change your mind about doing that if I told you I was on the job?" Matt asked.

The Traffic cop, who was old enough to be Matt's father, looked at him dubiously.

"You're a 369?"

Matt nodded.

"Where?"

"Special Operations," Matt said.

The Traffic cop, shaking his head, removed the citation.

"What did you guys do?" he asked, nodding at the Porsche. "Confiscate that from a drug dealer?"

This is not the time to tell Daddy that I chopped down the cherry tree.

"Yeah," Matt said. "Nice, huh?"

The Traffic cop shook his head resignedly and walked off without another word.

Matt drove to City Hall and parked the Porsche in an area reserved FOR POLICE VEHICLES ONLY.

I would not be at all surprised, the way things are going today, that when I come out of here, to find a cop, maybe that same cop, putting another ticket on me here.

He went inside the building and trotted up the stairs to the second floor. Thirty seconds after that he spotted Detective Jason Washington walking toward him. From the look on Washington's face, Matt could tell he was not overcome with joy to see him.

"What are you doing here?" Washington asked in greeting.

"Inspector Wohl sent me to find you," Matt said. "He wants to see you right away."

"Keep looking," Washington said. "You didn't find me yet."

"Okay," Matt said, with only a moment's hesitation. "I didn't."

"In ten minutes, give or take, you will find me in the ground-floor stairwell, on the southeast corner of the building."

"Yes, sir," Matt said.

"It's important, Matt," Washington said. "Trust me."

"Certainly."

Wait a minute! If my intention is to put Dolan off-balance, the kid can help. Dolan doesn't like him.

"I don't have time to explain this, even if I were sure I could," Washington said. "But I just changed my mind. I want you to come with me. I'm looking for your friend, Sergeant Dolan."

Matt's face registered surprise.

"I don't want you to open your mouth, understand?"

"Yes, sir."

"You any kind of an actor?"

"I don't know."

"Let us suppose that I have caught your friend Dolan doing something he shouldn't have," Washington said, "and I told you. Do you think you could work up a smug, self-satisfied look? So that Dolan would think you know he's in trouble and are very pleased about it?"

"If that son of a bitch is in trouble, I wouldn't have to do very much acting," Matt said.

"Just keep your mouth shut," Washington said. "I mean that. If I blow this, we could both be in trouble."

"Okay," Matt said.

"And there, obviously at the intervention of a benign deity," Washington said softly, "is the son of a bitch."

Matt looked over his shoulder. Sergeant Dolan was coming down the crowded corridor. At the moment Matt looked, Dolan spotted them. He did not look very happy about it.

"Sergeant Dolan," Washington called out, "may I see you a moment, please?"

He walked over to him with Matt at his heels.

"What's on your mind, Washington?" Sergeant Dolan asked.

Washington turned to Matt and handed him two of the three large manila envelopes.

"Give one to Chief Lowenstein and the other one to Chief Coughlin," he said.

"Yes, sir."

"But I'd suggest you stick around, Matt, until we have Sergeant Dolan's explanation."

"Yes, sir."

"You know Officer Payne, don't you, Sergeant? He's Inspector Wohl's special assistant."

"Yeah, I know him. Whaddaya say, Payne?"

Matt nodded at Sergeant Dolan.

"Sorry to bother you again, Sergeant," Washington said. "But I've come up with some more photographs. I'd like to show them to you."

He handed Dolan the third envelope. Dolan opened it. His face showed that what he considered the worst possible scenario had begun to play.

"So?" he said with transparent belligerence.

"I was hoping you could tell me who those two gentlemen are," Washington said.

"Haven't the faintest fucking idea. They was just on the street."

"I was wondering why those photographs weren't included in your report, or in the photographs you showed me."

"They wasn't important."

"You wouldn't want to even guess who those two gentlemen are?"

"No, I wouldn't," Dolan said.

"Let's stop the crap, Dolan," Washington said. "This has gone too far."

"Fuck you, Washington," Dolan said, his bravado transparent.

"Payne, get on the phone and tell Inspector Wohl that Sergeant Dolan is being uncooperative," Washington said. "And ask him to please let me know whether he wants to take it from here or whether I should take this directly to Chief Lowenstein. I'll wait here with Sergeant Dolan."

"Yes, sir," Matt said.

"Washington, can I talk to you private?" Dolan asked. "It's not what you think it is."

"How do you know what I think it is?"

"It's dumb but it's not dirty," Dolan said, "is what I mean."

Detective Washington's face registered suspicion and distaste.

"Come on, Washington," Sergeant Dolan said, "I've got as much time on the job as you do. I told you this isn't dirty."

"But you don't want Payne to hear it, right?" Washington said. "So you tell me about it, and later it's your word against mine?"

"That's not it at all," Dolan said.

"Then what is it?"

"Well, okay, then. But not here in the fucking corridor."

Washington let him sweat fifteen seconds, which seemed to be much longer, and then he said, "Okay, Dolan. I know you're a good cop. You and I will find someplace to talk. Alone. And Payne will wait here until we're finished."

Dolan nodded. He looked at Matt Payne. "Nothing personal, Payne."

Matt nodded.

Washington took Dolan's arm and they walked down the wide, high-ceilinged corridor. Washington opened a door, looked inside, and then held it wide for Dolan to precede him.

Matt waited where he had been told to wait for three or four minutes, and then curiosity got the better of him and he walked down the corridor. Through a very dirty pane of glass he saw Washington and Dolan in an empty courtroom. They were standing beside one of the large, ornately carved tables provided for counsel during trial.

Matt walked back down the corridor to where he had been told to wait.

A minute later Washington and Dolan came out of the

courtroom. Dolan walked toward Matt. Washington beckoned for Matt to follow him and then walked quickly in the other direction, toward the staircase. Dolan avoided looking at Matt as he passed him. Matt thought he looked sick.

Washington didn't wait for Matt to catch up with him. On the stair landing Matt looked down and saw Washington going down the stairs two at a time. He ran after him and caught up with him in the courtyard. By then Washington was in his car, and had taken the microphone from the glove compartment.

"W-William One, W-William Seven," Washington said.

"W-William One."

"Inspector, I'm at City Hall. Can I meet you somewhere?"

"I'm headed for Bustleton and Bowler. Did Payne find you?"

"Yeah. But I would rather talk to you before you get to the office."

"Okay. I'm at Broad and 66th Avenue at the Oak Lane Diner. I'll wait for you there."

"On my way. Thank you," Washington said, and put the microphone away. He looked at Payne. "You ever read *Through the Looking Glass*?"

Matt nodded.

"Profound book, although I understand he wrote it stoned on cocaine. Things really are more Curiouser than you would believe. If I lose you in traffic, Wohl's waiting for us in the Oak Lane Diner at Broad and 66th Avenue."

He pulled the door closed and started the engine.

Matt ran across the interior courtyard to the Porsche. There was an illegal parking citation under the windshield wiper.

He didn't see Washington in traffic, but when he got to the Oak Lane Diner, Washington's car was parked beside Wohl's. When he went inside, a waitress was delivering three cups of coffee to a booth table, on which Washington was spreading out the eight-by-ten photographs he had shown Sergeant Dolan.

Wohl looked up.

"Mr. Payne, well-known tracer of lost detectives," he said, "sit." He slid over to make room.

Washington was smiling.

"Okay, I give up," Wohl said. "What am I looking at?"

Matt looked at the photographs. A neatly dressed man carrying an attaché case and looking in the window of the cocktail lounge of the Warwick Hotel. A bald-headed man driving a Pontiac. The first man getting into the Pontiac. There were a dozen variations.

"Your FBI at work," Washington said.

"What?"

"They were apparently—what's the word they use, surveilling?—surveilling Mr. DeZego."

"Where'd these come from?"

"Sergeant Dolan."

"Why haven't we seen them before?"

"You're not going to believe this," Washington said.

"Try me."

"Sergeant Dolan does not like the FBI."

"So what? I'm not all that in love with them myself," Wohl said.

"So he decided to zing them," Washington said.

"What does that mean?"

"He wanted to make them squirm, to let them know that their surveillance was not as discreet as they like to think it is."

"You've lost me."

"He sent the FBI office pictures of themselves at work," Washington said. "In a plain brown envelope."

"Jesus Christ, that's childish!" Wohl said disgustedly.

"I would tend to agree," Washington said.

"Didn't he know Homicide would want to talk to these guys?" Wohl asked, and then, before there could be a reply, he thought of something else: "And the goddamn FBI! They must have known what went down. Why didn't they come forward?"

"Far be it from me to cast aspersions on our federal cousins," Washington said dryly, "but it has sometimes been alleged that the FBI doesn't like to waste its time dealing with the local authorities—unless, of course, they can steal the arrest and get their pictures in the newspapers."

"I'll be a son of a bitch!" Wohl said furiously.

"Can I say something to you as a friend, Inspector?" Washington asked.

"Sure," Wohl said. "I just can't *believe* this shit! God damn those arrogant bastards! DeZego was murdered! Assassinated! And the fucking FBI can't be bothered with it!"

"Peter, go by the book," Washington said.

"Meaning?"

"There is a departmental regulation that says any contact with federal agencies will be conducted through the Office of Extradepartmental Affairs. There's a captain in the Roundhouse—"

"Duffy," Wohl said. "Jack Duffy."

"Right. Go through Duffy."

Wohl looked at Washington for a long moment, his jaws working.

"When you're angry, Peter," Washington said, "you really give the word a whole new meaning. You get *angry*. And you *stay* angry."

A faint smile appeared on Wohl's face.

"You remember, huh, Jason?"

"I'm one of the few people who knows that it's not true you have never lost your temper," Washington said.

"Now Sherlock Holmes knows too," Wohl said, nodding at Matt Payne. "He tell you about the pimp?"

"No."

"What pimp?" Matt asked.

"That's right," Wohl said. "You don't know, either, do you?"

"No, sir."

Wohl related the whole sequence of events leading up to the death of Marvin Lanier.

"So what I think you should do, Jason," he concluded, "is get on the radio and get in touch with Tony Harris, and see what, if anything, they—he and D'Amata—have come up with. And then tell Tony I saw the mayor this morning, and he wants the Magnella shooting solved. I wish he'd get back on that."

"You saw the mayor? I saw your car at City Hall."

"Just a friendly little chat, to assure me of his absolute faith in me," Wohl said dryly.

"Yes, sir," Washington said. "You want me to take Payne with me? Or have you got something for him to do?"

Wohl gathered the photographs together, stacked them

neatly, and put them back in the envelope. "Payne, you go out to Bustleton and Bowler, driving slowly and carefully, obeying all the speed limits. When you get there, telephone Captain John J. Duffy at the Roundhouse and tell him that I would be grateful for an appointment at his earliest convenience."

"Yes, sir."

"And then contact me and tell me when Captain Duffy will be able to see me."

"Where will you be, Inspector?"

"Around," Wohl said. "Around."

"Come on, Peter!" Washington said.

"You made your point, Jason. Leave it," Wohl said. He bumped hips with Matt, signaling he wanted to get up, then picked up the envelope with the photographs. When Matt was standing in the aisle, Wohl dropped money on the table and started to walk away. Then he turned. "Good job, Jason, coming up with the photographs. Thank you."

"Just don't do something with them that will make me regret it," Washington said.

"I told you to leave it, Jason!" Wohl said, icily furious. Then he walked out of the Oak Lane Diner and got in his car. Neither Jason Washington nor Matt Payne was surprised to see him head back downtown rather than toward Bustleton and Bowler. The Philadelphia office of the Federal Bureau of Investigation was downtown.

"Until a moment ago," Washington said, "there was an element of humor in this. Now it's not at all funny."

"So he tells the FBI what he thinks of them. So what?"

Washington looked at him, as if surprised that Matt could ask such a stupid question.

"I really don't understand," Matt said.

"The FBI doesn't like criticism," he explained. "Especially in a case like this, where it's justified. So instead of admitting they acted like horses' asses, they will come up with a good reason why they didn't happen to mention to us that they had men on DeZego. 'A continuing investigation' is one phrase they use; 'classified national security matters' is another one. And they go to Commissioner Czernich and say, 'We thought we had an agreement that whenever one of your people wants something from us, he would go through

Captain Duffy's Office of Extradepartmental Affairs. Your man Wohl was just in here making all kinds of wild accusations and behaving in a most unprofessional manner.' ''

"But they were wrong," Matt protested.

"We don't like to admit it, but we need the FBI, use it a lot. The NCIC is an FBI operation. They have the best forensic laboratories in the world. They sometimes tip us off to things. They pass out spaces at the FBI Academy. You get an FBI expert to testify in court, the jury believes him if he announces the moon is made of green cheese. The bottom line is that we need them as much, maybe more, than they need us. For another example, the FBI was 'consulted' before we got the federal grant to set up Special Operations. If they had said—even suggested—that we wouldn't use the money wisely, we wouldn't have gotten it. So we try to maintain the best possible relationship with the FBI."

"And Wohl doesn't know that?"

"Wohl's angry. He has every right to be. He doesn't get that way very often, but when he does—"

"Shit," Matt said.

"Let's just hope he cools off a little before he storms through the door and tells the SAC what he thinks of him and the other assholes," Washington said.

"The what?"

"SAC, special agent in charge," Washington explained, translating. "There are also AACs, three of them, which stands for assistant agent in charge. But as pissed as Peter is, he's going to see the head man, not one of the underlings."

He slid off the seat and stood up.

"If you hear anything, let me know, and vice versa," he said.

"If that goddamn Dolan hadn't gotten clever—"

"Don't be too hard on him," Washington said. "I think one of the reasons Peter Wohl is so angry is that he knows that if he had a chance to take pictures of a couple of FBI clowns on a surveillance, he would have mailed them to their office too. I've pulled their chain once or twice myself. There's something in their anointed-by-the-Almighty demeanor that brings that sort of thing out in most cops."

He smiled at Matt and then walked out of the diner. Matt got in the Porsche and turned right onto North Broad Street.

A minute or two later he glanced at the passenger seat and saw that he still had the two envelopes with duplicate sets of photographs Washington had given him in City Hall.

He felt sure that the order to "give one to Chief Lowenstein and the other to Chief Coughlin" Washington had given him was intended only to unnerve Sergeant Dolan.

Since the pictures were of two goddamn FBI agents, they really had no value at all.

A moment later he had a second thought: *Or did they?*

Two blocks farther up North Broad Street, in violation of the Motor Vehicle Code of the City of Philadelphia, Officer Matthew Payne dropped the Porsche 911 into second gear, pushed the accelerator to the floor, and made a U-turn, narrowly averting a collision with a United Parcel truck, whose driver shook his fist at him and made an obscene comment.

"May I help you, sir?" the receptionist in the FBI office asked.

"I'd like to see Mr. Davis, please," Peter Wohl said.

"May I ask in connection with what, sir?"

"I'd rather discuss that with Mr. Davis," Wohl said. "I'm Inspector Wohl of the Philadelphia Police."

"One moment, sir. I'll see if Special Agent Davis is free."

She pushed a button on her state-of-the-art office telephone switching system, spoke softly into it, and then announced, "I'm sorry, sir, but Special Agent Davis is in conference. Can anyone else help you? Perhaps one of the assistant special agents in charge?"

"No, I don't think so. Were you speaking with Mr. Davis or his secretary?"

She did not elect to respond verbally to that presumptuous question; she just smiled benignly at him.

"Please get Mr. Davis on the line and tell him that Inspector Wohl is out here and needs to see him immediately," Peter said.

She pushed another button.

"I'm sorry to bother you, sir, but there's a Philadelphia policeman out here, a gentleman named Wohl, who insists that he has to see you." She listened a moment and then said, "Yes, sir."

Then she smiled at Peter Wohl.

"Someone will come for you shortly. Won't you have a seat? May I get you à cup of coffee?"

"Thank you," Peter said. "No coffee, thank you just the same."

He sat down on a couch in front of a coffee table on which was a glossy brochure with a four-color illustration of the seal of the Federal Bureau of Investigation and the legend, YOUR FBI in silver lettering. He did not pick it up, thinking that he knew all he wanted to know about the Federal Bureau of Investigation.

Ten minutes later a door opened and a neatly dressed young man who did not look unlike Officer Matthew W. Payne came out, walked over to him, smiled, and offered his hand.

"I'm Special Agent Foster, Inspector. Special Agent in Charge Davis will see you now. If you'll come with me?"

Wohl followed him down a corridor lined with frosted glass walls toward the corner of the building. There waited another female, obviously Davis's secretary.

"Oh, I'm so sorry, Inspector," she said. "Washington's on the line. I'm afraid it will be another minute or two. Can I offer you coffee?"

"No thank you," Peter said.

There was another couch and another coffee table. On this one was a four-color brochure with a photograph of a building on it and the legend, THE J. EDGAR HOOVER FBI BUILDING. Wohl didn't pick this one up to pass the time, either.

Five minutes later Wohl saw Davis's secretary pick up the receiver, listen, and then replace it.

"Special Agent Davis will see you now, Inspector," she said, then walked to Davis's door and held it open for him.

The FBI provided Special Agent in Charge Walter Davis, as the man in charge of its Philadelphia office, with all the accoutrements of a senior federal bureaucrat. There was a large, glistening desk with matching credenza and a high-backed chair upholstered in dark red leather. There was a carpet on the floor; another couch and coffee table; a wall full of photographs and plaques; and a large FBI seal. There were two flags against the curtains. It was a corner office with a nice view.

Walter Davis was a tall, well-built man in his forties. His gray hair was impeccably barbered, and he wore a faint gray plaid suit, a stiffly starched white shirt, a rep-striped necktie, and highly polished black wing-tip shoes.

He walked from behind his desk, a warm smile on his face, as Peter Wohl entered his office.

"How are you, Peter?" he asked. "I'm really sorry to have had to make you wait this way. But you know how it is."

"Hello, Walter," Wohl said.

"Janet, get the Inspector and I cups of coffee, will you, please?" He looked at Wohl. "Black, right? Don't dilute the flavor of good coffee?"

"Right. Black."

"So how have you been, Peter? Long time no see. How's this Special Operations thing coming along?"

"It's coming along all right," Peter said. "We're really just getting organized."

"Well, you've been getting some very favorable publicity, at least."

"How's that?"

"Well, when your man—how shall I put it—*abruptly terminated* the career of the serial rapist, the publicity you got out of that was certainly better than being stuck in the eye with a sharp stick."

"I suppose it was," Wohl said.

"Nice-looking kid too," Davis said. "I'm tempted to try to steal him away from you."

You would, too, you smooth, genial son of a bitch!

"Make him an offer," Peter Wohl said.

"Only kidding, Peter, only kidding," Special Agent in Charge Davis said.

"I never know with you," Wohl said.

Davis's secretary appeared with a tray holding two cups of coffee and a plate of chocolate-chip cookies.

"Try the cookies, Peter," Davis said. "It is my means of teaching the young the value of a dollar."

"Excuse me?"

"My daughter makes them. No cookies, no allowance."

"Very clever," Wohl said, and picked up a cookie.

"So what can the FBI do for you, Peter?"

"The nice-looking kid we're talking about is at this moment setting up an appointment for me with Jack Duffy. When

Duffy can see me, I'm going to ask him to arrange an appointment with you, for me. So I am here unofficially, okay?''

"Officially, unofficially, you're always welcome here, Peter, you know that," Davis said, smiling, but Wohl was sure he saw a flicker of wariness in Davis's eyes.

"Thank you," Wohl said. "You've heard, probably, about the shooting of Anthony J. DeZego?"

"Only what I read in the papers," Davis said, "and what Tom Tyler, my AAC for criminal matters mentioned *en passant*. I understand that Mr. DeZego got himself shot. With a shotgun. That's what you're talking about?"

As if you didn't know, you son of a bitch!

"On the roof of the Penn Services Parking Garage, behind the Bellevue-Stratford. DeZego was killed—with a shotgun. It took the top of his head off—"

"Why can't I work up many tears of remorse?" Davis asked.

"And a young woman, a socialite, named Penelope Detweiler, was wounded."

"Heiress, the paper said, to the Nesfoods money."

"Right. What we're looking for are witnesses."

"And you think the FBI can help?"

"You tell me," Peter said, and got up and walked to Davis's desk and handed him the manila envelope.

"What's this?" he asked.

"I was hoping that you could tell me, Walter," Wohl said.

Davis opened the envelope and took out the photographs and went through them one at a time.

"These were taken here, weren't they? That is the Hotel Warwick?"

"And the Penn Services Parking Garage," Wohl said.

"I have no idea what the significance of this is, Peter," Davis said, looking up at Wohl and smiling. "But I have seen these before. This morning, as a matter of fact. Did you, or one of your people, send us a set?"

"None of my people did," Wohl said.

"Well, someone did. Without, of course, a cover letter. We didn't know what the hell they were supposed to be."

"You don't know who those men are?" Wohl asked.

"Haven't a clue."

I'll be a son of a bitch! He's telling the truth!

"Where did you come by these, Peter? If you don't mind my asking?"

"We had plainclothes Narcotics officers on DeZego," Wohl said. "One of them had a camera."

"But they didn't see the shooting itself?"

Wohl shook his head.

"That sometimes happens, I suppose," Davis said. "God, I wish I had known where these pictures had come from, Peter. I mean, when the other set came over the threshold."

"Why?"

"Well, I finally decided—my criminal affairs AAC and I did—that someone was trying to tell us something and that we'd really have to check it out. So we went through the routine. Sent copies to Washington and to every FBI office. Real pain in the ass. It's not like the old days, of course, when we would have to make a copy negative, then all those prints, and then mail them. Now we can wire photographs, of course. They're not as clear as a glossy print but they're usable. The trouble is, they tie up the lines. A lot of the smaller offices don't have dedicated phone lines, you see, which means the Bureau has to absorb all those long-distance charges."

"Well, Walter," Wohl said, "you have my word on it. I'll locate whoever sent those photos over here without an explanation and make sure that it never happens again."

"I'd appreciate that, Peter," Davis said. "We try to be as cooperative as we can, and you know we do. But we need a little help."

"I'm sorry to have wasted your time with this," Peter said.

"Don't be silly," Davis said, getting up and putting his hand out. "I know the pressures you're under. Don't be a stranger, Peter. Let's have lunch sometime."

"Love to," Wohl said. "One thing, Walter. You said those pictures have already been passed around. Do you think you'll get a make?"

"Who knows? If we do, I'll give Jack Duffy a call straight off."

"Thank you for seeing me," Peter said. "I know you're a very busy man."

"Goes with the territory," Special Agent in Charge Davis said.

• • •

"I'm sorry, sir," the rent-a-cop sitting in front of Penelope Detweiler's room in Hahneman Hospital said as he rose to his feet and stood in Matt Payne's way. "You can't go in there."

"Why not?" Matt asked.

"Because I say so," the rent-a-cop said.

"I'm a cop," Matt said.

He felt a little uneasy making that announcement. The rent-a-cop was almost surely a retired policeman. He remembered hearing Washington say that one of the rent-a-cops the Detweilers had hired was a retired Northwest Detectives sergeant. He suspected he was talking to him.

"And I've been hired by the Detweiler family to keep people away from Miss Detweiler without Mr. or Mrs. Detweiler's say so."

"You've got two options," Matt said, hoping his voice sounded more confident than he felt. "You either get out of the way, or I'll get on the phone and four guys from Highway will carry you out of the way."

"There's a very sick girl in there," the rent-a-cop said.

"I know that," Matt said. "What's it going to be?"

"I could lose my job letting you in."

"You don't have any choice," Matt said. "If I have to call for help, I'll charge you with interfering with a police officer. That *will* cost you your job."

The rent-a-cop moved to the side and out of the way, watched Matt enter the room, and then walked quickly down the corridor to the nurses' station, where, without asking, he picked up a telephone and dialed a number.

"Ready for water polo?" Matt said to Penelope Detweiler. *Christ, she looks even worse than the last time I saw her.*

"Hello, Matt," Penelope said, managing a smile.

"You feel as awful as you look?" he asked. "One might suppose that you have been out consuming intoxicants and cavorting with the natives in the Tenderloin."

"I really feel shitty," she said. "Matt, if I asked you for a *real* favor, would you do it?"

"Probably not," he said.

"That was pretty quick," she said, hurt. "I'm serious, Matt. I really need a favor."

"I really wouldn't know where to get any, Penny. Your supplier's dead, you know."

"What's that supposed to mean?" she snapped.

He handed her one of the manila envelopes of photographs.

"What's this?"

"Open it. Have a look. The jig, as they say, is up."

"I thought you were my friend, that I could at least count on you."

"You can, Penny."

"Then do me the favor. I'll give you a phone number, Matt. And all you would have to do is meet the guy someplace."

"You're not listening," he said. "Bullshit time is over, Penny. Look at the photographs."

"You're a son of a bitch, you always have been. A son of a bitch and a shit. I hate you."

"I like you too," Matt said. "Look at the goddamn pictures."

"I don't want to look at any goddamn pictures. What are they of, anyway?"

She slid the stack of photographs out of the envelope.

"Oh, Jesus," she said, her voice quavering.

"Got your attention now, have I?"

"Have you got him in jail?"

"In jail"? What the hell does that mean? Why should we have the FBI guys in jail?

"Looks familiar, does he?"

"He's the man who shot me, who killed Tony," Penelope Detweiler said. "I'll never forget him—that face—as long as I live."

Jesus H. Christ! What the hell is she talking about? What am I into?

"We know all about you and Tony, Penny," Matt said. "As I said, you can stop the bullshit."

"Who is this man? Why did he kill Tony?"

"Who knows?" Matt blurted.

"He won't tell you?"

"He's being difficult," Matt said. "I don't think he believes that you're alive. If he had killed you, there would be no witnesses."

I don't know what the fuck I'm doing. I'm just saying the first thing that pops into my mind. Jesus Christ, why did I do this? I'm going to fuck the whole thing up!

"I'll testify. I saw him. I saw him shoot Tony, and then he shot me."

"Why didn't you tell us before?"

"I couldn't hurt my father that way," Penelope said, making it clear she considered her reply to be self-evident. "My God, Matt, he thinks I'm still his little girl."

"And all the while you've been fucking Tony DeZego, right?"

"That's a shitty thing to say. We were in love. That was just like you, Matt. Always thinking the nastiest thing and then saying it in the nastiest possible way."

"Tony the Zee had a wife and two kids," Matt said. "Little boys."

He couldn't tell from the look in her eyes if this was news to her or not.

"I don't believe that," she said.

"I told you, precious Penny, bullshit time is over. You were running around with a third-rate guinea gangster, a *married* guinea gangster with two kids. Who was supplying you with cocaine."

"He really was married?" she asked.

Matt nodded.

"I didn't know that," she said. "But it wouldn't have mattered. We were in love."

"Then I feel sorry for you," Matt said. "I really do."

"Does Daddy know about Tony?"

"Not yet. He knows about the coke. But he'll have to find out about DeZego."

"Yes, I suppose he will," she said calmly. "If I'm going to testify against this man, and I will, it will just have to come out, and Daddy and Mommy will just have to adjust to it."

She looked at him and smiled.

Jesus Christ, he thought, *she's stoned.*

He saw that her pupils were dilated.

Has she been getting that shit in here? In a hospital?

She's on cloud nine. I think the technical term is "euphoric." She didn't even react when I called DeZego a guinea gangster, or when I told her he's married and has two kids. The first should have enraged her, and the second should have . . . caused a much greater reaction than it did. She didn't deny it when I said DeZego was supplying her with cocaine, and she didn't seem at all upset when I told her I know her father knows about the cocaine and will inevitably learn about her and DeZego.

Ergo sum, Sherlock Holmes, she doesn't give a damn about things that are important, and is therefore, almost by definition, stoned.

It could be, come to think of it, that she is stoned on something legitimate, something they gave her for the pain. Or possibly that Dr. Dotson gave her a maintenance dose, having decided that this is not the time or place to detoxify her, either because of her condition or because he'd rather do that someplace where a lot of questions would not be asked.

So where are you now, hotshot? What do you do now?

"Penny, are you absolutely sure that the man in those photographs is the one who shot you?"

"I told you I was," she said.

"And you are prepared to testify in court about that?"

"Yes, of course," she said.

"Well, what happens now, Penny," Matt explained—*I don't know what the hell happens now*—"is that I will ask you to make a statement on the back of one of the photographs."

"What?"

"Quote, 'Having been sworn, I declare that the individual pictured in this photograph is the individual who, on the roof of the Penn Services Parking Garage, shot Mr. Anthony J. DeZego and me with a shotgun,' unquote. And then you sign it and I sign it. And then soon, Detective Washington will come back here and take a full statement."

" 'Killed,' " Penelope Detweiler said. "Not just 'shot,' 'killed.' "

"Right."

"You write it down and I'll sign it," Penny said agreeably.

"It has to be in your handwriting," Matt said. He rolled the bedside tray in place over Penny, selected one of the photographs, and showed it to her. "This him?"

"Yes, that's the man."

He spotted a Gideon Bible on the lower shelf of her bed-side table and held it out to her. She put her hand on it.

"Do you swear to tell the truth, the whole truth and nothing but the truth?"

"I do," Penny said solemnly.

He handed her a ballpoint pen.

"Write," he said.

"Say that again," Penny said.

He dictated essentially what he had said before, and she wrote it on the back of the photograph.

"Sign it," he ordered. She did, and looked at him, he thought, like a little girl who expected her teacher to give her a Gold Star to Take Home to Mommy.

He pulled the bedside tray away from the bed, read what she had written, and then wrote, "Witnessed by Officer Matthew Payne, Badge 3676, Special Operations Division," and the time and date.

And now what?

"Penny, as I said before, someone will be back, probably Detective Washington and a stenographer, and they will take a full statement."

"All right," she said obligingly.

"And I have to go now, to get things rolling."

"All right. Come and see me again, Matt."

He smiled at her and left the room.

Dr. Dotson, the rent-a-cop, and two hospital private se-curity men in policelike uniforms were coming down the cor-ridor.

"I don't know who you think you are, Matt," Dotson said furiously, "or what you think you're doing, but you have absolutely no right to go in Penny's room without my per-mission and that of the Detweilers."

"I'm finished, Dr. Dotson," Matt said.

"See that he leaves the hospital. He is not to be let back in," Dotson said. "And don't you think, Matt, that this is the end of this."

NINETEEN

"Inspector Wohl's office, Captain Sabara," Sabara said, answering one of the telephones on Wohl's desk.

"This is Commissioner Czernich, Sabara. Let me talk to Wohl."

"Commissioner, I'm sorry, the inspector's not here at the moment. May I take a message? Or have him get back to you?"

"Where is he?"

"Sir, I'm afraid I don't know. We expect him to check in momentarily."

"Yeah, well, he doesn't answer his radio, and you don't know where he is, right?"

"No, sir. I'm afraid I don't know where he is at this moment."

"Have him call me the moment you see him," Commissioner Czernich said, and hung up.

"I wonder what that's all about," Sabara said to Captain David Pekach as he put the phone in its cradle. "That was

Czernich, and he's obviously pissed about something. You don't know where the boss is?''

"The last I heard, he was on his way to the mayor's office."

"I felt like a fool, having to tell Czernich I don't know where he is."

"What's Czernich pissed about?"

"I don't know, but he's pissed. Really pissed."

Pekach got up from his upholstered chair and went to the Operations sergeant.

"Have you got any idea where Inspector Wohl might be?"

"Right at this moment he's on his way to see the commissioner," the sergeant said.

"How do you know that?"

"It was on the radio. There was a call for W-William One, and the inspector answered and they told him to report to the commissioner right away, and he acknowledged."

"Thank you," Pekach said. He went back in the office and told Sabara what he had learned.

Staff Inspector Peter Wohl arrived at Special Operations an hour and five minutes later. He found Officer Matthew W. Payne waiting for him in the corridor outside the Operations office.

"I'd like to see you right away, sir," Matt said.

"Have you called Captain Duffy?"

"No, sir. Something came up," Matt said, and picked up the manila envelope containing the photographs.

"So I understand," Wohl said. "Come in the office."

Sabara and Pekach got to their feet as Wohl entered his office.

"We've been trying to reach you, Inspec—" Sabara said.

"I had my radio turned off," Wohl interrupted.

"The commissioner wants you to call him right away."

"How long ago was that?"

"About an hour ago, sir," Pekach said. He looked at his watch. "An hour and five minutes ago."

"I've seen him since then," Wohl said. "I just came from the Roundhouse." He turned to look at Payne. "We were discussing you, Officer Payne, the commissioner and I. Or rather the commissioner was discussing you, and I just sat there looking like a goddamn fool."

Pekach and Sabara started for the door.

"Stay. You might as well hear this," Wohl said. "I understand you have been at Hahneman Hospital. Is that so?"

"Yes, sir," Matt said.

"I seem to recall having told you to come here and call Captain Duffy for me."

"Yes, sir, you did."

"Did anyone else tell you to go to Hahneman Hospital?"

"Inspector," Matt said, handing him the photograph on which Penelope Detweiler had written her statement. "Would you please look at this?"

"Did anyone tell you to go to Hahneman Hospital?" Wohl repeated icily.

"Those two guys weren't from the FBI," Matt said.

"Answer me," Wohl said.

"No, sir."

"Then why the *hell* did you go to Hahneman Hospital?"

"Sir, would you please look at the back of the picture?"

Wohl turned it over and read it.

"You're a regular little Sherlock Holmes, aren't you?" Wohl said. He handed the photograph to Sabara, who examined it with Pekach leaning over his shoulder.

"She positively identifies that man as the guy who shot her and DeZego."

"And now all we have to do is find this guy, bring him in front of a jury, convict his ass, send him off to the electric chair, and Special Operations generally and Officer Matthew Payne specifically will come across as supercops, and to the cheers of the crowd we will skip happily off into the sunset, is that what you're thinking?"

"Sir," Matt said doggedly, "she positively identified that man as the man who shot her."

"You did have a chance to buy uniforms before you came out here to Special Operations, I hope?"

"Yes, sir. I've got my uniforms."

"Good. You're going to need them. By verbal direction of the police commissioner, written confirmation to follow, Officer Payne, you are reassigned to the 12th District, effective immediately. I doubt very much if you will be assigned plainclothes duties. You are also officially advised that a complaint, making several allegations against you involving your visit to Miss Detweiler at Hahneman Hospital today, has been made by a Dr. Dotson and officials of Hahneman Hospital. It has been referred to Internal Affairs for investigation. No doubt shortly you will be hearing from them.''

"Peter, for chrissake, you're not listening to me!" Matt said. "She positively identified the shooter!"

"It's Inspector Wohl to you, Officer Payne," Wohl said.

"Sorry," Matt said.

"Matt, for chrissake!" Wohl said exasperatedly. "Let me explain all this to you. One, the chances of us catching these two, or either one of them, range from slim to none. On the way out here I stopped at Organized Crime and Intelligence. Neither of them are known by sight to anyone in Organized Crime or Intelligence—"

"You knew they weren't FBI guys?" Matt blurted, surprised.

"I have the word of the Special Agent in Charge about that," Wohl said. "They are not FBI agents. I have a gut feeling they are Mob hit men. Good ones. Imported, God only knows why, to blow DeZego away. Professionals, so to speak. We don't know where they came from. We can't charge them with murder or anything—unlawful flight or anything else, on the basis of some photographs that show them standing on a street."

"Penelope Detweiler swore that one of them is the guy who shot her and DeZego."

"Let's talk about Miss Detweiler," Wohl said. "She is a known user of narcotics, for one thing, and for another, she is Miss Penelope Detweiler, whose father's lawyers—your father, for example—will counsel her. They will advise her—and they probably should, I'm a little fuzzy about the ethics here—on the problems inherent in bringing these two scumbags before a grand jury for an indictment, much less before a jury. If I were her lawyer, I would advise her to tell the grand jury that she's really a little confused about what actually happened that day."

"Why would a lawyer tell her that?" Matt asked softly.

"Because, again presuming we can find these two, which I doubt, and presuming we could get an indictment—it isn't really true that any district attorney who can spell his own name can get an indictment anytime he wants to—and get him before a jury, then your friend Miss Detweiler would be subject to cross-examination. It would come out that she is addicted to certain narcotics, which would discredit her testimony, and it would come out that she was, tactfully phrased, romantically involved with Mr. DeZego. The press would have a certain interest in this trial. If I were her lawyer, I would suggest to her that testifying would be quite a strain on her and on her family.''

"Oh, shit," Matt said. "I really fucked this up, didn't I?"

"Yeah, and good intentions don't count," Wohl said. "What counts, I'm afraid, is that Commissioner Czernich believes, more than likely correctly, that H. Richard Detweiler is going to be furious when he hears about your little escapade and is going to make his displeasure known to the mayor. When the mayor calls him, the commissioner will now be able to say that he's taken care of the matter. You have been relieved out here and assigned to duties appropriate to your experience. In other words, in a district, in uniform, and more than likely in a wagon.''

"Oh, Christ, I'm sorry."

"So am I, Matt," Wohl said gently. "But what you did was stupid. For what it's worth, you probably should have gone to a district like anybody else fresh from the Academy.''

"Hell, I'll just resign," Matt said.

"You think you're too good to ride around in a wagon?" Wohl asked.

"No," Matt said, "not at all. That's what I expected to do when I got out of the Academy. Denny Coughlin made sure I understood what to expect. I mean, under these circumstances. I have fucked up by the numbers, and they'll know that at the 12th. I think it would be best all around, that's all, if I just folded my tent and silently stole away.''

"Today's Thursday," Wohl said. "I'll call the captain of the 12th and tell him you will either report for duty on Monday or resign by then. Think it over, over the weekend.''

"You don't think I should resign?"

"I don't think you should resign right now, today," Wohl said. "I think you would have made a pretty good cop. I think you were given too great an opportunity to fuck up.

But you did fuck up, and you're going to have to make your mind up whether or not you want to take your lumps.''

Matt looked at him.

"That's all, Officer Payne," Wohl said. "You can go."

When Payne had left and closed the door behind him, Wohl went to his coffee machine and poured himself a cup of coffee.

"Fuck it," he said suddenly, angrily. He opened a filing cabinet drawer and took out a bottle of bourbon and liberally laced the coffee with it.

"If anybody wants any of that, help yourself," he said.

"Inspector," Captain Sabara said, "I didn't want to open my mouth, but a lot of what happened just now went right over my head."

Wohl looked at him as if confused.

"Oh, that's right," he said. "You guys don't know about the FBI agents, do you?"

Both shook their heads.

He told them.

"So what Payne was really doing at Hahneman Hospital was less playing at detective than trying to get my chestnuts out of the fire," he concluded. "The poor bastard waited for me out there, in that pathetic innocence, really thinking that now that he had solved this shooting, it would get me off the hook for making an ass of myself with the FBI."

"Shit," Pekach said.

"If I was him, I'd quit," Wohl said. "But if he doesn't, I'll—I don't know how—try to get the word around the 12th that he's really a good kid."

"I know Harry Feldman over there," Sabara said.

"He's the captain?"

"Yeah. I'll have a word with him," Sabara said.

"Thanks. Not surprising me at all, it seems to have turned out that Payne's new boss hates my ass. Do you think Czernich knew that?"

"I know a couple of guys in the 12th," Pekach said. "I'll talk to them."

"What do you think is going to happen about the FBI?" Sabara asked.

"If Duffy doesn't know about the photographs yet, or of me going down there out of channels, he will shortly," Wohl said. "And from there, how long will it take him to walk down the corridor from his office to Czernich's?"

"Give Czernich Dolan," Sabara said. "That wasn't your fault."

"I might have done the same thing," Wohl said. "Those two looked like your standard, neatly dressed, shiny-shoes 'Look at me, Ma, I'm a G-man' FBI agents, just begging for the needle. I won't give Czernich Dolan. What he did was dumb, but not dumb enough to lose his pension over it, and that's what Czernich's reaction would be. Anyway, all Czernich is interested in doing is covering his ass in front of the mayor. I'm on his list now, so just let him add the photographs to everything else I've done wrong or shown a lack of judgment doing."

"Dolan won't do anything like that again, Peter," Pekach said.

"You're not defending the son of a bitch, Dave, are you?" Sabara asked.

"I should have added 'when I'm through with him,' " Pekach said.

"Well, what's done is done," Sabara said. "Let's go get some lunch."

"I've got to meet someone for lunch," Pekach said.

"Is that what they call a nooner, Dave?" Wohl asked mischievously. Then he saw the look on Pekach's face. "Sorry, I shouldn't have said that."

Pekach's face showed the apology was inadequate.

"What that is, Dave," Wohl said, "is a combination of a bad day and a bad case of jealousy. But I was out of line, and I'm sorry."

"I already forgot it," Pekach said. Both his face and his tone of voice made it clear that was far short of the truth.

"I'll buy lunch," Captain Mike Sabara said, "providing it doesn't go over two ninety-five."

Wohl chuckled. "Thanks, Mike, I really hate to pass that up, but I've got plans too. Maybe it would be a good idea if you hung around here until either Dave or I get back."

"You got it," Sabara said. "I'll send out for something. You want to tell me where you're going?"

"If you need me, put it on the radio," Wohl said. He

looked at Dave Pekach. "If you're still sore, Dave, I'm still sorry."

"I just don't like people talking that way about her," Pekach blurted. "It's not like what everybody thinks."

"What everybody thinks, Dave, is that you have a nice girl," Wohl said. "If anybody thought different, you wouldn't get teased."

"That's right, Dave," Sabara agreed solemnly.

Pekach looked intently at each of them. He smiled, shrugged, and walked out of the room.

When he was out of earshot, Sabara said, "But you were right, that's what you call it, a nooner."

"Captain Sabara, for a Sunday school teacher, you're a dirty old man," Wohl said. "I should be back in an hour. If something important comes up, put it on the radio."

"Yes, sir," Sabara said.

Martha Peebles was on the lawn, armed with the largest hedge clippers Dave Pekach had ever seen—they looked like two of King Arthur's swords or something stuck together—when he drove into the drive. She waved it at him when she saw him.

He parked the car in the garage, where it wouldn't attract too much attention, and walked toward the house. She met him under the portico.

"Hello, Precious," she said. "What's the matter?"

"Nothing," he said. "What are you going to do with that thing?"

She pointed the clippers in the general direction of his crotch and opened and closed it. Both of his hands dropped to protect the area.

"Oh, come on," she said. "You know I wouldn't want to hurt that."

"I don't know," he said. "I hope not."

"Something is wrong," she said. "I can tell. Something happen at Bustleton and Bowler?"

"Nothing that anybody can do anything about," Pekach said.

"Well," she said, taking his arm. "You can tell me all about it over lunch. I made French onion soup. Made it. Not from one of those packet things. And a salad. With Roquefort dressing.''

"Sounds good," he said.

"And there's *nobody* in the house," she said. "Which I just happen to mention *en passant* and not to give you any ideas.''

"I always wonder when I eat this stuff," Jason Washington said as he skillfully picked up a piece of Peking Beef with chopsticks and dipped it in a mixture of mustard and plum preserves, "if they really eat it in Peking, or whether it was invented here by some Chinaman who figured Americans will eat anything.''

"It's good," Peter Wohl said.

"They use a lot of monosodium glutamate," Washington said. "To bring the taste out. It doesn't bother me, but it gets to Martha. She thought she was having a heart attack—angina pectoris.''

"Really?"

"Pain in the pectoral muscles," Washington explained, and pointed to his pectorals.

"She went to the doctor and told him that whenever she had Chinese food, she had angina pectoris. He said, in that case, don't eat Chinese food. And then, when she calmed down, he told her that making diagnoses was his business, and about the monosodium glutamate.''

"I didn't know that," Wohl said, "about monosodium glutamate.''

In his good time, Wohl thought, *Jason will get around to telling me what's on his mind. He didn't ask if I was free for lunch because he didn't want to eat Peking Beef alone.*

"I feel really bad about Matt Payne," Washington said. "If I had any idea he was going to see that Detweiler girl, I would have stopped him.''

So that's what's on his mind.

"I know that," Wohl said. "He went over there to help me.''

"He thinks you're really something special," Washington said.

"He thinks you make Sherlock Holmes look like a mental retard," Wohl replied.

"If I was Matthew M. Payne and they put me back in uniform and in a 12th District wagon or handed me a wrench and told me to go around and turn off fire hydrants, I would quit."

"I think he probably will."

"We need young cops like that, Peter," Washington said. "So?"

"I have a few favors owed me," Washington said. "How sore would you be if I called them in?"

"You'd be wasting them," Wohl said. "Czernich decided the way to cover his ass was to jump on the kid before the mayor told him to. He knew that would piss off a lot of people. Denny Coughlin, for one. If Coughlin goes to the mayor, and I really hope he doesn't, it would make the mayor choose between him and Czernich. I'm not sure how that would go. And while I agree, I would hate to see Matt resign, and I would *really* hate to see Denny Coughlin retire. I'd like to see Coughlin as commissioner."

"So you're saying, just let the kid go, right? 'For the good of the Department'?"

"Pekach and Sabara say they know people in the 12th. They'll put in a good word for him."

"You won't?"

"Feldman is the captain. When I was working as a staff inspector, I put his brother-in-law away."

"Christ, I forgot that. Lieutenant in Traffic? Extortion? They gave him five to fifteen?"

Wohl nodded. "I really don't think Captain Feldman would be receptive to anything kind I would have to say about Matt Payne."

"Interesting, isn't it, that Czernich sent Payne to the 12th?"

Wohl grunted.

"You think I could talk to Payne, tell him to hang in?"

"I wish you would. I think you might tip the scales."

"Okay," Jason Washington said, nodding his head. And then he changed the subject: "So what's the real story about DeZego and the pimp getting hit?"

"It's your job, you tell me," Wohl said.

"You haven't been thinking about it? That something

smells with Savarese pointing Pekach at the pimp? Doing it himself?''

"I've been thinking that it smells," Wohl replied.

"Intelligence has a guy, I guess you know, in the Savarese family."

Wohl nodded.

"I talked to him about an hour ago," Jason Washington said.

"Intelligence know you did that?"

"Intelligence doesn't even know I know who he is," Washington said. "He tells me that the word in the family is that Tony the Zee ripped off the pimp, the pimp popped him, and Savarese ordered the pimp hit. I even got a name for the doer, not that it would do us any good."

"One of Savarese's thugs?"

"One of his bodyguards. Gian-Carlo Rosselli, also known as Charley Russell."

"Who has eight people ready to swear he was in Atlantic City taking the sun with his wife and kids?"

Washington nodded.

"Tony the Zee ripped off the pimp?" Wohl asked. "How?"

"Drugs, what else?" Washington replied.

"You don't sound as if you believe that," Wohl said.

"I think that's what Savarese wants the family to think," Washington said.

"Why, do you think?"

"I think Savarese had DeZego hit, and doesn't want the family to know about it."

"Why?"

"Why did he have him hit? Couple of possibilities. Maybe Tony went in business for himself driving the shrimp up from the Gulf Coast. That would be enough. Tony the Zee was ambitious but not too smart. He might have figured, who would ever know if he brought a kilo of cocaine for himself back up here in his suitcase."

"Interesting," Wohl said.

"He was also quite a swordsman," Washington went on, "who could have played hide-the-salami with somebody's wife. They take the honor of their women seriously; adultery is a mortal sin."

"Wouldn't Savarese have made an example of him, if that was the case?"

"Not necessarily," Washington said. "Maybe the lady was important to him. Her reputation. Her honor. He might have ordered him hit to remove temptation. It didn't have to be a wife. It could have been a daughter—I mean, unmarried daughter. If it came out that Tony had *dishonored* somebody's daughter, she would have a hell of a time finding a respectable husband. These people are very big, Peter, on respectability."

Wohl chuckled.

"You never heard of honor among thieves?" Washington asked innocently.

They both laughed.

"Why the hell are we laughing?" Wohl asked.

"Everyone laughs at quaint native customs," Washington said, and then added, "Or both of the above. Bottom line: For one or more reasons we'll probably never find out, Savarese decided Tony the Zee had to go; he didn't want his family to know that he had ordered the hit, for one or more reasons we'll probably never find out, either; imported those two guys in the photos Dolan took to do the hit; and then had Gian-Carlo Rosselli, aka Charley Russell, hit Lanier, conveniently leaving the shotgun the imported shooters had used on Tony at the crime scene; and finally, pointed us at the pimp. We would then naturally assume that Lanier had gotten popped for having popped Tony DeZego and tell Mickey O'Hara and the other police reporters, which would lend credence to Savarese's innocence. He almost got away with it. He would have, if it hadn't been for Dolan's snapshots and those two Highway cops hassling the pimp and coming up with another shotgun."

Wohl exhaled audibly.

"One flaw in your analysis," he said finally. Washington looked at him curiously. "You said, 'He almost got away with it,' " Wohl went on. "He did get away with it. What the hell have we got, Jason? We don't know who the professional hit men are, and we're not likely to find out. And if we did find them, we don't have anything on them. The only witness we have is a socialite junkie whose testimony would be useless even if we got her on the stand. And we can't hang the Lanier murder on Rosselli, or Russell, or whatever he calls himself. So the bastard did get away with it. Goddamn, that makes me mad!''

''You win some and you lose some,'' Washington said, ''that being my profound philosophical observation for the day.''

''On top of which we look like the Keystone Kops in the newspapers and, for the cherry on top of the cake, have managed to antagonize H. Richard Detweiler, Esquire. Christ only knows what that's going to cost us down the pike. *Damn!*''

''What I was going to suggest, Peter,'' Washington said softly, ''presuming you agreed with what I thought, is that I have a talk with Mickey O'Hara.''

''About what?''

''Mickey doesn't like those guineas any more than I do. He could do one of those 'highly placed police official speaking on condition of anonymity' pieces.''

''Saying what?''

''Saying the truth. That Tony the Zee was hit for reasons known only to the mob, and that What's-his-name the pimp, Lanier, didn't do it. That would at least embarrass Savarese.''

Wohl sat for a long moment with his lips pursed, tapping the balls of his fingers together.

''No,'' he said finally. ''There are other ways to embarrass Mr. Savarese.''

''You want to tell me how?''

''You sure you want to know?''

Washington considered that a moment.

''Yeah, I want to know,'' he said. ''Maybe I can help.''

''So what you were telling me before,'' Martha said to Dave, interrupting herself to reach down on the bed and pull a sheet modestly over her, ''is that although it's really not Inspector Wohl's fault, he looks very bad?''

''Goddamn shame. He's a hell of a cop. I really admire him.''

''And those gangsters are just going to get away with shooting the other gangster?''

''That happens all the time,'' Pekach said. ''It's not like in the movies.'' He tucked his shirt in his trousers and pulled up his zipper. ''Even if we somehow found those two, they would have alibis. They'll never wind up in court, is what I mean."

"I don't know what you mean."

"Sometimes some things happen," Pekach said.

"Precious, what in the world are you talking about?"

"Nothing," he said. "What makes Wohl look bad is the shot cop. We don't have a damn thing on that. And that's bad. It makes the Department look incompetent, stupid, if we can't get people who murder cops in cold blood. And it makes Peter Wohl look bad, because the mayor gave him the job."

"I understand," she said. "And there's nothing that he can do?"

"There's nothing anybody can do that isn't already being done. Unless we can find somebody who saw something—"

"What about offering a reward? Don't you do that?"

"Rewards come from people who are injured," Dave explained. "I mean, somebody knocks off the manager of an A&P supermarket, A&P would offer a reward. The Department doesn't have money for something like that, and even if there was a reward, we'd look silly, wouldn't we, offering it? It would be the same thing as admitting that we can't do the job the taxpayers are paying us to do."

"*I* don't think so," Martha said.

He finished dressing and examined himself in the mirror.

His pants are baggy in the seat, Martha thought. *And that shirt doesn't fit the way it should. I wonder if that Italian tailor Evans has found on Chestnut Street could make him up something a little better? He has a marvelous physique, and it just doesn't show. Daddy always said that clothes make the man. I never really knew what he meant before.*

Pekach walked to the bed and leaned down and kissed Martha gently on the lips.

"Gotta go, baby," he said.

"Would you like to ride out to New Hope and have dinner along the canal?" Martha asked. "You always like that. It would cheer you up. Or I could have Evans get some steaks?"

"Uh," Pekach said, "baby, Mike Sabara and I thought that we'd try to get Wohl to go out for a couple of drinks after work."

"I thought Captain Sabara wasn't much of a drinking

man," Martha said, and then: "Oh, I see. Of course. Can you come over later?"

"I think I might be able to squeeze that into my busy schedule," Pekach said, and kissed her again.

When he left the bedroom, Martha got out of bed and went to the window and watched the driveway until she saw Pekach's unmarked car go down it and through the gate.

She leaned against the window frame thoughtfully for a moment, then caught her reflection in the mirrors of her vanity table.

"Well," she said aloud, not sounding entirely displeased, "aren't *you* the naked hussy, Martha Peebles?"

And then walked back to the bed, sat down on it, fished out a leather-bound telephone book, and looked up a number.

Brewster Cortland Payne, Esquire, saw that one of the lights on one of the two telephones on his desk was flashing. He wondered how long it had been flashing. He had been in deep concentration, and lately that had meant that the Benjamin Franklin Bridge, visible from his windows on a high floor of the Philadelphia Savings Fund Society Building, could have tumbled into the Delaware without his noticing the splash.

It probably means that when I'm free, Irene has something she thinks I should hear, he thought. *Otherwise, she would have made it ring. Well, I'm not free, but I'm curious.*

As he reached for the telephone it rang.

"Yes, ma'am?" he asked cheerfully.

"Mr. and Mrs. Detweiler are here, Mr. Payne," his secretary of twenty-odd years, Mrs. Irene Craig, said.

Good God, both of them?

"Ask them to please come in," Payne said immediately. He quickly closed the manila folders on his desk and slid them into a drawer. He had no idea what the Detweilers wanted, but there was no chance whatever that they just happened to be in the neighborhood and had just popped in.

The door opened.

"Mr. and Mrs. Detweiler, Mr. Payne," Irene announced.

Detweiler's face was stiff. His smile was uneasy.

"Unexpected pleasure, Grace," Payne said, kissing her cheek as he offered his hand to Detweiler. "Come on in."

"May I get you some coffee?" Irene asked.

"I'd much rather have a drink, if that's possible," Detweiler said.

"The one thing you don't need is another drink," Grace Detweiler said.

"I could use a little nip myself," Payne lied smoothly. "I'll fix them, Irene. Grace, will you have something?"

"Nothing, thanks."

"We just came from the hospital," Detweiler announced.

"Sit down, Dick," Payne said. "You're obviously upset."

"Jesus H. Christ, am I upset!" Detweiler said. He went to the wall of windows looking down toward the Delaware River and leaned on one of the floor-to-wall panes with both hands.

Payne quickly made him a drink, walked to him, and handed it to him.

"Thank you," Detweiler said idly, and took a pull at the drink. He looked into Payne's face. "I'm not sure if I'm here because you're my friend or because you're my lawyer."

"They are not mutually exclusive," Payne said. "Now what seems to be the problem?"

"If five days ago anyone had asked me if I could think of anything worse than having my daughter turn up as a drug addict, I couldn't have imagined anything worse," Grace Detweiler said.

"Penny is not a drug addict," H. Richard Detweiler said.

"If you persist in that self-deception, Dick," Grace said angrily, "you will be compounding the problem, not trying to solve it."

"She has a *problem*," Detweiler said. "That's all."

"And the name of that problem, goddamn you, is addiction," Grace Detweiler said furiously. "Denying it, goddammit, is not going to make it go away!"

H. Richard Detweiler looked at his wife until he cringed under her angry eyes.

"All right," he said very softly. "Addicted. Penny is addicted."

Grace nodded and then turned to Brewster C. Payne. "You're not even a little curious, Brewster, about what could be worse than Penny being a cocaine addict?"

"I presumed you were about to tell me," Payne said.

"How about getting rubbed out by the Mob? Does that strike you as being worse?"

"I don't know what you're talking about," Payne said.

"Officer Matthew Payne of the Philadelphia Police Department marched into Penny's room a while ago—past, incidentally, the private detective Dick hired to keep people out of her room—and showed Penny some photographs. Penny, who is not, to put it kindly, in full possession of her faculties, identified the man in the photographs as the man who had shot her and that Italian gangster. And then she proceeded to confess to him that she had been involved with him. With the gangster, I mean. In love with him, to put a point on it."

"Oh, God!" Payne said.

"And he got her to sign a statement," H. Richard Detweiler said. "Penny is now determined to go to court and point a finger at the man and see him sent to the electric chair. She thinks it will be just like Perry Mason on television. With Uncle Brewster doing what Raymond Burr did."

"What kind of a statement did she sign?"

"We don't know," Grace said. "Matt didn't give her a copy. A *statement*."

"I'd have to see it," Payne said, as if to himself.

"I think I should tell you that Dotson has filed a complaint against Matt with the Police Department," H. Richard Detweiler said.

"For what?"

"Who knows? What Matt did was wrong," Detweiler said. "I think he said, criminal trespass and violation of Penny's civil rights. Does that change anything between us, Brewster?"

"If you're filing a complaint, it would," Payne said. "Are you?"

"That sounds like an ultimatum," Detweiler said. "If I press charges, I should find another lawyer."

"It sounded like a question to me," Grace Detweiler said. "The answer to which is no, we're not. Of course we're not. I'd like to file a complaint against Dotson. He knew that Penny was taking drugs. He should have told us."

"We don't know he knew," Detweiler said.

"God, you're such an ass!" Grace said. "Of course he knew." She turned to Brewster Payne. "Don't you think?"

"Penny's over twenty-one. An adult. Legally her medical problems are none of your business," Payne said. "But yes, Grace, I would think he knew."

"Right," Grace said. "Of course he did. The bastard!"

"If there are charges against Matt—a complaint doesn't always result in charges—but if there are and he comes to me, I'll defend him," Payne said. "Actually, if he doesn't come to me, I'll go to him. One helps one's children when they are in trouble. I am unable to believe that he meant Penny harm."

"Neither am I," Grace said. "I wish I could say the same thing for Penny's father."

"I'll speak to Dotson," Detweiler said. "About dropping his charges. I don't blame Matt. I blame that colored detective; he probably set Matt up to do what he did."

"What Matt did *wasn't* wrong, Dick," Grace said. "Can't you get that through your head? What he was trying to do was catch the man who shot Penny."

"Dick, I think Matt would want to accept responsibility for whatever he did. He's not a child any longer, either," Payne said.

"I'll speak to Dotson," Detweiler said. "About the charges, I mean."

"As sick as this sounds," Grace Detweiler went on, "I think Penny rather likes the idea of standing up in public and announcing that she was the true love of this gangster's life. The idea that since they tried to kill her once so there would be no witness suggests they would do so again never entered her mind."

"Off the top of my head, I don't think that a statement taken under the circumstances you describe—"

"What do you mean, 'off the top of your head'?" H. Richard Detweiler asked coldly.

"Dick, I'm not a criminal lawyer," Brewster C. Payne said.

"Oh, great! We come here to see how we can keep our daughter from getting shot—again—by the Mob, and you tell me 'Sorry, that's not my specialty.' My God, Brewster!"

"Settle down, Dick," Payne said. "You came to the right place."

He walked to his door.

"Irene, would you ask Colonel Mawson to drop whatever he's doing and come in here, please?"

"Mawson?" Detweiler said. "I never have liked that son of a bitch. I never understood why you two are partners."

"Dunlop Mawson is reputed to be—in my judgment *is*—the best criminal lawyer in Philadelphia. But if you think he's a son of a bitch, Dick—"

"For God's sake," Grace said sharply, "let's hear what he has to say."

Colonel J. Dunlop Mawson (the title making reference to his service as a lieutenant colonel, Judge Advocate Generals' Corps, U.S. Army Reserve, during the Korean War) appeared in Brewster C. Payne's office a minute later.

"I believe you know the Detweilers, don't you, Dunlop?" Payne asked.

"Yes, of course," Mawson said. "I've heard, of course, about your daughter. May I say how sorry I am and ask how she is?"

"Penny is addicted to cocaine," Grace Detweiler said. "How does that strike you?"

"I'm very sorry to hear that," Colonel Mawson said.

"There is a place in Hartford," Grace said, "that's supposed to be the best in the country. The Institute for Living, something like that—"

"Institute *of* Living," Payne said. "I know of it. It has a fine reputation."

"Anyway, she's going there," Grace Detweiler said.

"I had a hell of a time getting her in," H. Richard Detweiler said.

" '*I*'?" Grace Detweiler snapped, icily sarcastic.

"Really?" Payne asked quickly. He had seen Grace Detweiler in moods like this before.

"There's a waiting list, can you believe that? They told Dotson on the phone that it would be at least three weeks, possibly longer, before they'd take her."

"Well, that's unfortunate, but—" Colonel Mawson said.

"*We* got her in," Detweiler said. "*We* had to call Arthur Nelson—"

"Arthur Nelson?" Payne interrupted. "Why him?"

Arthur J. Nelson, Chairman of the Board of Daye-Nelson Publications, one of which was the *Philadephia Ledger*, was not among Brewster C. Payne's favorite people.

"Well, he had his wife in there, you know," Grace Detweiler answered for her husband. "She had a breakdown, you know, when that sordid business about her son came out. Arthur put her in there."

"Yes, now that you mention it, I remember that," Payne said. "Was he helpful?"

"Very helpful," H. Richard Detweiler said.

"Dick, you're such an ass," Grace said. "He was not!"

"He said he would do everything he could to minimize unfortunate publicity," H. Richard Detweiler said. "And he gave us Charley Gilmer's name."

"Charley Gilmer?" Payne asked.

"President of Connecticut General Commercial Assurance. He's on the board of directors, trustees, whatever, of that place."

"Whose name, if you were thinking clearly," Grace Detweiler said, "you should have thought of yourself. We've known the Gilmers for years."

H. Richard Detweiler ignored his wife's comment.

"It was not very pleasant," H. Richard Detweiler said, "having to call a man I have known for years to tell him that my daughter has a drug problem and I need his help to get her into a mental institution."

"Is that all you're worried about, your precious reputation?" Grace Detweiler snarled. "Dick, you make me sick!"

"I don't give a good goddamn about my reputation—or yours, either, for that matter. I'm concerned for our daughter, goddamn you!"

"If you were really concerned, you'd leave the booze alone!"

"Both of you, shut up!" Brewster C. Payne said sharply. Neither was used to being talked to in those words or that manner and looked at him with genuine surprise.

"Penny is the problem here. Let's deal with that," Payne said. "Unless you came here for an arena, instead of for my advice."

"I'm upset," H. Richard Detweiler said.

"And I'm not?" Grace snapped.

"Grace, shut up," Payne said. "Both of you, shut up."

They both glowered at him for a moment, the silence broken when Grace Detweiler walked to the bar and poured an inch and a half of Scotch in the bottom of a glass.

She turned from the bar, leaned against the bookcase, took a swallow of the whiskey, and looked at both of the men.

"Okay, let's deal with the problem," she said.

"We're sending Penny up there tomorrow, Colonel Mawson," Detweiler said, "to the Institute of Living, in an ambulance. It's a six-week program, beginning with detoxification and then followed by counseling."

"They know how to deal with the problem," Mawson replied. "It's an illness. It can be cured."

"That's *not* the goddamn problem!" Grace flared. "We're talking about Penny and the *goddamn gangsters*!"

"Excuse me?" Colonel H. Dunlop Mawson asked.

"Let me fill you in, Dunlop," Payne said, and explained the statement Matt had taken and Penny's determination to testify against the man whom she had seen shoot Anthony J. DeZego.

Colonel Mawson immediately put many of the Detweilers' concerns to rest. He told them that no assistant district attorney more than six weeks out of law school would go into court with a witness who had a "medical history of chemical abuse."

The statement taken by Matt Payne, in any event, he said, was of virtually no validity, taken as it was from a witness he knew was not in full possession of her mental faculties, and not even taking into consideration that he had completely ignored all the legal t's that had to be crossed, and i's dotted, in connection with taking a statement.

"And I think, Mr. Detweiler," Colonel Mawson concluded, "that there is even a very good chance that we can get the statement your daughter signed back from the police. If we can, then it will be as if she'd never signed it, as if it had never existed."

"How are you going to get it back?"

"Commissioner Czernich is a reasonable man," Colonel Mawson said. "He's a friend of mine. And by a fortunate happenstance, at the moment he owes me one."

"He owes you one what?" Grace Detweiler demanded.

Brewster C. Payne was glad she had asked the question. He didn't like what Mawson had just said, and would have asked precisely the same question himself.

"A favor," Mawson said, a trifle smugly. "A scratch of my back in return, so to speak."

"What kind of a scratch, Dunlop?" Payne asked, a hint of ice in his voice.

"Just minutes before I came in here," Mawson said, "I was speaking with Commissioner Czernich on the telephone. I was speaking on behalf of one of our clients, a public-spirited citizeness who wishes to remain anonymous."

"The point?" Payne said, and now there was ice in his voice.

"The lady feels the entire thread of our society is threatened by the unsolved murder of Officer Whatsisname, the young Italian cop who was shot out by Temple. So she is providing, through me, anonymously, a reward of ten thousand dollars for information leading to the arrest and successful prosecution of the perpetrators. Commissioner Czernich seemed overwhelmed by her public-spirited generosity. I really think I'm in a position to ask him for a little favor in return."

"Well, that's splendid," H. Richard Detweiler said. "That would take an enormous burden from my shoulders."

"What do we do about the newspapers?" Grace Detweiler asked. "Have you any influence with them, Colonel?"

"Very little, I'm afraid."

"Arthur Nelson will do what he can, I'm sure, and that should take care of that," H. Richard Detweiler said.

"I don't trust Arthur J. Nelson," Grace said.

"Don't be absurd, Grace," H. Richard Detweiler said. "He seemed to understand the problem, and was obviously sympathetic."

"Brewster, will you please tell this horse's ass I'm married to that even if Nelson never printed the name Detweiler again in the *Ledger*, there are three other newspapers in Philadelphia that will?"

"He implied that he would have a word with the others," H. Richard Detweiler said. "We take a lot of advertising in those newspapers. We're entitled to a little consideration."

"Oh, Richard," Grace said, disgusted, "you can be such an ass! If Nelson has influence with the other newspapers, how is it that he couldn't keep them from printing every last sordid detail of his son's homosexual love life?"

Detweiler looked at Payne.

"I'm afraid Grace is right," Payne said.

"You can't talk to them? Mentioning idly in passing how much money Nesfoods spends with them every year?"

"I'd be wasting my breath," Payne said. "The only way to deal with the press is to stay away from it."

"You'r- a lot of help," Detweiler said. "I just can't believe there is nothing that can be done."

"Unfortunately there *is* nothing that can be done. Except, of course, to reiterate, to stay away from the press. Say nothing."

"Just a moment, Brewster," Colonel Mawson said. "If I might say something?"

"Go ahead," Grace said.

"The way to counter bad publicity is with good publicity," Mawson said. "Don't you agree?"

"Get to the point," Grace Detweiler said.

He did.

TWENTY

Matt Payne was watching television determinedly. PBS was showing a British-made documentary of the plight of Australian aborigines in contemporary society, a subject in which he had little or no genuine interest. But if he did not watch television, he had reasoned, he would get drunk, which did not at the moment have the appeal it sometimes did, and which, moreover, he suspected was precisely the thing he should not do at the moment, under the circumstances.

He had disconnected his telephone. He did not want to talk to either his father, Officer Charles McFadden, Amanda Spencer, Captain Michael J. Sabara, or Chief Inspector Dennis V. Coughlin, all of whom had called and left messages that they would try again later.

All he wanted to do was sit there and watch the aborigines jumping around Boy Scout campfires in their loincloths and bitching, sounding like brown, fuzzy-haired Oxford dons, about the way they were treated.

His uniform was hanging from the fireplace mantelpiece. He had taken it from the plastic mothproof bag and hung it there so he could look at it. He had considered actually putting it on and examining himself in the mirror, and decided against that as unnecessary. He could imagine what he would look like in it as Officer Payne of the 12th Police District.

If there was one thing that could be said about the uniform specified for officers of the Philadelphia Police Department, it did not have quite the class or the élan of the uniform prescribed for second lieutenants of the United States Marine Corps.

He had actually said, earlier on, "Damn my eyes," which sounded like a line from a Charles Laughton movie. But if it wasn't for his goddamn eyes, he would now be on his way to Okinawa and none of this business with the cops would have happened.

He would have gone to Chad and Daffy's wedding as a Marine officer and met Amanda, and they would have had their shipboard romance, as she called it, in much the same way. And things probably would have turned out much the same way, except that what had happened between them in the apartment would have happened in a hotel room or something, for if he had gone into the Marines, ergo, he would not have gotten the apartment.

But he had not gone into the Marines. He had gone into the cops and as a result of that had proven beyond any reasonable doubt that he was a world-class asshole with a naïveté that boggled the imagination, spectacular delusions of his own cleverness, and a really incredible talent for getting other people—goddamn *good* people, Washington and Wohl, plus of course his father—in trouble because of all of the above. Not to mention embarrassing Uncle Denny Coughlin.

And now, having sinned, he was expected to do penance. He had not told Wohl the truth, the whole truth, and nothing but the truth about whether he thought he was too good to ride around in an RPW hauling drunks off to holding cells and fat ladies off to the hospital. He didn't want to do it. Was that the same as thinking he was too good to do it?

Presuming, of course, that he could swallow his pride and show up at the 12th District on Monday, preceded by his reputation as the wiseass college kid who had been sent there in disgrace, what did he have to look forward to?

Two years of hauling the aforementioned fat lady down the

stairs and into the wagon and then off to the hospital, perhaps punctuated, after a while, when they learned that within reason I could be trusted with exciting assignments, like guarding school crossings and maybe even—dare I hope?—filling in for some guy on vacation or something and actually getting to go on patrol in my RPC.

Then I will be eligible to take the examination for detective or corporal. Detective, of course. I don't want to be a corporal. And I will pass that. I will even study to do well on it, and I will pass it, and then what?

Do I want to ride shotgun in a wagon for two years to do that?

Amanda would, with justification, decide I was rather odd to elect to ride shotgun on a wagon. Amanda does not wish to be married to a guy who rides shotgun on a wagon. Can one blame Amanda? One cannot.

There was a rustling, and then a harsher noise, almost metallic.

The building is empty. I carefully locked the door to my stairs; therefore it cannot be anything human rustling around my door. Perhaps the raven Mr. Poe spoke of, about to quote "Nevermore" to me, as in "Nevermore, Matthew Payne, will you be the hotshot, hotshit special assistant to Inspector Wohl."

It's a rat, that's what it is. That's all I need, a fucking rat!

"You really ought to get dead-bolt locks for those doors," a vaguely familiar voice said.

Matt, startled, jumped to his feet.

Chief Inspector August Wohl, retired, was standing just inside the door, putting something back in his wallet.

"How the hell did you get in?" Matt blurted.

"I'll show you about doors sometime. Like I said, you really should get dead-bolt locks."

"What can I do for you, Mr. Wohl?"

"You could offer me a drink," he said. "I would accept. It's a long climb up here. And call me Chief, if you don't mind. It has a certain ring to it."

Matt walked into the kitchen and got out the bottle of Scotch his father had given him.

"Well, I'm glad to see there's some left," Chief Wohl said.

"Sir?"

"I really expected to find you passed out on the floor," Chief Wohl said. "That's why I let myself in. People who drink alone can get in a lot of trouble."

"I'm already in a lot of trouble," Matt said.

"So I understand."

"Water all right?"

"Just a touch. That's very nice whiskey."

"How'd you know I was here?"

"Your car's downstairs. There's lights on. There was movement I could see—shadows—from the street. It had to be either you or a burglar. I'm glad it was you. I'm too old to chase burglars."

Matt chuckled.

"Why'd you come?" he asked.

"I wanted to talk to you, but I'll be damned if I will while drinking alone."

"I'm not so sure that drinking is what I need to be doing just now."

"And the pain of feeling sorry for yourself is sharper when you're stone sober, right? And you like that?"

"What the hell," Matt said, and poured himself a drink.

"I see you have your uniform out," Chief Wohl said. "Does that mean you're going to report to the 12th on Monday?"

"It means I'm thinking about it," Matt said.

"Which side is winning?"

"The side that's wondering if I can find anybody interested in buying a nearly new set of uniforms, size forty regular," Matt said.

"You going to ask me if I want to sit down?" Chief Wohl said.

"Oh! Sorry. Please sit down."

"Thank you," Chief Wohl said. He sat in Matt's chair and put his feet up on the footstool. Matt sat on the window ledge.

"I told Peter that I think he's wrong about you needing the experience you'll get—if you decide to go over there on Monday—at the 12th," Chief Wohl said. "Incidentally, Peter feels lousy about the way that happened. I want you to understand that. It was out of his hands. That's one of the reasons I came here, to make sure you understood that."

"I thought it probably was," Matt said. "I mean the commissioner's decision."

"Reaction, not decision," Chief Wohl said. "There's a difference. When you decide something, you consider the facts and make a choice. When you react, it's different. Reactions are emotional."

"I'm not sure I follow you."

"Right or wrong wasn't on Czernich's agenda. What he saw was that Jerry Carlucci was going to be pissed off at Peter because of your little escapade with the Detweiler girl. He wanted to get himself out of the line of fire. He *reacted*. By jumping on you before Carlucci said anything, he was proving, he thinks, to Jerry Carlucci, that he's one of the good guys."

Matt took a pull at his drink.

"You're not going to learn anything," Chief Wohl said, "if you decide to go over there on Monday, hauling fat ladies with broken legs downstairs—"

Matt laughed.

"I say something funny?" Chief Wohl snapped.

"I'm sorry," Matt said. "But I was thinking in exactly those terms—hauling fat ladies—when I was thinking about what I would be doing in the 12th."

"As I was saying, you won't learn anything hauling fat ladies except how to haul fat ladies. The idea of putting rookies on jobs like that is to give them experience. You've already had your experience."

"Do you mean because I shot the serial rapist?" Matt asked.

"No. As a matter of fact, I didn't even think about that," Chief Wohl said. "No, not that. That was something else. What I meant was the price of going off half-cocked before you think through what's liable to happen if you do what seems like such a great idea. The price of doing something dumb is what I mean."

"It's obviously expensive," Matt said. "I lose my job. I get my boss in trouble. I get to haul fat ladies. And because I was dumb, the scumbags who shot the other scumbag and Penny Detweiler get away with it. That really makes me mad. No, not mad. Ashamed of myself."

He became aware that Chief Wohl was looking at him with an entirely different look on his face.

"Chief, did I say something wrong?" Matt asked.

"No," Chief Wohl replied. "No, not at all. Can I have another one of these?"

"Certainly."

When Matt was at the sink, Chief Wohl got up and followed him.

"They may not get away with it," he said. "I have just decided that if I tell you something, it won't go any further. Am I right?"

"Do you think, after the trouble I've caused, that I am any judge of my reliability?"

"I think you can judge whether or not you can keep your mouth shut, *particularly* since you have just learned how you can get other people in trouble."

"Yes, sir," Matt said after a moment. "I can keep my mouth shut."

Chief Wohl met his eyes for a moment and then nodded.

"There is a set of rules involving the Mob and the police. Nobody talks about them, but they're there. I won't tell you how I know this, but Vincenzo Savarese got word to Jerry Carlucci that the Mob—Mobs, there's a couple of them—had nothing to do with the shooting of that Italian cop . . . what was his name?"

"Magnella. Joseph Magnella," Matt furnished.

"We believe him. The reason he told us that is not because he gives a damn about a dead cop but because he doesn't want us looking for the doer, doers, in the Mob. We might come across something else he doesn't want us to know. Since we're taking him at his word, that means we can devote the resources to looking elsewhere. You with me?"

"Yes, sir."

"Okay. The DeZego hit is different. Ordinarily we really don't spend a lot of time worrying about the Mob killing each other. If we can catch the doer, fine. But we know that we seldom do catch the doers, so we go through the motions and let it drop. The DeZego hit is different."

"Because of Penny Detweiler?"

"No. Well, maybe a little. But that's not what I'm talking about. The one thing the Mob does not do is point the finger

at some other Mob guy and say he's the doer, go lock him
up. That violates their Sicilian Code of Honor, telling the
police anything about some other mafioso. If a Mob guy is
hit, it's one of two ways. It was, by their standards, a justified
hit, and that's the end of it. Or it was unjustified and they put
out a contract on the guy who did it. This was different. They
pointed us, with that matchbook Savarese gave Dave Pekach,
at the pimp.''

''He was black.''

''More important,'' Chief Wohl said, a tone of impatience
in his voice, ''he didn't do it.''

''Yeah,'' Matt said, chagrined. ''Maybe they wanted him—
the pimp, I mean—killed for some other reason.''

''Could well be, but that's not the point. The point is that
Savarese tried to play games with us. Two things with that.
One, we wonder why. Two, more important, that breaks the
rules. He lied to us. We can't have that.''

''So what happens?''

''The first thing we think is that if he lied to us about the
pimp, he's probably lying to us about not knowing who killed
the Italian cop. So that means we can't trust him.''

''So you start looking around the Mob for who killed
DeZego and who killed Magnella.''

''Yeah,'' Chief Wohl said. ''But before we do that, to make
sure that he knows we haven't broken our end of the arrangement, we let him know we know he broke the rules first.''

''How?''

Chief Wohl told him. And as he was explaining what was
going to happen—in fact, had *already* happened, thirty minutes before, just after ten P.M., just before Chief Inspector
Wohl, retired, had shown up at the apartment—a question
arose in Matt's mind that he knew he could never raise:
whether the chief had been a spectator or a participant.

When Mr. Vincenzo Savarese's Lincoln pulled to the curb
in front of the Ristorante Alfredo right on time to pick up
Mr. Savarese following his dinner and convey him to his residence, a police officer almost immediately came around the
corner, walked up to the car, and tapped his knuckles on the
window.

When the window came down, Officer Foster H. Lewis

Jr., politely said, "Excuse me, sir, this is a no-parking, no-standing zone. You'll have to move along."

"We're just picking somebody up," Mr. Pietro Cassandro, who was driving the Lincoln, said.

"I'm sorry, sir, this is a no-standing zone," Officer Lewis said.

"For chrissake, we'll only be two minutes," Mr. Gian-Carlo Rosselli, who was in the front seat beside Mr. Cassandro, said.

Officer Lewis removed his booklet of citations from his hip pocket.

"May I see your driver's license and registration, please, sir? I'm afraid that I will have to issue a citation."

"We're moving, we're moving," Mr. Cassandro said as he rolled up the window and put the car in gear.

"Just drive around the block," Mr. Rosselli said.

"Arrogant fucking nigger—put them in a uniform and they really think they're hot shit."

"That was a *big* nigger. Did you see the size of that son of a bitch?"

"I didn't want to have Mr. S. coming out of the place and finding jumbo Sambo standing there. If there's anything he hates worse than a nigger, it's a nigger cop."

There was more fucking trouble with the fucking cops going around the block. There was something wrong with the sewer or something, and there was a cop standing in the middle of the street with his hand up. And they couldn't back up and go around, either, because another car, an old Jaguar convertible, was behind them. They took five minutes minimum, and the result was that when they went all the way around the block, Mr. S. was standing on the curb looking nervous. He didn't like to wait around on curbs.

"Sorry, Mr. S.," Mr. Cassandro said. "We had trouble with a cop."

"What kind of trouble with a cop?"

"Fresh nigger cop, just proving he had a badge," Mr. Cassandro said.

"I don't like trouble with cops," Mr. Savarese said.

"It wasn't his fault, Mr. S.," Mr. Rosselli said.

"I don't want to hear about it. I don't like trouble with cops."

Mr. Savarese's Lincoln turned south on South Broad Street.

Mr. Cassandro became aware that the car behind, the stupid bastard, had his bright lights on. He reached up and flicked the little lever under the mirror, which deflected the beam of light, and he could see the car behind him.

"There's a fucking cop behind us," Mr. Cassandro said.

"I don't like trouble with cops," Mr. Savarese said. "Don't give him any excuse for anything."

"Maybe he's just there, like coincidental," Mr. Rosselli said.

"Yeah, probably," Mr. Cassandro said.

Six blocks down South Broad Street, the police car was still behind the Lincoln, which was now traveling thirty-two miles per hour in a thirty-five-mile-per-hour zone.

"Is the cop still back there?" Mr. Savarese asked.

"Yeah, he is, Mr. S.," Mr. Cassandro said.

"I wonder what the fuck he wants," Mr. Rosselli asked.

"I don't like trouble with cops," Mr. Savarese said. "Have we got a bad taillight or something?"

"I don't think so, Mr. S.," Mr. Cassandro said.

Three blocks farther south, the flashing lights on the roof of the police car turned on, and there was the whoop of its siren.

"Shit," Mr. Cassandro said.

"You must have done something wrong," Mr. Savarese said.

"I been going thirty-two miles an hour," Mr. Cassandro said.

"You sure it's a cop?" Mr. Savarese said as they pulled up to the curb.

"It's that gigantic nigger that gave us the trouble before," Mr. Rosselli said.

"Jesus," Mr. Savarese said.

Officer Lewis walked up to the car and flashed his flashlight at Mr. Cassandro, Mr. Rosselli, and Mr. Savarese in turn.

"Is something wrong, Officer?" Mr. Cassandro said.

"May I have your driver's license and registration, please?" Tiny Lewis asked.

"Yeah, sure. You gonna tell me what I did wrong?"

"You were weaving as you drove down the street," Officer Lewis said.

"No I wasn't!" Mr. Cassandro said.

"Have you been drinking, sir?"

"Not a goddamn drop," Mr. Cassandro said. "What is this shit?"

"Shut your mouth," Mr. Savarese said sharply to Mr. Cassandro.

Officer Lewis flashed his light at Mr. Savarese.

"Oh, you're Mr. Savarese, aren't you?"

After a discernible pause Mr. Savarese said, "Yes, my name is Savarese."

"You left something behind you in the restaurant, Mr. Savarese," Officer Lewis said.

"I did? I don't recall—"

"Here it is, sir," Tiny Lewis said, and handed Mr. Savarese a large manila envelope.

"Please try to drive in a straight line," Tiny Lewis said. "Good night."

He walked back to his car and turned off the flashing lights.

"What did he give you?" Mr. Rosselli asked.

"Feels like photographs," Mr. Savarese replied.

"Of who?"

"There's two of them, Mr. S.," Mr. Rosselli said. "I adjusted the rearview mirror. I can see good."

"Two of who?"

"Two cop cars. The other's got a lieutenant or something in it. Another nigger."

"Get me out of here," Mr. Savarese said.

"You got it, Mr. S.," Mr. Cassandro said.

Officer Tiny Lewis watched until the Lincoln was out of sight, then drove to a diner on South 16th Street. Lieutenant Foster H. Lewis, Sr., drove his car into the parking lot immediately afterward.

A very large police officer, obviously Irish, about forty years of age, came out of the diner.

"Thank you," Lieutenant Lewis said to him.

"Don't talk to me, I haven't seen you once on this shift," the officer said, and got in the car Officer Lewis had been driving and drove away.

Officer Lewis got in the car with his father.

"You going to tell me what that was all about?"

"What *what* was all about?"

"Thanks a lot, Pop."

"You did that rather well for a rookie who's never spent sixty seconds on the street," Lieutenant Lewis said.

"Runs in the family."

"Maybe."

"You're really not going to tell me what that was all about?"

"What *what* was all about?"

The next day, Friday, Officer Matthew W. Payne was stopped twice by law-enforcement authorities while operating a motor vehicle.

The first instance took place on the Hutchinson River Parkway, north of the Borough of Manhattan, some twelve miles south of Scarsdale.

An enormous New York State trooper, wearing a Smoky the Bear hat sat in his car and waited until he had received acknowledgment of his radio call that he had stopped a 1973 Porsche 911, Pennsylvania tag GHC-4048, for exceeding the posted limit of fifty miles an hour by twenty miles per hour. Then he got out of the car and cautiously approached the driver's window.

Nice-looking kid, he thought. But twenty miles over the limit is just too much.

And then he saw something on the floorboard. His entire demeanor changed. He flicked the top of his holster off and put his hand on the butt of his revolver.

"Put your hands out the window where I can see both of them," he ordered in a no-nonsense voice.

"What?"

"Do what I say, pal!"

Both hands came out the window.

"There's a pistol on your floorboard. You got a permit for it?"

"I'm a cop," Matt said. "I wondered what the hell you were up to. You scared the hell out of me."

"You got a badge?"

"I've got photo ID in my jacket pocket."

"Let's see it. Move slowly. You know the routine."

Matt produced his identification.

"You normally drive around with your pistol on the floor-board?"

"It's in an ankle holster. It rubs your leg if it's on a long time."

"I never tried one," the state trooper said. "I always thought I would kick my leg or something, and the gun would go flying across a room."

"No. They work. They just rub your leg, is all."

"You working?"

"I cannot tell a lie, I'm on my way to see my girl."

"This is yours?" the state trooper asked incredulously, gesturing at the Porsche.

"We take them away from drug dealers," Matt said.

"You work Narcotics?"

"Until Monday I work in something called Special Operations."

"Nice work."

"Yeah. It was. Monday I go back in uniform."

"Into each life some rain must fall," the state trooper said. "Take it easy."

"I will."

"I mean that. Take it easy. I clocked you at seventy-one."

"Sorry," Matt said. "I wasn't thinking. I'll watch it."

"My sergeant is a prick. He would ticket Mother Teresa."

"I have a lieutenant like that," Matt said.

The state trooper returned to his car, tooted the horn, and resumed his patrol.

It wasn't that I wasn't thinking. I was thinking. And what I was thinking was the closer I get to Scarsdale, to Amanda, the worse of an idea it seems. This is not the time to see her. She would not understand anything I have to say to her. And the reason for that is that I have nothing to say to her. Nothing that makes any sense, even to me.

Shit!

He put the Porsche in gear, reentered the flow of traffic, and at the next intersection turned around and headed for Philadelphia.

The second time Matt Payne attracted the attention of police officers charged with enforcement of the Motor Vehicle Code on the public highways took place several hours later, on Interstate 95, just inside the city limits of the City of Philadelphia.

"Jesus Christ!" he said aloud as he pulled to the side of the road, "this is really my day."

He glanced at the floorboard. His revolver and holster were safely out of sight.

Two Highway Patrol officers approached the car.

"You're a cop?" one asked.

"You're Payne, right?"

"Guilty," Matt said.

"You better come back to the car with us," one of them said. "They're looking for you."

"Really?"

We have changed our minds about you, Payne. You are really an all-around splendid fellow, and we have decided that instead of sending you to the 12th, we are going to make you a chief inspector.

What the hell could it be?

If they've really been looking for me, then it's serious. Christ! Mother? Dad? One of the kids?

He leaned on the Highway car so he could listen.

"Highway 19. We have located Officer Payne. We're on I-95, near the Cottman Avenue exit."

"Wait one, Highway 19," radio replied.

"I really like your wheels, Payne," one of the Highway guys said.

"Thanks," Matt said.

"Highway 19, escort Officer Payne to City Hall. They are waiting for him in the mayor's office."

"This is 19, 'kay," the Highway guy on the radio said, and then turned to Matt. "What the hell is that all about?"

"I wish to hell I knew."

"Christ, if we had the lights and siren on that," the other one said, pointing at Matt's Porsche, "we could set a record between here and City Hall."

"We'll go ahead," the other one said, chuckling. "You can catch up, right?"

"I'll try," Matt said.

The Highway car was moving with its flashing lights on and the siren howling by the time Matt got back behind the wheel of the Porsche, but he had no trouble catching up with it.

Peter Wohl was waiting for him in the courtyard of City Hall.

"Well, you don't look hung over. Pull your necktie up."

"What's going on?"

"You ever hear that God takes care of fools and drunks? Just smile and keep your mouth shut. For once."

"Before we get this press conference started here," the Honorable Jerry Carlucci, mayor of the City of Philadelphia, said, "let's make sure everybody knows who everybody is. You all know Chief Lowenstein and Chief Coughlin, I know. Chief Coughlin's standing in for Commissioner Czernich, who's tied up and couldn't be with us, although he would have liked to. I'm sure most of you know the two who just came in: Inspector Peter Wohl, who commands Special Operations; and Officer Matt Payne, who is the Inspector's special assistant and who most of you will remember as the splendid young officer who . . . removed the threat to Philadelphia posed by the Northwest serial rapist. And standing beside me is a gentleman I'm sure most of you know and who is the reason I asked you to come here this afternoon. I would be very surprised if anyone here doesn't recognize Mr. H. Richard Detweiler, president of Nesfoods International, but in case . . . ladies and gentlemen, Mr. H. Richard Detweiler."

Detweiler and Carlucci shook hands, which seemed to sort of surprise Mr. Detweiler, who then moved to a lectern.

"Thank you, ladies and gentlemen, for coming here this afternoon," he said, reading it from a typewritten statement. "I am sure that most of you are aware of the tragedy that struck my family recently, with my daughter very nearly killed not six blocks from here.

"I am not here to talk about my daughter but about the Police Department. I am somewhat ashamed to admit that before my daughter was shot and nearly killed, I never paid much attention to the police. They were simply there. But my experience with them since my daughter was injured, an innocent bystander in what seems to be an incident of gangland warfare, has taught me how devoted to the safety and welfare of us all they are.

"Something even more shocking than the senseless shooting of my daughter has occurred in our city. I refer to the cold-blooded murder of Officer Joseph Magnella. That brutal, vicious act, the slaying of a police officer, poses a real, present, and absolutely intolerable danger to the entire fabric of our society, a threat we simply cannot tolerate.

"It came to my attention that one citizen, who wishes to remain anonymous, was thinking along the same lines. More important, she was prepared to do something about it. She was prepared to offer a reward for information leading to the arrest and conviction of those responsible for the brutal murder of Officer Magnella. The reward she offered was in the amount of ten thousand dollars. My wife and I have decided to offer an equal amount for the same purpose. I have a check here with me.

"I call upon—"

He stopped and fished in his pocket and came up with a check, which he handed to Mayor Carlucci, who shook his hand while flashbulbs popped.

That forgotten little detail out of the way, Detweiler continued. "I call upon my fellow citizens of Philadelphia to assist with the investigation of the murder of Officer Magnella. The police would prefer information, but if you have no information, certainly you can afford a dollar or two, whatever amount, to add to the reward fund and to demonstrate to the police that the people are behind them. Thank you very much."

Matt felt a tug at his arm. Wohl pulled him off the stage and out of the room.

"You are only partially forgiven," he said. "That whole ambience would be ruined if Detweiler tried to choke you. I know he'd love to."

"What does 'partially' mean?"

"What do you think it means?"

"I don't know."

"Put your uniform back in the mothball bag," Wohl said. "And forget the 12th."

"Thank you."

"Don't thank me. That came from the mayor."

"In other words, you'd rather not have me."

"I didn't say that," Wohl said. "Don't put words in my mouth."

Matt looked at him.

"My father thinks you'll make a pretty good cop," Wohl said. "Okay? Who am I to question his judgment?"

"Thank you," Matt said.

Two weeks and two days later, Staff Inspector Peter Wohl received a call from Walter J. Davis, Special Agent in Charge, of the Philadelphia office of the Federal Bureau of Investigation.

Mr. Davis told him that he had received word from the assistant special agent in charge (Criminal Affairs) of the Chicago, Illinois, office of the FBI that one Charles Francis Gregory, who was almost certainly the man in the photographs Wohl had shown him, had been found in the trunk of his automobile in Cicero, Illinois, having suffered seven large-caliber pistol wounds to the head and chest, probably from a Colt government model .45 ACP pistol.

Special Agent in Charge Davis said, unofficially, that the Chicago FBI believed Mr. Gregory to be a hit man and that the word was that Mr. Gregory had been shot because he had botched a job he had been hired to do.

"We've got to get together for lunch, Peter," Special Agent in Charge Davis said.

"We really should," Inspector Wohl replied. "Call me."